After leaving school at fifteen, **Mo Hayder** worked as a barmaid, security guard, film-maker, hostess in a Tokyo club, educational administrator and teacher of English as a foreign language in Asia. She has an MA in creative writing from Bath Spa University, where she now teaches.

She is the author of *Birdman* and *The Treatment*, which won the 2001 WH Smith Thumping Good Read Award, and *Tokyo*, which was shortlisted for the CWA Gold and Steel Dagger Awards for Novels of the Year, 2004. *Pig Island*, her fourth novel, was a *Sunday Times* bestseller.

For more information about Mo Hayder, please visit www.mohayder.net

BIRDMAN

Greenwich, south-east London.
Detective Inspector Jack Caffery is called to one
of the most gruesome crime scenes he has ever
seen on a wasteland near the Millennium Dome:
five bodies, all young women, each appearing to
have been ritualistically murdered.

'Hayder's vibrant narrative and crunchy
characterisation propel the book along to
its denoument with fearsome velocity'
The Times

'It'll scare the hell out of you'
Elle

THE TREATMENT

Midsummer: Donegal Crescent, south London.
A husband and wife are discovered bound and
imprisoned in their own home. They are badly
dehydrated, have been beaten, and the husband
is close to death. But worse is to come . . .

'The book is surprisingly hard to put down . . .
Hayder's horrible ability to make you fear for
your life is a very modern achievement'
Daily Telegraph

'Hayder's gory insights into the dark
side are compelling'
Guardian

TOKYO

Desperate and alone in an alien city, student
Grey Hutchins accepts a job as a hostess
in an exclusive gentleman's club.
There she meets an ancient, wheelchair-bound
gangster who is rumoured to rely on a strange
elixir for his continued health – an elixir
others want, at any price . . .

'Left me stunned and haunted. This is writing
of breathtaking power and poetry'
Tess Gerritsen

'Deeply felt and haunting . . . it sticks with
you well after the last page is turned'
Michael Connelly

PIG ISLAND

When journalist Joe Oakes visits a secretive
religious community on a remote Scottish island,
he is forced to confront the nature of evil and to
question whether he might be responsible for the
terrible crime about to unfold.

'*Pig Island* surpasses anything Mo Hayder has
written before. She's the bravest writer I know'
Karin Slaughter

'The twist in the tail comes like a hammer blow
right at the end, clever and unexpected'
The Times

Also by Mo Hayder

BIRDMAN
THE TREATMENT
TOKYO

and published by Bantam Books

PIG ISLAND

Mo Hayder

BANTAM BOOKS

LONDON • TORONTO • SYDNEY • AUCKLAND • JOHANNESBURG

PIG ISLAND
A BANTAM BOOK : 9780553814637

Originally published in Great Britain by Bantam Press,
a division of Transworld Publishers

PRINTING HISTORY
Bantam Press edition published 2006
Bantam edition published 2007

1 3 5 7 9 10 8 6 4 2

Copyright © Mo Hayder 2006

Set in 10.5/13.5pt Sabon by
Falcon Oast Graphic Art Ltd.

Bantam Books are published by Transworld Publishers,
61–63 Uxbridge Road, London W5 5SA,
a division of The Random House Group Ltd,
in Australia by Random House Australia (Pty) Ltd,
20 Alfred Street, Milsons Point, Sydney, NSW 2061, Australia,
in New Zealand by Random House New Zealand Ltd,
18 Poland Road, Glenfield, Auckland 10, New Zealand
and in South Africa by Random House (Pty) Ltd,
Isle of Houghton, Corner of Boundary Road & Carse O'Gowrie,
Houghton, 2198, South Africa.

Printed and bound in Germany by
GGP Media GmbH, Pössneck.

Papers used by Transworld Publishers are natural, recyclable
products made from wood grown in sustainable forests. The
manufacturing processes conform to the environmental
regulations of the country of origin

'And he laid hold on the dragon, that old serpent, which is the Devil, and Satan, and bound him a thousand years.'

Revelation 20:2

Part One

CRAIGNISH
AUGUST

Oakesy

1

The alarms first went off in my head when the landlord and the lobsterman showed me what had been washed up on the beach. I took one look at the waves breaking and knew right then that cracking the Pig Island hoax wasn't going to be the straightforward bit of puff I'd expected. I didn't say anything much for a few minutes, just stood there, probably scratching the back of my neck and staring, because something like that . . . well, it's going to get you thinking, right? However much of a big guy you think you are, however much you reckon you've seen in your life and however lairy you are about the mad stories that go round, looking down at something like that splashing around your shoes, it's going to make you scratch a bit. Why didn't I listen to those alarm bells, turn right round and walk away from the whole thing there and then? Don't. Just don't. I stopped asking myself that question a long time ago.

That summer what they called the 'devil of Pig Island' video had already been around for a couple of years. Disturbing thing, it was. Genius hoax. And trust me, I know hoaxes. It had been shot on a sunny morning by a tourist out on a boozy sight-seeing tour of the Slate Islands, and when it hit the public the whole country went off on one, whispering about devil worship and general bad shit happening on the remote island off the coast of west Scotland. The story might have run and run, but the secretive religious group that lived on the island, the Psychogenic Healing Ministries, wouldn't give interviews to the press or respond to the accusations, and with nothing to fuel it the story died. Until late August last year when, after two years of nothing, the sect decided to break the silence. They cherry-picked one journalist to stay with them on the island for a week to see how the community lived and to 'discuss the widespread accusations of Satanic ritual'. And that canny old git of a journalist? Meet me. Joe Oakes. Oakesy to my mates. Sole architect of the biggest self-fuck on record.

2

'Seen the old video, have you?' said the lobsterman. It was the first time we'd met and I knew he didn't like me. There were only four of us in the pub that night: me, the landlord, his dog and this moody old shite. He sat in the corner huddled up against the wood panelling, puffing away at his rollies, shaking his head when I started asking about Pig Island. 'Is that why you're here? Fancy yourself a devil-wrangler?'

'Fancy myself a journalist.'

'A journalist no less!'

He laughed, and looked up at the landlord. 'Did ye hear that? Fancies himself a journalist!'

The place had that leery feel you sometimes get in these struggling local holes – like any minute a fight's going to kick off behind one of the fruit machines even though the place is half empty. There were two alehouses in the community – the tourist one, with its picture window overlooking the marina, and this one for the locals, up a cliff path in the soggy trees. Stained plaster walls, stinking carpets and dingy, sea-dulled windows that stared out to where Pig Island lay, silent and dark almost two miles offshore.

'They'll not let you on the island,' said the land-lord, as he wiped down the bar. 'You know that, don't you? There's not been a journalist on that island in years. They're as mad as kettles out on Pig Island – won't let a soul on the island, much less a journalist.'

'And if they *did* let you on,' said the lobsterman, 'God, but there's not a soul in Craignish will take you out there. No, you won't catch any of us gaun out to auld Pig Island.' He squinted through the smoke out of the window to where the island lay, just a dark shape against the gathering gloom. His white beard was nicotine-stained, like he must've been drooling in it for years. 'No. Not me. I'd sooner go through the old hag's whirlpool, pure fatal or not, than go round Pig Island and come face to face with auld Nick.'

One thing I've learned after eighteen years in this trade is there's always someone who gains from supernatural phenomena. If it isn't money or revenge it's just good old-fashioned attention. I'd already been to Bolton to interview the tourist who'd shot the video. He had nothing to do with the hoax: poor beer-bloated sod couldn't see past the next Saturday-afternoon league tables, let alone set up something like that. So who was gaining from the Pig Island film?

'They own the island, don't they?' I said, twisting my pint of Newkie Brown round and round in the circular beer stain, looking at it thoughtfully.

'The Psychogenic Healing Ministries. I read that somewhere – they bought it in the eighties.'

'Bought it or stole it, depending on your position.'

'Was an awful fool, the owner.' The landlord leaned on the bar with both elbows. 'An awful fool. The pig farm goes belly up and what does he do? Lets all the farmers in Argyll dump their dodgy chemicals out there. Ended up a death pit, the place – pigs all over the island, old mine shafts, chemicals. In the end he has to give it all away. Ten thousand pounds! They could have stole it from him, it'd be more honest.'

'You won't like that,' I said, in a level, casual voice. 'People coming from the south and buying up all the property round here.'

The lobsterman sniffed. 'Doesn't bother us. What we *don't* tolerate is when they buy a place, then lock themselves away and get up to all their queer rituals. That's when it bothers us – them hunkering down out there, consorting with the de'il, doing nothing but eating babies and giving each other a rare auld peltin' whenever they've a mind to.'

'Aye,' said the landlord. 'And then there's the smell.'

I looked at the landlord. I wanted to smile. 'The smell? From the island?'

'Ah!' he said, throwing the tea towel over his shoulder. 'The smell.' He fished under the bar for a giant bag of crisps and opened it, shovelling a fistful into his mouth. 'Do you know what they say? What they say is the signature smell of the devil? The smell of the devil is the smell of shite – that's what it is. Now, you go to anyone out there –' He jabbed a crisp-covered finger at the window. Crumbs confettied on to his T-shirt. '– out on Jura or in Arduaine, and they'll all tell you the same thing. The smell of shite comes off Pig Island. There's no better proof of their rituals than that.'

I studied him thoughtfully. Then I turned and looked across the dark sea. The moon was out and a wind had come up and was whipping branches against the windowpane. Beyond our reflections, beyond the image of the landlord standing under the lighted optics, I could see an absence – a dark space against the night sky. Pig Island.

'They piss you off,' I said, trying to picture the thirty-odd people who lived out there. 'They do their fair bit to piss you all off.'

'You're right about that,' said the landlord. He came to the table and sat down, setting the crisps in front of him. 'Do their fair bit to piss us all off. They're not well liked – not since they fenced off that nice bit o' beach on the south-east of the island and stopped the young folk from Arduaine going out with their boats. They'd only be wanting a wee game of footy or shinty in the sand, the weans, Godsake, no need to be so stern about it, is my opinion.'

'Not your perfect neighbours.'

'No,' he said. 'They're not.'

'Where I come from, you behave like that you're asking for a hiding.'

'So you're starting to see my point.'

'If it was me I'd be trying to think of how to make their lives difficult.'

'We've been tempted!' The landlord laughed. He licked his fingers carefully, then put them to his eyes, like tears of mirth had gathered there. 'I don't mind telling you. Been tempted. Put some paraffin in their bottles of bevvy, maybe.'

'You know, if it was me, I'd – I'd – I don't know.' I shook my head and looked at the ceiling, like I was searching for inspiration. 'I'd probably try and set up some kind of . . . dodgy rumour. Yeah.' I nodded. 'I'd set up a hoax – spread a couple of rumours around.'

The landlord stopped laughing and rubbed his nose. 'Are you saying we're making it all up?'

'Aye. Takin' the piss, are ye?' The lobsterman sat forward, suddenly flushed. 'You takin' the piss? Is that what your message to us is?'

'I'm just saying,' I met his eyes seriously, looking from him to the landlord and back, 'it's got a smell about it, hasn't it? I mean, *devil-worshippers*? Satan walking the beaches of Pig Island?'

The colour in the lobsterman's face paled very slightly. He crushed the rollie in the ashtray and stood, drawing himself up to his full height. He took a few deep, fighting breaths, and looked unsteadily down at me. 'Laddie, tell me. Are you a man who is easily shocked? You're a big man, but I reckon you're one who'd shock easy. What do ye think?' he said to the landlord. 'Is he? Is he a man who'd go in a funk if he saw something peculiar? Because that's how it looks from where I stand.'

'Why?' I said, putting the glass down slowly. 'Why? What are you going to show me?'

'If you're so clever you don't believe what we're saying, then come with me. We'll see what kind of a *hoax* is gaun on.'

Pig Island, or as it's called in Gaelic Cuagach Eilean, lies in the small cup of sea at the edge of the Firth of Lorn, caught like a precious stone in a setting between Luing, Jura and Craignish Peninsula – like it's been placed to block the entry to the Sound of Jura. It's a weird shape: like a peanut from above, covered in grassland and dense trees, a wide rocky gorge running down the middle. Once, before the pig farm and the chemical dumping, there'd been a slate mine operating in the south of the island, with a community of miners and a regular ferry. But by the time I got there Pig Island was almost totally cut off. Once a week the Psychogenic Healing Ministries sent a small boat to collect supplies. It was their only contact with the world.

I knew a bit about that part of Scotland – wrote bits and pieces about it from time to time. But my bread and butter was debunking work. One of the things that comes as birthright to a Scouser is knowing the stripe of bullshit when you see it and I'm a natural sceptic, a full-blown non-believer: a Scully, a James Randi, an out-and-out hoax-buster. I've flown round the world chasing zombies and chupacabras, Filipino faith-healers and beasts in Bodmin; I've used glass vials to collect dripping milk from the breasts of Mexican virgin statues – and in that time I've worked up a hard skin. But even I had to admit there was something odd-looking about the Psychogenic Healing Ministries' island. If you were going to believe in devil-worship you'd picture it happening somewhere remote and sea-wreathed like Pig Island. That night, as we jolted and bumped along a dark path that led to the end of the peninsula, I stared out of the window at its dark, desolate shape and for a moment or two there I had to tell myself not to be an old tart about it.

The landlord had crammed me into the back seat of the lobsterman's beat-up rust-bucket of a car. We left the dog in the pub: 'Because he's a mad rocket when he comes out here,' said the landlord, as the car pulled off the road on to a thin, muddy beach. 'Makes him crazy and I'm not putting him in a paddy just because *you* won't take my word for something.'

We got out of the car and I paused. I hadn't been out on the lash or anything, but I'd sunk a fair old few in the pub and it felt good for a moment to fill my lungs with the night air. The beach was silent, and there was already a breath of autumn in the air. It was gone eleven but Craignish was so far north the sky was still edged with blue. You'd almost think that if you stood on tiptoe and squinted you'd see the land of the midnight sun peeping at you from over the horizon, maybe a reindeer or a polar bear on a giant mint.

'See the pipe?' The lobsterman walked away to the south, totally steady in spite of the whisky, his old shoes leaving dull prints in the mud, his moon-shadow long beside him. 'The wee stank over there?' He was pointing to the long, low shape of a sewage pipe straddling the beach ahead. 'You get the conditions right – a nice westerly, an ebb and a spring tide – then everything from out at Pig Island gets washed up, not in the loch or even on Luing, where you'd expect it, but here, on this side of the peninsula. Most of it gets caught on the other side of that pipe.'

The landlord hung back, giving me a dubious

look. His face was a little pinched seeming in the moonlight. He turned up his collar like it was suddenly dead cold out there. 'Sure you're ready for this?'

'Yeah. Why not?'

'It's not for the faint-hearted, what's caught up under that pipe.'

'I'm not faint-hearted,' I said, looking down the beach at the lobsterman. 'I've seen everything there is to see.'

We walked for a while in silence, only the sound of the waves breaking on the beach, and the tinkle of a halyard on a boat moored somewhere out in the sea. The smell hit me first. Even before I saw the lobsterman hesitate at the pipe, looking down on the other side, before I saw him shaking his head and leaning over to spit out something in the sand, I knew it was going to be one of those stomach-turners. One of those times I'd regret the last pint. I took a breath and swallowed, tapping my pockets as I got nearer, hoping I'd find a stray bit of chewy or something to take the taste away.

'Worse is it?' said the landlord, approaching the lobsterman. 'Got worse?'

'Aye – there's more. More than there was last week.'

I held my T-shirt up to my nose and peered down

on the other side of the pipe. Dark shapes bobbed and buffeted in a yellowish foam. Meat. Decaying chunks of flesh – impossible to tell in the slime where one piece ended and the next began. The breaking waves forced them into the crevice under the pipe, tangled them in ribbons of tasselweed. Decomposition gas fizzed from under the raised flaps of skin, sending bubbles to the surface.

'What the fuck's this?'

'Pig meat,' said the lobsterman. 'Dead pigs. Killt in one of them rituals on Pig Island and been washed off the island.'

'Police have seen it,' the landlord said, 'and they've not cared to do anything about it – can't prove where it's coming from and, anyway, a few dead pigs aren't hurting anyone, is their manner of thinking.'

'Dead pigs?' I looked up at the mouth of the Firth. The moon picked out the silvery tips of waves as far as the eye could see – to where Pig Island peeped round the end of Luing, silent and hunched, like a dozing beast. 'All of this is dead pigs?'

'Aye. That's what they say.' The landlord puffed out a series of short, dry laughs – like the world never ceased to amaze him. 'That's what the police say – everything here is just pig meat. But you know what I think?'

'What do you think?'

'I think that when it comes to the lovers of Satan you can never be too sure.'

3

Let's think about my mistakes with the whole Pig Island thing. Well, the first one was letting my wife come to Scotland with me. What was I thinking? I've had to stop punching myself in the face about it, because you have to find ways of hanging on to a bit of sanity, so I say whoever was to blame, Lexie was there with me. Course, I didn't know she was there for her own reasons, didn't know she had something on her mind. I thought she was totally made up with her job – a receptionist at a London clinic – besotted by the media-whore neurosurgeon who ran the place (you guessed I don't like him, right?). The last thing I expected was for her to want to leave London. But one minute I say, 'I'm coming to Scotland,' next thing she's on the web looking for holiday cottages.

She found a crappy one-bed bungalow on Craignish Peninsula that my budget stretched to. It was hot and unventilated and Lexie slept restlessly. The night I got back from the beach she was already in bed, turning over in her sleep, whimpering and pushing at the pillow. I got in silently and lay next to her, staring up at the ceiling. Tomorrow I'd be on Pig Island. I needed to think about what I was chasing. I was going to have to play it dead carefully. Going to have to concentrate, be ready for anything.

The Psychogenic Healing Ministries wanted me at their Positive Living Centre on Pig Island because of Eigg, the little Hebridean island fifty miles to the north. They hadn't said it, but I knew it anyway. On Eigg the tenants had raised the money to buy the island from the owner. They got donations from everywhere, all over the country – even the National Lottery. Booted old Schellenberg and Maruma out. And how did they manage that? Good publicity. Simple as that. Someone was there to spread their story to the world. And that someone was me. I'd been there – helped break the story in the press. How I saw it now was the Psychogenic Healing Ministries probably had some legal hassle they wanted to raise money for. Thought I could help. If they'd known I had history with their founder, Pastor Malachi Dove, if they'd known that eighteen years ago I'd written an article on him under the name Joe Finn, that he'd been so arsed off about it he'd tried to sue me for libel, I'd never have got even a little bit close to Pig Island. But, like I said, canny bastard, me.

I lay awake half the night ticking off kit in my head: MP3 player, camera, batteries, spare camera card, phone ... Didn't get to kip until three in the morning and the next day I was on edge. After breakfast, when I'd packed and was ready to set off for Pig Island, I got the laptop out one last time.

I never had found out what came first – the rumours that the Psychogenic Healing Ministries were practising Satanism, or the video. But when the public saw it they made up their mind it was an image of the devil, brought down on to Pig Island by the Satanic ritual of the PHMs. A great steaming pile of bollocks, naturally, but even I had to admit there was something dead creepy about the video.

First of all, it wasn't trick photography. It had been through every AV specialist unit in the country, passed every test, been torn apart frame by frame, but even with all that gadgetry thrown at it, it kept coming up clean over and over again. Whoever had cooked up this little bit of chicanery hadn't used trick photography: something had definitely been on the island beach that hot 18 July two years ago.

That morning I played it again on my laptop. I sat forward on the edge of my seat, concentrating hard. I'd seen it a thousand times and knew every frame. It started off kind of ordinary, with the camera lingering on the horizon out to sea, tilting gently as the single-engined boat bobbed on the waves in the

Firth of Lorn. I dragged the RealPlayer toggle to the bit where a shout went up on the boat. This was the exact moment when one of the other tourists saw something moving on the island. A few indistinct shouts came from the TV – a lot of camera movement as the surprised tourist whipped the videocam sideways, taking in one or two shocked faces on the boat, then focused across the bay on an indeterminate line of green-brown – the seaward shoreline of Pig Island. Someone close to the camera spoke. The words were totally unintelligible because of the wind on the soundtrack, but the BBC unit had added sub-titled dialogue to my copy: 'What in fuck's name is *that*?'

This was the important bit. You could feel the guys on the boat inching forward in curiosity, staring at the beach where a creature no one could put a name to moved ponderously through the foliage at the water's edge. It stood at about five foot eleven; the BBC technicians figured this out from comparative measurements using sun and trees. In most ways it appeared like a naked human being – the video showed its back from the waist down; the upper half was concealed in shadow. Except it *wasn't* human. There was something dangling from the base of its spine. Estimated to be about two feet in length, the same battered brown flesh as the body, it looked just like a fleshy tail. It banged once on the back of the creature's legs as it moved.

Even in that stifling bungalow, with the sun coming through the picture windows, lying in great squares on the dingy patterned carpet, and Lexie a few yards away in the kitchen, I got this crawl of discomfort across my skin. I leaned nearer to the TV and stared at the wavery brown line of empty beach, the camera holding steady on the island in case the beast reappeared. A full three minutes elapsed until the tourist gave up waiting and turned the camera back to the other men on the boat. They stood at the gunwales, all four of them in their Bolton Wanderers shirts, holding the stanchion line and staring in silence at the spot on the beach where the creature had been.

The people at the BBC reckoned it was an actor, someone in a costume. Their AV unit had worked on the Bluff Creek Bigfoot film, and they thought this video had some of the same hallmarks: Sasquatch, as we all knew, was just some guy in a Hollywood gorilla suit – and the technicians decided that was probably what was happening in the Pig Island film. The problem was, because the video was taken from a boat about two hundred yards offshore, because the 'creature' emerged from the trees at frame 1,800 and had disappeared into the foliage by frame 1,865 (at a rate of thirty frames per second that meant a shade over two seconds), and because the movement of the boat had the picture jumping all over the place, the Beeb couldn't get a good enough image to analyse it any closer. They could only say what it *appeared* to be.

Half beast. Half human.

'I'll put your lighter in the rucksack,' said Lexie, suddenly, from the kitchen. 'I'm putting it in the front pocket.'

I paused the video and turned to look at her. She was standing at the table, her hair held back in the Alice band she'd got for her snobby job, and a pair of shorts I had a vague idea I was meant to notice. I didn't answer her straight off. Her voice was kind of casual, but both of us knew how serious she was. I'd 'given up' smoking months ago and I reckoned I'd hidden the occasional sneaky rollie pretty well. Except now there was the lighter.

I watched while she zipped up the rucksack.

'It was in your jacket pocket,' she said, reading my mind.

'I got it for the stove. There's no pilot.'

'Yeah,' she said, laughing. 'You're so transparent.'

I laughed too. Just a bit. 'Transparent or not – I used it for the stove.'

'OK,' she said lightly. 'OK. I believe you. You're so believable.' She set her tongue at the back of her front teeth and smiled up at the ceiling. Her smiling made the sinews in her neck stand out. She'd got skinny recently. I waited a few more moments to see if we were going to pursue this. Not dropping the smile or taking her eyes off the ceiling, in that same high voice she goes: 'And there was tobacco in the shorts you had on yesterday.'

'You're going through my pockets now?'

'Yes. My husband lies to me about smoking so I go through his pockets.' She dropped her chin then and met my eyes and I saw she'd flushed a deep purplish colour – like her cheeks were bruised. 'My husband thinks I'm stupid. So I have to fight back.'

The most important thing about me and my marriage was I didn't fancy my wife any more. I'd known it for months and done nothing about it – it's one of those things you can stick in the back of your mind and ignore if you're clever enough. But, and this is true, I cared about her. Weird fuck I was, I did still care for her. And I cared, in some rusty old-fashioned way, about fidelity. Back in London half my friends were already blasting their way through first, second divorces: I was the sanctimonious one, believed in thick and thin, wasn't going to end up in a frigid, three-minute-egg of a marriage. *Touché, Joe Oakes, you pious arse. This'll teach you.*

I stood slowly and went to stand in the kitchen doorway, looking at her. 'I'm sorry,' I said. 'I am.'

She didn't move for a moment. Then her

shoulders slumped and she let out a sigh. 'That's OK,' she said, shaking her head and holding out the rucksack to me. 'It can't be easy, giving up.'

'No, but I'm working on it.' I pulled on the rucksack. 'Believe me.'

She forced a smile. 'I've put some water-bottles in, at the bottom, and some factor ten.' She smoothed down the rucksack straps across my chest and, finding an imaginary stain on my T-shirt, wet her finger and rubbed at it. A compulsive neatnik, Lex, this grooming, this shrimping, was her way of showing I was forgiven. 'Now,' she said. 'I know it's your turn to cook tonight, but you'll be exhausted, so I'll do a pasta salad. Avocado, bacon, olives. It'll save if you're late.'

'Lexie,' I said, 'I told you. Didn't I? I said I didn't know if I'd be back tonight. I told you this. Remember? I said I could be out there a few days.'

She bit her lip. 'A few days?'

'We talked about it. Don't you remember? I said I'd probably have to stay over and you said you'd be all right on your own.'

'Did I? Did I say that?'

'Yes.'

She shrugged. 'Well, don't worry about it. I mean I'd've loved some time with my husband on our holidays, and obviously I'd rather *not* be in *this* place on my own.' She opened her hands to indicate

30

the bungalow. She'd hated it at first sight. She'd booked it but turns out to be my fault it was so shitty. 'But, don't worry, it's all right, I'll be all right.'

'Lex. I said it was work, remember?' Remember how I said it was—'

'*Please!*' She cut me off, holding up her hand in the air. 'Please don't. Please just go. I'll be fine.'

'I'll call you. If there's a signal out on the island I'll call you. I'll tell you how it's going – when I'll be back.'

'No,' she said. 'Don't. Really – don't. Just . . . just go. Do your thing.' She drummed her fingers on the table, not looking up at me. 'Go on,' she repeated, when I didn't turn to go. 'Just go.'

I sighed and touched her shoulder, opened my mouth to say something, then thought better of it. I tightened the rucksack and left, not bending to kiss her goodbye, quietly closing the kitchen door behind me. That was how it went, these days. Outside I stopped. At the end of the bungalow's long, rhododendron-crowded driveway the land opened into a funnel. There, basking in the glittering sea, was Pig Island.

4

*'Rage against the Philistines of science. Do not
allow the arrogance of the medical community to
rape and subdue your natural self-healing powers.
Wrest control over your life.'*
     The Psychogenic Healing Ministries, volume 14,
                                        chapter 5, verse 1

The Psychogenic Healing Ministries would say my
problems with Lexie were all about my godlessness.
They'd say that if I only opened my heart to the
Lord, that if I'd only grow towards his cosmic love,
in no time I'd find myself growing back towards
Lexie. And she'd grow towards me too. I'd never
been to the Positive Living Centre on Pig Island, but
I knew more than I needed about what the PHM
would say about me and Lex. I knew their
philosophies like I wrote them myself.

What happened between me and their founder,
Pastor Malachi Dove, all starts back in Liverpool
twenty years ago. It's the mid-eighties. Liverpool's
the unemployment capital of Europe, and my cousin
Finn is the closest thing to a God I know. He's a
charm bird, totally does not look like my cousin
with his blond, mosh-pit hair and ratty nose. The
Kurt Cobain of Toxteth. He's the first in our family
to get into university and he comes home summer

holidays to Self-pity City talking like a Londoner. He tells us all about university and the birds he's shagged. He's going to be a journalist, travel the world. Everyone hates him. Me – I think I can see the sun shine when he bends over.

It's probably the girls that do it for me, because by the next year I've got a place at UCL and I'm ready to follow him down south. Me and Finn together, I'm thinking, the copping potential is unlimited. Then something happens. Something that changes the course of our lives. Finn's ma gets cancer.

Now, I've always really liked his ma, always thought she was totally sound. Actually, what I've always thought is, she's clever. But what does she do, good Catholic girl, when she's told she's dying? She refuses chemo. She scoffs down shark cartilage and flower remedies by the lorryload. She visits Lourdes. She ends up selling the house and trailing some faith-healer around the United States. His name is Pastor Malachi Dove. He believes in NO MEDICAL INTERVENTION. He believes in the power of prayer and positive thinking. Two months later she comes back to Toxteth and dies in agony in a hospice in Ormskirk. So it goes, as Vonnegut would say.

For me and Finn, religion's what you get twatted for. Aled up on a Saturday night it'll be Everton and Liverpool, or Papes and Prods that starts the fight.

And seeing Finn's ma die like that gives us a rage for Pastor Malachi Dove that won't go away. We get copies of *Charisma* magazine and find he's in the south-west US. With the money Finn's ma leaves we get on the next flight to New Mexico. We think we're gonzos. Bad Boys doing the Right Thing.

Oral Roberts has just told the world God will kill him if the congregation doesn't stump up eight million and Peter Popoff's just been outed on *The Johnny Carson Show*. We spend about a week on the breakaway-church circuit, trailing all these characters around the south-west, getting to know how it works: we meet rapture partisans, pretribulationists, preterists, post-wrathers and the midtribbers. We go to deliverance ministries and take part in prayer chains. Slowly we're narrowing it down to our target. And in July it happens. We meet Pastor Malachi Dove. Chief minister and founder of the Psychogenic Healing Ministries Foundation.

It's in a convention centre in Albuquerque. Aircon because it's hot as hell outside. Finn and me, we're about as out of place as you can get: there's me in my beanie and striker's donkey jacket, Finn in his Big Kahuna T-shirt and a mincy little Italian-style zip-up bag that would get him a good twatting in Seaforth; here it contains a loaded tape recorder and mic. We sit in row T, thinking everyone's staring at us. Thinking everyone knows for sure why we're there.

The first surprise is the stage. It's kind of empty and clinical. Feels like a hospital theatre, not a church. The helpers, all women, are a cross between angels and theatre technicians: eighth Dan judo pants and gleaming white plimsolls on bare feet. On stage a stretcher is wheeled up to a screen with a blue sky projected on it. Me and Finn sit there muttering between us, all ready to start snickering. Then Malachi Dove comes on stage and we get surprise number two.

First off, he's not American, he's English. (From Croydon, we find out later, son of a paperclip salesman.) And he's dead normal, not dressed in some huckster's suit: he's wearing a corduroy jacket and he looks more like a young teacher at a public school, with his soft, boyish good looks and thatch of blond hair flopping down over his forehead. Rimless specs on a tip-tilted nose and you can see his tendency is to get fat, not mean. Years later, when Leo DiCaprio is famous, me and Finn turn to each other and go, '*Malachi Dove. Malachi Dove and Leo. Separated at birth.*'

Malachi Dove doesn't bound on stage. He comes on quietly, sort of shuffling, clearing his throat and tucking the specs in his jacket pocket, like he's going to deliver a theology lecture. He sits on a little stool and looks seriously and thoughtfully into the dark auditorium while the place erupts: cheers, hoots, promises of undying love echoing off the walls. He waits till the noise dies down. Then he moves the microphone to his mouth, clumsily, banging it on his nose. He grins at the mistake. 'Uh – sorry,' he goes. 'Technology's not my strong point.'

The audience erupts again, applauds like crazy.

He holds up his hands modestly. 'Look . . . let me explain who I am.' The congregation goes quiet. The assistants take their seats at the edge of the stage. Malachi Dove waits. Then he fixes the audience with his pale eyes. There's silence in the place now. 'Whatever you think,' he says, 'we are all religious. We may believe in different prophets. My prophet is Jesus. Yours may be . . . I don't know, Muhammad perhaps? Or Krishna? Some of you may think you have no prophet at all, and that, too, is fine. We don't check your faith at the door.'

A murmur of laughter goes round the hall. They know that twinkle in his eye, that ironic twitch of a smile.

'But one thing is sure. We all believe in the same *God. I* know *your* God. And *you* know *my* God. Maybe by a different name, but you know him.' He breaks off and grins again, throwing a hand at the audience, like they just told him a risqué joke. 'OK, don't panic. I'm not going to quote the Bible at you.'

More laughter. Finn nudges me. He's got the mic poking out of the little zip-up bag now, like the nose of an animal, pointed in the direction of the stage. We're waiting for the wackiness to start so we can get outraged. On stage Malachi holds up his empty hands. He makes a great pantomime of studying first one bare palm, then the other.

'Nothing special about these hands. Is there? Just your average pair of hands. I don't pretend to have power in them. I can't send a lightning bolt from them. I know all about my hands because I, like you, have not been content to believe what the tent-show evangelists tell me. I have made it my business to study the subject. Did you know, for example, that a soldier in the victorious army will survive wounds that can kill a soldier in the defeated army? Did you know that? Do you understand the dance of chemicals in your body? Your body . . .'

He points a finger into the audience. He's smiling, and maybe he's already got to me on some level, because I ignore this sudden image I get in my head that he's not a human but a husky dog, staring into my eyes from the stage.

'Your body can heal itself. *It* has the knowledge. It only needs the right chemicals. Since the day I left my parents' home I have never crossed the threshold of a medical professional. *And I never will!*' He looks at his hands again, one at a time, like they're a mystery to him. 'My faith allows me to channel my endorphins. And with a faith this strong I can channel it to you, too.'

'*What crap*,' Finn mutters.

'*What bukkakes*,' I say. We both shake our heads. But we're subdued, and we're not meeting each other's eyes. We've both got a glimpse of what Finn's ma saw in Pastor Malachi Dove. Straight off when the lights come on, a healing line forms in the aisle going to the stage. The disabled are wheeled out and helped on to the stage by relatives. One of Malachi's helpers takes them by the arm: Asunción (we find out her name from the crowd), a total vision of horniness with her hair in a long squaw plait snaking down the back of her white judo jacket, keeps production-lining these invalids up on to the stage, keeping a hand on their arms, holding them back until Malachi is ready. Then she nudges them forward, half lifting them, half talking them up on to the stretcher where they lie on their backs staring up at Malachi, who stands above them, back to the audience, both hands on the stretcher, resting his weight there, his head bowed and eyes closed, like he's waiting for a migraine to go. He doesn't pray. He just waits. No hellfire. After a few moments he places his hand on the body part and closes his eyes again. Then he lifts his hands and whispers something to the patient, who gets up and leaves. Or is helped away by relatives.

'Go on,' whispers Finn, nudging me. 'Go on. Get up there.'

I get up and join the queue. I feel like a twat because I'm the tallest. All I can see in front and behind and to the side of me are Sunday hats, little blue and pink feathers quivering in the netting. After about half an hour waiting I'm up on the stage under the heat of the spotlights. Malachi glances at me, and for a moment, seeing my height and my strength, he hesitates. But if he thinks it's a trick he hides it.

'What's your name?'

'Joe.'

'What part of you has brought you here tonight, Joe? What part of your body?'

'Bowels,' I say, because that's how Finn's ma went and it's the first thing that comes into my head. 'It's a cancer. Sir.'

I get on the stretcher, thinking about Finn sniggering in the audience. Malachi stands above me, head bent, eyes closed, sweat coming out from under his blond thatch. I register the pores in his cheeks. I see he's wearing face powder or found-ation. Suddenly I'm totally interested in what he's going to say.

After what seems like for ever, he raises his head and frowns at me. 'How did they know?' he goes, in a hushed voice. 'How could they tell? When it's so small, how could they tell?'

I swallow. Suddenly I don't want to laugh any more. 'When what's so small?' I say. There's a lump in my throat. 'When what's so small?'

'The tumour. It's less than a centimetre across. How did they even know it was there?'

'What happened?' Finn says.

I've come off stage. I'm covered with sweat and my head's throbbing. 'Two weeks,' I mutter. I sit there sweating, rubbing my stomach under my jeans waistband. 'Two weeks. Then I come back to a prayer meeting, and I'm going to pass the tumour.'

'Pass the tumour? What the fuck does that mean, "pass the tumour"?' Then he stops. He's seen my face. 'Oakesy?' he goes, suddenly concerned. 'Oakesy, what is it?'

'I dunno,' I mutter, getting unsteadily to my feet. 'I dunno. But I want to get out of here. I think I want to speak to a doctor.'

The next ten days are a blur. I go from health professional to health professional. Finn trails along behind me, bemused and worried. I eat up half my aunt's inheritance trying to get a primary-care practitioner to refer me for a cancer test on the grounds a faith-healer has told me I'm dying. I end up stumping up for a faecal occult blood test in the Presbyterian hospital. The doctor, I remember, is called Leoni. It's in grey pastel letters on her badge. I remember staring at her name while she reads me the results, my heart banging in my ribcage.

Negative. No tumour. No cancer. Did I really believe what an evangelical preacher told me? She's got pity in her voice.

Well, that does it for me. If I hated him for what he did to Finn's ma, now I've got big fucking rocks in my head for Pastor Malachi Dove. By the time we go back to the Psychogenic Healing Ministries prayer meeting I want to do one thing: kill him.

This time we're in Santa Fe. The stage looks the same. Asunción's in an embroidered baptism shift, and when she spots me in the queue again – almost shaking, I'm so fucking pissed off – she takes my hand and leads me back through the crowd. 'Where are we going?' I can see the exit door approaching. 'What's happening?'

She doesn't answer. She just leads me, with this totally surreal calm, through the back door of the chapel and left through a door into the toilet block.

'Move your bowels, please,' she goes, pointing to one of the toilets.

'What?'

'Move your bowels to complete the treatment.'

I stand there stunned, looking from the bog seat to her then back again. 'I can't just—'

'I think you'll find it easier than you expect.'

I stare at her for a long time. I'd like to slap someone right now, but even at eighteen I'm clear enough to see a story when it comes my way. My hands hover on my belt. 'What about you? Where are you going to be?'

'I've seen it several times before.'

'You're going to *watch*? You have to be—' I break off. She's looking at me with one of those faces that doesn't need any words – eyebrows slightly raised, chin tilted down, arms crossed. An SS guard, may as well be. Her mouth is closed in a firm line: *Argue all you want*, it says. *I'm not budging*. I sigh. 'OK, OK. Just stand back a bit, for Christ's sake.' I unbutton my trousers, pull down my shorts and sit on the toilet, elbows on my bare knees, hands dangling, looking up at her. 'Well,' I say, after a while. 'I told you, nothing's going to happen—'

Before I know it, Asunción's conjured a wad of toilet paper out of thin air and is thrusting it down under my arse, forcing it up against me. There's a moment of uncomfortable slithering as I struggle, '*What the fuck do you think you're – get your hand out of—*' and an unfamiliar wet, cold sensation around my arsehole. Then she steps away, pushing her hair triumphantly out of her eyes, the tissue bunched in her fingers.

'You fucking lunatic!' I go. 'What was *that* about?'

'The tumour,' she says, holding the paper under my nose, making me recoil at the fucking awful smell. A wad of something black and slimy sits in the petal-white tissue, something that smells of putrefaction and death. 'You passed it.'

'Here,' I say, making a grab for it. But Asunción is too quick. She whips it out of reach and spins on her heel, throws open the cubicle door and stalks out. 'Hey – stop.' I follow, hopping, skipping and almost tripping over my unbuttoned trousers, trying to do up my belt and flies at the same time as push open the doors she's slamming her way through. In the hall as I catch up with her she's making a triumphant entrance, hand held high, titanic smile like a boxing-match ring girl, me stumbling after her as she marches up the aisle. Up ahead the pastor's staging a shocked pause in the proceedings, his eyes widening dramatically at the procession approaching him. 'Asunción,' he calls. 'Why the interruption?'

She mounts the stage. Dove uses his hand dramatically to cover his lapel mic and leans over so she can whisper in his ear – his eyebrows lifting almost to his blond hairline as he pretends to be amazed, delighted by what she's saying. He lifts his eyes to mine with a smile and he's half got his hand out ready to pull me victoriously on to the stage when he sees the expression in my eyes. His face falls.

'What're you fuckers up to?' I mount the steps two at a time. Under my feet the stage shakes a little. 'Give me that fucking thing.'

'Joe?' he says. 'What's the problem? What's the—'

'Give me that.' I make a grab for the tissue. 'Show me what you wankers are doing.' Asunción gasps and tries to wrench her hand away. A feedback scream shoots through the microphones, but I hold on tight to her wrist. The congregation jump to their feet, faces frozen and shocked. I dig my fingernails hard into Asunción's skin – *don't stop just because she's a woman* – and get her to release the tissue.

'Joe!' Malachi rips his microphone off his lapel. 'Joe!' He puts a hand on my arm, so close I can smell his face powder. He tries to turn us away so our backs are to the audience and he can talk confidentially. He's sweating now. Looking at what's in my fist and sweating. 'Leave the stage now, Joe,' he goes, licking his lips and putting his fingers out, itching to grab the tissue off me. 'Give me the tumour and leave the stage. Whatever your problem I'll speak to you off stage. Just give me the—'

He makes a move for my hand but I shake him

off. '*Listen, you little shit*,' I hiss. I turn and put my face close to his. 'I'd like to kill you. If I could get away with it, I'd kill you. Remember that.'

And that's it. I'm off, striding out of the hall with my prize, joined by Finn in the aisle. Outraged little black women hit us with their navy blue handbags as we go.

The tumour turns out to be a putrefying chicken liver. 'Probably been left to rot for a couple days,' says the Environment Department in Santa Fe. 'Where the hell did you boys get this little beauty?' It's such a great story I'm over the fucking moon. We've got him. Pastor Dove is ours.

But funny how life goes, isn't it? because Finn, the one who started the Albuquerque crusade, the one who was going to be a journalist, suddenly goes cold on it. He loses his heart to some girl he's met in a tequila bar, follows her home to Sausalito, California, and spends the next couple of years as a surfer dude. He gets himself sun damage and a phoney West Coast accent. When he comes back to the UK he publishes a surf mag for a while and ends up a literary agent in London. Turns out I'm the only one with a hard-on for getting Pastor Malachi Dove knobbed.

I take up my university place in London, and start casting around for a mag to take the chicken-liver article. But before I can place it, a rumble comes out of the New Mexico desert. The Psychogenic Healing Ministry is in crisis. The IRS are reviewing its tax-exemption status; Malachi Dove is admitted to hospital, suffering from manic depression. And then the proverbial shit hits the fan. The dominoes really start to fall: he's under suspicion of torching the house of a state trooper who's given him a speeding ticket; some of his female disciples go to the press – he banned them, they say, from bringing sanitary towels into ministry headquarters. He says feminine hygiene products are medical intervention; they say he does it to humiliate them, that he's a misogynist.

'I asked myself difficult questions when I was at my lowest,' Dove tells a journalist on the *Albuquerque Tribune*, when he gets out of hospital. 'I asked the Lord if He would, in His grace, take me to be by His side. The answer was no, but what was revealed to me was that I *will* control my death. My death will be significant to the human race.'

'We're talking about suicide,' goes the journalist. 'The Bible says it's a sin.'

'No. It *says*, "Thou shalt not kill." The translation is faulty. The Hebrew says, "Thou shalt not *murder.*"'

'I didn't know that.'

'Well, now you do. Every Sunday I will pray. I will ask if my time is here.'

'And when the time comes, how will you do it? Hanging?'

'Not hanging, and not jumping. As a Christian those methods have connotations of guilt for me. Relating to the death of Judas Iscariot.'

'Pills?'

'I don't take medication of any sort.'

Probably at this point he's sussed that whatever method of suicide he comes up with, it's going to put his manifesto under the glass, because after that he changes the subject. Ends the interview. There's a photo of him attached to the article and he looks fucking appalling. He's piled on weight and it's gone round his shoulders, neck and chest. His thatch of hair is yellow against his skin, which is red from either blood pressure or the New Mexico sun, and the only thing I can think when I see the photo is: Christ – looks like someone's *peeled* the bastard's face.

In London I work all the depression-suicide stuff into the article and sell it, at last, to *Fortean Times*. Maybe I have a premonition, who knows? because I publish under a pseudonym: Joe Finn. Two weeks after it comes out the *Fortean Times* gets a solicitor's letter. We're all in the shit. Pastor Malachi Dove is going to sue us all: the *Fortean Times* and, most of all, *the heretic who dares to call himself a journalist, Joe Finn.*

5

I was meeting my contact from the Psychogenic Healing Ministries at the convenience store in Croabh Haven where he came weekly to collect supplies for the community. As I walked I tried to imagine what sort of ritual would have a community discarding pig offal into the sea. No wonder they've got you down as Satanists, I thought, turning my eyes to the island. What are you getting up to out there then, you bunch of nutsos? What're you messing with?

Suddenly and brilliantly, the trees opened on to the vista of Croabh Haven. I stood for a moment, blinking in the brightness, thinking how different it all looked from last night, how difficult it was to square this picture-pretty marina, its glittering yachts and SUVs, with the swill of rotten meat next to the sewage pipe only half a mile up the shore.

The heart of the marina was the convenience store on the green, surrounded by vehicles gleaming in the sun, a dairy truck and tourists to-ing and fro-ing, lazy in their flip-flops, clutching carrier-bags full of fresh tomatoes and lettuce and *Hello!* magazine, seabirds pecking at ice-lolly wrappers on the grass. A guy in a striped butcher's apron was stacking boxes at the rear of the shop and inside, in the cool, a dimpled, smiling girl in a yellow halterneck served holidaymakers at the cash desk, loading their purchases into bags.

I'd never seen Blake Frandenburg before. He was one of the original settlers on Pig Island twenty years ago and I knew his name, but not his face. When none of the men in striped polo shirts and canvas hats approached me, I wandered the shop for a while, picking up odd extras I might need for the next few days: no Newkie Brown so a bottle of Stolichnaya in case I was on Pig Island for a long time, a few sticks of menthol chewing-gum (thinking of the smell last night again) and some Kendal mint cake, because you never knew what they'd feed you in those places. These are people who can get by on green tea and glasses of their own urine, don't forget.

I was at the cash desk, half-way through paying, when the shop girl paused. She lifted her chin and looked over my shoulder out of the window and, with a muttered ' 'Scuse me,' slipped silently out from behind the desk. I turned to see what had got her attention. There was nothing outside, just the neatly clipped green and beyond that bright pennants fluttering on the masts. At that moment a large woman in shorts and a bikini top came barrelling across the grass towards the shop, sweating and ushering in front of her a young boy, both of them casting anxious glances over their shoulders in the direction of the jetty. The shop girl stepped to the door and held it open for the woman to come inside, holding the child firmly, her hands covering both his ears. 'That's it, good boy. Inside. Good lad.'

The shop girl closed the door and raised the blind slightly, so that she could stand with her nose to the door and stare out. The large woman stood next to me, peering out of the window, mopping her neck, the child pressed into her hip. Outside, next to the green, a couple had parked their car. They had both opened their doors and the woman had one sandalled foot resting on the Tarmac when something made them change their minds. First the foot disappeared back inside, then the doors closed. You could hear the distinctive double clunk of a central-locking system engaging. Behind me, other shoppers had slowly turned to see what was happening and now a long silence descended on the shop. I was about to say something when, from nowhere it seemed, a face appeared on the other side of the glass.

'Holy Christ!' blurted the fat woman. 'He's insane.' At the back of the shop a small girl squealed with fear and hid behind her mother's legs.

The face pressed itself into the glass, its nose distorted, the eyes pulled open to show the pink inner rims, the lips pressed away from gums like a skull.

'*Booh!*' it said. '*Booh!* Run! Run from the bogey-man!'

And that was how I met Blake Frandenburg, the first of the thirty or so members of the Psychogenic Healing Ministries I'd encounter over the next few days.

He turned out to be even weirder-looking without his face pushed against a glass pane: he was miniature and suntanned with a very tight, thin skull that looked like it had been squashed sideways in a vice. His skin was rough and scarred, like a shark's, and he was dressed like he belonged half-way between a Florida hotel and a golf course: a yellow shirt and tie, white shorts, his feet in shin-high socks and pale laced-up golf shoes. When he first shook my hand outside the convenience store it was like holding the skeleton of a very dried-up fish.

'Sorry about the bogeyman thing.' He gave me a nervous grin. 'But I really want to impress this on you, Joe, they push you to it. They really do. It's been like this from scratch – they ain't done nothing but be antagonistic.' He was from the States, and when he spoke he smiled constantly with one side of his mouth – like the other side was paralysed – showing those white teeth you only ever get on a Yank. 'The things they say about us. If you want my opinion, it's just plain *antagonistic*.'

'They say you're Satanists. That's what they say about you.'

His fixed smile didn't waver. He continued shaking my hand, nodding up and down, up and down, nervously searching my face, like he wasn't sure if there was a sly joke going on or not. His palms were sticky with sweat. Just when it seemed it was going to go on for ever, he took a sudden step back, releasing my hand like it was hot. 'Sure,' he said. 'Sure. We'll get to that later.' He ran his palms down the front of his shirt – to smooth it or clean them, I wasn't sure – and shot me another quick flash of teeth. 'All in God's good time, all in God's good time.'

That edgy, noncommittal cheerfulness turned out to be Blake's thing. He kept it up all the way across the firth to the island, giving me cheery facts and figures about PHM: how many people it reached through its website, how they'd built generators and cared for the land, and worshipped daily. 'We live in Paradise, Joe. Thirty of us, living in Paradise. Only five people have left in twenty years and you'll see why. You, Joe, even *you* won't want to leave.'

I sat in the bows, facing the island, the cuffs on my shorts rolled up a bit to get some sun on my white, city-boy knees, watching the settlement on Pig Island gradually reveal itself to me: a vague pale line on the north shoreline, slowly blooming into a spit of sand: indeterminate patches of colour above it, which wavered and crystallized into twenty or more cottages huddling together, their windows reflecting back the morning sea like mirrors. Apart from the cliff that rose above the community, crowned with trees, the settlement didn't look very sinister now I could see it close up – not the place of devil-worshippers. Each cottage had once been painted a different ice-cream colour, like the seafront at Tobermory, but they had faded now and stood, like dying flowers, facing a central green. The only God-squad thing was a towering stone cross in the centre of the grass – Celtic, medieval, pagan-looking, and as we got closer I saw just how fuck-off enormous it was. At least forty feet tall. Taller than our house back in Kilburn.

The dory was quick. Even loaded down with a week's supplies it was a little sea rocket – the water slipped quickly away under us, oily engine fumes lacing the air. Blake nosed it into a small gap between the rocks and a jetty. Overhead was a trot-line with a pulley that he pulled down and clipped on to the bowline. He worked quickly, killing the motor and moving the fenders around so the boat didn't jostle against the rock. On the jetty I helped him unload the boat, stacking everything – the tinned stuff and the fresh milk, crates of vegetables and (oh, sweet relief) a healthy stash of Guinness tinnies and gin – into a large handcart. I pushed it for him because that was only fair, big hairy old me and tiny-guy him, and I followed him in silence up the narrow path that led away from the jetty, looking at the way the knotty veins in his calves pulsed black with the effort of climbing.

At the top of the path I dropped the cart and stopped, staring at the huddled settlement. It was like a novelty golf course with its neatly trimmed green and paths running off in different directions – like you'd expect a cuckoo-clock woman to wheel out on tracks any second. Set just behind the front row of cottages, where the land rose, was the roof of a long breezeblock building that looked a bit like the sort of community halls that sprang up everywhere in the seventies. Against it the cottages looked even more run-down, with their weathered roofs, the same greenish-grey as the earth, only freckled in places where a slate had been recently replaced. And it was silent. Not a sign of life except for the two of us.

'Here,' said Blake, pointing to the grass. 'Wait here. I won't be long. Please don't leave the green. For your own safety, please stay here on the grass.' Before I could stop him he headed away up a path, glancing left and right as he went, his golf shirt flapping against his skinny back.

At first I stood for a while in the centre of the

lawn, staring at the place he'd disappeared. Then, when I realized he wasn't coming back, I turned and looked around. With the exception of the waves breaking on the beach below, nothing moved. Everything stood still and hot and silent in the mid-day sun. The curtains in all the windows were tightly closed against the heat, and beyond their roofs rose the highlands, thick with trees. The west coast of Scotland is poxy with midges and I could imagine what it was like between those trees – thick with the fuckers, probably.

I went and stood in the shadow of the cross, pulled the mobile out of the rucksack, looked at it and thought, Shit, Lex, I'm sorry. No signal. Typical. I walked to the edge of the green to see if I could catch anything there. Nothing. I walked all round the grass, staring at the screen, holding the phone at arm's length, standing on tiptoe, standing on rocks, and then, when I still couldn't get a signal, I put it in my pocket and sat down again. I stared back at the mainland for a while, at the Craignish Peninsula, green and foamy and indistinct in the bright sea, a flash of silver where the marina was. Why was Blake making me wait? Probably a test to see if I'd stay where he put me. And, of course, me being working-class, as Lexie would point out, the exam ethic never does come easy: I just couldn't stay still. After about five minutes I had to get up. I had a lot to do in my time on Pig Island.

Weird to think that the letter I got twenty years ago was written on this island. Dove had sold the ministry's assets, given a whack to the IRS and come scurrying back to the UK, a handful of devoted disciples with him. He bought Pig Island and founded the Positive Living Centre.

'The only thing to mar my happiness,' he said in the letter, 'is the arrogance of certain members of the press. I remember you quite well, Mr Finn. I remember you in Albuquerque, and that you said you'd like to kill me. You should know that *I* will be in control of the end of my life. It will be a more beautiful, spectacular and memorable end than someone of your calibre could comprehend. And be glad! You will know when it happens! Because when I take my life I intend to *take your peace of mind with me*. I will, Mr Finn, in the final hour, run rings around you.'

The *Fortean Times* was not pleased. 'You'll end up selling space on the hatch, match and dispatch column at the *Crosby Herald*,' said Finn happily, while the magazine's legal department was girding its loins for a fight. But the summons never came. We waited. We all held our breath. Nothing happened. Weeks went by. Months. After almost a year my curiosity got the better of me. I wrote to the

PO box on the letter asking if Malachi was going to pursue the 'conversation raised in your last letter'. No reply. I waited weeks and wrote again. 'Looking forward to hearing from you.' Still no reply. On it went, letter after letter, and nothing but silence from Pig Island. Eventually, after six months, I got a curt little note from the treasurer: 'Dear Mr Finn. Sorry to inform you, but Pastor Dove is no longer with us.'

'No longer with us,' I asked Finn. 'What does that mean?'

'Dunno. Topped himself, probably. And if he's dead I'm glad.'

'He said his death was going to be memorable. Remember? Said we'd all know about it. Me especially. Said he was going to take my peace of mind with him.'

'Well?' said Finn. 'Has he?'

I paused. 'Don't think so. Don't feel any different. I mean, I'd like to know how he killed himself. I'd like to know if he went back on his manifesto, how he made it memorable, cos I always had this idea it was going to be somewhere public, you know? Somewhere everyone would see him. He's a showman.'

'You'll have to find his body. That's the only way to find out.'

'Yeah. And I think it's out on some shag-awful island in Scotland.'

After that I went on for twenty years as a free-lance journalist, but I never really took one eye off Pig Island. I did my paranormal work, and hack-work by the yard, but if anything came up on the Western Isles of Scotland, I'd be there. Which is how I came to do the Eigg revolution. And how I got invited, at last, on to Pig Island. Weird to think of Dove's body out there somewhere on this silent island. Weird to think what the Ministries might have done with his body. Built a mausoleum, maybe. Or left it lying in state for people to come and see, like Lenin or Jeremy Bentham. In a glass box somewhere out in those trees.

6

I crossed the clipped lawn in silence and set off along a small path that passed the backs of the cottages. Everything was neat and ordered – wheelie-bins lined up neatly against walls, a large re-cycling bin with flies circling its opening, and a shed where a ride-on mower sat with its bonnet folded open, piles of yellow gas tanks stacked beyond it. Nothing odd there. The path left the cottages, entered the trees. I could feel in the back of my legs that the land had begun to climb slightly.

Over the years I'd done a lot of work in the States, trailing evangelists, watching mad-haired women in housecoats draw UFOs in trailerpark dust – and that morning on Pig Island I was suddenly reminded of a wood I'd visited on that long trip. It was in Louisiana, just outside Baton Rouge, and I was interested because the local residents had had the shits put up them by someone sneaking into the wood at night and decorating all the trees for a half a square mile with tiny, ruby-eyed voodoo dolls. I only found out later that a killer had been operating in those woods at the same time. A killer of children. No one ever worked out for sure if the dolls were connected with the murders, or if they were completely coincidental, but they stuck with me. From then on I couldn't go into woods anywhere on the planet without remembering the red points of light reflected in their eyes, and wondering if the killer had put them there – or if he'd been watching me that day as I walked around. It all came back to me now, like a shiver: the whisper of Spanish moss and live oak, the faint twang of a stringed instrument.

I hesitated, feeling the hair go up on the back of my neck, and turned slightly to look back. Only a few yards below me Blake had appeared silently on the path. His hand was up in a friendly wave.

'Hi, Joe. Hi. Good to see you.' He flashed me his

ratty, lopsided smile. 'Do you recall, Joe, I asked you to wait on the green?' He laughed. 'Didn't I ask you to wait? Didn't I?'

I wanted to grin back, laugh, maybe slap him on the back like a buddy and say, 'Yeah, but you didn't really expect me to wait, did you? You set a test like that, what do you expect?' and that was nearly what I did. But the professional came back at me: *Don't bollix it up, Oakesy, old mate.*

'I thought you'd forgotten.'

He wagged his finger. 'You'll find we're very friendly, very friendly folk here at the Psychogenic Healing Ministries, Joe, but please believe that we have rules for your own protection.' He raised his eyebrows and flashed me another smile. 'We do it because we care, Joe. We want you to enjoy your time here, not regret it. Now, won't you join me for lunch?'

He led me back towards the cottages, his hands outstretched to show me the community – like he was trying to sell it to me. 'We'd like to get to know you,' he said, grinning over his shoulder, as we came back to the green and crossed it. He slipped down a path that led along the side of the breezeblock building, still speaking over his shoulder. 'We'd like you to stay with us and to get to know us. We want you to feel you're part of our family.' At the head of the path he paused, holding out his hand with a theatrical flourish. 'This way,' he said, with a wink – as if to say, 'I just know you're going to LOVE this!'

I stepped forward and turned the corner and saw, arranged at two trestle tables, thirty faces gleaming up at me. Dove's followers. One or two of them half rose from their seats, grinning broadly, not sure what the etiquette was – and from somewhere at the back someone applauded timidly. The tables were loaded down with food; a breeze moved among it, lifting festively coloured napkins and tablecloths, ruffling blouses and rocking the massive enthusiastic sign strung above their heads: 'WELCOME TO CUAGACH EILEAN!!!!'

'Joe,' Blake said, holding out his hand to indicate the diners, 'Joe Oakes. Meet the Psychogenic Healing Ministries. Welcome to our family!'

It was probably only then that I really believed no one on Pig Island had linked me to Joe Finn of twenty years ago, the great nemesis of Malachi Dove.

Everyone knows the story about Aleister Crowley, right? The one about when the 'Great Beast' Crowley tried to raise Pan? Well, it's dead simple. It goes like this: Crowley's disciples locked him and his son, McAleister, in a room at the top of a Parisian hotel, promising that under no circumstances would they re-enter the room until morning, whatever noises they heard. They waited downstairs, huddled together and wrapped in blankets because the hotel had gone inexplicably cold. All night they listened in horror as the ritual upstairs unfolded in a series of bangs, shouts and splintering of wood. Usual shite. At last, at daybreak, when silence had fallen, they ventured cautiously upstairs to find the door locked, the room silent. When they broke down the door they saw Crowley's ritual had been a success. His son McAleister lay dead at one side of the room and on the other crouched Crowley, naked, bloodied and gibbering. He needed four months in a lunatic asylum before he could speak again.

Well, it's famous, as stories go. Only problem is, *it didn't happen*. It's just a myth, just part of Crowley's impulse for self-promotion and show-manship. That's what Satanists are, in general – a bunch of theatrical types whose main aim, IMHO, is to get a crafty shag. So what was I expecting of the Psychogenic Healing Ministries? I can't remember exactly – but probably the usual shite: Gothic robes, altar rites, chanting in the trees at sundown. What I didn't expect were these ordinary, mostly middle-class people, dressed, on the whole, like they were off for a spot of shopping on a Saturday afternoon.

'You see, Joe, we're quite normal,' said Blake,

showing me to my seat. 'We're not going to eat you!'

'No,' laughed one of the other diners. 'Or try to convert you!'

And that was supposed to be the first impression I got – normality and sunny wholesomeness through and through, from the gingham tablecloth to the homey food: thick-crusted quiches sprinkled with chives, misshapen pork pies, large institutional metal bowls of potato salad. There was even wine in cloudy-looking carafes placed at intervals down the table, and everywhere I looked I saw pleasant-faced people grinning back at me, sticking out their hands and saying, 'Hi, Joe!' But no matter what they did, I couldn't help it, that REM song kept chuntering away through the old grey matter: *Shiny happy people*'. Something a bit sinister about anyone that happy . . . '*Shiny happy people*'. And the fucking sunshine, too. Sunshine in a bottle. That was what they wanted me to think.

What they were doing was staging this totally elaborate game of musical chairs. My neighbour kept changing every ten minutes. Everyone who sat next to me did this dead intense PR job on the community, working their nuts off to tell me about how much hard work went into maintaining the Positive Living Centre, how much love and honest brain-power had gone into Cuagach Eilean.

'Everything's done with total, like, sensitivity to the environment – we recycle, don't use pesticides or herbicides, we celebrate what Gaia and the Lord give us through Cuagach Eilean. We want to repay them in some small way. Those trees over there? The tall ones? Planted by us.'

'The more we love the soil the more it repays us. We grow all our own fruit and vegetables. If I say it myself, when it comes to size and taste our vegetables can give Findhorn's a run for their money.'

'See the refectory building? I made the windows. I was a carpenter by trade before I came here, through God's grace. It's all timber from renewable sources – some of it from Cuagach herself. I'm working on new doors for the cottages now.'

There was a tall African guy in a *dashiki*, who told me he'd arrived in England as a missionary to spread the word of the Lord to the British: 'This proud nation that has forgotten God.' (Get that? A Nigerian bringing Christianity to us – what a turn of the tables is *that*?) But no one had mentioned Dove's name yet, which I thought was kind of odd. I waited long enough so that when I spoke it'd sound like normal curiosity. Then I said, 'What happened to your founder, Malachi Dove? I don't see him here.'

The missionary was smiling at me, and when I

said the name his smile got a little fixed, his eyes a little distant. But he didn't stop beaming. 'He's gone,' he said, with a fake cheerfulness. 'He left years ago. He lost his way.'

'Suicide,' I said. 'Story goes he had a thing about suicide.'

He didn't blink. The smile got tighter, wider. 'He's gone,' he repeated. 'Long time now. Lost his way.'

'Thank you for asking about Malachi.' Blake was suddenly at my side. He put a hand on my elbow to turn me away from the missionary. 'Our founder, Malachi, the messenger. We hold his name dear, though many have forgotten it.'

'I did some homework and seems like he topped himself.' I looked across the table at the bloodless faces of the women eating, one of them methodically working a piece of gristle out of her teeth with a broken fingernail. 'Can't think why. On this Paradise.'

'No, no, no.' He flashed me that cookie-cutter smile – the one the missionary had just wheeled out for me. 'Our founder is not yet with the Lord.'

I paused. Now this was interesting. 'He's alive?'

'Oh, yes.'

'Then where the hell—' I stopped. 'Then where is he?'

'He's – he's gone. Gone, a long time ago.'

'Where? New Mexico?'

Silence.

'London?'

'Gone,' he repeated, the smile fixed, a veil coming down behind his eyes. 'Thank you, Joe, for your interest. In God's good time I will tell you all you wish to know about Malachi Dove. All in God's good time.'

While the sun crossed the zenith and the shadows of the trees on the cliffs moved like the hands on a clock, I met at least half of the community: big-chested men in denim smocks and Birkenstocks, who put their heads sympathetically on one side when they spoke; an elderly ex-professor of theology in wire-framed glasses, who had located the fresh-water well they used and created the pumping system that fed the community; serious-faced girl students in flowery skirts, who could talk intensely for hours about the theory behind the Psychogenic Healing Ministries.

I've got a trick, a way of nodding and keeping up the small-talk while another part of me detaches and floats free. I was smiling and nodding but inside I was off, unravelling what Blake had said: Malachi not dead. Was that why I still had my peace of mind? How had he just slipped off the radar like that? If he'd started up another ministry somewhere else I'd have known about it. I thought of all the places he could have gone, the connections he had. He was from London. Weird if he'd been living in the same town as me for the last twenty years.

Whatever had happened to their founder it wasn't on the minds of the Psychogenic Healing Ministries members. Once you tuned into it, it was as plain as anything. There was something else happening here. There was a division. Trouble in Paradise.

At the far end of the table a group of about eight people sat morosely, not making the effort to come and introduce themselves. I noticed them whispering nervously among themselves, and some couldn't resist glancing over their shoulders up at the cliff when they thought I wasn't watching. Blake saw I'd clocked them. He took his glass, patted my arm, and said, 'Come on. Let me introduce you to the Garricks. It'll have to happen sooner or later.'

Benjamin Garrick, the centre's treasurer, was a tall, pinched-looking man with a severe haircut and a buttoned-up grey shirt. His wife, who sat to his right, was big-boned, man-faced, dressed in a king-fisher blue kaftan and headscarf, gingerish ringlets peeking from the headscarf. They nodded, they greeted me, but I wasn't welcome. You could just tell. Susan Garrick especially would've liked to see me dead. She sat stiffly, pointedly averting her eyes, while her husband gave me stilted details of the community's financial situation, saying nothing, until about five minutes into the conversation she lowered her fork and sniffed the air. 'It's a southerly,' she said, the ringlets shivering and bouncing. 'We shouldn't have come out here if there was a southerly due.'

'Not now,' muttered a nearby woman in a battered straw boater.

Benjamin Garrick dropped his face, and subtly covered his mouth with his napkin, murmuring under his breath, 'Darling, let Blake deal with that.'

But she'd started something. Out of the corner of my eye I could see other women making faces and wrinkling their noses, one or two turning so their backs faced the cliff. I put down my fork and sniffed the air. There it was – the smell of something rotten. Dying vegetation? Or the community's septic tank? It was unmistakable – the smell that is the purest distillation of sickness and death. I thought about the rotting meat clotted behind the outlet pipe.

At the tables one or two of the women had pushed away their plates, others sat with unhappy expressions, trying to eat their potato salad. One pulled out a handkerchief and covered her nose.

'Hey,' said Blake, leaning over to them, using his knife to indicate their plates. He continued chewing, giving them a meaningful nod. They hesitated, and after a few seconds, wan expressions on their faces, bravely picked up their forks and pushed some food into their mouths, looking down at their plates as they chewed.

'What can you smell?' I said, leaning past Garrick so I could see his wife.

She shook her head and pinched her nose, glancing at Blake and muttering, 'Nothing, absolutely nothing,' under her breath.

'What is it?' I asked again, my eyes straying up to the clifftop where the sun was so strong it cut out the shapes of individual leaves, like cacti in the desert. 'Tell me.'

'All in good time,' Blake said, flashing me his reassuring smile. He lifted a carafe. 'More wine? We want you to enjoy yourself.'

'What's at the top of the cliff?' I said. 'I'll enjoy myself more if you tell me what you're all staring at.'

'You *see*?' Susan Garrick said abruptly, pushing back her chair and standing, her eyes locked on Blake. 'I *told* you he'd interfere. That's what journalists do. He's just going to tempt the—'

'*That's enough, Susan*,' said Blake. 'Hold your counsel.'

Benjamin put a hand on his wife's arm, drew her back to her seat. Slowly she subsided into the chair, staring red-faced at Blake as if she hated him more than anything in the world.

'Now,' Blake said with a smile, taking my arm

and raising me kind of forcefully to my feet, 'come along, Joe. Let's show you the rest of our Paradise.'

7

As the afternoon wore on all my questions were answered the same way. *Malachi is gone. Gone. He's left us. Blake will tell you everything in God's good time.* While the meal was cleared away by two elderly men in blue cambric aprons, I was treated to a tour of the community. You know the kind of thing: the generator, the sewage system, the orchards and the bean rows. I was handed unripe plums from the trees and a fresh oyster shucked off the rocks near the jetty. I was dragged into a giant barn and made to watch while slate was passed through cutting equipment, turned, polished and rubbed with linseed oil to make the Celtic crosses the community sold on the mainland for an income. A contingent of people came with me everywhere, hovering at my elbow, eagerly pointing out how well they took care of the place. But wherever we went we stuck to the slopes at the bottom of the cliffs.

'Where are the pigs?' I asked Blake, as we entered a small forest and at last started to climb a path in the direction of the cliffs. By now we'd been going for over two hours and the welcome party had dwindled to him and a sullen teenage girl with toothpick-thin arms who'd offered to hold my camera bag while I took photos. 'It's called Pig Island, but I haven't seen any pigs.'

'Yes,' he said, taking my arm with a smile, 'but that's just a nickname. The real name is Cuagach Eilean. "Limping Island." Nothing to do with pigs.'

'So there are no pigs here?'

He paused – seemed about to answer. After a moment's thought his face cleared and he said cheerily, 'Look at this!' He headed off along a path that led away from the one we stood on, off into the dark of the woods. 'Here we are! We're coming to the real heart of our community.'

I followed him, and a few yards along the path we came to a weathered clapboard church half hidden in the trees ahead, only picked out by patches of sunlight. It had a rectangular tower ending in a small steeple and two stained-glass, Gothic-style windows, several panes replaced with clear glass. Over the years ivy had clung to it and been removed so you could see where the suckers had been painted over, leaving strange textures like tidewater along the walls. Standing in a patch of sunlight in the grass to the left of the doors was a life-sized crucifix – like the Celtic cross on the green, it was carved out of stone. An effigy of Christ, it had been clumsily made: Christ's face was like the weird Filipino iconography I'd photographed in Manila, the skin drawn back from his teeth, like a howling animal in agony. His body was pocked with small darts and other marks. When I shaded my eyes and studied them I saw they were a series of numbers scratched into the skin.

'The projected populations of every country in the world in the year twenty twenty,' said Blake. 'Because of medical intervention in the natural cycle of life and death we believe that these numbers are branded in Christ's flesh, that even now where He sits with His father, He feels the agony of the planet. Come in.' He held the door open for me. I saw cool flagged floors in the gloom, and caught a whiff of camphor, wood polish and red wine. 'Walk past Him, Joe. He looks at you with only love. Only love and compassion. Walk past Him. Come inside.'

I was a bit weirded out to go so close to the crucifix. It was almost my own height and so lifelike that going past its eyes was like being in the presence of the dead. I looked straight ahead and ducked into the gloomy vestibule to where Blake stood facing me in the semi-darkness.

'I want you to see this, Joe.'

I stood still until my eyes got used to the light. The two Gothic windows behind me dropped coloured light on to the flagstone floor, but the rest of the chapel was in shadow. It took me a moment to understand why. I turned and looked back at the doors and saw that the weatherboard steeple was only a fascia containing the small vestibule – the remainder of the chapel, which stretched out past Blake into the darkness, had been hewn deep into the cliff face. Everything, the altar, the pulpit, the vaulted ceiling, even the pews, was carved from grey-veined rock. It was one of the hottest days of the year, but the chapel was colder than a meat-locker.

'We did this,' said Blake proudly, his voice echoing round the walls, 'with hammers and chisels and our own sweat. Three years it took from start to finish. Fifteen of us working round the clock. Can you imagine the love, Joe, the love that goes into a project like this?'

I fumbled out my camera, handing the bag to the girl, and fired off a few shots, resting the camera on a pew for stability because I didn't want to use a flash. A wooden cross hung on the far wall and below it, painted in a gold-leaf arc that spread like sunrays across the walls, were the words: 'Leave the world when the Lord calls you. Resist not his will. Accept his grace and feel it grow within.' The altar was very large and probably, looking at the imagery, carved by the person responsible for the crucifix outside. 'What happens in here?' I said, moving between the pews.

'What happens in here?' Blake gave a nervous laugh showing his long teeth, like he couldn't believe I'd ask such a dumb question. He glanced to the girl and back, sharing his disbelief with her. 'What happens in most Christian chapels? We hold our prayer meetings and services.'

'Prayer meetings?' I lowered the camera. 'Services?'

He studied me with his pale eyes. 'That's what I said. Have you ever been to a Christian service, Joe?'

'Yes, Blake, I have. Will I be invited to one of yours?'

'Oh, you will. All in good time.'

I smiled at him then, holding his eyes. We were playing a game now, Blake and me, and we both knew it. 'That lock.' I nodded back to the big main doors. 'That's kind of a serious lock.' I'd noticed it when we first came in – a huge iron one that could be opened from either side. The key was on the inside and it was supplemented with bolts all the way up the interior of the door. The windows had no catches because they had been built not to open. For whatever reason, the PHM felt a need to lock this chapel, miles away from the mainland. 'Pretty secure. Feels like a bunker.' I gave him a sly wink. 'But I think that's something else you'll tell me about. All in God's good time?'

Blake drew himself up to his fullest height and took a deep breath. 'You'll stay with us tonight, won't you, Joe? I've got no plans to go to the mainland. There's a bed made up in my cottage.'

I gave a short laugh. 'Of course I'm going to stay, Blake. Of course.'

8

After the tour Blake let me off the leash for an hour to get some photographs in – I was allowed to go anywhere, as long as I didn't stray further up the slope towards the cliffs. He sent the teenage girl along as a chaperone. She carried the bag when I was shooting, held the reflector for me, and didn't say much until we were out of sight of the cottages. I was busy changing a lens when she crept up next to me and said, almost in my ear, 'They're on the other side of the island.'

I stopped and looked at her. Her face was very pale. Her eyes were watery and cold blue, like a swimming-pool.

'The pigs. You wanted to know about the pigs. And I was just saying, they're over there.' She rolled her eyes in the direction of the cliff face, nodding up there, as if she'd have liked to point but thought she might get caught doing it. 'Over there. All the way across the other side. But no one's going to, like, just let you go over there or anything.'

I lowered the camera. 'Why? What's over there?'

'I can't tell you that. We're not supposed to talk to you about it. Blake's going to tell you.'

I studied her. She had lank blonde hair pushed behind her ears and was so pale and thin it was pitiful, with spidery fingers and her feet like a skeleton's, blistered and sore, crammed into pink jelly sandals. 'And who are you?'

She grinned and wiped her hand on her shorts and held it out to me. 'I'm Sovereign. Yeah, I know, *Sovereign*. It's what my parents called me. Because I was, like, so valuable to the community when I arrived. Apparently.'

'You were born here?'

'Yeah, and this place is *so* not what I'm about. The day I turn eighteen I'm total *history*.' She made her hand into a plane and glided it out into the air, off towards the mainland. 'Bye-bye, toot toot, train – you won't see me for dust. Only four months now.'

'Who are your parents?'

'The Garricks. You met them. The ones with the sticks up their butts?'

'Yes. I met them.'

'I know what you're thinking – like, geriatric ward, yeah?' She grinned, showing a missing canine in her left jaw. No medical treatment, my mind flashed. 'They waited until they were thirty-eight before they had me, totally ancient. How gross is that? But that's how it is round here. Bunch of retards.' She stopped smiling and took a few moments to look at me, jiggling her legs a bit, chewing her thumbnail. 'You know, you don't look anything *like* a journalist.' She took her thumb out of her mouth. 'Anyone ever tell you that? I watch a lot of TV and I know what a journalist should look like and the first thing I thought when I saw you was, uh, like no *way*, he *rully* doesn't look like a journalist.'

I glanced down at my battered shorts, my big stained hands and sandals all dirty and fucked from walking everywhere. I had to smile. She was right – in spite of the psychology degree, the cushy detached house and the job, somehow I never had got the Merseyside docker out of my bones. I only did it once over the summer, helping my old man out, but it was in my family and stuck inside me like DNA. 'I know,' I said. 'I look like a docker.'

'Yeah, you do. You look like a docker.'

I snapped on the lens cap and studied her carefully.

'Sovereign,' I said, 'what goes on here? What happens in the church? What rituals was it made for?'

She laughed. 'I know what you're thinking. I know about the video. I told you: we see TV.'

'Then what is it? The thing on the beach. Who is it?'

'That depends on who you ask. One person says one thing, someone else says something else.'

'What about you? What do you say?'

'I say we're not Satanists. Nothing happens in the church except the usual shit. Prayer meetings, tambourines, Mum and Dad making total muppets of themselves. It's, like, so boring it's not true. And cold. Mum's stopped making me go, except on Sundays.'

'What about the locks on the doors? Those are some serious locks. Makes it look like they want to stop someone getting out.'

Sovereign blinked, confused. Then her expression cleared and she gave a short laugh. 'Duh, Joe!' She tapped her temple, as if to say, 'How stupid are you?' 'Not out! *In*. They're not trying to stop anyone getting *out*. They're trying to stop something getting *in*.'

'You're not going to answer any of the questions I want answered. You don't want to talk about your rituals or the rumours going round. Or about why everyone is so antsy about whatever's at the top of that cliff. Instead you're giving me a pretty good press release on how well the PHM is taking care of Cuagach Eilean.' I leaned across the table and helped myself to another shot of Blake's gin. It was late – nearly midnight – and we'd come back to his cottage after the evening meal in the refectory. We sat at the kitchen table near the window that faced the cliff. It was dark outside, and all we could see in the glass were our reflections – our faces lit from underneath by the small table lamp. Sovereign had given me clues: I needed Blake to give me the truth.

'And you know what?' I said, pushing back the bottle and settling in my chair, nursing the drink. 'It crosses my mind that this has only happened to me once before. Almost ten years ago. The Eigg revolution.'

Blake rested his head sideways on his thumb, a cigar burning between two outstretched fingers, and looked at me levelly. 'Yeah. And?'

'I was one of the journalists who broke the story. Got them the publicity they needed.'

Blake nodded silently, waiting for me to continue. I smiled at him. 'Malachi Dove's money bought this island, right? You moved here with him, but he's not here now – and no one wants to talk about him. So, I'm going to make a little leap of faith here, *Blake*, and call me forward, but I'm going to *suggest* you've got me out here on false pretences.' I pointed my finger at him, smiling slyly over the top of it. 'See, I don't think I'm going to hear much about Satanism. Or the video. What I think is that Malachi left you all here to go wherever it is he's gone – and you're insecure about that. You want to raise the money to buy Cuagach from him. You're not going to make it from selling those crosses so you've got to appeal for donations. You want me to do for Cuagach what I did for Eigg.'

'You're a sharp one, Joe.'

'Yes, Blake.' I downed the gin, put the glass neatly on the table in front of him and met his eyes. 'I am.'

There was a long silence. I wanted him to squirm a bit. After a long time he cleared his throat and lowered his eyes, tapping his cigar in the ashtray and shifting uncomfortably in the seat. 'We're cold out of luck here, Joe. Things have not been good.'

'It's OK.' I sighed. 'It's straightforward. You give me the story I want – that's the Satanism one – and I'll attach a sob message to it, get one of the nationals to run it as a feature and before you know it you'll have the nation crying with you. Is Dove ready to sell?'

'No. But if we can raise the legal fees and prove he's insane we can get him into something like the Court of Protection, here or in England. Get a judicial factor appointed, then we've got power of attorney and we can buy the island. We won't cheat him – we'll give him what he paid for it.'

'Insane?' I bent to light a cigarette, screwing up my eyes. 'On what grounds?'

'On the grounds he's practising Satanism on Cuagach Eilean.'

I paused. The lighter faltered and went out. I raised my eyes to Blake. He looked back at me steadily.

'I said on the grounds that he's practising Satanism on our—'

'I heard you.' I flicked on the lighter again, lit the cigarette and raised my head. 'He's still on Cuagach? Is that what you're telling me? He hasn't gone back to the States? London?'

Blake pushed back his chair with a loud, scraping noise. 'You'd better come through, Joe.' He beckoned me with his cigar. 'Come through here.'

We went into the corridor at the back of the house.

'I was one of Malachi's first disciples,' he said. 'Me and Benjamin Garrick and Susan, his wife. This cottage was the first place we built on Cuagach and this was our meeting room. I haven't had the heart to change it.'

He unlocked a heavy, planked door, switched on the light and let me into a small annexe to the house. It was built in the same stone as the rest of the cottage, with a small mullioned window, but it was cold and unswept – unlived in, the carpet thin and patchy. The walls were decorated with 1970s Malachi Dove tour posters and I walked slowly round the room, studying them: Dove on stage, a spotlight creating a halo behind him, a studio portrait of him, his chin resting on hands, looking into the camera with a frank, intimate expression. Another showed him laid out on his back, eyes closed, hands on his chest, like he was in his coffin. I peered at the picture carefully. He was bloated and old without his glasses. Under the photo were printed the words: 'When God calls me I will go to His side.'

'What's he doing?' I said. 'What is this?'

'He's praying. This position, on his back, was the only way he could concentrate. Still does, for all I know.'

I squatted down to sort through a stack of framed photos leaning against the wall. More pictures of Malachi Dove, but this time they all seemed to have been taken on the island. One showed him with a young Blake and the Garricks, arms linked and smiling into the camera. Behind them the cottages were all freshly painted. Mrs Garrick was ringleted in a piecrust-collar Laura Ashley dress. Only Malachi seemed wrong. He looked tired and flabby, his eyes distant behind his glasses. He wore a kaftan to disguise his weight gain, and there was something tight and shiny about his face, like maybe he'd had a lift.

'He looks ill.'

'He was agitated. He was suing a journalist in London. He was very depressed by it.'

'A journalist?' I didn't look up. Didn't want him to read my mind. I closed the stack of photos. 'When was this?'

'Nineteen eighty-six. But he never followed it up. Events stopped him.'

'These are the events you're going to tell me about?'

Blake leaned over and pulled from the stack of photos a gilt-framed one showing Dove with his arm round a woman in a drawstring Greek-style blouse. 'His wife,' said Blake, tapping the glass. 'Asunción. A good Christian girl.'

Oh, Asunción, I thought. Light of my life. So you married her. A reward for all those old ladies' arses she had to stick her hand up.

'They prayed for a child. But when it happened Malachi's faith collapsed.'

I raised my eyebrows. Blake shrugged. 'Yeah – I know. We didn't expect it, but Malachi was weaker than any of us thought. When Asunción went into labour you could tell by the way she was breathing there was a problem. It was right here, in this room, it happened.' He pushed the frame back into the pile and straightened, brushing off his hands. 'Malachi prayed that night. He prayed hard with the other disciples to find strength. We sat at that kitchen table, where you and I were sitting just now, the three of us talking to him, holding his hands . . . Holding his hands, but trying, in our own ways, Joe, to hold his heart. Even with God's love we couldn't persuade him to keep his vows. After twenty-four hours he put Asunción into the boat and took her to a hospital on the mainland.'

'Even though that was against what the Psychogenics stood for?'

'Even though that was against *everything* we stood for.' He gazed down at the floor, his arms out a bit at his sides, and then, like he was disappointed not to see Asunción and Malachi's ghosts marked out on the carpet, he dropped his hands and looked up at me with red-rimmed eyes. 'Believe me, Joe.' He touched his heart with his little finger. 'It didn't make me happy, what came next.'

'Why? What came next?'

'At first we didn't see him. Not for weeks. When he did come back he was alone – torn apart. The boy was just torn apart. Came in and sat at that table and poured his heart out to me: how badly he felt to have broken his vow, how it had been too late anyway – the Lord had called the tiny baby to His side, stillborn it was, and Asunción was refusing to come back to the island. She didn't want anything to do with the Positive Living Centre or the PHM, and after what happened maybe you couldn't blame her.' He stopped then, his finger tapping his forehead and his eyes lowered, like he was too choked to continue.

'But he's still here? In the village?'

Blake shook his head. 'No,' he said, in a tight voice. 'He couldn't stay in the community, not after that. He was too – too ashamed of his weakness.' He took a deep breath. 'But the island was his home, of course.'

'So he stayed?'

'He found himself an old miners' barracks over by the slate mine. Three miles away. On the south tip of Cuagach. The side facing the sea. Sometimes a shop in Bellanoch does supply runs for him, but he doesn't speak to them or even see them. He's completely isolated.' Blake went to the curtain, drawing it back and opening the window. He leaned out, looking up at the cliff face, his breath clouding the air. It was silent and hollow out there, and mist was beginning to come down, shifting across the cold stars above. 'We've carried on his teaching, but we haven't seen him in the village for twenty years. Twenty years he's been out there. Twenty years on his own.'

I came to stand next to him, opening the other

window and ducking to stick my nose out, staring up to where the cliff rose hard into the night. I tried to picture the island stretching out between here and the south tip – miles of uninhabited land, poking into the sea like a finger. So, Malachi, you live with the pigs, I thought. And do you cut them up too?

'What's he getting up to over there, then, Blake?' I murmured. 'What did the tourist photograph that day?'

When Blake answered his voice was so low that I had to strain to hear. 'Something has gone very wrong for Malachi. Things are happening at that end of Cuagach I try not to think about too hard.'

There was a full moon that night, and the air was so crystalline, so salty and cool that, lying in my bed in the cottage next to the firth, I could have been in my tomb. I stayed awake listening to the wind picking up outside, thinking of the trees on the slopes above, leaning and bending in the wind, about all the secret places their movements revealed. Malachi Dove, alive and only three miles away. I kept coming back in my mind to the path I'd been walking up when Blake had stopped me – *Where does that go, then, Blake? Where does that path go?* When at last I gave up trying to sleep and slid out of bed the display on my mobile phone read 02:47.

I hauled on my filthy old army shorts, grabbed

my rucksack, and crept down the stairs. The house was silent. The smell of our drinking session still hung in the kitchen and the two half-empty glasses stood on the table. At the back door there was a heavy torch on the worktop, a Post-it taped above it – Blake reminding himself to check the batteries. I took the torch and stepped out into the starry night, closing the door carefully behind me.

Outside it was cold. The cottages were frosty and shuttered-looking in the moonlight. The only light was an old-fashioned harbour lamp on the jetty, twinkling through the trees, and beyond it, high in the sky above the silver-capped firth, clouds were gathering in a shape like sprawling seaweed, one tendril snaking out to the island, the other angling down above the Craignish Peninsula where the bungalow was, like they were trying to connect the two landmasses. I pictured Lexie, curled up on the bed, her yellow pyjama top bunched up a bit to show her long back, her face pleated against the pillow. Sorry, Lex, my love, I thought, pulling out my mobile, checking it for a signal. Nothing. When we first met it wouldn't have mattered that I'd left her on her own – she'd have been out with her friends or in bed with a bottle of wine, watching all the shite TV I hated. But everything was different now. The way she talked about my job, these nights away were like me putting fingers into an open wound. Still, I thought, pushing the phone back into my pocket, someone has to do it. I hitched up the rucksack, and was about to set off along the path when a faint sound made me pause.

What the—?

I turned and stared at the dark, ragged shape of the cliff, darker than the sky. The sound had come from that direction. It had been so brief, so momentary and faint, I thought I must've dreamed it. *You're hearing things, Oakesy, old mate.* But then it came again – clearer this time, sending a neat finger of fear down my back. It was thin and lonely, very, very distant, and I knew instinctively it wasn't human. Instead – and I got this instant picture of the rotting meat under the sewage pipe – it sounded like a animal squealing. Or howling.

Pigs.

I looped my fingers into the rucksack straps and turned my face to the sky, standing still for a long time and straining to listen. But minutes passed and the sound didn't come again. The cliff face stood hard and silent, only the occasional toss and buffet of the trees disturbing it. At length, when it felt like I'd waited for ever, I hitched the rucksack up again and, casting occasional glances at the cliff, set off along the path, the torch shining on the ground ahead.

I turned on to the narrow lane that wound up into

the woods, the memory of the one lousy family holiday I'd ever had coming back to me – a caravan in Wales – the brilliant treachery of being out at night as a kid, the pancake-grey luminescence of the road. Who'd have thought Tarmac could look so pale in the darkness? About a hundred yards past the maintenance shed the Tarmac gave way to earth and I was into the woods, climbing now. Up and up for a good ten minutes into the dark woods and for ages all I could hear were my footsteps and the thump of my heart. Then, dead sudden, the trees opened, the moon came out, and I was in a clearing.

I stopped. A wire fence stood in front of me, rising up against the stars. Tall. At least nine feet of it. Like something from a zoo. I stared at it for a long time. A zoo or Jurassic Park. In the middle of it, directly in the path, was a tall gate. It had a heavy-duty padlock, and even before I went forward and rattled it I knew it wasn't going to open. I stood for a few moments, shining my torch to left and right along the fence, to where it stretched uninterrupted into the darkness. Then I pressed the torch into a hole in the wire and shone the beam through it to where the path continued on, identical to the path I stood on, winding away, higher and higher into the trees.

'OK,' I muttered, thinking of the maintenance shed I'd passed the previous morning. 'This, dear

Father in heaven, is why you invented wire-cutters.'

'Wait!'

I'd found the cutters in the shed and was half-way back to the gate when I heard the voice. I halted in my tracks, heart sinking.

'I said *wait*! What do you think you're doing?'

I turned, shoving the cutters into my pocket. Blake was running up the path behind me, flushed and puffing, an expression of outrage on his face. 'What in – in *heaven's* name do you think you're doing?'

'I'm having a look round.'

'No! You do not just "have a look round" on Cuagach. It's against the rules.' He caught up to me, and stood, breathing hard and shaking his head. He was wearing a sports jacket over a long purple T-shirt, his naked feet shoved hurriedly into unlaced trainers. 'You can't leave the community. Do you understand?' He switched on a pen torch and shone it into my face, then on to my rucksack, then up the path. 'Where were you going?'

'Over there,' I said amiably. 'Was just on my way to speak to Dove.'

'No, no, *no*, Joe!' He snatched at my sleeve, holding it between thumb and forefinger to stop me moving. 'Oh, no. You can't just *go and speak to him*. It's not a good idea. Not a good idea at all.'

I stared at the hand on my sleeve. 'Well, you know,' I said slowly, the instinct to thump him twitching briefly in my chest, 'maybe you're right – maybe it isn't a great idea. But I'm going to do it anyway.' I pulled my arm out of his grip and began to walk away.

'No!' he cried, starting to run again. I was going fast but he managed to insert himself on the path in front of me, holding out his arms and trotting backwards, trying to prevent me going any further. 'Over my dead body.'

I stopped and looked down at his scrawny legs, his weird, squashed skull. He weighed about half what I did. I shook my head, amused. 'You're not really saying you want to fight me?'

'Don't laugh at me,' he said savagely. 'Don't you dare laugh, boy. If I can't fight you then the others will. They'd be here in minutes.'

'Well, that sounds like a deal-breaker. It sounds like you don't want me to do your publicity after all.'

He paused and bit his lip. We regarded each other in silence, and after a few moments, without speaking, I pushed past him and continued up the path. At first I thought he was going to let me go. Then I heard his footsteps behind, running to catch up. I stopped.

'*OK*,' he said, panting hard. 'OK. I'll take you.

But this path ends at the gorge, and that's where we stop.'

'The gorge?'

'Yes. It's impassable, totally impassable – especially with a storm coming.' Almost on cue the moon went behind a cloud, dropping us into darkness. 'See?' he said, switching on the torch and shining it on his own face, so he looked like a Hallowe'en pumpkin. 'I told you. There's a storm coming.'

'What can we see from the gorge?'

He shot his eyes up to the sky to where the tendrils of cloud were splitting like mercury, running away in fragments across the moon. 'If this moon holds,' he said, shadows flitting across his face, 'you'll see everything. Everything you need to see.'

I continued on to the gate while Blake went back to the cottage for the keys. When he came trotting back he was dressed in jeans and a turtleneck, a pair of binoculars slung round his neck. You could tell he was still pissed off with me. He unlocked the gates without a word and for a while we walked in moody silence, through the gates and up the path, cresting the cliff in the darkness, the only sound our footsteps and the wind stirring the branches around us. Clouds flitted across the moon, sending huge animal-sized shadows scuttling out of the trees, across the path under our feet, and disappearing back into the woods. Blake switched on his torch, and after about ten minutes so did I, occasionally turning the beam and shining it into the trees when the wind shook a branch or snapped a twig.

The further we went, the more anxious Blake got. He walked with his neck very stiff, his eyes scanning the woods at either side, occasionally looking over his shoulder, like he was checking nothing was making its way up the path behind us.

'Hey,' I said, when we'd been walking for more than half an hour. My voice sounded very loud. 'Are you nervous?'

'No,' he said, in a whisper, not looking at me, keeping his eyes on the woods. 'No. Why would I be?'

'Because of what's on the video.'

He glanced at me. 'That video is all a big misunderstanding.'

'A misunderstanding? I've seen it. There's some weird fucking creature on it, walking through these fucking forests. What kind of misunderstanding is that?'

At first he didn't answer. We kept walking and I was about to ask him again when he stopped, switched off his torch and looked up at me. '*Listen*,' he whispered, standing very close. I could smell something bitter on his breath – like his fear was coming out as ketones. '*Let's get this straight. It was Malachi on the video.*'

'Malachi?'

He held a finger up to quieten me. '*Yes*. Malachi himself. Doing – I don't know, but doing something that means nothing to us, but everything to him.'

'What? In some fucking pantomime-cow costume with a— ?'

'The idea—' he interrupted, casting glances up and down the path. 'The idea that you can – can conjure Beelzebub, or Pan or Satan, is garbage. You know that and so do I. It was Malachi in the video.'

'Except not everyone agrees with you. Do they?'

'*Please*,' he hissed. 'Keep your voice down.'

'Why are the Garricks so scared?' I whispered. 'Susan's crapping herself, thinking I'm going to start something, tempt something. Now, Blake, *you* might think it's Malachi on the video – but they don't. They think he's brought Satan to Cuagach, don't they?' I raised the torch briefly and shone it off into the tree-trunks, the beam distorting and making strange shapes and shadows. 'They think—'

'*Sssssh!*'

'They think there's something unhuman out there.'

'It was a big decision inviting you on to the island,' Blake put a hand on my torch and pulled

94

the beam gently away from the trees. 'Some people are very superstitious – Benjamin and Susan and some others. They think that the less said about what is happening on Cuagach the better – that to talk about it to anyone outside could be ... provocative.'

'Yeah. I got that bit.'

'Believe me, Joe.' He pushed his face close to mine. 'Believe me, there have been times today when I have questioned ever getting you involved. Now,' he switched on his torch again and aimed it down the path, 'let's get this over with.'

He began walking again, a bit faster now, like he wanted to put distance between himself and the words 'Beelzebub', 'Pan', 'Satan', like they'd hang there in the branches behind us – proof he'd uttered them.

I went after him down the silvery path, and had caught up and was about to speak again when I registered something pale and small sitting in the centre of the path ahead.

'*What the*—' I came to a halt and quickly swung the torch beam on it. It was small and hunched, stood about two feet high and wasn't moving. It had a shape like a very small human with its back to us. 'What the fuck, Blake?' I murmured, approaching carefully. I walked past it, turned and shone the beam into its face. 'A gargoyle?'

'Yes,' he muttered impatiently. 'They're supposed to—'

'I know what they're supposed to do. They're supposed to ward off the . . .' I let the sentence trail off and turned to look along the path ahead. It continued for a few yards, then was swallowed by the trees. Somewhere beyond it lay the gorge and Dove's house.

'I see,' I said, turning back to the gargoyle. It had weird glass eyes, like the voodoo dolls in Louisiana. 'It's blocking the path. The Garricks put it there. It's to stop the devil coming along this path, isn't it?'

'*Leave it*,' Blake whispered. 'We need to keep going. We're nearly there.'

He started off again, leaving me standing staring at the gargoyle, picturing Susan or Benjamin coming up here, positioning it to face the south, blocking the path. *Christ*, I thought, shooting a look into the dark trees, Dove had done a cracking job of convincing someone in the community the devil was real. Good enough to get them so scared they'd turned their church into a fortress in case they ever had to take shelter there.

I clicked off the torch and headed off after Blake, imagining the gargoyle's eyes watching my retreating back. The path descended for a while, the land on either side of it rising steadily, until I was walking in a narrow ravine. Then the path ahead opened dramatically to show the sky and the moon, swollen and drenching everything in its icy light, Blake standing in front of it, waiting for me. I came down the last few steps and stopped next to him, staring at Cuagach spread out below us.

'Jeee-*sus*,' I breathed. '*Jesus*.'

We were standing on a long ledge about twenty foot from the top of an escarpment. The land dropped straight from our vantage-point about a hundred feet to what had the look of a very wide, dry riverbed studded with boulders as big as houses. About a third of a mile away it rose up again, marked by a distant line of trees. The gorge between the two slopes was as barren as a desert, unmarked by any shrub or tree, as otherworldly and lonely as a distant planet. Scattered among the boulders were odd brown shapes, reflecting an occasional glitter as clouds scudded across the moon. It took ages for me to understand what I was looking at.

'Barrels? Drums?' I said. 'Is that what they are?'

'This land was a chemical dump before we came here.'

I shot a few photos, then looked left and right along the ledge we stood on – at the ghostly squatting forms. 'More gargoyles.' They were planted at intervals of ten feet, all facing bravely across the gorge, their glass eyes glittering expectantly. Behind the ledge we stood on, the upper part of the escarpment formed a wall, and along its length ten-foot-tall letters had been sprayed in red paint that had dripped.

Get thee behind me, Satan. Get thee behind me, Satan. Get thee behind me, Satan.

'Jesus,' I said faintly, pulling out my camera, staring at the letters. 'Jesus fucking Christ. Someone here is really scared.' I squatted and fired off a few shots. Then I stood and faced across the gorge. The letters were so big they were difficult to understand this close up – they weren't designed to be read from the place we stood. They'd only be clear from a distance. Like if you were to stand in the tree-line on the other side of the gorge.

'That's it,' I said, staring at the trees. 'He lives over there, doesn't he? That's why you've got all this – this shit lying around up here.' I went to the edge of the gorge and squinted down into the darkness. 'Can we get down there? I want to go nearer.'

'No. The only way to get to Malachi's side of the island is in the boat and – *don't lean over, please.*' He plucked at my shirt, trying to pull me back. 'Joe – please – this is *very* dangerous. If you went down there you wouldn't make it back alive. And anyway—'

I turned. 'Anyway what?'

He hesitated. His face in the moonlight was pale. He knew he'd said too much. 'Nothing. It's very dangerous. Very dangerous.'

'No.' I straightened and looked at him, a bit amused. 'No. You weren't going to say that. What were you going to say?'

'Nothing.'

'Yes, you were.'

'No,' he said firmly.

I sighed. 'Well, if you're not going to tell me I'll have to find out for myself.' I started off along the ledge, dodging the gargoyles, shining the torch at the edge, trying to find a place to clamber down the escarpment.

'Stop!'

I looked back at him. 'Only if you tell me what you were going to say.'

He paused, biting his lip, his eyes lowered, shifting uneasily from foot to foot. 'A non-harassment order,' he muttered, not meeting my eye.

'What? What was that?'

'I said *a non-harassment order*. Malachi took out a non-harassment order on us. He went to court for it.'

'He went to court?' I echoed. 'Oh, Blake,' I leaned a bit closer to him, giving him a faint smile, suddenly enjoying this, 'what *did* you do to deserve that?'

'*Nothing*. Malachi is very unwell. We've done nothing wrong.'

'So why'd he get a restraining order on you?'

'*Because he is insane!* Insane. We've done nothing wrong!' He paused, breathing heavily, wiping his face like it was difficult to control himself. He ripped his binoculars off his head, thrusting them out to me. 'There. Look. His place is a fortress.'

I let the camera dangle on my chest and lifted the binoculars, focusing, moving them through a kaleidoscope of landscapes: the side of a boulder, a pile of rusting drums, the yellow flash of a hazardous-substance label. The opposite escarpment was of a darker rock: it looked geologically totally different from the land we stood on – blacker and more compact. I raised the binoculars and found a consistent line at the point where the trees started and, above it, a faint impressionistic cross-hatched pattern.

'What's that? Another fence? He's got a fence just like you?'

'Yes.'

'And when did he put up that little beauty?'

'Two years ago. Can you see the video cameras? They're trained on us now, Joe.'

I moved the binoculars slowly. The fence ran the length of the top of the escarpment, and mounted in front of it, like H. G. Wells's tripods, were at least forty video cameras, all pointing out across the moonlit gorge, glinting at us like silent, unblinking eyes.

'If he picks us up on those video cameras then

we're in breach of the order and we'll never get power of attorney.'

'This is your Gaza Strip wall? This is where it all happens?' I was about to drop the binoculars when they swept past something I couldn't put a name to. I quickly moved them back, the cross-hatching of the fence blurring with the movement, and—

'Blake? *Blake*, this is fucking weird shit.'

I was looking at a pair of eyes. Smeared and hollow. Below them a snout. A pig's head. Mounted on top of the fence. When I moved the binoculars to the right I found another – the same pushed-in features, the same hatch-like eyes, lolling tongue. I dropped the binoculars and stared out at the tree-line. Now I could see them – faint blobs of light, one after the other on top of the fence, lined up like heads on medieval battlements, one every ten feet or so just like the gargoyles on this side – stretching away into the distance. 'Where the fuck have they come from?'

'I *told* you – Malachi's very sick. He wants us to be scared.'

'And if I asked Benjamin Garrick, what would he say?'

Blake let his gaze drift out across the gorge. There was something resigned about his voice when he spoke. 'If you asked Benjamin he would say that Pan put them there. He would say that Pan can tear a living pig apart with his bare hands.'

9

The Garricks, it seemed, had a small following. They had convinced at least fifteen other members of the community that Pan was living on Pig Island, under Malachi's control. Or worse, not under it. Blake knew I wasn't going to be put off so the next morning he took me over to their cottage to speak to them. The storm he'd promised had arrived: overnight the island had been caught in a grey squall that sat like a cartoon cloud above it, circling it in grey mists and humid rains. When we set off at eleven, it seemed like the village had disappeared, only the dim orange glow of electric lights on in the cottages coming through the mist.

The Garricks lived at the end of the path that led down to the jetty. Once, their cottage had been painted peppermint green, but now it was faded almost to white, patched in places with grey filler and wet with condensed mist. It was the only cottage with a television set and the aerial rose, spidery, into the mist above the roof. We sat in the well-lit kitchen, with its cheerful gingham blinds, drinking steaming mugs of coffee and eating Susan's home-made brownies. Sovereign sat on the arm of the sofa in the adjacent room. She didn't speak but I was conscious of her watching me, an amused, knowing smile on her face. She was wearing a black Avril Lavigne T-shirt and a buckled, pleated mini-skirt. Her long thin legs kept jiggling up and down, like she was dancing to a tune in her head.

I settled back and opened my notepad. 'The only way I can help you is if you tell me everything,' I said. 'We're going to talk about Malachi – and you're all going to tell me what you know.'

Susan Garrick flushed a very bright red. She looked from me to Blake and back again. 'I don't like this, Blake,' she said. 'I don't like this attitude. What happened to our agreement of March 2005?'

'Susan, there wasn't an agreement,' he said levelly. '*You* said you wouldn't talk about it to outsiders, but I didn't make that promise. I'm acting in the interests of the whole community.'

'Well, I can't help it,' she said, running her hands over her arms where goosebumps had risen up. 'I can't help thinking that if Malachi knows we've talked about it he'll send that – that *thing* over here again. I'm not happy about provoking him.'

'Mr Oakes,' Benjamin said to me, 'do we have to do this? All we want is for you to tell our story. To tell how difficult it's been on Cuagach – but how devoted we are to it. We just want Malachi off the island so we can go over there and exorcize whatever it is he's tempted into living there.'

'Benjamin, Susan,' Blake put down his coffee and leaned across the table, taking their hands in his, 'Susan, Benjamin, this is important. Joe has told me that he won't do the story unless we talk about it.'

Susan stared at me. 'Is that true?'

'It's important to get the readers' interest,' I said, Joe-diplomat wise. 'They need to be drawn into a story.'

She looked at her husband, who shook his head and shrugged. 'Blake always does get his own way,' she said sullenly, dabbing at the few brownie crumbs on her plate. 'It's always been the same.' She turned her eyes to him. Her parrot-blue shirt made her face look old. 'If I speak, Blake, please try not to undermine me. I know you only do it because you're scared, but it wounds me.'

'I won't undermine you, Susan. Just tell yourself that if the public knows about Malachi's madness it can only strengthen our case.'

'But that's just it,' she said, appealing to me. 'He's not mad. He's evil. He's dabbling in things that no Christian should be in involved in and everyone, even Blake, knows it.'

'Dabbling?' I said. 'What's he dabbling in?'

She fixed me with her pale green eyes. 'Where

there is light, Mr Oakes, there is darkness in equal measure. Let me put it simply: this is no madness. Malachi has learned how to summon the biforme.'

'The biforme?'

'Half man, half beast.' She lowered her voice and leaned a bit closer to me, searching my face accusingly. 'Why? Don't you think it's possible? Where do you think those mine shafts in the south lead to?'

I opened my mouth to answer. Then I closed it. Basic hack rule: never express doubt or ridicule. When someone says they've seen Elvis's face in the roof insulation, don't laugh. 'Mrs Garrick,' I said carefully, uncapping my pen and writing 'biforme' on the pad. I could feel Sovereign in the other room eyeing me, waiting to hear what I'd say. 'Blake suggests that the – the *biforme* on the video is Malachi himself. Disguised, maybe. He thinks that—'

'I know what Blake thinks,' she said crossly, 'but *he* hasn't seen that monster. And *I* have.'

'You've *seen* it?'

'Ah,' she said, pleased with herself. 'You see? I *told* you to take me seriously.' Smiling now, she got up and went to a drawer in the painted dresser that stood against the wall, returning to the table with a sheaf of papers. 'Almost three years ago, long before that wretched video came out.' She placed the papers in front of me. 'It was late. Everyone was already in bed and it was my turn to get the laundry from the kitchen. I was walking down that path over there . . .' She leaned forward and pointed out of the window in the direction of the refectory. The mist outside was rolling in thin spirals. '. . . when I had a feeling . . .' She hesitated. 'I had this dreadful feeling that I was . . .' She put her hand to the back of her neck, like she was reliving the moment. Grey shadows of raindrops on the window dribbled down her face like tears.

'Yes?' I murmured. 'You had a feeling that you were . . . ?'

She coughed and shook her head. 'That I was being *watched*. All the hairs went up here – you know – on the back of my neck and I looked up and I saw it. Sitting in a tree, like a lion or something.'

'OK,' I said levelly. I put down my pen and picked up the top sheet, unfolded it and flattened it on the table. 'And this is . . .' I was looking at a charcoal drawing, slightly smudged and creased in places, but kind of skilfully drawn. Most of the paper was filled with sketched leaves, but a few branches showed through, and on one of these a carefully sketched human foot gripped the branch with the prehensile strength of a monkey. Squashed in next to it was a buttock and . . . Oh, Christ, I wanted to smile . . . a *tail*. Dangling down at least two feet below the branch.

'Can you see how it was sitting?' She lowered herself to a squat next to my chair, holding on to the table for balance. In the other room Sovereign blew air out of her nose, disgusted by her ma. 'See? Like this.' Susan lifted her blouse so that I could see her haunches in the brown leggings pressed down against the hiking boots and tweedy socks she wore. 'I could see all of this part.' She drew a vague circle round her foot and buttocks. 'From here to here. I couldn't see here – where the tail joined to the body – because it was hidden in the trees, but I could see the tail itself.'

'How long was it in the tree?' I picked up the next sheet. The same image, a slightly different scale.

'Not long after I screamed. It scuttled away.'

'We searched the whole of this side of the island,' said Benjamin. 'Couldn't find it. And, believe me, we looked.'

I riffled through the sheets, seeing the same image over and over again. 'The feet are human.'

'Yes – and all of it's got skin like a human, even the tail. Quite brown – you know, a sort of leathery brown. I saw it close enough to know.'

'It's latex. A clever costume,' said Blake. 'Malachi must have his reasons.'

'Well,' Susan said, straightening and putting her hands on the table, leaning forward to look Blake in the eye, 'answer me this, Blake. If it was a costume how did he make the tail move?'

'It moved?' I asked. 'What do you mean, it moved?'

'It twitched.' She used her hand to imitate a muscular flick. I thought immediately of a snake or a shark. 'You know, like a cat does.'

I dragged my eyes away from her hand and looked at Blake, waiting for an explanation. 'Look,' he said, impatiently, 'you can write it any way you like – it doesn't really matter what's going on over there. Just make sure that the message is clear. Malachi is behaving intolerably. He's insane. With enough contributions we can turn this island over to the people who care about it.'

'I want to know what else Susan's seen. You know about the pigs' heads on the fence?'

'Everyone's seen those,' said Benjamin. 'But there's more.' He turned in the chair to look to where Sovereign had been sitting in silence. 'Tell Mr Oakes what happened to you.'

But Sovereign wasn't paying attention to her father. She was smiling at me in that disconcerting, knowing way, like she was laughing at me, her feet in their pink plastic sandals tapping away distractedly. Benjamin turned and followed her gaze, as if it was a solid entity stretching across the room, and when his eyes landed on me his expression changed.

'Sovereign!' he said sharply, making her jump. 'Did you hear me?'

'What?' she said, blinking like she'd been asleep. 'What?'

'Tell Mr Oakes what you caught in the trap. The trap.'

Her face cleared. She smiled at me. 'After Mum saw – well, you know, after she saw all that weird stuff, I was like, my God, this is so cool, so I made this – this, like, *trap* thing.' She nodded out of the window. 'Out there in his forest. Because I'd, like, *never* seen Malachi, right? Only in photos, y'know? So I'm, like, I've really got to get to the bottom of this, see what this dude's up to, and so I went over there and dug a hole and I had it all covered up like some jungle thing – kind of cool, actually – and I left it for a few days. Then I went back.'

'Shall we show him what you found, Sovereign?' said Susan, getting to her feet and pulling a fleece from a peg on the door. She had changed since I first arrived in her kitchen: she had a victorious air to her, like she knew she was close to winning the argument. 'Shall we go to the freezers and show him?'

We took umbrellas. They didn't do much good – the rain was like a mist, atomized like we were standing near a jungle waterfall. It got into everything – our ears, our eyes. In the short walk to the refectory we were all covered with a fine dew.

'I'm so into photography,' Sovereign told me, as we walked. 'I'm the girl for you if you ever need someone to carry your bags, hand you lenses and shit. When I did the trap I had this totally wicked idea. I made this, like, tripwire thingy? Hooked it up to a camera – stuck the camera in the tree above the trap, so that if anything went into it I'd get a photo.'

'But Malachi ripped it down,' said Blake, as we stepped inside the refectory. 'He found it, didn't he?'

'*Something* ripped it down,' Benjamin said. 'We don't know it was Malachi. We haven't established who or what did it.'

'You should have seen that camera, Joe,' Sovereign said, shaking out her umbrella. 'I bet you've never seen a system like it. You'd be like, wow, this is so flare.' She led us through the refectory, where the trestle tables all stood, dis-infected and shining, past the kitchen where the two men who always served dinner were moving around, rattling pans and plates, and into a side room. She switched on the light. Inside, three large chest freezers hummed quietly, and she rested her hand on one, looking at me, with a slight smile. 'This was what was in the trap. It totally does my head that there's a photo of it falling in on that camera he snatched.'

She lifted the freezer lid and a stale cloud of cold air floated up. We all gathered round. A pig lay on its side, half covered with drifts of flaky white ice. 'A pig,' she said, smiling at me with a glint in her eye. 'My very own pig. Do you like it?'

'Show Mr Oakes the other side,' said Benjamin. 'Come on – turn it over.'

She sighed and dug her hands into the ice, trying to get a grip on the huge creature. 'Well, help me, then.'

We all gathered round, plunging our hands in and rolling it on to its back. Its trotters stood up in the air, a frozen mixture of mud and grass caught in the clefts of its hoofs.

'On its side,' said Benjamin, and we hefted it up again, dropping it down with a crash, sending a fine spray of ice out of the freezer.

I peered at it, fumbling out my camera. In the centre of its flank, branded neatly into its flesh with something hot, was the symbol beloved of witches and *soi-disant* Satanists the world over: a pentagram. I rolled off a few shots of it.

'Blake,' I said, snapping on the lens cover when I was finished, 'the next thing is for me to get over there. I want to speak to Malachi.'

'It can't be done. The boat can't run in this weather. You'd be asking me to commit suicide.'

'You're not going over there at all.' Susan's big

face was twitching with anger. 'By boat or otherwise. You know everything you need to know for your story. You must not, absolutely *not*, go over there and disturb him. It's the most dangerous thing you could do.'

10

In the end it was Sovereign who helped me. During lunch I left the table to get another notepad from Blake's cottage, and on the way back through the mist I heard someone hiss my name. When I back-tracked a few paces I saw her standing between two cottages, one finger to her lips, beckoning me with the other hand. She had a denim jacket pulled round her shoulders and dark circles of makeup round her eyes, like she was going on a date. I glanced over my shoulders to make sure I wasn't being watched, then stepped into the alley.

'I'll take you over there,' she said, leaning forward eagerly. 'I know how to get to Malachi's side without the cameras seeing us. There's a blind spot.'

'You mean the boat?'

'No. Through the gorge. I've been looking at those cameras and I'm sure we can do it.'

'When?'

'Now.' She grinned, her eyes shining with excitement. She pointed to a rucksack that lay up against the cottage wall. 'Bottled water and walking-boots. It'll drive Mum 'n' Dad crazy, but I've got to live a little.'

I looked back over my shoulder down the narrow alley to the square of milky fog at the end. How long would it be before I was missed? Another ten minutes maybe? 'OK,' I said, bending to pick up her rucksack. 'But let's go quickly.'

'No – wait. I need some money.'

'*Money?*'

'Yes. Twenty quid and I'll do it.'

'What'll you do with twenty quid?'

'I'm saving up for when I leave. Twenty quid or forget it.'

'Jesus.' I thrust the rucksack at her and began patting my pockets for my wallet. 'You're a businesswoman, Sovereign, I'll give you that.'

'I know,' she said, her eyes on my wallet, as I found a couple of battered tenners and held them out to her. She grabbed them, like they might disappear, and shoved them into her jacket pocket. Then, instead of turning to go, she bit her lip and raised her eyes to mine. 'And something else.'

'What?'

'I want a quick feel too.'

I paused, the wallet half-way into my pocket. 'A *what*?'

'A feel. You know what I mean.' She glanced up to the end of the alley and leaned closer to me. I could smell her breath – a bit caramelly, like toffee. 'A quick grope.'

'Let me get this straight,' I said, kind of awed by her. 'You want a grope. And for that you'll take me through the gorge?'

'Yes.'

I pushed the wallet into my pocket. 'And what does that mean? *I* grope *you*, or *you* grope *me*?'

'Both.'

I gave a short, disbelieving laugh. 'You're joking, aren't you?'

'No,' she said. This time she was a bit uncertain. A bit hurt-sounding. 'I'm serious.'

'Come on,' I said. 'You can't be—' I stopped. Her face had dropped. All the bravado was dissolving. She looked suddenly smaller, like a kid, like she might cry. 'Sovereign?' I said. 'Sovereign, listen. It wouldn't be right.'

'What wouldn't be right?' she said, her lip trembling now. 'Why wouldn't it be right?'

'Because . . .' I held out my hands: *do I have to spell it out?* 'Because I'm *thirty-eight*, Sovereign. That's, what? More than *twice* your age.'

'I'm *nearly* eighteen.'

'You're nearly eighteen, and you're very pretty, Sovereign, but you – you can't go around saying things like that to men my age.'

'Why not?'

I looked up at the sky, lost for the answer. Me and Lexie had been together for five years. We'd kept our vows, but in my imagination I'd been unfaithful about a million times. I'm not going to lie: in my head I'd done it with boatloads of them – the businesswoman with the ibook next to me on a long-haul to California, the girl who wrapped up organic chicken in the butcher's in Kilburn, the nurse who once took my blood pressure when I had chest pains after a trip to Mexico. Even, strike me dead, some of Lexie's friends. The list was endless. And, card-carrying pervert me, some of those girls were Sovereign's age. Younger, maybe.

'Why?' she repeated, like she knew what I was thinking. 'What's wrong with it?'

'It just *is*,' I said lamely. 'And, anyway, I'm married.' I held up my hand, showing her my ring. 'It wouldn't be fair to my wife.'

Sovereign sniffed and pushed her hair behind her ears, biting her lip and staring at the ring. I could see tears in her eyes waiting to fall. 'It's so, *so* shit out here, Joe,' she said, in a shaky voice. 'There's no one – no one. I mean, who am I supposed to have it off with? *Blake*, for Christ's sake?'

I looked at her pityingly, resisting the impulse to put a comforting hand on her arm or shoulder. 'Things'll be better when you leave.'

'But it's *four months*.' A tear broke and she pushed it away with her fingertips. 'And all I want is—' She paused, an idea striking her. 'Can't I at least *smell* you? That wouldn't hurt.'

'Sovereign—'

'I won't touch you, Joe, I promise. It's just – I don't even know what men smell like. I know what Dad smells like, but I want to know . . .' She hesitated. 'I want to know what *you* smell like.'

I glanced up along the alley. I'd been gone more than five minutes now. Soon Blake would start to wonder what had happened and here I was, trapped by a teenager who wanted to *smell* me. She was gazing up at me, her eyes big and wet. The whole baby-seal, no-fur campaign flashed through my head. I sighed, shook my head, thinking, I can't believe this is happening, and pulled off my sweat-shirt. 'Be quick.'

She paused, looking at my chest in the T-shirt, running her eyes down to my bare arms. 'Yeah, I'm a manky old sod,' I said, looking down at her. 'Bath shy. Don't go thinking we're all this gamey.' She didn't answer. She pushed away the last of the tears and stepped forward, stopping just a pace away. I was ready to take a step back, thinking she was going to throw her arms round my neck, when instead she closed her eyes and pushed her face forward, inhaling deeply. I looked down at the skin showing through the thin hair, thinking how weird this must look, me with my chest forward, arms back, and Sovereign in front of me, moving her head in slow circles, a smile spreading across her face, breathing in like she was smelling fine wine and not my stale old body. Blissed-out ecstasy. How totally, totally sad – this girl, with all her swank and ballsy nature, sniffing a guy's dirty T-shirt in an alley. How was she going to cope when she left Cuagach? She thought she was totally sorted, streetwise, but she had no idea, *no* idea the fucking bunfight it really was out there.

'All right?' I said, ready to pull my sweatshirt back on. 'Get the picture?'

She stepped back, smiling dreamily, her eyes still closed. 'Yes. I get the picture.' She opened her eyes. 'Joe?'

'What?'

'I can't wait to get to the mainland. I think I'm going to love it.'

I stopped at Blake's cottage – still no sign of a posse ponying up and coming for me – and got my rucksack, shoving in my camera and some water. The wire-cutters were still at the bottom, but we didn't need them to get through the gate – Sovereign used a key she'd stolen months ago. She was in a good mood, light-hearted, and the trip was much easier than it had been the night before. Even with white fingers of mist sidewinding through the trees the path up to the gorge was smooth and unchallenging. We passed the first gargoyle.

'Mum's idea,' said Sovereign, giving it a dirty look. She skirted it like it might bite. 'You see them and think they're sane parents, but trust me, they've got secret freak bones a mile long. Sorry, but you can't take Mum seriously. I mean, all that stuff about the devil and mine shafts – I ask you.'

'There're things she can't understand,' I said, keeping my voice low, I don't know why. I didn't want to discuss this on our way to Malachi's land. 'That's what ninety per cent of my work is about, thinking about things people can't explain.'

'There are things she needs to drama-queen off about, more like.'

We came out on to the ledge and suddenly the misty drizzle of the forest vanished, leaving the sky above the gorge hot, dry and cloudless. The land below looked parched, the light so bright you had to squint. Sovereign wasn't interested in the view, Malachi's escarpment, wavering in the heat. She took a right along the ledge and walked fast, breathing hard, waving her hands as she talked.

'That's why I put the pentagram on the pig. Never thought everyone would fall for it.'

I stopped in my tracks. 'What?'

She turned back to me. 'Don't look at me like that – I know I made things a whole ton worse, but I just had this, like, uncontrollable *itch* to freak her out.'

'And the pig?'

'Nope.' She shrugged, turning and starting up the slope again. 'That really did happen. Found it in the mantrap. And the stuff about the camera too – Malachi really did rip it down.'

'Is that why he got a restraining order on the village?'

'It wasn't just me, it was everyone coming over here and bugging him. But I think the trap was the worst. Think of it: I might have caught him wearing his strap-on tail.'

We went almost half a mile, dwarfed by the huge red letters at our side, until we reached a dried-up streambed cutting into the escarpment. 'Blake was lying when he said there was no way down,' she said. 'He just doesn't want you going across there and getting caught on Malachi's video.'

We half climbed, half slithered down the streambed, sending sprays of pebbles ahead of us. At the bottom you could feel how big the place was – the land seemed to go on for ever, chemical drums grouped in piles all over the place, rusting and falling apart, the yellow decals with their skull and crossbones flashing in the sun. Underfoot, the ground felt dead rubbery, like you might sink into it at any moment, and the few trees dotted around were dead and dried up, their naked branches fingering the sky like scorched scarecrows, one or two rattly dead brown leaves clinging to them.

Every now and then Sovereign paused and stared up at the video cameras on the far slope, her hand shading her eyes from the intense white light. 'I swear, Joe, if we get caught on camera Blake's going to *kill* us.' She kept stopping and starting, changing her mind and heading off at an angle, or even reversing her footsteps. It was so hot I had to keep wiping my face with the bottom of my T-shirt. But at last, when my watch told me two hours had passed, we slipped under the range of the video cameras and began to scale the opposite slope.

The fence glinted from between the trees above, the pigs' heads like strange, luminescent patches against the thick green leaf cover. It was a much gentler slope than on the centre's side, and it wasn't long before the parched yellow land began to give way to a slatier rock and vegetation: first, patches of heather and plantain, then stubby grass and the occasional wild flower. We arrived suddenly at the fence – before we knew it, it was less than ten feet ahead of us and rose at least fifteen in height. At the top, peering down at us from the trees, was a pig's head, a halo of flies circling it, like a stain in the air. Its eyes had been eaten away by decay and maggots, but the teeth were still there, big and bare, like polished bone. The smell that had drifted across the island the day before was stifling now. I cleared my throat and ran my tongue round my mouth. Malachi, oh, Malachi, I thought, is this where you get up to your little rituals, you mad old bastard?

'Hmmm,' said Sovereign, brazenly, looking up into the trees inside the fence to where hazes of midges wafted among the trees. A weak breeze came off the sea and ruffled the branches. 'You don't suppose he's put cameras inside the fence, do you?' She squatted down and craned her neck up at the tops of the trees, narrowing her eyes. 'Hello, Malachi, you old bonehead. Come and give it to us. Show us your strap-on tail.' Beyond the fence the undergrowth was so thick that I couldn't see more than a few feet – everything in there hung eerily still, like the heat of the day was trapped in the heavy leaves. There was no flicker of movement, just a low-level buzz of insect life deep in the trees that made me wonder about stagnant water.

'I've never been this close,' she said, 'not since he put the fence up. He might be dead for all we know, in the trees somewhere – decomposing.' She stopped. 'Joe?'

I didn't answer. I had straightened, my chin up, staring intently over her shoulder.

'What is it?'

I put a finger to my mouth, my eyes locked on the enclosure, and slowly, disbelievingly, turned my head a bit to one side, wondering if I was seeing a trick of the light. Past the alarm tripwires, beyond the heavy-duty fence, something paler than its surroundings lay on the ground. It was the size and shape of a large snake, and the colour of weathered human skin. It seemed to emerge from the leafy shadow of a large tree-trunk. The hair all over my body stood up like a cat's.

'*Joe?*' Sovereign was whispering. '*He's behind me, isn't he?*'

I blinked. 'Yeah,' I whispered.

'He's watching.' She lowered her voice until it was almost inaudible. 'Isn't he?' She turned slowly and stared into the forest, to where the trees beyond the wire fence were silent and still, only the haze of insect life moving in patches through the shadows, while the strange piece of flesh lay inert on the ground. '*Oh,*' she breathed. '*Oh.*'

Silently I fumbled my camera out of the rucksack and crouched next to Sovereign, hastily fitting on the lens and pulling off the cover. Maybe flesh has a way of communicating its authenticity through channels and senses we don't know anything about

– because I was certain, I'd have put money on it, we were looking at something living. I raised the camera and was focusing when, suddenly, the tail gave a small twitch. Just like a cat. It twitched again, and next to me Sovereign leaped to her feet, breathing hard.

'*Fuck fuck fuck*,' she hissed. '*Did you see that?*'

Her voice alarmed the creature. The tail twitched again, then slid away into the trees and disappeared with a rustle, leaving nothing but leafy patches of shadow and sun.

'Shit,' I said, lowering the camera and staring at the place where it had been, trying to make sense of the light and shade.

Next to me Sovereign was backing away, whispering in a shaky voice, 'What the fuck was it? What was it?'

'Sssh!'

'Joe, I want to go. Let's go.' She grabbed at my T-shirt, trying to haul me to my feet. 'NOW! Please, I want to go home.'

Well, that was the choke point, of course. For the Psychogenic Healing Ministries, the moment Sovereign came fleeing across the gorge, crying and stumbling and covered with dust, I was instantly elevated to most-hated-individual status. By the time I'd given up waiting for the creature to re-emerge and had gone after her, the posse had arrived. They were watching us from high up on the graffiti ledge, and when Sovereign saw her parents she raced towards them, crawling up the streambed, scraping her knees bloody, throwing herself, sobbing, into her father's arms. Benjamin stared at me accusingly over her head. As I climbed wearily up the last few feet Blake came forward and looked me in the eye.

'I am so out of patience with you, Joe,' he muttered. 'As soon as the mist lifts I'm taking you back to the mainland.'

So there I was, the social equivalent of dogshit, excommunicated to Blake's cottage, waiting for the weather to lift. But he wasn't getting his wish: by nightfall the mist was still there, the island still shrouded like a ghost ship, and I was stranded, lying on my bed, empty supper plate on the floor. Downstairs they'd mounted a guard – Blake and the Nigerian missionary – in case I tried another great escape. As darkness fell outside the window I closed my eyes, my fingers resting on the lids, and tried to replay the few seconds of rustling wood, the way I'd replayed the tourist's video time and again. How had Dove done it? I went through every imaginable Frankensteinian scenario: Dove in mad-scientist garb, galvanizing a shaved animal tail with an electric shock; Dove plotting in his lab over a cleverly engineered robot limb, maybe wrapped in meat. There wasn't an end to my imagination on this one.

At ten I heard them spend a long time going round the house, dragging furniture about. By eleven the cottage was silent, and when I went downstairs I found a chest of drawers pushed up against the back door, the Nigerian asleep on a Zed Bed next to it, Blake in a chair next to the front door, like a sentinel. I stood looking at him for a while, his chest rising and falling. He was clutching an iron fire poker to his stomach – he must have thought he might have to batter me. Me, half his age and twice his size. I held up my hand to say a silent goodbye, feeling a moment's pity for him – for his fear and for his ambition.

The drop from my bedroom window wasn't bad. I lowered myself to a dangle under the sill, then kicked off, landing OKish on the grass, my kit banging on my back. Outside, like a silent sign from the sky, I was doing the right thing: the mist was beginning to clear, leaving a cold, moonlit night. As I headed off, wire-cutters at the ready, the only sound was the waves crashing distantly on the beaches. From time to time, going alone through those woods, across the gorge with its ghostly piles of drums, I broke into a soft whistle to keep my spirits up. Dead girlie of me. There was an explanation for what I'd seen behind the tree, I just couldn't think what it was.

By midnight I was back at the place where me and Sovereign had stopped. The smell of the rotting pigs' heads was stronger than it had been earlier. I began to walk along the perimeter, flashing the torch beam into the trees on the other side of the fence and sniffing the air. Dove's land was very quiet, only a vague, vague squeak coming from somewhere deep inside, like the sound of rusting machinery moving in a breeze. The mine? I wondered. The old slate mine? I walked for more than five minutes, and must have been nearing the end of the gorge because I could hear the sea from beyond a bluff ahead of the fence. I thought about a decomposing body, about Malachi lying in the trees, his hands folded on his chest like he did in his prayers. I pulled off my sweatshirt, tied it round my nose and mouth, hauled the wire-cutters from the kit and went straight through the grass towards the fence, ready to go.

Like I said, the big thing with me is that I'm not a superstitious guy – nothing much rattles me. Which was why, as I got close to the fence and felt all the hairs on my arms and face stand up, bristling, at once, I paused, taken aback. I stared down at my hands, turning them over and holding them up so that the moon lit the hairs. What sixth sense had touched *that* off? Not like me – not like me at all. I peered through at the trees beyond the fence. No movement – nothing except the creak of machinery. And the wind had died to a breeze, so it wasn't that stroking my pelt the wrong way. Frowning, I opened the cutters, reached for the fence, and as the blades met, the answer came hard on the heels of the current, *static electric field, you stupid fuck*, a millisecond too late – five, six, seven hundred volts and fuck knew how many amps, spasming my pectorals and slamming my biceps up so hard that my arms shot out sideways, kangarooing me backwards across the rocks, slipping helplessly, my sandal strap snapping, the wire-cutters flying in a hot silver arc above my head.

SEF. Static electric field – makes your hairs stand up.

I lay on my back in the grass, like Scouser Tommy in army shorts, with my arms out to the sides where they'd fallen, only my eyes moving, tracking the clouds going across the stars and wondering about the heaven that half the world believes is beyond them. *It's a warning, old boy, a warning for the very dense.* My nerves are dying, I thought, and the idea made me huff out a breath of laughter – the first clue that I'd live. OK, I thought, not dying, but breaking – my first nervous breakdown. My first electric shock. It burns a path through you. A big path of burned meat that they never know about until they cut you open on the slab. That's what Finn reckons. That they can put a finger right through it and see which way the electricity went, just the way they can put a pen through a bullet path in a wall.

It was my left foot that came to life first. First my left foot, then a travelling, crackling wave of warmth – and now it was my left leg and the left side of my body. The fingers on my left hand flexed and I could feel my nose and ears twitch. Then, suddenly I could cough. With an effort I rolled sideways, on to my side, and spat into the heather, my right arm hanging like a length of dead meat against my back – like it had nothing to do with me. I raised my chin stiffly and looked around. I must have been lying on my back for a long time. Hours. The moon had moved and there was the beginning of a pink light in the east. Dawn. I wrenched my head sideways and stared over my shoulder at the fence. No warning. Military-compound gear and not a single high-voltage sign for the whole of the stretch I'd walked.

'Hoo hoo,' went something from the other side of the fence. 'Hoo hoo.'

I froze, all the hair on my body standing up like a cat's.

'Hoo hoo.'

With my good leg I treadmilled myself round on the ground so I was facing the enclosure. The trees were dark, harlequined in shadow. Above me, one of the pigs' heads, with its ever-moving halo of flies, looked down at me. I tucked my chin in and squinted painfully, arrows going up my neck. A rustle. A break of a twig. Then silence. I held my breath.

'Haven't they told you . . . ?'

My pulse rocketed. I scrabbled round like a beached fish, flailing on the ground trying to face the direction of the voice. Someone was in there – a few feet inside the fence. I could see him: a pale, bloated shape down among the trees, low, like he was crouching. A pair of eyes moved rapidly in the darkness.

'Didn't they warn you about me?'

It was him. I knew, straight off. I could see a foot in a worn-out trainer and a white hand clamped round the handle of something. A weapon. Every instinct said I was in deep fucking shit. It was something about that froggy crouch – like he was thinking of pouncing. I thrashed like crazy on the ground, trying to get a response out of my body. When nothing would move I lay back, panting hard.

'Didn't they tell you? Don't you know about—'

He broke off and there was a long pause. His breathing got louder, more congested, like an old man's, and I could feel his interest tighten and close on me. This is it, I thought, panicking. He knows who you are. He got to his feet. I tensed, expecting his face at the fence, but instead he went backwards, disappearing between the trees. His huge body moved heavily against the branches. There was a crack of twig and a faint rustle, then nothing. The world went silent.

With all my energy I forced myself on to my side and stared into the dark space he'd left, heart thudding like a train, wondering if I'd imagined seeing him in there. The rocks, grass and trees were motionless. After what seemed like for ever, when nothing in the trees moved, and I'd been lying there so long that it was like the world had ticked a degree or two further into morning, I took a deep breath and, with all the strength I could find, pushed myself clumsily into a slumped sitting position.

I sat there, blinking in the pink dawn, digging my good fingers into my right biceps, trying to wake it up. I looked to my side, down the long expanse of fence. Silence. Was there a gate in the fence to let him out on to my side? Was that where he was heading? My rucksack – fuck knew where that had got to, but my torch was lying on the ground about ten feet away, its dying beam lighting up the sparse heather. And there, glinting in the beam, the wire-cutters. I swivelled round, propelling myself on my arse, like a baby that hadn't learned to walk, scraping my legs in the rough heather. Wire-cutters. *Get up, Oakesy, old mate. Do it now. Get the fuck up and get to them.* I grabbed my numb right leg, moved it to one side out of the way and rolled clumsily on to my good left knee. 'Come on. Come on.' Somehow I got my left foot under me and straightened the leg, my right leg dragging uselessly. But I didn't have the strength or balance to get any further. The effort had half killed me and I couldn't get upright. I had to stay there, arse in the air, staring at my grazed kneecaps, swaying a bit, trying not to faint. Wondering whether to throw myself on the ground in the direction of the wire-cutters.

I saw him between my legs. Upside down and silhouetted against the pink sky. He crested the hill calmly, at his leisure, a huge shadow, like a mountain, blocking my vision. I had a moment where I couldn't move, where I was frozen, clocking all these details. He was massive, wearing something threadbare and filthy, and over the years he'd grown himself man-breasts. There was no strap-on tail dangling between his legs. But he was carrying an axe. Yeah, I thought, my leg going weak. It is an axe. An axe.

'*Come on,*' I hissed at my kneecaps. 'Straighten up, you fuckers.' But I couldn't. I'd lost it. I had to stay there like a fucking hairpin, swaying from side to side and shivering like I was drunk, while he came calmly up behind me. He didn't change his pace or run or bulldozer me, he just walked up to me and casually bumped into me from behind.

I couldn't stop myself: I went down, landing face first in the grass, my hands under my stomach, the sound of my nose crunching echoing through my head. A noise barked out of my mouth. 'Uhhh.' I lay for a second, head spinning, face mashed against the earth, a long rope of bloody mucus drifting out of my nose, like it was attaching me to the ground. '*Uhhhhohjesusuuh.*'

He got down on his knees behind me and gently, methodically, manoeuvred his body so he was lying on top of me, all his weight on my back, breathing against my neck like he wanted to fuck me. I lay there, heart hammering, forcing myself to breathe in and out with his weight on me, too scared to move, waiting to see what he was going to do. But he did nothing, just lay there on top of me, in this weird, kind of companionable way, with his face turned sideways so it lay against my cheek. A strand of his hair fell down the side of his face, just in the field of my vision. It looked about a hundred feet thick.

I flexed the fingers on my left hand feebly. You can probably still move, old mate, I told myself. I clenched my mouth a few times, trying to get my jaw to click. You probably can. I swallowed the blood that trickled down the back of my throat. If I rolled my eyes back I could just see the beam of the torch. The wire-cutters were right next to it. On top of me, Dove stiffened.

'Whad?' My voice came out of me thick and loud, like I had a heavy cold. 'Whad you doing?'

'Your peace of mind,' he whispered. 'Remember your peace of mind, Joe Finn? Well, now I'm fucking with it. I'm fucking with your peace of mind, Joe.'

He pushed himself off me and I rolled sideways, lungs sucking up air, arms coming up convulsively. He grabbed the axe, and before I could even begin to sit up he was swinging it down, blunt side first. I made a weak grab for it, blindly, my left wristbone colliding with the head and getting a slippery grip for a second before he hefted it away and I dropped back, my hands bleeding, the world rocking and bucking all around me.

And that was it. *Bang bang!* Maxwell's silver hammer came down on my head. And, bang, bang, down went old Oakesy. Not dead, of course. But pretty fucking close.

11

It was three weeks before I got back on to Cuagach. I never stopped thinking about it, not once. All the time I was lying in bed, too weak to get up, half asleep, half dreaming about Dove's Beelzebub, I never once stopped thinking about how to get revenge on the gobshite. Turned out he'd given it to me good. He'd split a big chunk of my scalp away and fractured my skull. Not an open fracture, no bits of bone forced into the brain tissue, but bad enough – a three-inch-long hairline fault in the 'parietal bone', whatever the fuck that is. And, bad fracture or good fracture, he took out a large chunk of my memory too. What I remember about the first forty-eight hours is almost nothing.

Christ knows how I got back to the community. Probably Blake raised the alarm, came over and found me lying on my back in the heather where Dove had left me, flies circling above my face like planes in a stacking pattern over Heathrow. I've got flashes of being carried through trees, and of being so cold my bones were shaking: I remember the taste of blood too, and every five minutes puking all over myself (try getting the human stomach to tolerate uncooked blood: it just won't do it). I know that at one point I was taken somewhere freezing and dark and laid out like the dead on a stone floor for what seemed like fucking-ever while Blake and Benjamin argued nearby, their voices echoey, like we were in a tomb: Blake wanting to call the police on Dove – saying this was attempted murder – and Benjamin screaming like a girl that he wanted nothing to do with it: '*We should never have had a journalist on Cuagach in the first place!*' Eventually someone – I imagine it was Blake – must have put me in the boat and got me to the mainland (he didn't take the card out of my camera – you never really know who's on your side, do you?), because the trusty lobsterman found me at six o'clock the next morning, lying under a blanket on a jetty outside Croabh Haven.

Later Lexie said, when she opened the door to find me standing supported by the lobsterman in the doorway, my left hand cupping the right like a dead animal, my head caked with blood, puke all over my T-shirt, the first words out of my mouth were 'Bolt-cutters, Lex. Insulated handles. I need you to get me some.'

She thought I'd had a stroke, seeing my face, and I've still got a memory of the Hallowe'en mask I saw when she held up a mirror to me: the right side of my face had slackened, like melted candlewax, and my right eye was hanging so loose I could see the red bottom of my eyeball. Sometimes that face comes to me still, mixed in with all the other nightmares. But

I refused point-blank to go to the police or the hospital – I wasn't having the police coming along and arsing it all up before I'd had a chance to get back to the island – and over the next few days, whenever I had the strength to speak, me and Lex argued about it. They all ended as class arguments, just like we always had, her raging around the room throwing her arms in the air and mourning the upper-class husband she should have married: 'I don't believe this! You've never trusted the police because you and Finn grew up little criminals and you think we're all living in some Orwellian bloody dictatorship where you can't trust the authorities – and because of this *perfectly reasonable* thinking, you're not going to report an attempted murder.'

'Lex—'

'*I* for one was brought up to *respect* authority. It'll come back to haunt you, Oakesy, not reporting this. Listen to what I'm saying. *It will come back to haunt you . . .*'

She was far, *far* more pissed off with me than she was with Dove. The only time she stopped shouting was when she brought me food, or changed the sheets, or wiped the caked blood out of my hair and tried to tape together the two sides of my scalp. It was weird the mixture of affection and fury she lavished on me. On the second day – 2 September – she crawled naked under the sheets, her feet cold against my calf, and slid her hand on to my knob. I lay there in silence, my eyes closed, knowing I'd never get a hard-on in that state, and after ten minutes of lying there, neither of us speaking, she burst into tears and jumped out of bed, running out of the room and slamming doors. For the rest of the night I heard her in the living room, sobbing loudly – loud enough for me to hear it. Which, of course, I was supposed to do.

Even if I could've got out of bed I wouldn't have known what to say to her. I couldn't tell what I'd fallen in love with any more: Lexie or a particular black mini-skirt she was wearing the night I first met her. The mini-skirt, and the kind of distant look Finn got on his face when he saw her in it. I married her two months later – the bride and the Neanderthal are just coming up the aisle, the bride looks stunning in organdie, the Neanderthal has got his hand up her dress. *Now* my friends tell me they never liked her – *now*, not from the get-go. Cheers for the caveat, so-called mates. That night in the bungalow I lay there, staring at the ceiling, while she cried and cried. From time to time I heard her push open the living-room door. Probably poking her head out to check I was listening.

We had a couple of silent days after that. I watched a lot of TV. The owner of the bungalow came over and I negotiated two more weeks' rental.

After ten days the paralysis and swelling had gone and I let Lexie take me to the hospital for X-rays, making up a load of old toss about a biking accident. Turns out Lex was a good nurse. All that time she spent at the clinic, I guess. The fracture was healing fine: I didn't need treatment or stitches. So, I ruffled my hair over the scar and began making plans to get back to Cuagach. I went to Lochgilphead and bought a pair of insulated heavy-duty bolt-cutters. Course, could I find *one* fisherman or boat-owner prepared to drop me on the south of the island and wait? Could I fuck. Eventually, after four days of searching, I found someone in Ardfern who was prepared to rent me a small outboard for a massive deposit. But just as I was all set to go the weather turned. Autumn had already descended on Scotland – the day I was carried off the island it seemed to pounce in an hour: one moment there was balmy Indian summer, the very next the temperatures dropped and there was even snowfall in the Highlands. Now it got worse. The winds picked up and howled round the coast; the sea threw itself at the beaches day after day. If I didn't want a battering on the rocks off Luing, I'd have to sit it out.

And what a wait it turned out to be. It was a week before I woke up to see chilly sunrays sparkling off the waves of the firth.

* * *

It's weird, but the clearest memory I have of Lexie during the whole sorry episode isn't what you'd think: it isn't any of the nightmare stuff, it's actually something kind of benign in comparison. It's from the morning she came down to the jetty to see me off. Even now it's as clear as anything. She was furious I was going back to Pig Island; she almost couldn't speak she was so angry, and I've got a perfect mental snapshot of her standing with one hand on her hip, pushing her sunglasses up her nose and staring out at the island because she couldn't bring herself to look at me. She'd had her hair cut in London before we left – and still a bit of suntan across her nose from the summer – and all in all she didn't look exactly like my wife that day, I thought, glancing at her sideways.

'Why don't you go back to London?' I said. 'Get a taxi and take the train.' She didn't answer. She shrugged and crossed her arms, keeping her attention on the island. I watched her for a moment, then got into the boat and started up the engine. 'There's cash in my computer case if you need it,' I called, as I slipped the bow line and the boat began to edge away. 'In the front pocket.'

She didn't bother waiting. When I got the boat out of the moorings and looked back at her, wondering briefly whether to make a romantic-guy display – take the boat back, leap ashore and kiss her without a word – she'd already turned away and was heading up the sea steps, and the moment was gone. *C'est la vie*, folks. I tapped out an irritated rhythm on the tiller arm as I watched her go. It goes to show you never can tell.

The tide was with me. I was washed straight out of Craignish loch into the firth, where whirlpools bounced tennis-ball-sized knots of foam on the surface and goats watched me from deserted islands. Spanish Armada goats: they'd been stranded on these islands for centuries, poor fuckers – and Sovereign thought she had it bad. It was rough for a while, and I had images of being sucked into the mighty Corryvreckan whirlpool, chewed up and spat out. But then I caught a drift of something and before I knew it the water was calm and the sea almost rolled me, like the gentle hands on a prayer book, around to the deserted side of Pig Island.

As I drew close to the shore I could see a small, derelict jetty, a white, salt-dried fishing-net tangled round it and pebble beaches stretching out as far as the eye could see. About a foot outside the tree-line stood a wire fence that must have been a continuation of the one in the gorge. Maybe it was there to stop the PHM landing by boat. Or maybe it was a cage to stop something getting out.

I tied the boat to the jetty, hefted the bolt-cutters

on to my shoulder and stood for a moment, staring inland, past the fence, half expecting Dove to materialize out of the trees. There was silence, just the creak and yaw of the boat moving against the sun-bleached timbers of the jetty. After a while I picked up my kit and set off along the beach, trying to find somewhere secluded to make the break. A breeze had picked up: a cold, unnatural breeze with a fishy scent to it, which made the trees come alive, a lazy flex and sigh travelling the length of the fence. By the time I'd reached the rocks at the end of the beach it had turned into a strong wind that flattened my hair sideways and made my head ache in a way it would never have done before I got that tap on the head from Dove's axe. In the daylight it was nothing like the gloom of the last time I'd been up here, but it felt like the twigs and scraps of heather pirouetting in the wind were just the outriders of something more powerful coming out of the enclosure. I was glad of the weight of the bolt-cutters on my shoulder.

I approached the fence, stopping only inches away and holding up my hand, waiting for the crawling sensation of the electric field lifting the hairs in their beds. But this time they remained flat, not responding, only moved by the occasional blast of wind. There was none of the faint buzzing I remembered from last month and now it occurred to me that although I couldn't have broken the circuit I could have caused Dove to close down the supply so he could repair the damage.

I positioned my hands carefully on the insulated handles of the cutters, checking the way my thumbs lay along them. There was a chance the fence was dead, but that didn't stop my heart thudding like a pile-driver. I lowered the bolts, bringing them closer and closer and closer to the wire. I let them touch, ready to have them jolted out of my hands. But they didn't. They lay inertly, occasionally moving sideways in the wind, the sun winking white off the jaws. I shook my head and gave an ironic smile, half laughing at the sinking feeling in my chest. *No excuse now, old mate* . . . I ran the cutters down the fence in one movement to check for a rogue current, and when they landed with a bang on the floor, no sparks or jolts, I crouched and began to sever the wire.

Compared to Blake's snippers, the cutters went through the fence like a hot knife through butter. In less than three minutes I'd made a hole from top to bottom. If someone was watching me from in there, hiding in the trees, they weren't going to have any doubt about my intentions. I picked up the kit and stepped through, resting the cutters on my shoulder so I could either carry them comfortably or circle them down in one move, crack them out of the air like lightning.

The first thing that struck me about the forest was the pig dung. The pellets were everywhere, piles of them, some trampled, some perfectly oval and crusted like manufactured dog biscuits. I kept passing shallow grooves in the earth, wind-battered snarls of hog-hair caught on twigs and stones where the pigs had come to scratch themselves. Every time the wind changed direction I got a blast of a smell too – not the rotting pigs' heads, but digested grass and leaves.

Deeper in the forest the wind couldn't reach and for a while everything got weirdly still, the trees motionless, loaded with silence. I paused to get my bearings, ears roaring in the quiet. Ahead, between the trunks, I could see patches of sunlight, like there was a large clearing out there. I could make out shapes – a rusting old hopper, a blondin rope suspended high in the air with an old pulley dangling from it. The slate mine.

I poked my head out of the trees and checked the clearing for signs of life. Deserted. The pulley creaked back and forward in the breeze – the same eerie squeaking I'd heard from outside the fence. I picked my way across the mine, peering into shafts, giving the hopper a shove, making rust flake into the air. In the side of a rock face a shaft entrance was half concealed by a rusting water tank. It gave off a stink of decay, like a sewer – when I shone my torch into it I came face to face with a dead pig. I stared into its flat eyes for some time, thinking that it was a weird place for it to have crawled. It must have been pushed in. And it wasn't as decomposed as it smelt – it looked kind of fresh. Maybe this was one of Malachi's disposal places. I remembered what the Garricks had said, that he had access to hell through these shafts: I was thinking of crawling inside to dislodge it when something made me stop.

Someone was laughing.

I backed silently from the shaft, clicked off the torch and sat back on my haunches, looking around at the trees. It was a heinous laugh – like a cartoon witch's – echoing around the deserted rocky hollow. My skin tightened. The laughter stopped and another noise joined it – of someone speaking in a long, low, uninterrupted monologue. There was something about the quality – something so familiar that—

I stood slowly, a smile on my face. *Television*. I was sure of it. Somewhere up ahead, among the deserted rocks, a television was playing.

The house was like a large Victorian cottage – bizarre out here on its own in the woods. Maybe it was built for someone senior in the mine. It stood on a weed-cracked hard-standing; the paint had been allowed to peel and drop and the windows were mossed and dirty. But there were signs of life: lace curtains tacked up, oil drums stacked against the generator at the side and a television – an old black-and-white movie, from the Celia Johnson accents – playing beyond an opened downstairs window.

I stared at that window. Something about the lace curtains lifting on the cool breeze, something about the darkness inside – the way it seemed almost designed to suck in the attention – made every nerve ending sing out '*Trap*'. Slowly I raised the bolt-cutters above my head. *You're not the fucking Special Squad, old mate. Don't get your head stove in for nothing.*

I approached, cautious step by cautious step, coming from a wide angle, meeting the house at the far end of the wall and sliding along with my back to it, conscious of the warmth of the bricks on the back of my neck. Hardly breathing now, cutters still raised, I bent slowly, slowly, to peer into the room. It was in disarray – filthy, crisps packets, dirty cups and empty yoghurt pots scattered around – the sunlight falling on sedimentary layers of dust. The back of the TV was to the window, and beyond it, facing me, was a sofa, worn shiny in the place opposite the screen. Beyond that another window, closed, its matching lace curtains hanging silent in the autumn sun, embroidered with dead-fly carcasses.

Using the tip of a finger I gently touched the door. It swung open to reveal the length of the tiled hallway. I took a step inside, my sandals sinking into the filth. In the room ahead the *Neighbours* theme tune started up, making me think incongruously of my soup-and-bread-roll lunches in Kilburn, when Lexie was out at the clinic and I was home working. I stood still and listened. Beyond the noise of the television, nothing stirred, only the occasional click of the net curtains moving in the breeze.

I stepped into the living room. It was small and clogged with furniture and rubbish. A reproduction of Blake's *Christ* hung above the fireplace, thick with dust, and in an alcove stood an almost life-size plaster statue of the Virgin Mary, the sort of thing I'd seen for sale in the Tijuana immigration lines, every inch of her painted a different colour, her cowl blue, her lips and cheeks red, her eyes a brilliant cornflower. She'd been draped with things – flower stems and tinsel trailed from her on to the floor. The house of a religious maniac, I thought. Just the sort of thing I'd—

Behind me something whirred to life.

The word *trap trap trap* went through me with a crack. I turned, bringing the cutters up ready to strike, expecting Dove or worse. But the living room was empty. In a plant pot on the windowsill a child's seaside windmill, lolling at an angle, had caught the breeze and was zipping round and round and round. I stared at it, blinking, as it speeded, slowed, speeded and slowed again, winding down with a lazy clickety-clickety-click, until I could see the individual colours, red and yellow, and at last came to a rather uncertain halt.

I didn't move. I stared at the windmill and let my heart thump out the remainder of the adrenaline. After a while I lowered the cutters. The house was still again, only the television still churning out its drama behind me. Clenching my teeth, I glanced at the pile of clothing in the hallway, then back at the windmill. Some of those clothes belonged to a child – there were a little girl's clothes in that pile. I entertained a brief, electrifying thought: that a child, or children, was here – maybe imprisoned. I raised my eyes to the ceiling, let the thought stay, and then, knowing that if I was going to keep sane I couldn't go forward in my imagination, I went into the front hall and started to search the cottage.

It turned out to be empty. Not a soul in the place. All I was getting from the cottage was that Malachi was as looped as they come. He had no regard for hygiene or civilization. And that maybe women, or a woman, or even children had been in the house at some time. One of the rooms was weirdly clean compared to the rest, a single bed made up neatly, curtains secured back, books lined up on the shelves. Where the occupants were now I didn't want to think. The second I was off this island I was calling the bizzies and getting them to check their missing-persons records.

You're a smart one, Oakesy. A smart one.

I stood at the edge of the clearing, my back to the cottage, breathing hard and wishing to Christ I hadn't let Lexie come to the marina. I hadn't had a chance to pick up any tobacco and, right now, I'd have given my kidneys for a tug on a rollie. I was staring at a trampled path that led away from my feet into the woods in the direction of the gorge, and I knew it had been walked along recently. The bad thing was that *I* was going to have to follow. On the heels of Dove's crooked beast. His *biforme*.

Time to drop this dread in my heart. I made a fist and knocked myself on the head with my knuckles. *Get going, you fucking arse.* I hiked up my kit, chucked the bolt-cutters on to my shoulder and set out.

The path wound and detoured, but I knew it was taking me in the direction of the gorge. The trees cloaked the air, warming it and deadening sound, making even my footsteps sound muffled. After half an hour I saw, glinting through the trees ahead, the fence. I picked up speed, sensing the gorge in the way the air had started to move. The wind would blow down the clefts in those rocks like through a tunnel. I could feel my sweatshirt and shorts starting to press against me, then flap and billow away, snapping and whipping around like sails. About twenty feet from the fence the trees cleared and I found I was standing on a stretch of grassland, the blades pressed down into random shapes with each gust. A dead pig lay next to the fence in a flat, deflated way, the shrunken skin lying tight and leathery against its ribs, the grass hugging it one moment, the next rolling back to reveal its mummified jaw and teeth. Something about its position made me think it had been thrown on to the ground, and then I noticed the black smudge on its snout – the stain of electrocution. I raised my eyes grimly to the fence, to where it glinted and creaked in the wind, and saw that a path had been trampled through the grass to a gate which stood open. My heart picked up speed.

I pulled up my kit, stepped over the pig's corpse and approached, looking out over the gorge. Someone or something had come through here recently.

The wind was blowing the dead trees, making them bow and scrape; the sun glinted off the old chemical drums. Almost a quarter of a mile away, above the PHM's scrawled message – *Get thee behind me, Satan* – the trees billowed and heaved, and for an odd moment that side of the island was almost as alien as this enclosure had once seemed. I looked behind me at the wind going through the trees, dipping in and blowing open holes in the leaf cover, revealing patches of different colours beyond, flashes of more trees and sky. There was no one on this side of the island and suddenly I was more sure of that than I had been of anything. I turned back to the gorge, gazing at the far escarpment, at the gate standing wide, and a weird feeling crawled across my skin, the words coming to me like a whisper: *Dove's gone to the village. And he's taken his devil with him.*

12

It took me three hours to cross the gorge. By the time I got to the edge of the community I had finished all my water and my tongue was a piece of raw meat in my mouth. There were blisters on my feet and an ache in my shoulder from carrying the cutters. I'd been on the island for four hours and the sun had dropped low in the sky. The wind, which in the gorge had twice set me off balance, had fallen quiet on this side of the island, almost like a memory, leaving my ears ringing and my face burning.

I came down the wooded path that led into the community and paused. The gate stood wide open. The shadows were getting long, evening wasn't far away, and there was an odd silence. An unearthly stillness. I rested for a bit, then headed through the gate, trying not to think about what it all meant. As I came down the wooded path, the rooftops appearing from out of the leaves, I knew something was wrong. Usually at this time of day there would be a prayer meeting, or someone busying across the green with a bowl of vegetables to be peeled, but now all I could see were empty windows and, beyond the cottages, the deserted green.

About a hundred yards to my right something moved. I became very still, concentrating. It was down near the ground, in a small, V-shaped depression, which continued in a straight line like a dried-up river, then disappeared between two cottages. It was something a bit paler than the surrounding grass. I took a few steps forward. It was a pig, snouting in the ground, its excited tail curling and uncurling like fishing bait. I approached silently, not wanting to disturb it. It was eating – its snout fixed in one spot while its hindquarters circled and shuffled and circled, trying to get a purchase on the food. I took a few more steps forward and—

'Shit.'

I shrank into the trees and sat down on the

ground, staring blankly at it. The animal looked up in mild interest – not fear. It wasn't going to be scared away from this meal. Its snout was smeared with something that looked like vomit, but must be, I thought, my heart falling, the stomach contents of the human being it was eating. *Fuck fuck fuck*. I stared at the thin white foot in the pink plastic sandal. *Sovereign?*

'Oh, shit,' I said again, gripping hold of my ankles and dropping my head. Not much fazes me, it's true, but now I gave in to a violent fit of trembling.

It was the same with dogs, I remembered later. Dogs were omnivorous: they always went for the victim's stomach first, for whatever half-digested plants and seeds and nuts they found, before moving on to the meat and bone. Maybe man had done the same, back in his hunting days. After a long time I got up and began to gather up stones, feeling like I might keel over every time I bent down. I straightened, took aim and was about to start hailing stones at the pig when I wondered suddenly if I was being watched.

I lowered my hand, turned and studied the wood I had come through. My ears were buzzing, my head pounding. That gate was open. But there was no one here. Except a corpse. The pigs hadn't killed her – they're not predators – but had they been the ones who had ripped her to pieces like that? I rubbed my head hard with my knuckles, trying to dislodge the thought. I looked down at the cottages. Everything silent, motionless. The cafeteria block was only a hundred yards away – the sliding doors stood open, reflecting back the beginnings of a sunset. I couldn't see anyone in there.

More adult pigs appeared from the trees, the same blunt feeding expression in their eyes, and began to strip the flesh from Sovereign, pulling long lumpy strings from inside her, ripping at the silvery connective fascia. I watched, in a detached way, as one, a junior from its size, made do with a leg. It bit through the bones with a splintering noise, then trotted away almost jauntily with the foot, pink plastic sandal and all, into the trees where I could hear it gnawing for what seemed like for ever, choking and gagging on the plastic. I dropped the stones, pulled out my mobile and checked the display for the faintest chance that a signal had appeared on Cuagach overnight. But no, just the no-signal icon. Shit, I thought, pocketing the phone and rubbing my forehead, what now?

After a long pause, I sighed and got to my feet. I hefted up the bolt-cutters, hesitated. I wanted to run, but I didn't. I walked. I kept my eyes on the cafeteria, my ears open to the woods, the expanse of silent grass on either side of me, the bolt-cutters held at just the right angle if anything rushed me.

There is no such thing as the devil. No beast. No biforme . . .

Then what the fuck did *that* to Sovereign?

It was late and shadows were falling between the cottages. I got to the refectory windows and turned to check over my shoulder. The woods were totally silent: nothing moved. The sun was dropping below the treetops. I turned back and squinted into the gloom of the refectory. It was dark in there, shadows gathering in the corners and niches. All I could make out were the trestle tables, empty of any cutlery, the surfaces scrubbed clean and shiny with disinfectant, just like the community always left them after dinner. I opened the door and stepped inside, a brief glimpse of my reflection: an anxious face floating out at me, sunburnt, trails of sweat like pencil lines in the dirt. I closed the door behind me and stood for a bit, my eyes getting used to the gloom.

For almost thirty seconds I thought I was alone. The kitchen door at the far end was open a crack and I could see the plates all stacked, the tea-towels hanging in a line above the cooker to dry. I took a step forward, was heading towards it, when something made me stiffen. My hands tightened on the cutters. I turned, raising them, ready to defend myself. Blake was watching me from the shadows to my left.

He was sitting in his usual place at the head of one of the tables, his back to the big fireplace. Dressed in a neat polo shirt, with both hands placed flat on the table. His head was at a slight angle, a bit back and to the side. It took me a few thudding heartbeats to realize that he wasn't going to lurch at me, screaming and yelling. He was dead. His mouth was open, his neck sinews tightened up. The staring eyes were almost opaque and the bottom of his shirt was streaked with blood.

I didn't breathe. After a few moments, when I was sure that he wasn't going to snap his mouth closed and stand up, I lowered the bolt-cutters and approached, stopping about a foot away. I stared at him, hardly breathing. Then I bent to look at what he was sitting on, and I immediately saw how he had died. He was seated on a chair. The flesh of his stomach and half of his trousers were missing. I could see a splintered bone in the wound. Part of his pelvis? Something had ripped his stomach out. Your first thought: if this wasn't Cuagach, it would have been an accident with farm machinery.

I looked over my shoulder to the evening gathering on the grass outside the paned glass. Now I could see – *Why didn't you notice that before?* – a bloody trail that led here from the door, like Blake had been attacked outside and was already wounded when he staggered in here. Trying to escape from something . . . Unexpectedly my legs seemed to loosen in a way that I couldn't picture anatomically – I had to grab the table to get my balance and stop myself falling to the floor.

I blinked a few times, staring at my blurry reflection in the polished tabletop. *What the fuck is going on here, old mate? What the fuck have you walked into?* I wiped my forehead, raised my eyes to Blake again and across at the trail going to the door.

I pushed myself away from the table and went to the small window that opened on to the green. From here I had a clear view of the community, the landing-stage, the cottages, some with their curtains drawn. Everything was eerily still: nothing moved. The sea, which earlier had been white-capped, bouncing and alive, was calm now in the coppery evening light and I could just make out the mainland: a few lights coming on in a necklace strung out along the horizon, the sudden sweeping cone of car headlights on the coast road. Lower down, where the sea met the land, there was a pale smudge on the coast: Croabh Haven, where Lexie might even be sitting, watching the sun go down.

When there seemed nothing else to do I went to the kitchen. I put my face under the cold tap, rubbing myself clean of the leaves, dirt and sweat, drinking until I couldn't drink any more. Then I dried myself off with a tea-towel and went back into the refectory where Blake was sitting. I watched him for a moment, half expecting him to speak.

'Is there any way I can get out of this?' I said to him. 'Any way I can just fuck right off and not deal with it?'

I went to the sliding doors and stood there, something swooping helplessly in my chest, thinking about all the windows in the village that someone could watch me from. *Is there any way you can just stay in here until it gets light?* No. I closed the door behind me, took a deep breath, tightened my fingers round the bolt-cutters and stepped outside.

I walked. Controlled and in silence with the bolt-cutters at the ready, the only sounds the breaking of the tide on the rocks below and the creaky in-and-out of my own breath for company. I didn't look over my shoulder or away from the path. If I was being watched I was fucked if they were going to know I was scared. The lantern on the jetty wasn't lit as it usually was. I had to get very close to see that the boat was gone.

I stood for a while, staring down at the sea sloshing around under the trotline, my heart thumping deafeningly. *Fuck, fuck fuck fuck*. I turned, my back flat against one of the jetty piles, and looked back at the cottages. There were no lights on in any of the windows, no movement in the trees to my left: absolutely no sign of life. *What now?*

157

My choices were narrowing. I either had to get back to my boat on the other side of the island – through the gorge in the dark, not knowing what the fuck was wandering through the woods – or, and the idea was even worse, find somewhere in the village to lock myself up and stay there until daylight.

'Ha,' I said aloud, slithering down to sit with my back to a piling. I stared morosely at the freezing water. 'Or swim, old mate. Or swim.'

It was the cold that made me think of the chapel. I sat huddled on the jetty for a long time not knowing what to do, watching the sun go down over the cliff and pinprick stars sneak into the sky. The village was silent. Absolutely silent. What had been a chilly, sunny day, was turning into a freezing night, and a memory of that freezing cold chapel, locks on the big oak door, came to me. And I'd laughed when Sovereign told me they locked themselves in there to hide from something.

I got up awkwardly from my frozen position against the jetty piling and headed back up the path, going between the cottages like a shadow, slipping past windows. I could be silent when I wanted – even with my legs numb from the cold I could move like a cat. At a glance you'd say the community was totally undisturbed: through windows I got brief, half-lit glimpses of normality – stacked chairs, an old-fashioned computer, a bowl of fruit on the Garricks' kitchen table. All stood empty, perfectly preserved like dolls' houses with the furniture positioned only for appearance, not to be used. Behind the cottages the wheelie-bins were lined up in their usual places on the path, and in the maintenance shed the big ride-on mower sat as usual, its engine housing hinged open. Everything as normal. Until I got to the chapel. And that was when I began to learn about real fear.

A few yards up the path I came to an abrupt halt, my heart thudding noisily in my skull. The moon was sending flittery shadows of leaves across the clearing, and I knew instantly that something was dead wrong there. Instead of coming to safety I'd done the opposite: I'd stumbled into the heart of whatever had happened on Pig Island in my absence.

I slipped silently off the path, crept invisibly through the woods, and stopped, behind a tree, standing stock still, thinking I'd blend into the patches of moonlight. Twenty yards away the top of the spire hung crookedly against the stars, like a broken limb, like it had been hung on by something heavy. The crucifix next to the front door had toppled face first into the grass, one arm snapped off. There was a sound too. The sound of cave water plinking into the darkness.

When, after a long time, nothing had moved, I pushed myself away from the path and came so close to the chapel I could see the huge oak door. It had been destroyed, slashed and shredded, like a giant claw had been taken to it, nothing remaining but one or two lolling pieces of wood creaking outwards on the hinges. On the floor, half in and half out of the chapel, was a shape that some crude instinct in me recognized instantly, even in this low light. I breathed in and out a few times, my mouth open, flushing the shock out of my cells, waiting for my heart to stop hammering. I dropped my rucksack and fumbled out a torch. I wedged the bolt-cutters between my legs, took a deep breath and switched on the torch.

I aimed it at the open door, counting loudly in my head to keep myself steady, ready to dart back into the trees if the beam made something move. Nothing happened. I moved the light down on to the shape. A body. I could tell almost instantly that it was the Nigerian missionary. In his pyjamas – unmistakable with his tyre-like middle and his wedge-shaped limbs – he lay on his face, one of his legs turned out from the hip socket so it lay at a weird angle, the little toe snapped so it stood straight up like a finger pointing to the stars. His right arm was missing – ripped off just like Blake's belly. He looked like he'd been trying to crawl out of the chapel when he died.

I steadied the beam as intently as a marksman and forced myself to stare, keeping up the monotone counting, sixty-one, sixty-two, sixty-three, trying to keep calm. I could smell him, I realized shakily, and it was much worse than the smell of the pigs because it was rawer. It was the smell of the sawdust in a butcher's shop, chill and coppery. And then it hit me what the sound was. Not water at all. Slowly, slowly, I raised the torch to the door.

The chapel was full of human flesh. Things caught in the shaky torch beam, things shivering, hanging from the walls and the light fittings. It was blood, not water, dripping on to the stone floor. I stood like a toy soldier, torch pushed out in front of me like it was a bayonet, frozen solid, my eyes taking it all in, heartbeat going bam bam bam *bam* in my temples. There was something on the back of one of the pews that looked like a face, torn off and dropped like one of those Salvador Dalí clocks. I'd never known skin behaved like that – that a whole face can be peeled off like rubber. That face still jumps out at me in my sleep. Even today.

You let things like this into your head and you either start building walls to contain them or you lose it big-time. It's that simple. As I was standing there, all of a sudden all these fucking tears just dribbled out of me. I wiped my eyes with my sleeve and waited for a few moments, studying the torch in my hands, eking out a few minutes pretending to myself that I was smoothing out the rubber casing on the handle. I hadn't cried in years, and it was weird, this feeling, because of how gentle it was: not violent or choking. More like there was a water-table in me that had got a bit full and was rising up behind my eyes. I clicked off the torch and stood in the dark, swallowing hard, still counting to myself, trying to keep it all together. I stopped when I got to two hundred and twenty and saw how pointless everything was. I turned and limped back to the refectory. Fuck knows why I went there – maybe because Blake was there. Maybe Blake dead was better than nobody at all.

'Don't know what to do for you, old mate,' I said, standing there in the dark, staring at his silent body. Suddenly I wasn't scared any more. I'd got past it. I knew I was going to die. 'I'm sorry.' Then, because I thought I was going to cry again, I went into the kitchen and wrenched out the cutlery drawer, with its knives and a heavy rolling-pin. I took the bolt-cutters into the corner and dragged a few things round me – a table, a steel pedal bin – a kind of barrier, and sat down to wait.

Didn't really know what I was waiting for. Morning to come? No. Not morning. I was beyond that. I was waiting to die.

13

It was a bit after midnight when I heard something. I'd been watching the stars moving through the window when it happened, listening to the waves on the shore for four hours and wondering about all the faiths and beliefs and lives I'd laughed at over the years.

There it was: a click or a shuffle from the refectory to my right. I sat bolt upright, my trance broken. The knife almost slithered from my fingers but I caught it, my hands sweating, hurriedly grabbed the bolt-cutters, moved aside the pedal bin and went silently to the door, my heart thudding. Careful not to make a sound I rested my ear against the door. I imagined Blake, sitting upright in the chair, his eyes wide, hands on the table. I imagined a beast next to him, rising up tall in the refectory, almost to the ceiling, pawing the ground. A sweat broke out all over my body. Another noise, slightly muffled, the kind of noise you'd expect if someone was sliding a chair back. *OK, OK*, I told myself. *It's nothing. It's all going to be straightforward*. Blake was dead. The noise was probably just a pig. Probably just a pig.

Except . . . you closed . . . the fucking door . . .

I shook my head, like something was clinging to my hair, took a breath and stepped out into the cafeteria, the bolt-cutters raised above my head. '*Come and fucking get it, Malachi*,' I yelled, teeth bared. '*Come and fucking have it!*'

I stopped. The sliding door stood slightly open, and beyond it the sweep of grass was grey in the starlight. Blake was exactly where he'd been, motionless in the dark, but now something tall and stooped was bending over him, its back to me. It was wearing an old and filthy man's coat and heavy boots, and dragging from under the coat, as it straightened from Blake's bloodied remains, was the tail. There was just time for a thought to flash at me, *It's feeding, I've interrupted its meal*, then it was gone, bounding away to the door, slipping away into the night.

I stood, paralysed, my mouth drooping. I was there for almost a minute, my hands above my head, not breathing or moving or blinking, only staring at the point in the darkness where it had disappeared. It wasn't Malachi. It wasn't Malachi in a strap-on tail. It was too tall and sinewy. My chest was about to burst. I let out all my breath at once, swung the cutters down and bolted after the beast.

At the top of the slope above the community I stopped and scanned the forest ahead. I had a good idea this chase was leading me back to the gorge. Even before I saw the dull shape moving away from me down the path, going rapidly through the trees and heading to the ledge, I knew I was going to end the night back at the mine. If I'd had any sense at all I'd've turned the other way and locked myself into the refectory. Lexie or the boat-owner would've raised the alarm eventually. But something was in me. Lex would've called it dumbness. I went forward.

I dropped myself over a boulder, down where the path snaked a few feet below, scattering gravel. I paused just long enough to get my balance, then I was off along the path, the bolt-cutters bumping along beside me. The thing was fast – it knew its way: I was getting glimpses of it ahead, moving unhesitatingly along paths through the trees, flowing kind of, like a ghost. I bolted noisily after it, branches breaking underfoot, up the path. I was covering ground fast – past the gargoyle, and suddenly, so suddenly it was like a flash of the moon, I burst out into the gorge, coming to a juddering halt on the ledge.

I stood there, panting hard, scanning the ledge, thinking I'd lost it. Then I saw it – a movement: a dull patch below me, a moving part of the rock that was slightly paler than the rest heading away into the gorge.

'*You fucker!*' I bellowed, looping the bolt-cutters round my neck so the jaws were hard against my throat, the handles sticking out over my shoulders like bony wings. I wasn't wasting time going across to the streambed: I was going straight down here. I turned my back to the drop and fell to my knees, throwing my feet out backwards into the darkness, over the lip. I paused for a second, my eyes screwed up, thinking about the drop below, feeling the fuck-awful thrill of adrenaline weaken my fingers. *Just do it . . .*

And I was off, dropping into the darkness, at best half crawling like a spider, at worst bumping and sliding for what seemed like miles, my T-shirt ruck-ing up to my chest, the rocks and gorse tearing into my thighs and stomach. I was ripped to pieces, pouring blood by the time I hit the bottom, but I didn't stop. I was up, running into the gorge with that indistinct shape ahead of me, dodging the drums, my feet springing off the chemical skin. My heart wanted to burst out of my chest, my throat was raw flesh and my tongue was huge in my mouth. But I'd drop dead right here and now before I left the chase. On and on I went, my moon-shadow running along beside me companionably.

It was a lifetime before I got to the other side and threw myself at the slope, going at it like a lizard, legs and arms pumping up and down like pistons, using the sore inside of my calves to get traction, losing my grip every few feet and sliding back, grabbing on to gorse and heather to get purchase. At the top I allowed myself exactly one minute to rest – lying on my back, panting and sweating, counting the sixty seconds with metronomic severity. I was running with blood but my head was clear, my thinking tight as a drum. Fifty-eight, fifty-nine, sixty – and I was up, dragging my feet a bit as I started, still bent over low with my arms hanging, but picking up speed until I was upright. Through the open gate. And there again, that wisp-like flash of something among the dark trees ahead. Proof that I was on it – still going. The air and the trees rushed past my face. I pumped my arms. 'FUCKING MOVE!' I screamed at my legs. 'Keep. Fucking. Going.'

Suddenly I was there, in the opening next to the cottage, coming to a juddering halt just in time to see the dull yellow movement of the beast disappearing round the corner, just in time to hear the door slamming, the sound of bolts being thrown.

I dropped my head and rested my hands on my thighs, shaking my head and spitting on the ground, waiting for my heart to stop pounding, for my lungs to stop stinging. It didn't matter now, no need to run. The fucker was mine – trapped in the cottage. When at last my legs had stopped trembling and I raised my head, I saw the window was being silently, secretively closed, a shadowy figure reaching out a hand under the lace curtain.

'NO,' I roared, launching myself at the house. '*No!*' I grappled for the window. But I was too late: it had closed neatly and tightly against the frame. Furious, I jumped away, almost dancing with rage, swinging the bolt-cutters to one side and then back, in a perfect golfer's swing, straight into the pane. The glass shattered in a star shape, broken pieces tinkling down into the living room. Quickly I pulled off my sweatshirt, wrapped it round my fist, punched out the remainder of the glass and unhooked the window. I was inside in seconds, slithering through like a worm, falling on my shoulder, rolling on to my side in the scattered glass. With a clumsy, crabby motion, I pushed myself up into a crouch, squatting bright-eyed and alert, moving my head side to side in a series of jerks. I was alone in the living room.

The child's windmill on the shelf rotated creakily, like it was pleased to see me. Slowly, moving very quietly, I drew the bolt-cutters along the floor towards me and straightened. Around me the cottage had gone totally silent.

I went quietly to the wall, switched on the light, then stood very still in the centre of the room, trying to focus on all the air in the cottage, feeling its vibrations move along my skin. Nothing. No movement, and no sound. I turned, my head on one side, my skin crawling with concentration. Slowly I lifted my chin and looked up at the ceiling. Something had moved up there, only a few feet above my head, a subtle, infinitesimally small creak of a floorboard. I opened my mouth in a smile, breathing out, whispering softly, 'Ah, *there*. I've got you, ya beaut.'

Stealthily, the cutters at the ready, I moved towards the staircase. The night was absolutely silent now, a cobweb on the light-fitting above floating spectrally over my head, like a draught was coming through. I placed my hand on the banister and, slowly, slowly, testing every inch of every step, crept up the stairs. I paused at the top. I could see three doors ahead – two open and one, on the left, closed.

The word *trap, trap* came back to me, making my skin crawl. I ground my teeth, giving in to a moment's nerves, then inched forward along the corridor, stopping at the closed door, facing it with my feet a pace apart, solid – ready for something to come tearing out at me.

I took in five long, deep breaths. *You can still walk away, mate* . . . raised the cutters above my head and, in one quick move, booted the door in. It flew open, a rush of stale air and darkness, and I saw the creature instantly. It was in the corner, its back to the wall, crying and shrinking away, its feet pedalling furiously. 'It', I saw instantly, was a 'she' –

a woman in her teens or early twenties. Her hands were over her head, a terrified keening noise coming from her mouth.

'Who the fuck are you?' I stood with the cutters at the ready – out in front of me like a sword – ready to swing them if she moved so much as an inch towards me. My breathing was coming so rapidly that I had to stop between each word. 'I said, *who the fuck are you*?' When she didn't answer I made a fake lunge into the room, raising the cutters like I was going to attack. 'Tell me – NOW – tell me who you are. *Who are you*?'

'Don't don't don't!' She shrank back against the wall, her hands out to defend herself, her face streaked with tears and blood. She probably wasn't much past her teens with chopped-around black hair so short you could see the scalp in places. She had the underfed, dingy look of a thirteen-year-old boy on drugs. Whatever the tail trick was, she had either disposed of it or had it tucked neatly down beneath her. All I could see were the tops of her bare knees, crusted with hardened, white skin. 'Please don't!'

'Stand up!'

'I can't!'

'I said –' I made another lunge towards her '– *stand up*!'

'No!' she sobbed. 'No. I can't stand up.'

'Stand up or I'll hurt you.'

She shook her head and sobbed louder. I approached, my eyes on her hands, bending cautiously. Her nails were bitten, the tips of her fingers red and sore. Before she could see what I was doing I grabbed her right hand, wrenching it so high and so quickly that she was caught off balance. '*NO! No no – please please please*.' She flailed, trying to grab me with her left hand, but I dropped the cutters and grabbed that too, yanking it up to meet the other, crunching the wristbones together.

'NOO! Leave me alone. *Please DON'T!* Let me go.'

'SHUT UP!' I slammed her hands into the wall above her head. 'Now, you're going to—' She wriggled, trying to kick me, to jerk her hands away. '*Stop that!* Now just fucking *stop* struggling and *stand* the *fuck* up.'

'I can't.'

'Do it. Fucking *do it*.'

I rammed her hands against the wall again, harder now, and this time she stopped struggling. She raised her eyes to mine and we studied each other, both breathing hard. She had these swimmy, inflamed eyes the colour of mud, and a tilted-up, defiant nose.

'Well?' I was trembling so hard I could almost feel my teeth chattering. 'Are you going to stand up?'

Her mouth moved shakily, but no words came out, only a scratchy murmur. I shook her again. 'Are you?'

'I – I will. I'll stand up if you don't hurt me.'

'I won't hurt you.'

She dropped her eyes, her whole body trembling, and shuffled her feet together, tucking them as tight under herself as she could. Pushing her head forward so her weight tipped over her toes, slowly, stiffly, she began to straighten. I raised her hands, lifting her, running them up the wall, drawing her up, my arms arching over her head. She was tall – almost six foot at a guess, and as she straightened I was aware that a part of her, something heavy and fleshy, didn't come with her and dropped heavily on to the floor. I could see it in the light coming from the hallway. I released her, grabbed up the cutters, and was back where I could see her properly.

'Don't move,' I said, holding up the cutters.

She dropped her face into her hands and stood pitifully in the centre of the room, her shoulders drooping. 'Don't kill me. Please don't kill me.'

'I'm not going to *kill* you, for fuck's sake.' I licked my lips. 'Take a step forward.'

She obeyed, not dropping her hands, shuffling forward dejectedly.

'That's it. Stop. Now . . . take your coat off.'

She unbuttoned it and let it fall. She was wearing

a man's shirt that reached to her knees and you could see her arms and chest, thin as a young boy's. Her bare, muscular legs were crammed into a pair of lace-up boots. I took a sideways step, circling her, staring in silence at what dangled from under the shirt – like something she had deposited there: an obscene, fleshed growth, the skin pale, rather yellow in places. It hung loosely between her legs, all the way down to the floor, ending in an odd, spatula-like shape of flesh. I could see instantly it wasn't a trick. This belonged to her. There was a vein in the top of it that was pulsing from the effort of the chase.

'Please,' she begged, making a grab for it, trying to conceal it. 'Please don't look.'

I stared for a long time, not knowing what to do or say. I realized I was holding my breath. I let it out in a long sigh, shook my head. 'My God,' I muttered, lowering the cutters to my side. 'What the fuck is going on in this place?'

'I don't know – *I don't know. Please let me sit down – please!*'

I nodded to the bed. 'Go on.'

She dropped down, pulling the coat over her. She arranged the duvet hurriedly, so that whatever the growth was, it was squashed out of view just behind her left leg, making her sit slightly tilted to one side. I stared at the place it was hidden, my mind racing.

173

When I looked up I found her staring back at me, like she was saying, '*I can't do anything about it. It's not my fault.*'

'Oh, Christ,' I said, a wave of tiredness taking my feet out from under me. I sat on the floor with a bump, rubbing my eyes. 'What is going on? Who are you?'

'Angeline,' she said. 'Angeline. I can't help it.'

'Angeline?' I said the name distantly, like it was the strangest name I'd ever heard. '*Angeline?*' I frowned. There was an odd, muffled quality to her voice – something sticky about the consonants, something I couldn't place – like she wasn't used to speaking.

'Angeline?'

'Yes?'

'Are you deaf, Angeline?'

She shook her head.

'Not deaf?'

'No. I can hear you.'

I narrowed my eyes. 'And what the fuck have you been doing today? Eh?' I nodded to the window. 'What did you do to Sovereign? And to Blake? What was that all about then?'

She dropped her hands and blinked at me. 'What have *I* been doing?' she said, wiping her nose. 'No – not me. *I* haven't done anything.'

'Someone has.'

'Dad,' she said, hurriedly rubbing at the tears on her cheeks. 'My dad. He's gone crazy. There was an explosion and—'

'*Dad?*'

'I followed him. He waited until they were in the chapel and then he—' She wiped her nose with her shirt sleeve. 'He *nailed* them inside. He knows about explosives. *He's always known how to blow things up*. I saw it. I saw it all.'

'And who the fuck's your – Jesus Christ.' I dropped my hands disbelievingly. It was all coming straight now. What a mangled fucking truth. 'No shit,' I muttered. 'No shit. Malachi? He's your father?'

She stared back at me, her face closed and defensive. 'They couldn't get out. *Are they going to think it was me?*'

Part Two

DUMBARTON
SEPTEMBER

Lexie

1

Dear Mr Taranici

I certainly hope you are coming to understand why I had to cancel last week. Apparently you said I didn't give you enough warning to waive the fee and, of course, I apologize for that, but I really think you should try, as a professional, to understand just what things are like up here. They are so . . . I don't even know how to say it . . . so completely *awful* that I have absolutely no idea when I'll be back in London. So maybe you can see why one cancelled appointment doesn't seem all that *catastrophic* to me. (By the way, just for the record, being nagged by your receptionist didn't help. I mean yes, surprisingly, I do know I've got to pay you. Haven't I always paid on time? And don't you remember why I'm here in Scotland in the first place? To find a way to tell Oakesy about it all, my job and everything? I've told you I'm going to get him to help me with my bills, but your secretary rubbing it in that I haven't got any money is just making my anxiety levels *rocket*.)

Do you recall saying if I hit an anxiety barrier a good coping mechanism would be to write things down? Remember? To soothe myself? Well, that's what I'm doing now. Writing it all out. How about we treat this letter as my session? Then I won't be paying for empty time after all and we'll both be happy. The other thing I've been doing is reading the chart you gave me (filling it in religiously every day, actually) and trying to identify the 'life/situation/relationship/practical problem' that triggered this catastrophic anxiety. And what do I find? Surprise surprise, at the very root of it all is the usual thing: you-know-who, and his *#%*$* job and his total inability to take me seriously or even *notice* me. God knows how I'll ever get him on to the subject of money. Especially with all that's happened to *him*.

You remember I told you we were up here for him to cover a story on Cuagach Eilean? Pig Island? Well, yes, I can just see your face now because you must have heard that name in the news this week. I

assume you've already put two and two together
and guessed who has managed to get himself
caught up in the whole dreadful thing. And now
he's the centre of attention and I'll never get
listened to or my needs met.

Honestly, it's been horrible, just horrible, from
the moment we got here. I'd spent ages choosing
my wardrobe for this holiday – I mean, the
attention I paid to detail. I bought three sets of
shorts, quite shorty ones. Yes, I can hear you saying, 'Alex, are you sure you should be sexualizing
another negotiation?' Well, you'd be very pleased
with yourself in this instance, because the shorts
didn't work. He just spent the whole time on his
computer, hardly noticing I was there. And to cap it
all he left me on my own in this horrible bungalow
with water that's piped down through peat so it's
an awful brown colour and makes the toilet look
dirty, and this huge picture-window, which lets the
sun come in and bake everything until you can't
breathe. You couldn't imagine it in your worst
nightmares. Fake beams, squares of cardboard
daubed with pink ant-killer in every corner, not a
soul for miles around.

How long do you think he was gone for? One
day? Two days? Ha! No. Try again. *Three. Three
days* I was there, miles from the nearest house, with
nothing to do but go back through my credit-card

statements for the zillionth time, or stare out at the clouds of midges in the trees. Just when I was really panicking, when I'd gone through nearly all the money he'd left and was thinking there was no point in hanging around in Scotland at all because he wasn't going to be interested in talking to me anyway, suddenly he turns up on the doorstep.

Well, that was almost the end for me. He'd been in a fight. He was totally unrecognizable – half paralysed and bloody, half his hair missing where it had been pulled out. I really had to struggle to keep my temper with him. Oh, I put him to bed and did the devoted-wife number, but I was furious. It turns out that Malachi Dove (you've heard *that* name in the papers a few times this week, I bet), Oakesy's nemesis for years, is alive and kicking and living on Pig Island. And, typical of Oakesy, he's gone out of his way to provoke a confrontation with him. Honestly. He could have been killed.

It's a class thing, Mummy says. Remember I told you she's got this bee in her bonnet about Oakesy being my rebellion against her? That marrying outside my class is a guarantee cracks will come to the surface sooner rather than later? Well, I've got to the point where I'm almost agreeing with her. I mean, why does he have to drink so much? Where are his social graces? (Incidentally, I'm convinced this is why there were such sparks between me and Christophe –

and whatever you say there's no doubt there were sparks. It's a simple fact of life. We looked at each other and recognized someone from the same class, and that's all there is to it.)

It took Oakesy two weeks to get back on his feet. And then he was straight back out there, hiring a boat to take him to Cuagach. But if I thought that put me on edge, sent my stress hormones into overdrive, I had no idea of the *nightmare* that was about to start. Early Sunday it was, and I was asleep when the phone rang. It was you-know-who calling from his mobile, shouting above the noise of a boat engine, saying something about getting dressed because we were going out when he got back. I propped myself up on the pillow and looked at the clock. It was four in the morning.

'I'll be home in half an hour,' he shouted. His voice kept going in and out of range. Fading away. He hadn't even waited to get a good signal. 'Get . . . and don't . . . in a hurry. Get dressed.'

'For heaven's sake,' I mumbled. My head was all thick and cottony with sleep. 'For heaven's sake . . .'

'*Just do it. Get dressed.*'

And when he said that it really jolted me awake. I sat up in bed, suddenly thinking about Malachi Dove, about all the nightmares I'd been having. '*Oakesy?*' I said, scared now, looking up at the window, at the curtains and thinking of the silent woods out there and the long driveway surrounded by rhododendrons. 'What's the matter? What's happening?'

'Wait next to the front door. I won't be long. And, Lex, don't take this the wrong way, but it might be a good idea to—'

'Yes? Might be a good idea to *what*?'

'To lock all the doors and all the windows.'

'What? *What do you mean*? Oakesy?' But the phone hissed static back at me. '*Oakesy*?' He was gone, leaving me sitting bolt upright in the dark, clutching the receiver, staring at the window.

You know how level-headed I am. Don't you? You know it takes a lot to rattle me. But with that twenty-second phone call he'd got me scared – really anxious about how dark the bungalow suddenly seemed. I got out of bed and went shakily to the kitchen, getting the first knife I could find out of the drawer and standing with it pointing out in front of me in the darkness. *Don't take this the wrong way, but lock everything.* I went round the bungalow without switching on a single light, holding the knife in both hands, double-checking every lock, my hands shaking. When I tested the window locks I did it really quickly, only slightly opening the curtains, not the whole way. I didn't want to find a face staring back at me through the glass.

In the bedroom I put the light on and got dressed with my back to the wall so I could see the window and the door, my hands shaking so hard I could barely do up my jeans. I got my shoes on and went to sit in the living room, on a chair against the wall between the window and the front door, the knife still clutched in my hands. I kept thinking of the acres of wood surrounding me, pressing in on the bungalow. Every sound was magnified a hundred times: the strange click-click-click of the immersion-heater coming on in the airing-cupboard, a bird walking across the shingled roof. When the phone rang again I snatched it up, my heart thundering.

'*Yes? Is that you?*'

'I'm outside. I'm going to let myself in.'

I heard the key in the lock. The door opened and he came in wearily, dropping his rucksack on the floor.

'*What is it?*' I jumped up and stood in front of him. 'What's happening? You're frightening the life out of me.'

He didn't answer. He stood there, looking at me with bloodshot eyes, his T-shirt torn and covered with blood. Hadn't shaved, of course, and his skin was all leached and sick-looking under the tan. There was a pause and then another figure shuffled in from the darkness and stopped just inside the door, blinking and turning round in a confused circle. It took me a moment to realize it was a woman because her hair was really short and black, with these patches of skin showing through, and she was very tall, almost as tall as Oakesy. She was wearing this awful belted imitation-leather coat, and a denim skirt that reached all the way down to her chain-store trainers – you know the sort, with flashing lights in them, except the lights didn't seem to be working. When she turned and caught sight of me she put her hands up defensively as if I was going to pounce on her from the darkness.

'My wife,' Oakesy said. He slammed the front door and bolted it. 'Lex.'

She subsided a little. Slowly she lowered her arms and turned her head sideways, a wary eye fixed on me. She would have been quite pretty in a way if her hair didn't look like it'd been cut with pinking shears and she hadn't got that closed-up, sullen scowl on her face. She had the appearance of those teenage white boys you see hanging around the town centre in Oban sniffing glue, with their washed-out skins and shadows under their eyes.

'Who's she?'

'Angeline,' he said. 'She's Angeline.'

'Angeline?'

'Angeline Dove.'

'Angeline Do—' I stopped. I wasn't sure I'd heard him right. 'Angeline *Dove*?'

'His daughter.'

I turned to stare at her. 'Is that true?' Oakesy had never said anything about children. 'Is it?' She didn't answer. She just went on studying me doubtfully as if she was ready to run away. 'Hey,' I said, waving a hand to get her attention, 'hello-oh. I asked you a question.'

'It's true,' she muttered quickly. 'It's true.'

'It's all right, Lex,' Oakesy said.

I swivelled my eyes to him. 'All right?'

'She's cool.'

'Cool?'

'Yes. Really.'

I shook my head, putting my fingers to my temples. I've lived with all the stories about Dove for long enough and I think I can be forgiven if I was a little taken aback. Can't I? 'Oakesy?' I said, turning from him to Angeline, and back again. 'Do I deserve to be told what's happening?' I stared at her coat – filthy and cheap and covered with grass stains – then at him: just as bad with his T-shirt all stained and ripped, his bare legs grazed, dirt and gravel embedded in the congealed cuts. 'Why is *she* here? What's happened?'

'I'm sorry.' He sounded so sad. I've never heard him sound like that before. 'I'm sorry, Lex, we've got to go to the police.'

2

Outside the world was silent, as if it was holding its breath. It was still dark but there was a faint flush of morning starting at the horizon. We stood in the doorway, blinking out at the trees, listening for movement. It was silent. No dawn chorus, no flutter of wings in the branches. Oakesy paused for a second then hurried us out – *come on, come on* – across to the cold little Fiesta, our feet crunching in the gravel, ushering us into the car.

He wasn't telling me what had happened. He wasn't telling me why he was scared, why he locked all the doors as soon as we got into the car. He started the engine really quickly and we were off – jolting down the driveway, out on to the dark lane that led to the top of the peninsula. When we got out on the coast road he kept leaning forward to peer out at the forests and the little rocky coves rushing past outside as if he was searching for something, slowing at one point as we passed a pebble beach to study a boat pulled up there.

'Oakesy? What's happening?'

But he shook his head as if he was concentrating on something very important – the sort of focused look he'd get if he was trying to balance something on the top of a very thin stick. He wouldn't answer. And in the back Angeline Dove was as silent as he was. She sat awkwardly cantilevered over on to one side, her hand up to grasp the seat in front of her as if she was injured. I glanced at her from time to time in the wing mirror. She had her nose to the window and was staring really hard at Pig Island with her shadowy eyes. Whenever we turned a corner and it disappeared behind the headland her eyes went blank, as if she'd retreated back into herself. *She's cool*, Oakesy had said. *Cool*. Cool? Well, she wasn't like her dad, that was certain – she looked like she'd lived in a dungeon all her life: her skin was pinched and sallow, and now it was getting light I could see she had a rash of acne round the corners of her mouth. The haircut was so bad there were bits of curls in one place and patches of scalp next to them. My God, what a mess. I wondered who her mother was.

We'd gone about three miles when Oakesy started tapping his fingers agitatedly on the steering-wheel and swallowing noisily.

'What is it?' I said, looking at his hands. 'What's the matter?'

But before I could finish the sentence he swerved the car off the road, pulling it into a layby with a spume of gravel. He threw the door open, jumped out and walked away from the car half bent over, his hands pressed to his stomach. Oh, God, I thought, here we go, he's going to be sick. I got out of the car. It was really cold and still outside. My breath was hanging in the air as I crunched across the layby towards him. He heard me coming and turned, and I saw that he wasn't being sick, he was *crying*. His face was swollen and red. His nose was running.

'I shouldn't,' he said, hunching his shoulders and wiping his face on the sleeves of his sweatshirt. 'I shouldn't – I mean, look at her. She saw the whole fucking thing and she's not crying.'

'What whole thing? What *whole thing*? How can I talk to you if you won't tell me what happened?'

'It's all my fault, Lex.' He wiped his nose with the back of his hand and shook his head, taking deep breaths, slowly getting the crying under control. 'If he'd never found out they let me on that fucking island in the first place—' He took another few shaky breaths, then drew himself up, red-eyed. He raised a hand towards the firth, glittering and twitching pink in the dawn. 'People are dead, sweetheart.' He shook his head, sad and exhausted. 'Out there, on Cuagach, people are dead.'

I'd taken a breath to answer before his words sunk in. When I realized what he'd said I closed my mouth and turned my head to one side, lowering my voice. '*Dead?* Is that what you said? *Dead?*'

'Yes.'

'*What do you mean dead?*' I took him by the

sweatshirt, at a point just above his belly-button, and turned him so he had to look me in the eye. 'You said people are *dead*. Dead how? Oakesy? Tell me this isn't what those types in the pub were telling you about.'

He closed his eyes and sighed. 'You don't want to know, Lexie, please, believe me you—'

'*Don't patronize me, Oakesy*. Whatever's happened to you out there I can promise you I've seen it before. Don't forget who I work for. Now, tell me.'

And in the end he did. He sat down wearily on the freezing gravel on the side of the road and while Angeline peered at us through the steamed-up car window, and the sun spread orange and molten across the horizon, he told me.

I'm sure you think you know what he said because it's all been in the papers this week, and everyone probably imagines they know exactly what happened, but I can promise you don't know the half of it: some of the things he kept coming back to – over and over again as if they'd got stuck on a loop in his head. I mean, you never saw in the newspapers about a face peeled off, did you? But Oakesy kept coming back to that, showing me with his hands how big it was, the way it had been hanging, drooped over the edge of something. And you never read in the *Sun* about pigs tearing apart a teenage girl and carrying her foot away. Or the way her foot had tried to stay attached to her leg bones. Or the guy blown by the blast on his side, just his little toe facing the ceiling, or – I could go on and on – the people with no heads, their necks just red stalks, a bit of vertebra protruding from the flesh, half a skull with its contents sucked away by the explosion . . .

I can say it all quite calmly now, a few days later, but as much of a professional as I am, as much as I've seen with Christophe's work, I'm not completely atrophied, you know. I couldn't even look at Oakesy as he told me. I listened with my eyes locked on the frozen blades of grass at the edge of the layby, my arms folded, half of me wanting to scream at him, '*Shut up.*' When he was finished I was quiet for a long while, feeling my heart knocking deep against my stomach. Then I turned round to where Pig Island just peeped out beyond the headland. It was too far away to see anything, of course – not the village or the chapel or anything – just this great silent shape taking all the light away.

'Lex?' He put his hand on my foot. 'You OK?'

I looked down at his hand. 'I've seen things, you know. At work.'

'I know,' he said, rubbing his eyes. 'I know.'

There was a bit of a silence while we both thought about the island. Then he stood and felt in the back pocket of his shorts. He pulled out a crumpled piece of paper and passed it over. I took it, my eyes not leaving his face.

'Well?' I said. 'What's this?'

He didn't answer. He put his hands in his pockets and stared out to sea, as if he'd just handed me one of those awful private-detective photos – him with another woman. I unfolded the paper shakily, my heart thumping.

'It's the rental agreement for the bungalow.'

'Yes.' He bent his head and scratched the top of his scalp hard – the way he always does when he knows he's done something wrong. For a moment I thought he was going to start crying again. 'Found it in Dove's cottage,' he said, his voice all thick. 'I took her to get a bag packed and I found it. I never said, but it was missing from my rucksack – after he gave me that twatting.' He paused. 'You know what it means?'

My blood was racing now. Oh, yes. I knew what it meant. Now *everything* made sense. Like why he'd called me and told me to lock the doors. Like why he was so anxious. 'My God,' I said faintly. My legs felt like jelly. 'He knew where I was? All that time?'

'I'm sorry.'

'All that time.' I looked back down the long, empty road in the direction of the bungalow. I was scared out of my mind. I kept picturing the woods surrounding the bungalow, thinking how close I'd been. Maybe he'd been out there, watching me. Maybe he was *there now*. 'My things. Oakesy, I left all my things in the bungalow.'

'Yeah.' He got to his feet and put his hand on my back. 'The police'll deal with it.'

The walk back to the car was only a few yards – but it felt like miles. I kept my back stiff, resisting the impulse to whip round. I knew if I turned all the mountains and clouds would be glaring down at me, scrutinizing my back. As Oakesy put his hand on the driver's door he stopped and looked round quite suddenly as if someone had called his name. He stared up at the mountains, at the dark green, almost black ribbons of trees on the upper slopes.

'*What?* What did you hear?'

'Nothing,' he said. He gave a long, violent shiver as if he wanted to shake something off his back. He threw a glance out at Pig Island, then got into the car, locked his door and leaned across me to lock mine. 'Come on,' he said. 'Let's go.'

3

I don't know if this is a good time to point something out, but you may as well know, if you haven't already guessed: your comments about Christophe really hurt my feelings.

'Lexie, would it be very difficult for you to accept that Mr Radnor wanted nothing more than a professional relationship with you?'

That's what you said. Remember? Well, I've thought about it and the other day I remembered an incident I should have told you about before. It's something that *absolutely proves* there is more to Christophe's relationship with me than *you* could ever guess at.

It was one morning when I'd been at the clinic for only about a month. He came in early because that was his habit – all clean and scrubbed and smelling of aftershave – his *Telegraph* tucked under his arm. Usually he'd just raise a hand as he passed my desk, but that day, maybe because no one else was around, he stopped and looked at me curiously.

'Good morning,' he said, as if he'd never seen me before and was impressed with what he saw. I was wearing a very neatly pressed white blouse with a matelot collar and a rather sweet black skirt that ended mid-thigh. But Mr Radnor is too much of a gentleman to be staring at my legs. Instead he pretended to be admiring the vase of fresh yellow ranunculus I'd placed on the counter-top. 'This all looks very attractive,' he said, taking in the gleaming floor, the magazines lined up neatly, the plasma screen monitor polished carefully. 'Yes,' he repeated. 'All very attractive.'

Well, off he went into the lift and that was where the exchange ended, short and polite and not very remarkable. But I'm not stupid. I knew quite well the message he was sending. His choice of words, *very attractive* (used twice), wasn't lost on me. From that day on I kept the reception area shining and bright, squirting perfume into the air and sweeping the floor every time a patient walked leaves and dirt in from the street. Every day Christophe came breezing through; no matter how late he was or how stressed, he always found time to comment on how attractive it looked, and every day I worked harder at it, always thinking ahead, trying to do what would please him.

I think I've told you – and you probably knew anyway – about all his *pro bono* work, the fabulous things he's done for people around the world too poor to pay for operations? Well, I'd saved a lot of the press cuttings, interviews and photos of him with the people he's helped, and it suddenly occurred to me how nice it would be to have them framed. I found someone in Tottenham Court Road to do them quite cheaply and two weeks later I got to work early and spent an hour hanging them around the reception area until they looked perfect.

Then I polished everything, swept the floor, straightened my blouse and sat neatly, waiting for him to come in

He was a few minutes late. He came in, shaking his umbrella and propping it in the corner. 'Good morning, Alex.'

'Morning, Mr Radnor,' I said, my smile getting wider. I could hardly keep still I was so excited. 'What filthy weather.'

'Dreadful.' He looked up, and when he saw all the pictures arrayed behind me, his expression changed. He paused, then came forward slowly, a hesitant smile on his face. 'Those are nice,' he said uncertainly. He stopped at the desk, unbuttoned his raincoat and seemed to be thinking hard. Then he said, 'Maybe not *entirely* suitable in Reception? I wonder if they look a little – uh – showy. Do you think?'

My smile faded. 'You've got a lot to be proud of, Mr Radnor.'

'I tell you what,' he said kindly, 'don't you think they'd look rather good in my office?'

'Your office?' And then, of course, I understood. He wasn't upset or angry – he was being modest. That's the sort of man he is. I stood up behind the desk, very erect and proud. 'Yes. Your office. Your office it is.' I turned and began to take them down, piling them efficiently on the counter. 'I'll carry them up for you.'

'Oh, no no no – no need for that.'

'None of the staff'll be here for half an hour. I can lock the door.'

'It won't be necessary.'

'But I'd *like* to.'

I stood on tiptoe to reach the top ones, and here I blame myself – because I didn't give a thought to what it might do to him to see my skirt ride up and reveal the tops of my legs in my black tights. When I got the last picture down and turned to him, his expression had hardened. He was red in the face.

'Come on, then,' he said, picking up half of the pictures. 'I'll get the lift.'

I'd never been in his office because that dragon of a secretary guards it like Cerberus. Well, it was absolutely *exquisite*, with oak-panelled walls and elegant curtains and a marvellous view of the rain-spattered roofs of Harley Street. You could even see the tops of some of the trees in Regent's Park. I stopped and sighed, looking around me.

'Oh, it's *lovely*, just lovely, up here. It's exactly what I expected.'

'Thank you,' he said, taking off his raincoat and hanging it on the hatstand behind the door. 'You can put them on the window-seat. I'll deal with them later.'

So I took the pictures to the window-seat, with its lovely raw-silk cushions in a dusty apricot colour, and put them in a pile. Then I loitered for a moment or two, next to the window where the sun could come through and show the highlights in my hair. Christophe sat down at his desk and switched on his computer.

'Was there anything else?'

I smiled and stretched up on tiptoe once or twice, my shoulders up, I was so full of excitement. This was like a secret game we were playing.

He smiled, a little tightly. 'Sorry. I said – was there anything else?'

'Your secretary's got a great job,' I said. 'It's the sort of job I'd love.'

He nodded, and looked at the door, then at the computer screen. Then he rubbed his top lip a little anxiously, with the side of his finger.

'Don't worry,' I said, because I know that's the thing with men and sex – it overwhelms them, like a wave. He needed time to come down to earth. 'I'm going. Call me if you need anything. I finish at five.'

I stopped at the door and turned round to give him a last little wave, but he was busy with the computer, clicking through his appointments – like the professional he is – so I went back to my desk and spent the whole day glowing with that amazing feeling you get when you know you've met someone who is going to change your life.

I didn't tell you any of this before out of respect for Mr Radnor – the medical community is like a grapevine, isn't it? And, God knows, it's not easy for a man of his age, struggling with these feelings. But don't think I'm dismissing what you said: in fact, when you said, 'professional relationship', I think you were closer to the truth than you realized. Because in the last few days it's become very clear to me: what Christophe needs is an *excuse* to have a closer professional relationship with me. He needs a bit of breathing space to relax around me, so the real thing between us can develop. What's ironic is I didn't see any of this until what happened that awful morning with Oakesy and Angeline Dove.

4

Sometimes you surprise yourself. When we drove away from the layby I was trembling with shock. But then I wound down the window and put my face into the slipstream, the cold air racing up my nose and into my lungs and I thought of one thing. *I thought about Christophe.* I thought about the things he's endured – the human tragedies, the danger, the disaster zones – all the appalling conditions he's confronted (without, incidentally, *ever* being reduced to *tears*). The sun floated free of the horizon and warmed my face, and suddenly I felt very close to him. I had the strange feeling that what had happened on Cuagach was going to unite us in some way. By the time we got to Oban I wasn't trembling any more. If anything, I was excited. I was in the middle of something enormously important. No one at the clinic would be able to ignore that for very long.

The seaside town was absolutely silent: aside from the early Mull ferry in the harbour, lit up like a Christmas tree, the only sign of life was the remains of last night's drinking sessions – chip-wrappers blowing along the cobbled street, a seagull tugging at a half-eaten kebab in the gutter. Oakesy parked in a back alley and we all got out of the car, our faces stony and shocked in the early sun. Angeline took a little longer getting out, struggling a bit. I think it was then I realized there was something wrong with her.

Earlier I suppose I must have thought she'd hurt herself on the island and that was why she was sitting strangely. It's amazing that, with all my experience at the clinic, I didn't give it much thought. But now, as we walked to the police station, I studied her out of the corner of my eye and it dawned on me that something was very wrong. She limped slightly, lurching a little, as if her right leg was shorter than the left, and once or twice held her hand up, as if to reach for something to catch her balance, the hem of her coat swaying. She kept up with us – but whenever I slowed down to try to get a glimpse of her from behind she slowed too, so I couldn't see. But I was getting an impression, even out of the corner of my eye, of a strange bulk at the back – looking at her, you'd think she was wearing a bag strapped under her coat.

The police station was in a dark brick building on a main street, and while we waited in Reception for someone to come to the desk, she stood with her back to the wall, arms folded tight round her, eyes darting from side to side as if she expected to be ambushed. The man behind the glass shield was friendly enough until Oakesy told him why we were there. Then his smile froze and the friendliness left him. He looked from Oakesy, to me, to Angeline and back again, as if he was sure we were having him on. 'Wait there,' he muttered, and disappeared for a while. When he reappeared he didn't meet our eyes, but ushered us through a door, down a corridor and into an office, a small stale room at the back of the police station, full of filing cabinets, with chipped mugs on the desk. 'Wait in here,' he said, switching on the light. 'DS Struthers is out on a call, but he's coming back to speak to you. I'm going to get you some coffee.'

We sat in the office waiting for our coffee, none of us speaking. Oakesy spent the time bent over, inspecting his legs, running his fingers down the messy long grazes already scabbing over. I kept watching Angeline. She could hardly keep still she was so nervous: swallowing over and over again and putting her coat sleeve up to dab at the sweat that kept popping out on her forehead. It was strange the way she was sitting, half on her right leg, one hand clutching the seat as if she was sore or something.

After about five minutes a sleepy-looking man in a rather creased suit appeared in the open doorway. We all glanced up at him expectantly, but he didn't say anything, just stood there, studying us all. He was young, probably only about twenty-nine, and slightly overweight (what do they say about the Glaswegians? That they've got a lower life expectancy than the Ethiopians or something?). His hair had been shaved at the back of the neck, with the front all spiked up and the tips bleached yellow.

'I'm DS Callum Struthers,' he said, after a while. 'The desk FSO told me your story and what I'm wondering is . . .' He looked from one of us to another, taking us in. '. . . is it true?'

'It's true.'

'You were out on old Cuagach? The three of you?'

'Just me,' said Oakesy. He nodded to Angeline. 'And her.'

'And what are you going to tell me? You saw the devil of Cuagach? A wee maddarous beastie creeping through the forests?'

Next to me I felt Angeline stiffen. She dropped her face and began to scratch compulsively at her shorn head. Her chest was rising and falling, her mouth moving noiselessly; she was muttering something under her breath as if she was talking herself into not getting up and running away. Oakesy turned to Struthers. He had that heavy, red-eyed look that he gets when he's angry.

'Are you sure your desk sergeant told you what happened?'

Struthers lowered his lids and nodded. 'Aye. But to be fair with you, it's not the first time I've heard this story. People love a good hoax call when it comes to old Cuagach. Human remains washing up on the Craignish Peninsula? I mean, what do they think we are?'

'Don't say that word again.'

'What word?'

'Hoax.'

Oh-oh, I thought, there's going to be another fight. But then Struthers seemed to back off a bit.

He came in and sat down, studying Oakesy very carefully for a while.

'Our dispatchers in Govan have got a lad nipping out to Cuagach for a keek at what's happening out there.' He glanced up at the big map on the wall. 'They'll've sent someone out of Lochgilphead and he'll've chartered something out of, I don't know, Ardfern or somewhere, because the launch won't come up from the Clyde, not for a ho—' He paused. 'Not until we know what's happening. So that'll be . . .' He sucked in a breath through his teeth and looked at his watch dubiously. 'What? Two hours before we know how the land lies out there?'

'This isn't a hoax. Do we look like teenagers?'

Struthers didn't say anything for a moment or two. Then he opened a filing cabinet and pulled out a folder, kicking the drawer closed. 'Tell you what. Why don't I do the right thing? Get your statements. Get it all clear in our heads.'

Oakesy went first, leaving the room with Struthers, wooden, still containing his anger. Angeline and I were left with some undrinkable coffee in polystyrene cups that the desk sergeant had brought. We didn't speak. She sat opposite me in an uncommunicative huddle. She'd stopped that compulsive scratching and had her hands pressed between her knees. Her closed little face was lowered, but from time to time she looked up at the door as if she expected someone to come running in. I tipped my head forward, resting it on my fingertips so that she wouldn't be able to see me sneaking glances at her. She was all tilted and awkward, as if she was sitting on a large cushion or something. I thought about the way she'd reacted to what Struthers had said and suddenly my heart started to race, my hands sweat. Something incredible – something strange and unbelievable – was in my head. Something about the mass she was carrying around under the coat. *Why doesn't she take that coat off? She must be baking in it . . .*

The video.

A human tail – it sounds like a fantasy, doesn't it? But you as a doctor will know that actually *hundreds* of children a year are born with tails, it's just that most of them are removed in the first few hours. The sacrococcygeal growth. The vestigial human tail. I'd seen a paper about them in one of the journals at the clinic. There are all these differ-ent kinds of human tails, some are haemangiomas – I stared at her with this fixed smile on my face, all the scientific stuff going through my head – and some have something to do with spina bifida. There had been photos in the journal. One was of a little boy in India with a long, skin-covered tube of fat dangling from the bottom of his spine. What was the term they used? *Occulta? Spina bifida occulta?* But his tail had been quite small in comparison: no bigger than a large worm. So what about something as big as what was on the video?

And then, with Christophe's face in my mind and all these ideas racing around, something else occurred to me. It went click-click-click into place, and I almost smiled. This dreadful thing might have a silver lining, after all. Oakesy was sitting on something big with this story, much better than a feature on the Positive Living Centre. This would be tabloid front-page stuff – the end of our financial troubles. Angeline would give Oakesy everything he needed to know about Malachi. But it wasn't just Oakesy she could help: this was a story Christophe would kill to be involved with. I could just imagine his face, smiling out of the newspaper from Angeline's post-op bedside, maybe holding her hand. And I'd be the one who had found her for him. An excited little itch was starting in the palms of my hands.

I glanced at the door, then sat back, sipping my coffee and smiling at her. My heart was beating, very cool and hard, because I knew Angeline Dove was going to help us. First she'd help Oakesy. And then she'd help me.

5

It didn't take two hours, as Struthers predicted, but just fifty minutes before the news came through from the dispatcher. Then everything changed. In the time it took for Oakesy to give his statement, the station was transformed from a sleepy back-water to a place full of noise: people busying around, carrying forms and bulging folders, phones ringing in distant offices, doors slamming, police radios firing off bursts of white noise. They were supposed to use a courtroom in Lochgilphead, but that was being renovated so they were setting up an incident room here in Oban, in a building that was too small, and by lunchtime there were arguments raging up and down the corridor between the local police officers and the women in the HOLMES team, who'd just arrived from Glasgow with their computer equipment: there weren't enough parking spaces – where in the name of God were they expected to leave their cars? And *what*? Only one ladies' lavvy? In the whole building? 'And that's got a broken water-heater that'll scald you if ye're not careful.'

For lunch me and Oakesy sat in silence at Struthers's desk and ate supermarket sandwiches, like office workers on a rainy lunch-hour. Angeline couldn't eat. She tried but you could see it was like trying to swallow pebbles. When Struthers came to get her to give her statement she stood, but she was shaking so much they had to call a female officer to come and help her away.

'She's in shock,' Oakesy said. 'Take it easy with her.'

Ten minutes later he was taken off by a detective who said he was the 'senior identification manager'. He needed help in making up a list of missing persons. Well, that took almost two hours during which time guess who was left alone in the office, with nothing to do but read through the Strathclyde Police leaflets from Reception – *Loch Safety*; *What Happens If I'm Arrested?*; *Cadet Programme: So You Think You're Too Young to Join the Police?* – and stare at the area map. Nobody said anything about getting our stuff from the bungalow, no matter how many times I asked, and I didn't have my phone with me to send a text.

'No one's even offered me a cup of tea,' I told Oakesy, when he and Angeline came back to the office. 'Not a thing since lunch. I wouldn't mind a cup of tea.'

At four p.m. an intimidating team of plain-clothes men arrived from Dumbarton, silent, grim-looking in their suits. At their helm was the subdivisional chief inspector: a bit older than Christophe, maybe mid-fifties, very thin and austere, the height of a basketball player with the long, serious face of a professor. When he came into Struthers's office he didn't say hello or anything: he went past us to the window, put his nose to the pane and studied the view thoughtfully. I knew what was out there – God knows, I'd had enough time to look out at it: a little parking area behind the station, two marked cars and a row of dustbins. Beyond that the back-street rooftops . . . then purplish, heather-pocked hills, deserted and alien.

After a few minutes he closed the blinds, twisting the slats so they met each other neatly and didn't let any daylight through. Then he switched on the fluorescent lights and came to sit down opposite us. He didn't speak for a while, just studied us carefully, one after the other.

'I'm Peter Danso,' he said eventually. 'I'm the police incident commander, which means, for your purposes, I'll be heading up the investigation. I'm sorry it's taken me some time to come and speak to you. There's been a lot to – to deal with.' He leaned over and shook our hands. We all said our names in turn, like children at register time. It was making me nervous, the way he seemed so worried about us. He turned to Oakesy and Angeline. 'I've read your statements and there are a few things I want to say to you both. A lot of issues around your mental welfare and what we can do to support you, of course. But what's on my mind, what I'm here for now, is to discuss your plans.'

'I'm staying,' said Oakesy. 'I'm staying here.'

Danso nodded slowly, taking him in: his scabbed knees and battered hands. The measured look in his eyes. 'You know there's nothing to stop you just getting out of Strathclyde right now? I'm not going to lie, you're crucial to our investigation, and in a perfect world I'd have you stay, both of you.' He looked at Angeline who was staring at the floor, bright red in the face. 'But I want this clear – all I can do is *advise* you to stay. I can't force you.'

'I know,' Oaksey said. 'I'm staying.'

'OK, OK.' Danso propped an elbow on his desk and scratched his ear uncomfortably. 'Look, I don't need to tell you how serious this is. And reading through your statements just now one or two red flags came up for me that made me want to think carefully about your safety. With the trouble this lass's father is in . . . well, in my experience it makes him dangerous.' He met Oakesy's eyes and held them. 'Very dangerous indeed. In the next few hours someone'll be thinking about doing an impact assessment and that'll address just how worried we should be . . .'

On Danso's belt his phone rang. He checked the display, put it on to answer and looked back up at us.

'We had a vehicle stolen from the car park at Crinian Hotel on Saturday night – at about eleven. Do you know Crinian? It's one of the places boats put in to when they come off the islands.'

'He took the little dory, the one they had at the centre. It was missing.'

'Aye, and my head's telling me the stolen car is just some kids come up from Glasgow, but my ticker's got a mind of its own on the subject. Now, you've got history with him, Mr Oakes. He's already injured you once.'

'Yes.'

'He knows where you live? And he threatened you?'

'Yes.'

Danso sighed and rubbed his temple. He dropped his hand away from his head in Oakesy's direction. 'It's a pity you didn't report it. If you'd reported it at the time we could have—'

'I know, I know. Tell me about it. It's gone through my head about a million times – if I'd told you then, you could've done something about it.'

Danso nodded. He studied Oakesy for a long time without speaking, as if he was trying hard not to say something nasty. My heart was still going fast, thinking about the close call I'd had, but I had a moment's faint satisfaction. I'd begged Oakesy to report it, but would he? *It will come back to haunt you, Oakesy.*

'Look,' Danso said eventually, 'I'm going to be honest. I don't have a lot of experience with endangerment of witnesses, but . . .' He pulled out a drawer in the filing cabinet, rummaged a bit and found a folder. He held it up, clearing his throat and giving us an apologetic look. '. . . Strathclyde Police has got a dedicated witness protection scheme. Sorry to come over like a PR exercise, but we're one of the only forces that has.' He opened it and distributed a set of stapled papers to each of us. I looked at the top page in my lap. 'These are the unit's criteria forms. I think it'd be worth filling them out and sending them down to Headquarters to see what they think.'

Oakesy flipped through the pages, his face tense. Angeline took her copy without meeting Danso's eyes. She read in silence, the paper in her lap, her hands up to her face.

'It's not going to happen overnight. Even if it comes back from Pitt Street with a tick in the box it's still going to take time to process, so in the meantime my lads back in Dumbarton have been calling the locals to find somewhere safe for you. They've come up with a place – on my home patch, as it happens. My feeling is, it'll be better than anything the witness team can offer you.'

'A safe-house?' I said. 'Is that what you mean? A safe-house?'

Danso looked up at me and smiled. His face was suddenly pleasant, not austere any more. 'Hen, if you want to call it that then be my guest. I hope you won't be disappointed. It's a property we use for visiting police officers. It used to be a hidey-hole for victims to give their evidence. Vulnerable victims, if you're with me: racial harassment, child abuse, rape.' He let that sink in. 'Put it this way, it's not the Hilton.'

'All my things are still at the bungalow. He knows the address.'

'We've got someone out there already, having a look round. When we've cleared it we can pick your stuff up.'

'Or this could be a good time for you to go and see your mum, Lex?' Oakesy said, turning to me. 'This is going to be over in a few days and then I'll drive down and get you. We'll take her to that tapas place she likes and—'

'No. That's OK – I'll stay. I'll come to the safe-house.'

'I think you'd be better off—'

'I mean it,' I said, cutting him off. 'I'm not going anywhere. I'm staying with you. And . . .' I leaned over and put my hand on Angeline's arm. She dropped her hands from her face in surprise at the touch and stared down at my fingers, white and clean-looking, the nails quite pink and nice next to her earth-stained skin. '. . . and you must come with us too,' I said. 'You really must. You need to be with someone who can care for you.'

6

Angeline's mother, it turned out, had been dead for two years. Angeline had been on the island all her life and she had no contact with friends or relatives on the mainland. There was nowhere else for her to go. Danso said, 'Look, hen, a doctor can examine you if you want, see if you need any psychiatric care or medical attention.' Here, he glanced vaguely down at her hips, then back at her hair, which looked, I agreed with him, diseased. But for all his offers she just stared ahead of her, occasionally looking warily at him and grunting an answer. It was only after about ten minutes that she spoke. 'Him,' she said stiffly, nodding at Oakesy. 'I want to go with him.'

A plain-clothes officer came with us in the Fiesta to the bungalow. They'd had a team out there, checking the place, and they said it was clear. Oakesy wanted to go back and collect our things, then go on to the safe-house. Danso had to take us out the back of the station because by the time we were ready to go – after Oakesy and Angeline had given their fingerprints – the press had gathered in front, growing in number from two or three incongruously battered cars at ten a.m. to forty or fifty now, all lined up in the seasidey street, their drivers' doors open, the occupants waiting patiently, a BBC television van in their midst. 'Fucking hyenas,' Oakesy muttered, apparently forgetting what *he* does for a living. 'Grubby little shits.'

Oakesy drove – I went shotgun. The 'babysitter', a small shaven-headed man in a poloneck who had shadowy patches on his fingers that looked as if they might have once been LOVE/HATE tattoos, sat in the back with Angeline. He didn't speak much. All the way through the narrow back-streets he hooked his hand on the back of the seat and stared out of the rear window, watching the other cars.

The nights were drawing in, and by the time we got to the bungalow it was dark. There was an unmarked car at the foot of the driveway and a marked one parked at the top, the blue lights flashing silently on and off, lighting up the interior of the woods like an electric storm. Oakesy stopped the Fiesta and he and the babysitter got out and went to speak to the driver, leaving Angeline and me sitting in the car with the engine still running. Our headlights made yellow cones, reflecting off the police car and the men's faces, but beyond this halo of light the woods, the driveway and the bungalow were cloaked in the sort of compressed, borderless darkness that you never see if you live in the city. I stared in the direction of the bungalow, my eyes swimming in and out of focus it was such an impenetrable black, wondering why I hadn't thought to leave a light on before I left. It wasn't like me not to – I *always* leave a light on. So why had I forgotten to do it this morning? I shuffled forward in the seat and put my hand against the windscreen, shading my eyes and trying to see past the lights up to the bungalow, my breath steaming up the glass.

The driver had got out of the marked car and all the men were standing at the side of the driveway now, just at the very edge of the pool of light, all peering at something on the ground. Oakesy said something, and both policemen glanced at his face, then looked thoughtfully back along the driveway for a while, then at the police car. The driver went to it and got down on his haunches to examine the front wheel, pulling a pen out of his pocket and digging into the tread as if he was searching for something. The other two men watched him, exchanging a sentence or two, and after a while the driver stood up and shook his head. Oakesy and the babysitter came back to the car.

'What?' I said as they climbed in, bringing a whiff of night smoke and the chill of an early frost on their clothes. 'What did you see?'

'When?' said Oakesy, turning his eyes to meet mine.

'Just now. Over there.'

'Nothing.' He disengaged the handbrake and swung the wheel round. 'Just tyre marks.'

'Tyre marks? Whose tyre marks?'

'His.' He nodded at the marked car. 'That's all.'

I stared at the car as we drove slowly past it. The policeman was in the driver's seat now, studying something – a map or a notebook, a penlight shining down, making a reddish blur of his profile. 'Are you sure?' I said, trying to keep my voice level. Earlier I was sort of excited. But now it was beginning to be nasty all over again. 'Are you sure they were his? Could he have got them confused?'

'I'm sure.'

He stopped at the bungalow and switched off the engine and we all leaned forward and peered at our reflection in the huge plate-glass window for a moment or two.

'Has anyone been inside?'

'Checked it before we got here and it was all locked. No sign of anyone.'

'Do you think they switched the light off?'

'I don't know. Probably.'

The other policeman started the engine of the car behind us and switched on the headlights, coming up the drive and stopping behind us, the lights dazzling us all.

'Bastard,' said the babysitter, holding his hand up to shield his eyes from the glare bouncing off the rear-view mirror.

'Coming?' Oakesy opened the door.

I shivered and glanced up at the bungalow. 'No, thanks.'

'OK. Won't be long. Ten minutes. Going to take a meter-reading for the landlord too.'

'Don't crease my clothes. Lay them flat.'

He looked at me for a long time, as if he was trying to decide what to say. Then he sighed. 'Don't worry,' he said, climbing wearily out of the car. 'I won't crease your clothes.'

When they'd gone the car began to get colder and colder. The officer in the car behind switched off his lights and the engine and, slowly, silence came down. The darkness seemed to stretch round the car and the bungalow. Behind me Angeline sat chewing a nail and staring blankly out of the window. For ages it was just me and her, and our breathing, which seemed to get louder and louder in the quiet.

'Angeline?' I said, after a while. 'Do you think your father's going to try to find Joe? I mean, do you think he could have been here? In these trees?'

There was a pause. 'Don't know.'

I waited for her to go on, but she just went silent again. So, I thought, no more communicative than when we were at the police station. I dropped my head back against the seat and put my hand in my shirt pocket where I usually kept my mobile, but of course it was still inside the bungalow. It was so odd to have no contact with the outside world. With Mummy or Christophe. I had a picture of Christophe in my head. I tried to keep it there, so I didn't have to think about the woods around us.

Eventually I sat up and swivelled round in the seat. Angeline hadn't moved. She was sitting near the window, holding the handle above the door, using it to lift some of her weight off her backside. A little stray light was shining off her forehead, which looked big and domed because of the weird haircut. In the car behind, the silhouette of the police officer was motionless. 'Angeline,' I said carefully, 'what do you think the detective meant? DS Struthers? About the devil? The devil of Pig Island – do you know what he was talking about?'

At first she didn't answer. She just looked out at the bungalow, at the door where Oakesy had gone, her eyes fixed, the skin round her mouth tightening.

I put my elbow on the back of the seat and lowered my chin on to it: watching her.

'Angeline? I was asking if you knew what he meant. Because I think *I* know. I think I've seen what he was talking about. I've seen it on a video.'

There was a moment's silence. Then she turned very quickly and stared at me. I could see a vein beating rapidly in her temple.

'Didn't you know? There's a video, Angeline, a video of something. Walking along the beach of Cuagach. It's a bit blurry. But there's no doubt what it is. It's a creature on the beach – half man, half beast.' I licked my lips and glanced out of the window at the police car. Suddenly it seemed important that no one was watching me too carefully. 'Or maybe,' I said, in a low, clear voice, leaning over the seat and pinning her gaze meaningfully, 'maybe it was half beast, half *woman* . . .'

7

Lightning Tree Grove (*God*, doesn't the name just say it *all*?) is the nearest thing to hell on earth. It's an abandoned estate between Dumbarton and Renton, one of those wretched fifties and sixties examples of bad urban planning, and it's basically already dead and just waiting for the undertaker's hearse to arrive. Number twenty-nine Humbert Terrace is a three-bedroom semi at the edge of the estate and when I lift up my head from writing this letter and look out of the window, what do I see? Three hundred houses shivering at the edge of miserable, deserted fields, some of the windows grilled up by Environmental Services because they've found asbestos in the attics, all the walls covered with graffiti, tiles flapping around on roofs, and a cul-de-sac where cars come from Dumbarton to fly-tip, so that the streets are littered with Buckfast tonic-wine bottles and dirty nappies. It's going to be concreted over so they can build a leisure centre, but there are still about twenty people clinging on to their pitiful lives here: mostly squatters and asylum-seekers – lots of women in headscarves loping along the streets with long, timid faces. God knows what *they* must think of the place. Talk about out of the frying-pan and into the fire.

Of course, when we first arrived it was dark so we had *no idea* how horrible it was. It just seemed very, very quiet and deserted. The babysitter unlocked the door, struggling a bit with the un-familiar keys, and let us in, clicking on the light. We all filed in behind him, to this horrible, damp little house. Oakesy went straight to the windows and began rattling them, checking the locks, and Angeline, who hadn't said a word on the journey, shuffled sideways and sat down on the nearest sofa with her coat pulled tight round her, glaring at the floor. I stood in the middle of the room, looking around feeling really depressed.

It was much, much nastier there than at the bungalow, I could see that straight away. Everything was rather stiffly positioned, as if it had been doing a mad dance in the dark before we arrived and had to freeze when the babysitter's key rattled in the lock: two peeling fake leather sofas sat at untidy angles, and a dust-covered TV on a black veneer video cabinet was pushed into the corner. All still and noiseless, you could imagine the place was waiting for us to leave, tensed, hating our intrusion. It was open-plan, the ground floor, and beyond the seating area was a kitchen someone had tried to make cheery with bright yellow-papered walls and turquoise tiles, primrose yellow mugs on a rustic mug tree. But it felt like a deserted institution: '*Do NOT use the grill!!!!*' said a sign taped to the oven. '*The grill has been disabled for your safety!!!!!*'

'Aye.' The babysitter wandered over to the corner, where a bundle of wires poked out of the ceiling above an empty bracket. He hooked a finger round the bracket and gave it a small tug. 'Used to be a camera here. And over there. Which means *somewhere* there'll be a . . .' He opened a cupboard in the kitchen, peered inside, then closed it and went into the hallway where he opened a door under the stairs. 'Yes, here. The console room.' Oakesy and I crowded round and saw a little control panel, all the electronics ripped out, the holes pocked with spider-webs. An ageing rota sheet was thumbtacked to the wall. 'Yes.' He put his hands on the doorframe and leaned his head back outside the cupboard, craning his neck to follow the wires that led up the wall and out of sight under the stair carpet. 'They told me this used to be the rape suite.'

'The what?' I said. 'The *what* suite?'

'Rape suite.' He turned to me and the instant he saw my face his expression changed. 'Yeah,' he said hurriedly, ducking back out and closing the door. 'I know. Daft expression. It's just what the lads call it. Some of the lassies who used to come here had been—' He broke off, blushing and scratching his head in embarrassment.

'Raped, you mean? We know. The chief inspector told us.'

'It's somewhere safe, isn't it? Safer than being in the station. You're safe here.'

'Are you sure?'

'Of course. And, anyway you can coorie down here better. It's more cosy here than the station.'

I rubbed my eyes and sighed. Cosy? *Cosy?* It was horrible. Just horrible. If you ask me, all those raped girls and abused children and victims of racial harassment must have left something behind them in the house – some of their distress still clinging to the rag-rolled wallpaper – because when I did the rounds that night shivers went down my spine, just as if something very bad had happened there. Or was going to happen. At the back of the house, behind the kitchen, there was an examination room, still with a couch in the corner, as if we needed reminding what the place was once used for. None of the rooms had been properly cleaned – there was a stained baby's cot in one of the bedrooms with a patch of dried vomit on the wall behind it, dead flies all over the carpets and a used condom in the kitchen sink. *Viva* bureaucracy, I say. I hooked the condom out with the end of a spoon and dropped it into the bottom of a white bin-bag, where it lay, dried out and brown, as transparent as old human skin.

8

When the police had gone we carried our bags upstairs and chose rooms – Oakesy and me took the front room, Angeline the one at the back. Later, when I went in there, I saw she'd unpacked the bag she'd brought with her and put all her clothes on hangers arranged along the plaster picture rail. Dreadful things she had: long denim skirts and ageing blue and white Kappa T-shirts, all washed so many times they'd faded or gone grey.

Downstairs we made a dinner from the things we'd brought from the bungalow, a bit of tomato sauce that I poured over some sausages and called a casserole. I wished I could have put some broccoli or something on the plate because she didn't look as if she'd ever had a vitamin inside her. She ate a little bit, not looking at either of us, her head down so all we could see was that big, chapped forehead. It was only much later when I was at the window, my back to the room, peering out at the broken windows and the police car parked at the top of the street, and Oakesy was in the kitchen washing glasses, that she spoke. 'I think,' she said, out of the blue, 'I want to see the video.'

I dropped the curtain and turned – disconcerted to hear her voice after all this time. In the kitchen Oakesy had stopped what he was doing and was looking at her in surprise, the glass he was holding dripping water on to the floor. She was sitting on the sofa, her shoulders slumped, her head hanging, and although she'd said it quite clearly you could be forgiven for thinking she hadn't spoken at all, because her eyes were on the floor and she was chewing her lip, that paranoid, defensive look to her as if she'd never be able to meet another person's eyes.

'Did you say something?' said Oakesy.

'Yes. I want to see myself.'

He blinked. 'You know about it?'

'I want to see it.' She raised her eyes to him. 'If I'm in it I want to see it.'

There were a few moments' silence while Oakesy took this in. He turned to me.

'She had to know,' I said, opening my hands. 'Someone was going to tell her eventually.'

He didn't say anything. I think he was too tired to argue – or maybe he could see the sense in what I was saying. He went resignedly to the hallway and picked up the laptop from where we'd leaned it against the wall. He brought it back to the kitchen, pulled one of the chairs away from the table and spoke to Angeline. 'Sit down. Here.'

She hesitated, then got up and limped over unsteadily, resting her hands on the table to hold her weight and tentatively lowered her awkward body on to the tiny aluminium chair. Oakesy switched on the laptop and put it in front of her. He got a beer from one of the carrier-bags and switched off the kitchen light so the screen was the only illumination and Angeline's face was bathed a greenish-blue.

I sat next to her at the table, hunched forward, my chin cupped in my hands. I made it seem as if I was concentrating on the computer, but I wasn't. My eyes were rotated sideways to watch her. I got very close to her until I could see every detail of her face – the colourless skin, the big forehead illuminated by the computer, and the small nose, like a young boy's.

'This was taken west of the island.' Oakesy leaned between us and clicked on the RealPlayer icon. The video started. 'Two years ago. Before the fence went up. Here.' He pointed to the end of the tree-line. 'Just here – watch this bit.'

I didn't turn to the screen – I'd seen the video enough times before. This time I watched its mirror image reflected in the glassy curve of Angeline's left eye: the bobbing motion of the boat, the men in their football shirts holding up beers to the camera, and then the long grey expanse of Pig Island's flank rising above the waves, below it the woods coming down to meet the beach. I knew exactly the place on the screen where the blurry figure would appear, with its lurching walk, coming out of the trees for one or two steps on to the sand. I knew the pause, the quick turn back, the disappearance into the trees, the shouts of the men on the boat.

When it was over Oakesy leaned over and stopped the video. I sat motionless, staring at her eye, fascinated by the way it was flickering from side to side as if it were trying to escape. Then a clear disc of liquid appeared, bulging rapidly, trembled for a moment on top of the iris, then broke and fell down her face. She put her palms together, the tips of her fingers on her nose, and started trembling, as if the temperature in the room had plummeted.

'You all right there?' Oakesy said. 'You want to—?'

'I was born like it,' she said. She pushed the chair back with a screech and put her fists to her eyes, pushing at them as if she'd like to punish them for leaking. *'It's not my fault. I was born like it. You can't blame me for it. You can't.'*

Oakesy and I exchanged a look. He leaned forward a little and I think he was going to touch her, but something must have stopped him because his hand got half-way to her shoulder then stopped and went uncertainly back down to the table. 'Listen,' he said, 'nobody thinks it's your fault.'

'They'll think I'm trouble. Like they did on Cuagach. They thought I was a—' She broke off, took deep breaths. Her face was bright red now and there were two lines of snot coming out of her nose. 'They said I was an abomination. That's what they said. They said I—'

229

'You didn't really believe all that,' I said. 'You're disabled, that's all.'

'Lex,' Oakesy said.

'Well, Oakesy, we've all seen it now, the three of us. There's no point in being coy. And anyway . . . I'm sure there's something that can be done for you, Angeline.'

When I said that she went really still. She stopped crying and all the colour drained out of her skin. She lowered her hands and stared at me with an odd, cracked look, her irises slightly off-centre as if her eyes had broken.

'It's true. I see people every day with spinal injuries and deformities and I'm sure there's a very simple operation you can have.'

'To make me normal?'

'I can help you. My friend's a neurosurgeon – the best in the country. Would you like that? Would you want him to look at you?'

'I – I . . .' She pressed her palms to her cheeks, taking a few deep breaths, looking from me to Oakesy and back again. She was trembling so hard her teeth were almost chattering. 'I don't know. I don't *know*.'

Oakesy stood up and switched on the light. He rustled through the carrier-bags we hadn't unpacked yet and pulled out the bottle of Jack Daniel's he took everywhere with him. He went through the cupboards until he found a child's plastic cup with Spiderman on it, filled it half full with JD and pushed it in front of her.

'Oh,' I said. 'Alcohol – I don't think that's a very good—'

She picked up the drink and without even sniffing it, or questioning it, swallowed it in one. I closed my mouth and watched her, amazed. She pushed the beaker back across the table to him. He filled it again and she drank another two beakerfuls down in one. Well, I thought, someone's done *that* before. Oakesy kept filling it up, watching her face as she drank. A slow flush spread long fingers up her neck towards her chin and by the fourth beaker she'd stopped trembling. Instead of knocking this one back, like the town drunk, she took one or two sips and returned it to the table. Then she straightened a little and wiped her nose, gathering her courage, her eyes going nervously from me to Oakesy and back again.

'You all right?'

'Yes.' She paused. 'Have lots of people seen it? The video.'

'Lots,' Oakesy said, not meeting her eyes, the way he does when he's embarrassed. 'Lots of people know about it.'

'The police? The one that said "devil". In the police station he said devil.'

'Yes. The police. They know too, I suppose.'

She took a long breath through her nose, letting this sink in. She looked up at the laptop screen and seemed to be putting it all together in her head. 'And – and that's why you were on Cuagach in the first place? To write about me?'

He looked awful now. Really guilty. 'Uh, yeah,' he admitted. 'That's why I was there.'

'Dad didn't know that.' She shook her head and gave a short laugh, staring at her hands on the table. Her fingers were pale and bitten, with red tips. 'He thought you'd come back to haunt him.'

'To haunt him? What does that mean? Why would he think that?'

She closed her eyes and opened them, as if it were a trick question and she needed to think about her answer. She glanced over at his camera sitting on the kitchen worktop. Then she looked at the laptop, then back at him. 'Um – because you're Joe Finn?'

He stared at her, his mouth open a little.

'You are? Aren't you?'

'Yeah,' he said hurriedly. 'Yeah, I . . . How did you know?'

She looked surprised – as if to say, 'Didn't you know this already?' 'But I've always known about you,' she said. 'I've known about you all my life. I've always known one day I'd meet you.'

9

There comes a time in every person's life when an opportunity presents itself. The test of character is how one chooses to respond to the challenge . . .

Downstairs Oakesy was watching the news and Angeline was in bed, the door to her room closed tight. I was in the front bedroom, sitting on the damp, lumpy bed with Oakesy's laptop open on my knees, tapping at the keys. The curtains were open with the orange streetlight coming through and falling on the computer screen. The police car was still out there – I'd checked, and a man was sitting in the dark watching us. According to Danso, we didn't really need him: he was just there to make us feel secure.

Today I find myself in just such a position [I wrote]. *Today I have been presented with a riddle, an opportunity. And the challenge is – do I attempt to solve the riddle myself, or do I pass it to someone I trust, someone whose professionalism and skill is better suited to deal with it than mine? Someone who will benefit enormously from involvement in this fascinating, high-profile case . . .*

I'd titled the email 'Unusual Spinal Abnormality.

High Media Interest' and sent it under an anony-
mously set-up Yahoo account, because I knew if I
used my real name that that witch of a secretary
would leap on it and rip it out of Christophe's
inbox in a flash. I still blame her for what happened. I mean, who was it who tried to make
something sinister out of my relationship with him?
Turning it round, telling people I was making a
nuisance of myself? That I'd 'bombarded Mr
Radnor with correspondence on the clinic's
intranet'. Which is a wild exaggeration, of course,
because I'd sent little more than a few good-luck
messages when he was off on one of his overseas
trips, once for the tsunami and once to help a little
spina bifida boy in the Ukraine. Oh, and a couple
of copies of my CV. It was probably those CVs that
did it. She *knew* I was a good contender for her job
– she *knew* she'd need to pull up her socks with me
around. And there was that poisonous little
comment I overheard her whisper on the day I'd
announced my resignation: 'Jumped before she was
pushed.' It was probably her who dumped all the
photos I'd framed. I found them – did I tell you? –
in the clinic's waste along with all the shredded
office documents and Pret à Manger sandwich
bags.

   'In my opinion,' I wrote, trying hard to remember the language of the referral letters I'd seen at the

clinic, trying to combine it with the article in the journal, 'this anomaly will almost certainly prove to be associated with spina bifida and therefore of great interest to you. In order to decide what can be done for the patient it will be vital to assess how much "tethering" there is in the spinal cord. To that end I suggest we make an appointment to meet as soon as possible.'

I nibbled my cuticles, wondering if I should say anything about Cuagach, about what had happened out there. But in the end I decided 'high-profile' would be enough to pique his interest. I finished the email: 'I very much look forward to working with you on this, a case that can only cement your reputation as a surgeon of repute and integrity.' I clicked send and sat back, waiting for the out-of-office acknowledgement to pop up on the screen.

My head was tingling. I was going to be back at the clinic by the end of the year.

Oakesy

1

I dreamed about Pig Island. Cuagach Eilean. I dreamed of dark clouds trailing long fingers down to stroke the cliffs, I dreamed of helicopters flying over the gorge in the moonlight, of tree branches, like hands, reaching up to grab them. I saw a police launch bouncing across the waves, blue lights flashing, I heard the words 'improvised explosive device' over and over again, echoing from the mouths of women and men, a chorus of moving lips.

I woke with a jolt on the sofa – dry mouth, stiff neck and a whisky stain on the carpet where the glass had dropped in my sleep. The curtains were drawn, the TV was on, flickering across my face – replaying my dreams: Pig Island in daylight, pictured from above, a shoreline rising up from the sea, familiar grass-covered cliffs, white tents dotted around the village. The words 'improvised explosive device' again. The helicopter banked and dipped above it, then the shot switched to show a small ferry bobbing in the waves close to a shingle beach. An aluminium pontoon connected it to the land. Two soldiers were winching an army truck up it.

I pushed myself upright, blearily, my body creaking, shaking myself out of the dream. On screen Danso appeared seated at a trestle table, a directional mic on the table in front of him, another on his lapel. A blue thistle, the Strathclyde Police logo, was projected on to the backdrop behind him. 'Crinian is one area we're looking at closely and—' He lifted his chin to listen to an inaudible interruption from the press floor. 'That's right – from the car park of the Crinian Hotel . . .'

'Shit, shit, shit.' I pushed myself upright and staggered to the kitchen, hating the way it all had to come back – had to force itself back at me. I hung my face over the sink, waiting, wondering if I was going to puke. I thought of the senior identification manager, a short guy called George who'd spent two hours with me in Oban carefully filling in his yellow 'misper' forms, one for each missing PHM member, thirty in all. Yesterday I'd made a promise to him – a poxy promise when I thought about it: I'd promised I'd go out to Cuagach today to identify bodies. The thought of it made my head ache – like there was something hard and egg-shaped inside it.

I turned on the tap and stuck my face under it, letting the water splash in my hair, my face, my mouth, staying there for more than a minute, getting colder and colder. By the time the mobey rang in my back pocket my face was numb with cold. I straightened, fumbling for it.

'Yeah?' I lifted the hem of my T-shirt to rub my face. 'What?'

'You're alive, then?'

'Finn,' I said. 'Hi.'

'Thanks for calling to tell me you're still breathing.'

'Why wouldn't I be?'

'Why wouldn't you be?' He sighed. 'Switch on the TV, Oakes. That fucker Dove, he's all over the fucking headlines.'

'Yeah,' I said, scanning the miserable little kitchen for a kettle. I needed coffee. 'I know.'

There was a moment's silence. 'You know?'

'Yeah. I was there.'

'You were *there*? What? On the *island*?'

'Yeah. It was me called the police.'

'*Shit*, Oakesy – you *serious*?'

'As a heart-attack.'

'Holy fucking Christ.' There was a long silence while he took this in. I could picture him in his World's End office at his leather-topped desk. When we did the States together he'd been pure Seattle Sound: prison jeans, flannel shirt and Soundgarden T-shirt, one of the first people in the world to wear Converse sneakers. Now he was establishment: he was losing his hair and every day he went to work in a suit he hated. 'What're you going to do with it? The nationals are popping veins trying to figure out what was happening on the island—'

'That's easy.' I tucked the phone under my chin and carried the kettle to the sink, sticking it under the tap. 'He had a harassment order on them – I showed up, he put two and two together, figured they were trying to get him into the court of protection. Which they were, by the way.' I plugged the kettle in, went to the window and opened the curtains. It was a bright, blustery day, a cold sun glinted off the police-car windscreen and the broken windows in the house opposite. I looked to the right, out across the playing-fields, all blistered and brown-looking, a stiff cold wind blasting across it. A good day for viewing dead people. 'But,' I said, 'I can't sell it.'

'Why the fuck not?'

'No. Can't put my head above the parapet.'

'Why not?'

'Did you see them on TV say they've got him? They've found him?'

'No.'

'And who do you think he's got the horn for now? Me. They've got us in emergency accommodation. Strathclyde's answer to an Amish village.'

He was quiet again, thinking. 'Oakesy?' he said cautiously, like something was just coming to him. 'Listen . . . I think this is . . . I don't think it's bad. I think . . . I think it's good. Yes, you know what? It is. In fact it's . . .' He must have jumped up then and almost dropped the phone, because the line got muffled for a moment. When he came back on he was shouting. 'It *is*. In fact it's unreal – fucking unreal.' He took a few breaths and I knew he'd be standing now next to the arched window above the King's Road traffic, moving his arm up and down to calm himself. 'Right – cool thinking, cool thinking, Finn. Oakes, if you don't sell it to the papers, right, if you can keep the story down until it's all over, there's a book in it – OK? As long as you keep it from the papers.'

'You're my agent now?'

'Yes. *Yes!* Listen, Oakesy, *listen* . . . This is what we do. I'm going to have a natter with some

WIN a set of Mo Hayder's bestselling crime novels

We are giving away **50 sets of novels** from highly acclaimed crime-writer,
Mo Hayder – *Birdman*, *The Treatment* and *Tokyo*.

To enter, simply fill in this card and send it in to arrive before **15 May 2007**. The winners
will be the **first 50 entries drawn** at random after that date, and will be notified within 7 days
of the closing date. There is no cash alternative. Open to residents of the UK & Eire only.

I am: Male ☐ **I am:** under 18 ☐ 18-24 ☐ 25-34 ☐ 35-44 ☐
Female ☐ 45-54 ☐ 55-64 ☐ 65+ ☐

My other favourite writers are:

My favourite daily newspapers are:

My favourite Sunday newspapers are:

My favourite magazines are:

My favourite websites are:

My favourite TV programmes are:

What I like about Mo Hayder is:

I buy most of my books at:

What made you buy this book? Please tick any that apply:

Recommended by a friend ☐   Received as a present ☐
Saw an advertisement ☐   Read a review ☐
Already a Mo Hayder fan ☐   Impulse purchase ☐
Other (please specify)

Thank you for taking the time to fill in this card.

Name:
Address:

Postcode:
Email:
☐ Please tick here to receive news on our Crime & Thriller titles.

MO HAYDER READER SURVEY
FREEPOST PAM 2876
TRANSWORLD PUBLISHERS
61-63 UXBRIDGE ROAD
LONDON W5 5BR

interested parties and in the meantime I want a two-page synopsis and the first fifteen K words. It's so fucking easy. I'm telling you, you can write an article, you can write a book . . . You can do that – can't you?'

I opened the window and breathed in the cool air. I didn't blame him – you have to see the reality of death before you understand the chill weariness that comes over you. Thirty-six hours ago, the moment I saw a pig dragging Sovereign's foot into the trees, my work head had switched off, powered down. But I'd had a night's sleep and now Finn was making it twitch again. Old Gorgon Joe-journalist inside me was waking up, giving a sleepy kick, and lifting its ugly, sticky head. I was thinking about the story that was out there in the sunshine. I was remembering why I'd come to Cuagach in the first place.

'Can't you? Tell me you can.'

I dropped the curtain. 'Yeah,' I said. 'I can do it.'

'Dude. We're *made*! We. Are. Made. Get it?'

While he talked I got myself ready. I went to the hallway, got my digital camera from my jacket pocket and put it on to charge. I made coffee in the kitchen, and listened to him plan-making. This was the project we were always meant to do together – we were going to celebrate with a slammer party; we were going to pay off our mortgages.

'So,' he said, 'before the crap hit the fan did you get to the bottom of it?'

'The bottom of what?'

'Y'know – the video and shit. The hoax. The devil of Pig Island. Did you figure out what it was?'

I paused, the coffee cup half-way to my mouth. 'Yeah,' I said. 'I did.'

'Well? Well?'

I didn't speak for a moment. I lowered the cup and turned my eyes to the stairs, thinking of the door to Angeline's room – closed so tight it was like a statement.

'Oakes, come on! I'm waiting. I want to know what you're thinking . . .'

'It was a kid,' I said, tipping the coffee down the sink and turning on the tap. I didn't want it now. I wanted tea. 'Just some local kid got himself out to the island in some outfit he cooked up with his mates. Like I always said.'

2

'Have a look at this for me,' DS Struthers shouted, above the boat engine. He was sitting wedged up against the cabin bulkhead of the chartered pleasure-boat, his legs crossed, one arm resting along the gunwales, the other holding up a Polaroid. 'Might be interesting.' He sat forward and pushed it under my nose. 'Might be very interesting.'

I had to raise my hand against the sun and squint to see that the photo showed an outboard motorboat pulled up at an angle on a beach.

'Recognize it?'

I took the photo from him, ducked into the cabin out of the sun, studied it and knew immediately: it was the orange-striped dory, a bit battered, resting on the beach, its bow line trailing in the shingle. I stepped back on to the deck and handed him the Polaroid. 'Where d'you find it?'

'Ardnoe Point. An off-duty woolly pulley out walking her pooch. Naughty lass – spends her days off fiddling with the police scanner if you ask me. Some people just can't leave their job behind, can they? What I think is, she's heard about it last night on the scanner and then, six o'clock this morning, she's walking her dog and finds she's staring at it in the flesh. So what's she going to do? She's got to phone it in.'

'And Ardnoe Point is . . . ?' I turned and looked back at the mainland.

'That way.' He waved a hand to the south. 'It's making our missing car look a little nicer because it's not far from Crinian where the car disappeared on Saturday. A long way. It's where you'd drift to with the tide they had that night, so maybe he was heading there. Or maybe he just didn't know how to drive the thing.'

'Near Crinian . . .' I murmured, gazing at the coastline. In the morning sun it looked fresh and cold, the granite fingers on the shore eerie and architectural. The trees billowed like they'd been melted down and poured across the landscape. What are you doing out there, Dove baby? I thought, staring south at the firth glittering in the distance. Where are you heading? What's in Ardnoe Point, then? I like that you went south and not north towards the bungalow . . .

'I think you can relax,' shouted Struthers, behind me. 'You're not going to see Pastor Malachi Dove again.'

I turned. He had put the Polaroid away and was leaning against the bulkhead, his head back, his eyes scrunched up, scanning the mainland.

'I'm not going to see him again?'

'No. Too close to the edge now, isn't he? He'll be a suicide.' He nodded, wiping salt spray from his face. 'Aye – in my professional experience he's going to be a suicide. Some hill-walkers'll find him, all maggoty and shit. Or he'll be dangling off some bridge, or bumping around in a weir with his face all smashed to fuck. Yes. That'll be the next time we see Malachi Dove.'

'In your professional experience?'

He tapped the side of his nose and smiled. 'Got a copper's nose. Always have had, since I was a bairn. I'm telling you he'll be a goner by now.'

I gave him a cold smile. As an undergraduate, when I was getting the chicken-liver article finished, I had a fantasy, or a fear, that I knew Malachi Dove as well as I knew my own bones. It came back to me now that I was connected to him in a way that none of the others were – maybe even Angeline – and I knew Struthers could have no idea what was really in Dove's head. He was right: Dove was thinking about how to end it all. But it wasn't going to be that easy. *I will, Joe Finn, in the final hour, run rings around you . . .* When he'd said he'd fuck with my peace of mind he didn't mean what he'd done in the chapel.

'Aye. Lost the plot, hasn't he? If you ask me—' He broke off and licked his lips. 'If you ask me, that lass is an orphan by now. As if she hasn't got enough problems.'

I looked thoughtfully at Angeline. She was sitting in the stern, arms crossed, chin lowered, staring into the middle distance and pulling sullenly at her lower lip. The bits of skin you could see through her patchy hair were red and chapped.

'Hey,' Struthers whispered, leaning close to me so I could smell his breath. He was squinting at her, taking in the faded football shirt you could just see peeping out from under the coat, the worn-out trainers. 'Something I wanted to ask you.'

I didn't meet his eyes. I knew what was coming.

'She told the boss she had polio. That's what she told him.' He licked his lips again. 'But it's not polio, is it? It's something else.'

I closed my eyes slowly, then opened them.

'Is it? It's not as simple as polio and I think—'

'Do you know,' I murmured, 'what would happen if the press knew about her?'

I felt him smile. 'Oh, yes,' he whispered. 'Which is why you're one lucky bastard, Joe Oakes. We can't talk to them about you because you're "vulnerable", according to the procurator fisk, which gives you the exclusive as soon as you want to crawl out from under your stone. I've got about a hundred good friends in the press up here who'd give up their bairns for the chance you've got. Not that I'll hold it against you.' He laughed and gave me a slap on the arm. 'Right,' he said, looking over his shoulder. 'The Semper Vigilo. We're nearly at the press cordon.' He stood and held his arm out to Angeline, beckoning her. 'Time to get you both in the cabin. Come on, hen.'

I stood. Ahead, bobbing in the waves, thirty or so chartered boats hovered in an untidy pack, surreptitiously nosing their way forward. Facing

them, throwing up glittering spumes, bucking and
rotating like a bull in the ring, a fluorescent yellow-
painted police launch held them at bay.

'I mean *now*,' said Struthers. 'If you don't want
them to see you, do it now.'

So we all crowded into the fume-filled cabin with
the skipper and stared in awe at Cuagach growing
bigger and bigger ahead of us, the army helicopter
banking above it, searching the cliffs and forests for
the one thing we all knew they weren't going to
find: survivors.

3

The police operation was massive. The army had
been called to make the island safe, and the nearer
we got, the more you could see how much they
were throwing into this. There were about eight
launches moored off the shore and everything on
Pig Island seemed covered in police tape and
tarpaulins: from the moment we got to the jetty
and gave our names to the officer on guard there, it
was like walking on to a movie set.

It had totally fucking changed – beyond recog-
nition. As we logged in at the rendezvous point and
came up the coast path the first thing we saw on the

village green, a hundred yards or so behind the
Celtic cross, was the force's HM40 helicopter,
crouched and silent, its rotor blades dipping gently
in the wind. The corpse of a giant insect. The grass
to the north – where the ferry had offloaded the
vehicles – was churned up and hatched with vehicle
tracks, and arranged in a circle round the green,
like a wagon train round a fire, were two army
trucks, four small inflated shelters and three white
and blue police Land Rovers, each with a photocopied sign taped to the side. 'Communications,'
said one. 'Casualty Clearing Station', another. The
signs flapped as we walked past. It was like being
at some weird village fête.

We headed to the top of the green in the direction
of a van marked 'Dockards and Vinty, Land
Surveyors. 3D Laser Technology'. Rubberized
power cables snaked out of it, linking it to a
generator, and behind it, parked so it blocked the
windows of the Garricks' cottage, stood a mobile
officer trailer, the Strathclyde logo printed on the
door.

'Control point,' said Struthers, mounting the
steps. 'Hey, boss,' he said, to the interior. 'I'm
back.'

The trailer creaked a bit, Danso maybe turning
to face him. 'Christ, Callum, have a word with
George, will you? Chief's given him a title, keep

him sweet – senior identification manager. Now he thinks he runs the show – says he needs a casualty bureau with six phone lines, ten staff and five more men out here at locus. That's *fifteen* men! Meanwhile *I*'ve got a procedures adviser on the phone to me every two minutes with a new bit of policy he's remembered, an incident room the size of my hand and a HOLMES team busy screwing every penny of overtime they can out of me.' He sighed audibly. 'You find me dead somewhere, Callum, look for the puncture marks on my neck because this Major Incident protocol is sucking the blood out of me.'

'I've got the witnesses.'

Danso stood up. He came to the back of the trailer and peered out at us. 'I'm sorry.' He jumped off the steps and shook our hands. He was wearing a fleece in place of his suit jacket and his skin was grey – like he hadn't slept. 'I'm sorry – I thought you were coming after lunch.' He peered at me. 'Well?' he said. 'Did you sleep OK?'

'It's warm. The house.'

He smiled. 'Good. And have you had your breakfast?'

I nodded, letting a kind of half-laugh come out of my nose. 'Now you're going ask me am I ready for this.'

'Aye. And what's the answer?'

'No. Of course it's no. I'll do it, but I'm never going to be ready.'

4

Turns out these Strathclyde lads aren't the genius bizzies they fancy themselves. They knew I was a journalist, Struthers had given me chapter and verse about it, but did anybody search me that morning on Cuagach? Did anybody find the mini digital camera stashed in my jacket? Did they fuck.

At ten thirty Angeline went away with Danso and a small bald man – 'The Crime Scene Manager', Struthers told me. She was going to show them where she'd been hiding when she saw her father pushing the explosives into the chapel window, which route he'd taken to arrive there, so they could sketch it out and get a laser 3D capture for Forensics. Someone brought wellington boots and gloves for me, and Struthers and me headed off to the north, following photocopied sheets that flapped on tree-trunks: *Body Holding Area This Way* —>

It was a leafy path I'd never been along before, quiet and cold. To its right, the land sloped down to the rocks and from time to time a wind came up off the sea and slapped us with its salty spray. On our left was the dark forest, where police tape fluttered among the tree-trunks. Beyond the tape I could see white lines laid out on the ground like a grid, each line numbered with a red marker.

'You know what I was thinking?' Struthers said. 'I was just thinking, this place must be covered with your prints, eh?'

There was something needling in his tone. I didn't look at him. 'Yeah, I suppose.'

'How about in the chapel?'

'I was in there once,' I said, 'for about five minutes. I told you yesterday. Remember? You got elimination prints from me at the station.'

'So, nothing else, then? The CSM's not going to find anything else, hairs or other – uh – *traces*?' He gave me an unhealthy smile, showing dull yellow teeth. 'I mean, old man, you were on the island for a few days, and things happen between people. Know what I mean?'

I stopped. He'd gone on a few steps before he realized I wasn't with him. He came to a halt and looked at me. The end of his nose and the tips of his ears were a bit red from the exercise. Behind him, out to sea, the horizon was a dark, unwavering blue.

'No,' I said coldly. 'I don't know what you mean.'

'Just trying to work out what sort of relationship you had with these people. Whether it was good or not.'

'It was good. But not so good that I fucked any of them, if that's what you're asking.'

Struthers laughed and turned, continuing down the path, his hands in the air. 'OK, OK. Just trying to get a feel for what the atmosphere was like out here. Sue me. There's a CAP 1 form back at the station.'

I didn't move. I let him go on ahead, watching his back, fleshy and broad-shouldered. We were destined not to get along, Callum Struthers and me. Star-crossed sparrers. He was everything I'd expected from a Strathclyde bizzy: overdressed, opinionated, vain. He tried to sound more intelligent than he was (why did he think it was smarter to say 'individual' and not 'person'?) and he smelt like he was on one of those diets that give you kidney damage. Struthers, for his part, had taken one look at me with my scabbing knees and my Scouse accent and I know the first thing that went through his head was *Is there any way I can make this guy's life really difficult?*

Now he disappeared round the bend ahead, leaving me alone on the path. And there, I saw, he'd given me a little gift, although he didn't know it. I counted off a few beats of time, then turned and peered into the trees. The chapel was somewhere in there, only a few hundred yards up, if I'd got my bearings right. 'Video,' someone was shouting from deep in the trees. 'Video, please. Over here – eighty-three/twenty. *Can you hear me, camera team? Need video at eighty-three/twenty.*'

I pulled out my camera, crouched under the police tape, steadied my hands on a branch – couldn't use flash – and rattled off ten photos. I shielded my eyes and checked the display. The zoom wasn't great, but you could just make out two ghostly figures in pale blue suits half hidden by the dark tree-trunks. The search-and-recovery team. Not outstanding as photos go, but not bad.

'Hey?' Struthers called from ahead. His voice was faint. 'You with me?'

I ducked out of the forest, pocketing the camera, back on to the path. It turned left, away from the cliff, and led upwards into the forest. There, about a hundred yards ahead, he was standing, watching me.

'This is it,' he said, as I joined him. 'I think this is it.'

We turned and looked down to where the land dipped, forming a natural hollow, cold and leaf-shaded, shielded on the coastal side by screens. One or two sharp blades of sun pointed like lasers through the tree canopy. It was weirdly silent, the only sound the low humming of the generator that powered two refrigeration trucks. We were looking at their roofs, the ventilators opened to the fresh air. Next to them was a packing crate the size of a small car. It had been opened so you could see the contents: grey fibreglass coffins, opaque like cocoons, piled one on top of another. A photographer, in a green fluorescent tabard, helmet and boots, stood in front of the crate, peering down at the display on his camera, scrolling through shots like I'd just been doing.

Struthers ran his hand across the back of his head. He didn't speak. You could tell from his face he didn't want to be here.

'Come on, then.'

We started down the path. We were half-way into the clearing when the doors of the nearest truck opened. George, the guy I'd spent the afternoon with at Oban, jumped out. He was wearing full body-suit and galoshes, and was followed by another man dressed the same. They both said something to the photographer, who lowered the camera and looked up into the woods in the opposite direction from me and Struthers. They all stood for a while, looking expectantly in the same direction towards the chapel. After a few moments there was a rustle of leaves and two members of the search-and-recovery team came quickly out of the trees, almost at a jog. Between them they carried something heavy wrapped in thick plastic, a pink form taped to the top of it. They lowered the package to the ground, said something to George, then swivelled and headed back into the woods at the same half-jog. The three men gathered round the package.

'This is where I start to earn my money,' Struthers muttered at my side, a bit sick-sounding. 'This is the bit no one wants to do. C'mon.' We came to the bottom of the path, out into the clearing, jumping down the last two feet. 'George,' he said, raising a hand in greeting.

'Yeah.' He didn't look up. 'With you in a minute, gentlemen. Just finishing with the doctor here.'

We stood for a few moments, a bit awkward, looking for somewhere to put ourselves while the photographer circled the package, clicking off photo after photo. The doctor crouched and untaped the pink form, handing it to George. He carefully unfolded the layers of plastic. Inside was a thick lump of flesh wrapped in cloth. I stopped breathing, thinking, *No way – this is a joke. Someone's got a bit of pig meat and put it in a T-shirt. Who are they trying to shake?* Next to me Struthers opened his mouth and started breathing through it. He tried to do it subtly, but I could hear it anyway.

George clipped the form to his board and began to tick off boxes. 'Right – what've we got? Number 147, grid ref 52–10.' He broke off, frowning at what he was reading. 'Oh, what's the sodding point?' he said, dropping the clipboard to his side in frustration. 'No one listens to a thing I tell them.'

The doctor looked up. 'What?'

'Look at this. Section twenty-two. Box ticked? Number one.'

'Yeah?'

'*Box number one*,' he repeated, nodding significantly at the parcel. 'How many times have I got to tell them? Box *two*. If it's just a body part, they tick box *two*. *Incomplete*.' He shook his head and corrected the mistake, then went bad-temperedly down the list, ticking off boxes as he went. 'So what've we got – the usual? Human. Life extinct—'

'Yes—'

'– at, let's see, eleven oh-four a.m. And what? Caucasian?'

'Yup. Male.'

'And you're saying it's . . . ?'

'Torso.' The doctor turned the meat over. He looked at the underside for a few moments then lowered it. There was a neat circle of bone under the skin – I knew what it was: it was a severed spinal column. I thought about Sovereign and her

256

pink jelly sandals and her dozy way of speaking. I imagined George piecing her brittle leg bones together on a trestle table. I thought about the old missionary and his broken toe pointing at the stars. I turned and sat quickly on a nearby tree-trunk, shaking. I had to spit, had to use my fingers to loop the taste out of my mouth and shake it off them, splattering it on to the ground. 'Malachi, you fucker,' I muttered. 'You arse.'

'Yeah, it's torso,' said the doctor. 'Half the thoracic, all of the lumbar section.'

'So what's that? Everything missing except oh-six and oh-seven?'

'That'll do.' The doctor peeled away the piece of torn T-shirt and held it up for George to inspect.

'A T-shirt.' He ran his pen down the list, tutting. 'When did Interpol write this? They've got a code for a corset, for Christ's sake, even one for a girdle. But is there a code for a T-shirt? They need a course in twenty-first-century living.' He wrote in large angry letters. 'T-SHIRT.'

'What colour would you call it?' The doctor said. 'Brown? Purple? Milly says I get my browns and purples mixed up.'

George peered over his glasses at it. 'Wine-coloured,' he said, after a while.

'Wine-coloured,' the doctor agreed, dropping the cloth into a bag. 'Exactly.'

George completed his form, the doctor initialled it, then the two men refolded the parcel, taped the form back on top and, facing each other, each taking one end of the plastic, shuffled sideways and lifted it laboriously into the lorry. Struthers didn't say anything. After a while he came and sat down stiffly next to me, not looking at me or speaking. Every other breath he made a sound in his throat, like he was trying to dislodge phlegm.

'Well,' he said eventually, 'that'll be a DNA jobby. More money. Boss'll be ecstatic.' A muscle in his face twitched. Just under his right eye, like a nerve was trapped in there. 'DNA,' he repeated carefully, like I might not have heard of it, coming from Liverpool and everything. '*D–N–A.*'

5

'Colour-coding. It's the only way to go. I've seen a file organizer with colour-coded compartments. The way I'm thinking is I can put my ante-mortem forms in the yellow tray, my PM forms in the pink tray. Looks like there aren't going to be any evacuee forms so I'd keep the blue compartment for when I've matched my PMs and mispers.'

Me and George were inside the refrigeration

truck. The doors were open behind us but the light was dim, so the photographer had given me a hand-held halogen lamp for the viewing. I waited in silence, the lamp dangling in one hand, the other pinching my nose while George moved around in the semi-darkness at the far end of the truck, opening and rearranging two fibreglass coffins, dragging them into the middle of the floor.

'What you said yesterday about them having no medicals, no dentals? Well, you were right. We're looking but so far no biopsies, no X-rays, not even a print on file. It'll be ninety per cent genetic IDing, because if we get a visual on ten per cent we'll be lucky bastards indeed. I'm going to be up to my pointy little ears in paperwork.'

I switched on the lamp and ran it over two piles of plastic-wrapped shapes pushed up against the right side of the truck, all milky and opaque from the cold. Some of the bodies had burned in the fire after the explosion, and in places I could see blackened shapes pressing against the plastic. A pink notice hung above the furthest pile: 'Incomplete 1–100'. I moved the light across the walls, the beam bouncing off the textured aluminium panelling. The sign above the second pile read: 'Incomplete 101–200'. I switched off the lamp, my heart thudding loudly.

'I've only got two for you today.' George

straightened and looked at me. The shadows on his face were etched and solid. In the gloom I could see he'd opened both coffins and folded the black rubber body-bag away to reveal the faces. 'The only two who made it out of the chapel after the blast. Must've been in the corners behind the others – that's how you get through an explosion. Someone else takes the force for you. Course, doesn't mean you survive in the long run.' He picked up his clipboard from the floor and showed me two yellow sheets. 'I got these out earlier. Our chat yesterday? Remember? I think I know who our two are. Still, I'd like you to give me the thumbs-up.'

I knew who he meant. The missionary and Blake Frandenburg. There wouldn't be anything of Sovereign left to identify. I switched on the light and approached, holding it down at an angle. In the first coffin lay the missionary, his face intact, eyes sunken. I looked at him in silence.

'Okonole?'

I nodded. 'Okonole.'

George wrote a neat three in a box at the top left-hand of the yellow form and tucked it with some satisfaction behind the other. We moved to the second coffin where Blake Frandenburg lay, his eyes like holes, his leathery face emaciated, like death had taken half his body weight. One of his hands poked stiffly out of the body-bag as if he was reaching for something – a light, or the sky maybe. I stared at that hand, thinking of him sitting in the cottage holding a fire poker, well ready to take me on at twice his size.

'You OK there?' asked George. 'Want some time on your own?'

I turned stiffly to him. 'Sorry?'

'Do you want to be alone?'

'Uh . . .' I stared at him. It took a moment or two but then the question set off a cog somewhere in my head. 'Uh, yeah,' I said. 'Yeah. Sure. Just a few minutes.'

He left the truck, going noisily down the aluminium steps. 'Hey, Callum,' I heard him say, 'when you get back to Oban get the station officer to look in the stationery catalogue, will you? Tell her page three hundred, there's a file organizer with colour-coded . . .'

I waited until the voices had moved round to the side of the truck. Working quickly, I fumbled out my camera. With the halogen light in my left hand, held up at arm's length and angled down to mini-mize the shadows, I squeezed off five photos of Blake's corpse. After each one I stopped, listening for the voices outside, wondering if the camera's mechanism could be heard out there. Then I photographed Okonole, and swung round to do the two piles of body parts. I shoved my camera into my pocket and got to the doors as George was coming back up the steps.

'How you getting on there? You feeling OK? We've got some bottled water here from the catering truck. If you want.'

'It's Frandenburg,' I said. 'Is that what you thought?'

He smiled and held up the yellow form on his clipboard. It read in capitals BLAKE FRANDENBURG. He took out his pen with a flourish and wrote a firm number '1' in the box. He put the pen away and nodded at me.

'See? That makes me happy. That's two for my green compartment.'

6

There was a catering truck on the island, if you can believe that, and at twelve thirty everything stopped for lunch. Like I said, you'd think we were on a film set. I queued for one of the plastic shrink-wrapped trays and carried it over to where Angeline sat with her back to the others, just at the edge of the lawn where the land sloped away and you could see the open sea above the police Land Rovers.

She was in a green director's chair, slouched on to her left side, her right leg crossed far over the other. Her dinner wasn't eaten: the tray rested on her thigh and she was sawing aimlessly at it with a serrated plastic knife. When my shadow fell on her she stopped sawing and went very still. I pulled a chair over to her, and after a moment or two she put down the knife and leaned forward, her body covering the tray, one hand crossing her chest and tucked into her armpit. The other hand she dropped to the ground and began to make idle sketches in the sand.

'What's up?' I said, sitting down. 'Not hungry?'

She shook her head and went on drawing in the sand. There were hot, sullen patches on her cheeks.

I unwrapped my tray and read from the sandwich label: 'Brie and grape on French bread. I mean, the bollocks these caterers come up with.' I dropped the sandwich into the tray and sat back, folding my arms. She still wasn't looking at me. 'So? They put you through your paces, then?'

She stopped drawing but she didn't look at me. She lifted her hand, tucked it under the other armpit and sank back down on to her thigh, crumpling the dinner tray.

'Well?'

'I told you – didn't I tell you?'

'Tell me what?'

'I said no one would trust me. They know who I am and they think I'm a liar.'

'Them?' I nodded over my shoulder in the direction of the police. 'Why? What did they say?'

'They definitely saw the video. It's like they think I'm . . .' She sighed and pulled moodily on her bottom lip. 'It's like they won't believe anything I say.'

'Who? Danso? Struthers?'

'Both. I showed them where I was hiding when I saw him – you know, what he did – and now they're saying because of where I was standing in that path over there, I couldn't've seen it was actually him who did it.' She sat up a bit and chewed the side of her thumbnail with her small teeth. 'Even though of course I knew it was him, because I'd followed him across the gorge and I could hear him banging in the nails, now they're saying I've got to get my story straight and the young one said—'

'Struthers?'

'He's going on about how I'm not a credible witness and how he's going to have to put in a supplementary statement or something.' She wiped her nose with the back of her hand. 'And I know it's because they've seen me on the video.'

I gave a short laugh. 'No, Angeline. They believe you.'

She looked up at me.

'They believe you. Really. They're just being cops. They're not thinking about how to catch your dad, they're a year ahead of us – in court already, thinking how your evidence is sounding.'

She studied me and for a while it was like she was going to say something. Then she changed her mind. She made a small, discontented grunt and went back to pushing her fingernail into the sand. Silence fell. A breeze chased through the grass and made the inflatable shelters behind us flap like sails. I unwrapped the Brie sandwich and ate. The lines in the sand at her feet got bigger and bigger, more and more complicated. I finished the sandwich, drank some coffee and ate a fruit salad out of a plastic cup with watermelon pips floating in the juice at the bottom. Then I screwed up the napkin and refitted the lid on the tray.

'Angeline?'

'What?'

'No one knew Malachi had a child. Did you know that? He let them think you were stillborn.'

She made a contemptuous snort. 'It would have been better if I was.'

'No,' I said, and thinking about it now, I'm amazed at how gentle my voice came out. 'It wouldn't be better. It really wouldn't.'

She was still for a moment. Then she raised her

eyes. There was a guarded, puzzled expression on her face, like she was trying to decide if I was joking. Her eyes had got very red round the inside rims. For a long time the only sound was the distant roar of the helicopter, hovering somewhere out of sight, searching the forests. When she spoke it was a whisper: 'Joe?'

'What?'

'No one would be interested, would they, if I told them what he did to me? No one would listen?'

I hesitated. I saw Finn, in his office, getting excited: *There's a book in this.*

'They'd listen,' I said, 'if you told it the right way.'

'The right way? What is the right way?'

'I don't know.' I glanced casually at the tray, then up at the sky. Folded my arms. 'But I suppose you could tell it to me. I suppose that's always an option for you.'

Danso and Struthers wanted Angeline to help them go through Dove's paperwork. I told Struthers he needed me to come too, to help with her, and he went for it without a thought. Somewhere over the last twenty-four hours I'd been appointed her minder. They put us into a police launch and took us to the south of the island.

It was fresh and chilly and the sky was a deep

blue, a string of baby-dragon-breath clouds chugging across the horizon in the west – perfect light for photos, I thought, squinting up. The launch bounced across the waves, its engine echoing back to us from the granite cliff faces of Pig Island's eastern shoreline, making flocks of black-back gulls wheel and croak out of the clifftops. The south of the island looked more parched than I remembered, a scorched red-brown after the green of the village, like a drought had come across and touched only this side. Even with the armed officers at the jetty talking on their radios a weird silence hung over the place.

A forensics team had been out there yesterday and they'd worked fast, releasing the site this morning at eleven. They'd collected hairbrushes, toothbrushes and dirty underwear, anything that would help them build up Dove's DNA profile. While they were at it, they'd uncovered a collection of aged quarrying dynamite and drums of fertilizer in an outbuilding half a mile from the cottage. Dove's explosives arsenal. The army disposal team had been there since dawn, sealing off ten acres on the eastern flank. As we clambered off the boat we got glimpses of them in the distance, wearing flak jackets, leading dogs around on short leashes.

Angeline hadn't said a word since our conversation. She walked around with her arms wrapped across her chest, moodily chewing the inside of her mouth, not looking at anyone. From time to time I'd get the idea when my back was to her she'd looked up and was watching me, and I'd turn, just in time to see her attention scuttle away like nothing had happened. But mostly she was still upset and embarrassed by what Struthers had said. When he stopped next to one of the galvanized-steel fence posts, and said, 'So, pet, who put this up for Dad?' she shrugged. She put her hands into her pockets and dropped her chin. Dug her toe into the soil and glanced self-consciously over her shoulder, like a teenager checking she wasn't being watched by her mates.

'Angeline?'

'It was him,' she muttered. 'Did it himself. Wouldn't've let anyone else come out here.'

'Good with his hands, was he? Knew his explosives – knew how to put a hole in granite?'

She shrugged again and stared off into the distance, like she wasn't connected with the words coming out of her mouth. 'Yeah. S'pose.'

It was kind of embarrassing the way she kept up with these monosyllabic answers – Yes. No. Maybe – not offering any more information than she was asked. She led us round grudgingly, showing us the handbarrow Dove used to bring the supplies dropped by the shopkeeper in Bellanoch up from the jetty, taking us to where he kept his outboard motor under a tarp near the jetty, tightly chained and padlocked.

Up at the cottage the generator had run out of oil, and when we came inside there were no lights. We all crowded into the small room at the front where Dove kept his paperwork, looking around ourselves at the torn curtains, the filthy windows, the two walls filled from floor to ceiling with battered notebooks and photos.

'He's taken the photos.' We all turned to look at Angeline then, because it was the first time she'd spoken without being asked. She was staring at two stained gaps on the peeling wallpaper. 'He's taken photos from there. And he's taken . . . *notebooks*. One. No—' She turned round, her finger out, tracing the air. 'No, two. He's taken two notebooks.'

'Which photos?' asked Danso, standing next to her and looking at the gaps really hard, like he'd pick up some supernatural vibes if he did. 'What did they show?'

'Him with Mother. And one of him praying.'

'Praying?'

'He looks dead,' I said. 'Lying on his back, hands over his chest. It was his habit.'

Struthers rolled his eyes. He'd spent a lot of his time in uniform in Glasgow dealing with crazies.

'What about the notebooks?' he said. 'Which ones are missing?'

Angeline lowered her eyes and pulled the coat round her like it was suddenly cold. 'The PHM philosophy on death,' she murmured. Behind her, Struthers and Danso exchanged a glance. 'It was always there – on that shelf. And another one – the PHM philosophy on suicide.'

'I told you so,' Struthers mouthed under his breath, giving me and Danso a slow, reptilian smile. He was over the fucking moon. He thought he was the only person in the world who'd predicted Dove's suicide. 'Didn't I tell you so?'

'If only,' I said. 'If only it was that easy.'

7

While Struthers, Danso and Angeline pulled note-books from the shelves, opening up the PHM's records, finding file after file of furious hermeneutical letters to the C of E synod, reams of Bible verses, written and rewritten in Dove's looping hand, I slipped outside, muttering something about needing a smoke. No one stopped me. I just walked outside, free as a bird, into the cold, bright day.

I went quickly, retracing our steps, getting photos of the outside of the cottage, the empty Scotch bottles piled in a mountain behind one of the sheds, the generator and the piles of rubbish. I went to the army cordon and got some long-lens shots of the explosives team working in the distance, then turned north, giving the cottage a wide berth and moving through the silent woods until I came to the mine. Today it was quiet, no wind reached the clearing, and an empty silence hung over the rusting old machinery.

I turned to face the south. In the distance, a long way past the treetops of Cuagach, I could just see the headland of Crinian, the sky above it stained with dark clouds. I pulled out the camera, switched it on and focused on that distant coast. None of them, not Danso, not Struthers, had the instinct I had for Dove. He wasn't going to commit suicide. Not until he'd finished with me. It was like I could feel him in my brain, creeping around making his plans.

Ardnoe Point? Crinian? What are you planning, Malachi? Why Crinian?

I clicked off some photos of the coast, then fitted a new lens and ambled around doing some shots of the mine: rusty wheelbases of long-forgotten vehicles, ageing barbed wire strung over adits. Every now and then I'd stop and look thoughtfully out at the coast. A swarm of flies hovered round the hole where the pig was wedged. When I flicked them away I saw maggots like moving rice grains in the pig's eyes and something brown and frothy coming from its snout. I took ten shots.

Why Crinian?

He hadn't drifted there because he couldn't start the boat engine, whatever Struthers thought. He had meant to go there. I cranked open the aperture for the light and moved round the pig, firing off shot after shot, my thoughts rolling out like ticks on a metronome: *What business have you got down there, Malachi? Why south? I was north. Does that mean you're not going to come after me direct? And if you're not going to do that, then what are you going to do? How else can you get to me? Or do you think I've gone back to London?*

A twig snapped behind me. I spun round, raising the camera, ready to swing out. It was Angeline, her face red, her breathing rapid, staring past me at the pig in the shaft. She'd got right up behind me without me hearing. She made a grab for my sleeve.

'Hey.' She caught me off-balance and I'd hopped along a few feet before I got my footing. 'Let go. Come on – let go.' I scrabbled at her fingers, trying to unpeel them. She resisted, then let out a gasp and snapped her arm away like it was burnt.

'Christ.' I closed my hand over the camera,

steadying it against my chest. My heart was racing. 'Don't do that again.'

She stood for a moment, half turned away, trembling, her hands crabbed up in front of her chest.

'What's up?'

'The pig.'

I wiped my forehead and looked over at the dead animal. 'What about it?'

A long shiver went up her body, something visible that travelled from her stomach to her shoulders, then kind of shook itself off into the air. She closed her eyes and put her hands over her mouth.

'It's dead,' I said. 'It won't hurt you.'

'*It looks like it's watching me.*' Her voice was quick and whispered, like she thought the pig might hear her. '*I know you'll think that sounds stupid but I mean it. It's watching me.*'

'Then walk away.'

'*It'll watch me.*'

I sighed, and clicked the lens cap in place. 'What do you want me to do?'

She shook her head, her hand over her mouth, her throat muscles working. '*I don't know. Just stop it watching me.*'

Pigs. Turns out to be pigs that had marked Angeline's life for the last six years. By the end of the day I'd understand why she thought they were watching her, why she wanted me to cover this one. I wasn't going to bury the fucking thing, not in the state it was in, so I hauled a rusting fertilizer drum out of the pile and wedged it across the hole to cover its face, kicking and punching the drum to seal the hole. It stank, the pig, worse than I remembered from two days ago, and while I was doing it I had to keep forcing saliva into my mouth – rubbing my tongue against the hard palate.

Angeline watched from the trees about a hundred yards away. She lowered herself awkwardly to a sitting position, using a branch to hold her weight, and was sitting there, half in the shadows, staring. When I'd finished I went and sat next to her. Her knees were pulled up, her dusty trainers tucked in tightly. The folds of the coat spread out behind her, concealing the deformity. She was still shaking.

'So,' I said, 'not a pig person, then?'

She closed her eyes and pressed her fingers into them, like she was trying to get rid of a picture in her head. There were beads of sweat on her forehead.

'Going to tell me about it?'

She shook her head, drawing in a long breath. I brushed the rust off my hands, rested my elbows on my knees, and looked up at the sky, watching the clouds. My head was racing, thinking, how the

fuck was I going to get her to talk? I needed her –
she was all I had. The instinct that has in the past,
I admit, allowed me to put my arm round the
mother of a hit-and-run victim and say, 'I feel your
pain. If you give me that photo of your lovely little
boy, the one on the mantelpiece, the reader will feel
it too,' – my journalistic instinct – was failing me.

'Look,' I started, but when I turned to her she
was looking at me. Her whole head was twisted on
her long neck. Her eyes were bloodshot, the whites
round the black irises spidered with red.

'He tried to pull me apart,' she said, 'the moment
I was born.'

I stared at her, my head buzzing, kind of knocked
off-centre by this. 'What? What did you say?'

'He thought he could pull it off me. My—' She
shivered and looked out at the clouds, at the way
they were gathering in a long train above the headland. 'My thing – my *tail*. He thought I would come
apart if he pulled hard enough.'

8

There was a narrow, tree-crowded path that went
from the cottage due west to the cliff edge. Angeline
led me down it, going fast, determinedly, her arms

swinging, sometimes steadying herself against the branches and tree-trunks as she went. Soaking bracken and rhododendron roots tugged at my calves and I had to struggle to keep up. Somehow, without me knowing exactly how or when, I'd come through the eye of the needle. Suddenly she wanted someone to talk to: she wanted me to know everything about the shitty life she'd lived out here on Pig Island. Maybe it was the way I'd hidden that pig. Stopped it staring.

She came to a halt and put out her hand to hold me back. The path had come out at the top of a cliff, hundreds of feet above the waves. We stood in silence peering out from the trees at the open sky. We were eye-level with clouds bouncing along the distant horizon.

'Nice drop,' I said.

She squatted down in the dust and fumbled a stick from the undergrowth. Streaks of colour from the exertion reached up her neck along the sides of her face like flames, and her eyes were bright. Not watery any more but hard and polished like wood. She poked the stick at the edge of the precipice where hummocks of grass splayed out like fingers. 'See?' She lifted the stick and showed me a clump of grass stuck to the end. It was clotted with some-thing tarry. 'See this?'

'Yeah. Smell it too.'

I wrapped my arm round a hawthorn trunk and leaned out cautiously over the drop. A hundred feet below, the waves crashed on a scrap of pebbled beach. From where I stood a wide, blackish smear extended down the screed to the beach; the one or two blighted bushes that clung to the cliff were sticky with matter. A warm decaying air rose and mixed with the stinging cold sea-smell of salt and fishing-net, making me think for some reason of kitchens. I tipped away from the edge, back into the trees.

'Pigs?' I said, pulling the lens cap off the camera and fiddling with the turret. 'His dead pigs?'

'He used to bring them here in buckets. What was left of them when he'd finished.'

'When he'd finished?'

'Butchering them.'

'For meat?'

'Meat?' She gave a half laugh. 'No. Not for meat.'

'For the heads? To put on the fence?'

'For that. But most of all . . .' She paused. 'Most of all for what he did with me. After Mum died.'

I stopped clicking through F-stops and raised my head. 'What he did with you?'

Her eyes dodged sideways, avoiding mine. She chewed the side of her thumbnail anxiously, pulling off tiny dry flakes of skin with her sharp little teeth.

'Well? What? What did he do with you?'

She held her sleeve up to her forehead like she was checking her temperature. The sea crashed and turned on the rocks below. After a while she used a branch to pull herself to her feet. She straightened her skirt and pushed her hands into her pockets, shrugging gloomily. 'Come on. I'll have to show you.'

About a hundred yards from the cottage there was a breeding shed where some of the equipment left over from the pig farm had been abandoned. It was down an overgrown path and so neglected it had shrunk back into the trees so you'd have walked right past it if you hadn't been looking. Its roof was crooked, the masonry was held together by ivy. 'Here,' she said, pushing the door open. 'This is where he did it.'

I stepped forward and peered into the gloom. It was cold and dark inside, a smell coming up from the floor. I leaned back out into the sunshine and looked at her.

'Well?' I said. 'Not coming with me?'

'No.'

'You sure?'

'What's the matter?' she muttered, looking at the floor, digging her toe into the earth. 'Don't you believe me?'

I studied her for a bit, her sullen mouth, the pale lids and big, serious forehead. I sighed and pushed the door open. As soon as I stepped into the freezing dark I knew why Angeline wouldn't come with me.

I flicked the switch but the overhead fluorescent strips were dead and the only illumination was the greenish daylight from a crumbling cobwebbed window about forty feet to my right, so I stood still and waited for my eyes to get used to the dark. Bad shit had happened in here. You could just tell. Slowly, shapes began to emerge. The roof was corrugated-iron, the floor cracked concrete, crisscrossed with gullies and holes where farrowing partitions had been ripped out. In the centre of the floor there was a livestock weighing crate, its paint chipped, the old-fashioned gauge rusty and worn. I went to the opposite wall where a tool rack was bolted at eye-level. Lined up neatly on the top shelf were axes, saws and chisels, a pair of orange salopettes hanging from a hook underneath – limp but weighty, like a half-stuffed bonfire guy. On the floor below was a bucket with a well-washed cloth draped over the side. Something made me stop and look at that bucket, then back at the tools, the salopettes. There was a smell coming from these things. It was like the smell of a sticking-plaster when you peel it off an infected wound.

I turned. Behind me, next to the door, was a low pine desk, sheets of A4 pasted on the wall above it. Arranged on it were a crucifix, a Bible, a small glass phial. The A4 sheets had inkjet words printed on them.

'*There met him out of the tombs a man with unclean spirit. And he cried with a loud voice and said: What have I to do with thee, Jesus?*'

I read the words twice, trying to place them. New Testament, one of the gospels.

'*What have I to do with thee, Jesus?*'

Something started to twitch at the back of my mind. I turned and looked across the shed. The livestock crate. A dark stain radiated out for several yards round it. One or two flies moved languidly on the floor, like it was sticky.

'*And there met him out of the tombs . . . a man with unclean spirit.*'

Overhead a bird or a squirrel scuttled noisily across the corrugated-iron. I went closer and peered at the other pieces of paper. The font was smaller and I had to squint to read it.

'*All wicked legions, assemblies and sects. Thou art an offence unto me, thou demoniac of Cuagach, for thou savourest not the things that be of God . . .*'

The hairs on my neck stood up. In the freezing air of this corrugated-iron shed sweat squeezed out

under my arms. I thought of the cliff, the dead pigs.
I thought of swine . . .

'*Beast, you beast. You fleeing piglet of Satan.
Prepare now, for your deliverance . . .*'

My skin was cold. It was coming to me what had
been happening in this freezing concrete shed, what
Dove had been doing to his teenage daughter, why
she didn't want to be in here ever again. I could see it:
a flickering light, his giant deformed shadow swaying
on the ceiling overhead, a ball-pein hammer in his
hands. Blood and the ghostly squeals of half-
butchered animals echoing off the bare walls.
Something I hadn't encountered for years. Not since
the bad old days in Albuquerque. '*My name is Legion
. . . all wicked legions, assemblies and sects . . .*'

'Joe?'

I jumped, like Malachi's shadow had run across
my shoulders. The scene was gone and I was back
in the farrowing shed, cold sweat pricking at my
scalp, Angeline at the door, whispering, 'Joe? Did
you say something?'

I opened the door and stepped outside, going
past her without a word. A few feet up the path I
stopped in a patch of sun, closed my eyes and put
my head back, opening my collar and rolling up my
sleeves to get some heat into my skin. I was so tired.
So weary with this insane wormcast of a human
being, Malachi Dove. I knew where the words on

the wall came from. '*My name is Legion . . .*' It was New Testament. It was the moment Jesus cast out the demoniacs of Gadarene. The moment he cast them out of a human and sent them into a herd of pigs. It was an exorcism.

9

The 'Deliverance Ministry' is the evangelical church's answer to the Catholic exorcist's Rituale Romanum. The darkest, most secretive of rituals. Around the same time I was in London trying hard to seduce Lexie, hundreds of miles north on Pig Island Malachi Dove had disintegrated to his lowest point. The only way he could see out of his problems was to exorcize the demon he'd convinced himself possessed his disabled daughter.

'He was insane,' I told Angeline, that evening back at the rape suite, 'but you know that, don't you?'

We were both sunburnt, our hearing dull from the constant roar of wind on the boat journey back. My sweater was torn, covered with rust from the drum I'd wedged into the shaft, but Lex wasn't around to complain. She'd left the light on in the kitchen and a note on the table:

Gone to bed.
Absolutely exhausted.
Thanks for the phone call.
Ha ha! Just joking.
Lex

I crumpled it and threw it into the bin. I took off my jacket and placed my MP3 recorder in the centre of the table, the mic facing Angeline. Then I got a fresh bottle of JD from the kitchen and filled two beakers.

'There,' I said, pushing one towards her. 'You need it.'

She sat down, picking up the JD and drinking it in one, seriously, like she was taking medicine. She handed the beaker back to me. I filled it again and she drank. On the fourth refill she sat back, shoved her hands into her coat pockets and studied me. The booze had made her flushed.

'You know who my mum was?'

I leaned over and pressed record on the MP3. 'Yeah. Asunción. I met her once. Twenty years ago.'

'She was pretty, wasn't she?'

'She was beautiful. I mean, really. Really beautiful.'

There was a pause. She looked at the winking red light on the recorder. 'I loved her, you know. She was the only thing I cared about ever. As long as she was alive I was safe.'

*   *   *

It's early evening in May, the honeysuckle is rambling across the little house near the mine and the sun is just finishing its long climb down the sky when Malachi, drunk, stumbles clumsily into the bathroom to find his teenage daughter standing in front of the window, naked except for the pink towel she's rubbing her face with. She freezes, the towel over her mouth, too shocked to cover herself. The two of them stand and stare at each other for over a minute. Waves of blood crawl up Malachi's face and Angeline's sure he's going to shout at her. But he doesn't. Instead, without a word, he turns and leaves unsteadily, closing the door behind him. Angeline is motionless for a long time, staring at the door, then at last she lowers the towel and wraps it round her body. Much later, when she looks back at this evening, she'll recognize it as the moment the trouble began.

At first it seems like nothing. Her father spends longer periods in his study, printing off page after page of biblical texts, and sometimes he lapses into silence at the dinner table. Both she and Asunción notice how much he's eating and how much weight he's gaining. His neck bulges above his collars, his corduroy trousers are too tight and he has to leave the waist unbuttoned. But it takes them a long time to find out what's at the root of all this. Almost four months. In the end it's Asunción who discovers what's really going on in her husband's mind.

'Start wearing something in the house.' One autumn night she calls Angeline into the study. Malachi is out, collecting generator oil from the jetty, and her mother is sitting at his desk, her serious face illuminated by the little Anglepoise. She is leaning forward. Her elbows are covering a pile of papers. 'I'm going to ask the shop to send some clothes, *mija*, we'll make you something proper to wear. I don't want your daddy to look at you no more.'

Angeline peers at the papers squashed under her mother's elbows. She can see Bible verses and a ripped-out bookplate: a medieval etching of a creature like a dragon standing up, straight as a man, wings sprouting from its shoulders. A woman is on her knees behind it, lifting its tail to kiss its buttocks. Before Angeline can look closer Asunción pulls the papers away and switches off the light. She doesn't want her daughter to see too much.

'Your daddy is losing his brains, *mija*.' She always elides the two words, *mi hija*, her pet name for Angeline. She stands, putting her hands on her daughter's shoulders and guiding her out of the study. 'He drinks too much. You keep your clothes on when he's around.'

For the next year Malachi's mental health

declines rapidly. His drinking accelerates and he'll spend hours lying on the sofa as if he's ill, eating and drinking, swelling like a giant marrow rooted there, and coughing long, dry coughs that sound almost intestinal. His face is patchy with broken veins and occasional bumps where he's fallen in the night, and at dinner he sits in silence, watching Angeline with bloodshot eyes. Sometimes in the living room the two women will go silent and watch his hands trembling as he turns the pages of the Bible.

Angeline has learned to be scared of him. It's never been said but she knows something has changed and she knows from instinct that it's only her mother who stands between them. Asunción makes sure Angeline is dressed when she's in the house – she allows her to take off the long uncomfortable skirts she's made only when they're away from it, on the days they wander the south of the island, making treehouses and teaching each other the names of flowers. Sometimes they sit for hours on the beaches, staring out at the sea, hoping to see a passing minke or a flock of cormorants, and if that doesn't happen they dare each other to go as far as the gorge and examine the chemical drums. On cold days they stay in Angeline's bedroom and read books or watch soap reruns on daytime TV. Angeline's room is lined with bookshelves.

Asunción was born in Mexico, but she thinks of Cuagach as her home, the place she was destined to be. She hasn't known much else in her life: she's been with Malachi since she was sixteen, on the island since she was eighteen, and she loves the place more than she loves anything. The island is in her bones. In her blood. But maybe she's wondering about what's on the mainland because Angeline notices her sentences have changed. There are a lot of We-coulds and If-wes, and Angeline knows she doesn't mean the three of them, but just the two. One day she finds a letter from a women's shelter in Glasgow addressed to Asunción thanking her for the 'enquiry'. This letter makes Angeline worry more about Malachi. If Asunción wants to escape, then maybe there really is something to fear.

But then, just as she's wondering how to ask her mother, something happens that changes everything.

'*Dios tiene sus motivos, dios tiene sus motivos . . .*'

It starts with pinprick moles all over Asunción's skin, as if she's walked through a shower of pepper. Then come the warts, pale brown things that dangle from her chin like berries. She plays with them all the time, twisting them in her fingers as if she'd like to snap them off. One on her temple gets bigger and bigger, spreading like a wine stain under

287

her skin until it's covering half of her eye and, before anyone knows it, lumps rise on her spine, like on a lizard – Angeline can see them even through her mother's embroidered blouses when she's in the kitchen opening cans of chopped tomato and chillies for casseroles. At night she hears Asunción praying. She takes out the note-books with the Psychogenic Healing Ministry's manifestos on death and healing from the study, and in her bed at night Angeline can hear her mother muttering like a witch, long liturgical sentences coiling out in the moonlight. In the day-time she stares at her mother's hands, covered with flour and chopped meat, the way she wipes her brow with the back of her wrists so it doesn't get into her hair. Nobody's said it, but she knows these are things she won't see much more of.

The day Malachi takes her to the mainland is in late summer. The wild fuchsia that carpets the forests is at its best today – hot and vivid beneath the trees – and Asunción is already awake when Angeline comes downstairs, sitting on the floor in the open doorway wrapped in a blanket, the blue day blazing away outside. When she sees her daughter she smiles. 'Come to me, *mija*.'

Angeline creeps nearer, putting a hand on her mother's arm and gazing up into her face. Asunción pulls a crucifix out of the blanket and holds it out, dangling it on her fingers. 'I always thought I'd have more to give a child,' she says. 'Don't let your father see it.'

She puts her arm round her daughter and they sit, looking down at their feet in their open-toed sandals. Angeline's are healthy and pink, Asunción's are greyish. A tear lands in the dust; no one mentions it. Her mother's body smells strange, Angeline thinks: sweetish and foul, like dead flowers in a vase. They sit like this for almost an hour, Asunción weeping quietly, until Malachi comes downstairs carrying a bag. He looks at them neutrally. 'It's time.'

When Angeline realizes where they're going she panics. He has to drag her away, peeling her fingers off her mother's arms. All the time she's screaming and begging him not to take her. 'No. Please *no*!' She hobbles along next to them, trying to head him off, all the way to the jetty, where his boat has been readied, the motor unlocked and mounted on the stern.

At the shore he takes her by the shoulders and turns her to face him. He puts his finger under her chin to lift it, trying to make her look at him. She resists, twitching her shoulders away and trying to get a glimpse of her mother waiting on the boat. 'We'll be back by tonight.' He shakes her, makes her look at him. His face is smooth and shiny and he smells of drink. There are two black sweat stains spreading across his shirt and some broken blond hairs at the temples. 'Now go up there, to the top of the beach, and wait for us.'

And so, at last, she's persuaded. She goes and stands obediently in the trees above the beach, staying for hours after they've gone, when the little dot of the boat has disappeared at last, leaving smooth water, with only the occasional cruiser from Ardfern crossing in the distance. When the sun goes down and they haven't come back she stays, standing straight and patient, waiting for permission to leave. It's only when dawn breaks that she understands she's been tricked. She goes back to the cottage. Her father's whisky bottles are piled in a crate next to the back door. She sits down next to them, staring at them.

From now on it's just her and Malachi.

10

If Finn had been there he'd have listened to Angeline spilling all the details and he'd've told me I was the meister. He'd say I'd finessed her, dolly-walked her into my trap. Funny that, I thought, as I sat, my chin resting on my hand, listening to her. Funny how I don't feel better about it.

Almost the very moment Malachi comes back from the mainland the deliverances start. Once a month he takes Angeline out into the breeding shed. There're always crucifixes and glasses of water waiting on the table and a pig in the rusting crate, squealing and hammering at the floor with its hoofs, making the crate rock and creak. Malachi uses the ritual he wrote for the PHM, muttering intercessory prayers and quoting the biblical rank of demons: thrones, dominions, principalities, powers and spirits. He makes her kneel on the concrete floor, bare knees, head bowed. She has to stay there for the ninety minutes it takes to complete.

Afterwards, when he lets her go, she runs straight back to the house and stands in the bath, the shower on full to drown the noises that are coming from the shed: the squeals, the boom of the pig colliding with the shed's corrugated-iron walls. She never sees what happens to the pigs, but she can guess from the evidence left in the morning. He puts down food and while they're eating he attacks them with the ball-pein hammer. Probably between the eyes because she remembers him saying that is the place a pig is most vulnerable. Then he slits them open and squats next to their opened ribs, inspecting their organs for black spots, for signs that the demons have been transferred. He usually waits a day or two to clear up after himself. Then he fills up buckets with gore and flesh, carries them to the cliffs and tips them into the sea. The heads he saves. She doesn't know what plans he's got for the heads. Maybe he doesn't even know himself.

For the first time in her life she thinks about escape. The only world she's ever known is the three square miles of forest on the south end of Cuagach. She's been to the gorge enough times and stared at it baking under the sun with its barrels and rusty streaks of chemicals leaching into the land. Crossing it would be like crossing to hell, and it's never entered her mind to break the boundaries her parents set. But now fear and desperation are pushing her to take unthinkable chances.

She crosses one afternoon in late August. She moves carefully between the chemical drums, stopping every now and then to check he isn't watching from the escarpment behind. The baked brown rock of the north side gets larger and larger by the hour. When at last she comes to the village it's so green she gets a fantasy she can drink the leaves. Dusk, and rooks are gathering in the trees above, dark clots of them, heads cocked on the side to peer beadily down at her. She moves trance-like along the path that leads to the community, and when she gets there she stops and stares down at it. It seems unreal, like a mirage in the desert, like something from the television – with its neat lawns and tidy, painted houses, a few lights coming on in the windows now that night is falling. Someone, a woman in a lavender headscarf, comes out of one of the houses and crosses the green. Angeline turns and drags herself clumsily up to the first branches of a tree, her heart beating hard. She wedges herself into the V of a branch, the bark digging into her feet, and watches.

The woman passes only a few feet below and enters a long, low building through sliding glass doors. A light comes on inside, and silence falls for a long time. Angeline's pulse is racing in her ears. This is the first human being she's seen who wasn't on television or loading supplies on to the jetty in the distance. She's thinking of slithering out of the tree and creeping to the building when the light goes off and the woman comes out of the building. She's carrying a metal bowl on top of a pile of folded tea-towels and as she turns up the path she pauses and comes to a halt.

For a moment she seems to be looking at the bowl, as if there's something in it she didn't expect, because her eyes are turned down, her mouth closed tight. Then, with a sideways twitch of her jaw, she slowly, very slowly, raises her eyes to the tree. Angeline holds her breath. Their eyes haven't met, but she knows she's been seen. There's a long, long pause, and although her heart is thudding she has a moment of hope. She pictures the woman putting down the bowl and holding out her hands. She pictures being led into the village, people coming out of their houses to greet her. She imagines a family kitchen, a fire, a meal on the table, and for the first time since Asunción left the island she can feel hope twitch in her chest.

But, of course, that's not what happens. What happens instead is that Susan Garrick drops the bowl. There's a pause as it rolls off the path and into the trees. It comes to a stop in the leaves and then Susan begins to cry. It's a cry of pure fear – of terror. It goes into Angeline's chest and stays there, winding into her heart as Susan swings round on the path. She hesitates as if she's not quite sure how to do this, then stumbles forward towards the houses, crying and shouting. Angeline is frozen, just for a second, then she drops out of the tree, as quickly as possible, the bark ripping into her leg. She turns and melts into the trees, back the way she came. It's the last time she'll go to the village until the night she follows Malachi and sees him put the explosives in the chapel.

Back at the cottage Malachi is in his study, the

light on, a bottle at his elbow. Angeline slips in silently through the back door and goes to the bathroom to drink water and wash the dried blood and dirt from her body. She's finished bathing and is climbing, shivering, into bed when a commotion starts outside the house, sending her instinctively scuttling to the top of the staircase. Someone's knocking on the door. Downstairs Malachi shoots out of the study in alarm.

'Go to your room,' he hisses. 'Don't move until I come for you.'

She scrambles back into her room, her heart thudding. Downstairs she hears him throw open the door. There's a moment's silence. Then, in such a strange voice she wonders if he's going to cry, he says, 'Benjamin. Benjamin – why are you here? I don't want you here.'

'*Malachi?*'

'Yes. I am Malachi. Why are you here?'

There's a few moments' silence. She knows who Benjamin is: Benjamin Garrick, she's seen his picture, and now she imagines the men staring at each other, thinking of the years that have passed. When Benjamin speaks again it's in an urgent whisper, as if he's afraid of something. 'Malachi? What has happened to you?'

'What has happened? Nothing's happened.'

'Malachi, terrible things are being said. Terrible

things are being suggested about what you are doing up here. Something evil has been seen in these woods.'

'Something evil? What does that mean, something evil?'

'The thing all Christians fear, Malachi, man's ancient enemy: a Pan, Malachi, a Dionysus, a *Satan*. Half beast, half man. A *biforme*.'

'I told you never to come here, Benjamin. Don't come here and tell me this babble. Get away now. Before I use my axe.'

Maybe he raises the axe to show how serious he is, because Benjamin staggers away from the door in shock. Angeline hears a barrel being knocked over, the sound of feet shuffling in the soil, then the front door slamming shut and Malachi's laboured, furious breathing in the living room. She leaps to the window, presses her nose to the pane and sees, from above, a man's head. The moon is close to the horizon, but there's enough light to make out the pale circle of skin showing through his thinning hair. He's wearing a dark green jacket and wellingtons and she stares at him in fascination as he moves his hands up and down in a strange spasmodic gesture. He turns in a complete circle, once, twice, as if he doesn't know what to do – whether to knock again, or run. Then he stops.

Only a few yards away, outside the fence, lies a

pig. Angeline hasn't noticed it before but from the odd angle of its head she guesses it's one of Malachi's sacrifices, not cleaned up yet from the deliverance on Sunday. She can't imagine what tools he's used for the slaughter, but he's split the animal into slices. When the insides came out he must have kicked them around in the dust because they are lying all over the place, already going a dark, hard red colour like dead liver.

Benjamin becomes very still, breathing quite hard, his shoulders going up and down. He takes a few steps forward, his hand up to his mouth, and peers down at the creature through the cloud of midges that have gathered above it. He mutters something, swishing the flies away. Hastily he holds his hands together in prayer, whispering feverishly, pointing to the heavens. She sees the creature through his eyes: she sees that its injuries look the work of a demon. It could be Faust's ripped-apart corpse. Asunción read *Faust* to her once, sitting at the edge of the bed, whispering the words because the book was a secret between them and they'd never mention the devil in Malachi's company.

The front door flies open behind him and Malachi steps out. Benjamin wheels round, a look of terror on his face: '*Malachi – please – what is this? What abomination is living on Cuag—*' He falters. Malachi's standing a few feet from the door, the axe held above his head, the moonlight glancing off it. '*Malachi*,' he stutters, all the colour going from his face. '*Malachi, please, I beg of you – what has happened to you? Who have you fallen into league with?*'

'Get away from my house.' Malachi takes a step forward. 'Do you hear? *Get away and never come back.*'

Benjamin looks at the axe. He looks back at the pig and raises his hands cautiously. 'I'm going,' he mutters, backing away. 'I'm going. But, Malachi, I beg you, you may have turned your heart against God but it's not too late. He who has flung headlong from the heights of heaven the reprobate dragon has not forgotten you and He—'

'Get away!' He takes another step forward, raises the axe a little higher, and at that Benjamin turns and staggers head first in the direction of the gorge, half stumbling and tripping over the fence. Malachi doesn't move. He stands in silence staring after him, at the point he's disappeared. The axe trembles in his hands.

Angeline shrinks against the wall, her head in her hands, all Benjamin's words coming back to her: *abomination* – a Pan, a Dionysus. *Satan*. The same words Malachi uses in the monthly rituals. Something lodges under her ribs – something thick she can't cough up or swallow. For the first time in her life she wonders whether Malachi may be right about her.

'And after that they kept coming,' she murmured. She was stony-faced, staring at the light blinking on the recorder. I didn't remember it, but now I could see she must have cried some time in the last half an hour because her eyes were red and puffy and she kept pressing a knuckle to her nose to stop it running. 'I – um, I found a tree to watch them from. They were like tourists.'

'Tourists?' I was still imagining the shock when Susan Garrick dropped the metal bowl. I could almost hear it. 'Trying to see you?'

'They'd even bring cameras. It was before Dad put up the fence. Benjamin – he came back and sprinkled holy water along the bottom of the escarpment.' She broke off and thought about this for a while, her muddy brown eyes moving from side to side like she was seeing it happen again. 'And that girl – the one you were with – she tried to trap me. Made a hole in the ground.'

'The one I was with?'

'Yes,' she said, her voice level. 'Don't you remember? "*Malachi, you old bonehead. Show us your strap-on tail.*"'

I stared at her. Sovereign. I remembered the way I'd stalked along the fence, desperate to get a shot of Angeline in the grass. Something pinched at me now. Something that must have been pity or shame or something. 'They wanted to kill you. They had plans.'

She shrugged, like this wasn't a surprise. She chewed a little more on her thumbnail. Her coat hung open and I could see under the football shirt that she was thinner than I remembered, sort of starved-looking. Lexie said she looked like she was on drugs. 'When they read what you write about me,' she said, nodding at the tape player, 'you know, in the papers, do you think people will still be scared of me?'

'No,' I said. 'Not at all.' I pressed pause on the machine and checked how long we'd been talking. Forty minutes. 'But it won't be yet. I can't go to the papers with this. Not until they find him.'

We were silent for a while, holding each other's eyes. And then, like we were both thinking the same thing, we turned and looked at the window. The curtains were still open, and outside the orange streetlight was flickering like it was going to short out any second.

'What do you think?' I murmured. 'Angeline? Do you think he's going to kill himself?'

She didn't turn back to me. She kept her eyes on the streetlight. 'Yes,' she said. 'He'll kill himself. But you're right. I think he's got something else to do first.'

11

When I went upstairs that night and started to get undressed in the damp bedroom at the front of the house, I saw Lexie was awake. She had her hand behind her head, the duvet pulled up to her chin, and was looking at me knowingly. I paused, the ripped sweater half way up my chest.

'You weren't asleep.'

'You made enough noise coming in.'

'You didn't want to come down? See how we got on?'

'Didn't want to interrupt.'

I pulled off the sweater and stepped out of my jeans. There was nowhere to hang them and my true instinct was to put them back on again and climb into bed. But she was watching me in silence. So I dutifully laid them flat on the floor and climbed into bed.

'She was talking to you.' Lex rested a hand on her chest, dropped her head sideways and looked at me. 'I heard her. She didn't stop talking.'

I rubbed my eyes. 'I've got the story – got it all. Tomorrow I'll speak to Danso.'

'Speak to Danso?'

'He needs to find her somewhere else to go.'

Lexie pushed herself up on her elbow and stared at me. 'No, she can't go, not yet.'

'She's not our responsibility—'

'Yes,' she hissed. 'She is. You *can't* just let her go.'

I turned to her. The broken streetlight outside was reflected orange in her eyes. 'What?'

'We can't let her go. Not yet. I've got someone to look at her. It's in Glasgow not London, because there are some – oh, some stupid professional hoops to jump through before we get her down to see Christophe, but it's next week so we have to keep her with us till then.' She bit her lip, searching my face. 'Oakesy? Just a few more days? Monday?'

I sighed. I put a fist into one of the appalling pillows, punched it – a pathetic attempt to get some air into it – and lay back on my hands, staring at the ceiling. I think I'd just realized how knackered I was. 'Go to sleep now. OK?'

But she didn't. She was still staring at me, chewing her lip. I closed my eyes and rolled away from her. 'Oakesy,' she said, tapping my shoulder, 'did she say anything? Did she say what's wrong with her?'

'I don't think she even knows herself. Can I go to sleep?'

'Hasn't she got an idea?'

'Don't think so.'

'Well, what about you? Haven't you got an idea?'

'Lex, please, I'm not a doctor.'

'Do you think she'd let me have a look?'

302

'Why don't you ask her?'

'You're not interested. Are you? You're just not interested.'

'I am,' I said. 'Of course I am.'

But I was lying. I didn't care what was wrong with Angeline. When I closed my eyes and fell back inside my head, the face I saw wasn't Angeline's or even Lexie's. It was Dove's.

Malachi. Malachi . . . My head was throbbing. *What is your plan?*

12

Danso was as scared as me about Malachi's plans. Instinct told him to listen to me, not to Struthers. But his head had gone further than mine and he'd started thinking about those suicide bombers in London, about all the capabilities Dove had, and whether his spectacular death would take out someone more than himself. The ACC had consulted with the home secretary, and over the next few days senior officers from London's SO13 terrorist team flew up to meet him. Suddenly the incident room at Oban was crammed with criminal profilers and explosives experts, tearing apart the community's computer. Every ex-member of the

PHM was being tracked down, every donor, anyone who had sent a letter or email in the last ten years. They'd got HOLMES actions raised to interview anyone who might have known Dove, even people involved in the arson or IRS investigations over in New Mexico. Some of the locals and national TV stations in Scotland had run appeals for sightings of the blue Vauxhall stolen from Crinian and the usual attention-seekers crawled out of the wainscoting – at least twenty people had seen the car and more than half of them had recognized Dove. They knew he was the Pig Island killer from the press, who were busy jumping up and down on Dove's sacred head. *Mystery of Missing Preacher: The Mad Monk of Pig Island*. All of which was funny, Danso said, because the force was still waiting for the procurator fiscal to let them name Malachi Dove publicly as their suspect.

'But what's good,' he said one morning, standing in the kitchen at the rape suite, still wearing his raincoat, 'what's good is we might know where he went after Crinian.'

It was Friday. Six days had passed since the massacre, and that, as everyone knew, wasn't good. The golden hours for a case, the first twenty-four, had passed. But now Danso was holding up a video-cassette for us to see. 'There I was, thinking it was all going down the cludgie, when this turns up.' He went to the TV on his long, awkward, ostrich legs, slotted the tape into the machine and stood back, aiming the remote at the video player. 'Inverary.' He looked at Angeline, who was sitting on the sofa, arms folded. 'It's about fifteen miles from Crinian. Ever heard of it?'

'No.'

'Dad never mentioned a friend in the area? Family? Someone who'd been with the PHM?'

'All the people he knew were in America. Or London. He was born in London.'

'You can watch it as many times as you need. Don't be afraid to say you don't know.'

Me and Angeline and Lexie all sat hunched round the TV, staring at the screen. It was grainy black-and-white CCTV footage but continuous action – easier to watch than the cut-price time-lapse of most shopping centres. The time code clicked away in the top corner and shoppers moved back and forward along the walkway, some stopping to sit on one of the four benches arranged round a concrete planter full of palm trees. A checkout girl in the window of Holland and Barrett opposite the camera gazed out at the passers-by, idly biting her cuticles.

'In about two seconds you're going to see him come from this side and – wait . . . wait . . . *there*. See him? Here?'

A man, the top of his head turned to the camera, appeared on the walkway. He shuffled across the screen, arms hanging listlessly at his sides. He was about to disappear off when something caught his eye in the window of a Superdrug shop. He turned his back to the camera and we had time to study his longish hair, the unremarkable sports jacket, the dark slacks.

'This is the best look you get at him. It was the sandals that did it. Sandals and socks. You both said sandals and socks in your statements. It's the kind of detail sticks in people's heads.'

I inched a bit nearer the screen, staring at the figure. If it was my own dad I wouldn't've been sure from this angle. I waited for him to face the camera. But he didn't. He peered through the chemist's window a little longer, then turned and continued off the screen. There was a long, silent pause. We all turned to Angeline. I'd expected her to look blank, but the second I saw her face I knew. She'd sat up a bit, her head was straight and she was staring at the screen. Her hands were on her knees, clenching and unclenching.

'Angeline?' Danso studied her. 'Want to see it again? There're a lot of these wee characters out in Inverary and—'

'No. Not again.' She blew out a long breath from pursed lips, a long *fooooo* sound, like she was trying to keep calm. 'Bastard,' she muttered at the TV. 'That bastard.'

It was the jacket she'd recognized. She'd washed it for him at the beginning of the summer and that was how she knew it was him. It had needed to be hand washed because there was blood on it from the pigs. Danso passed the news back to the incident room, then came and sat with me on the sofa. We had the shopping-centre video in the player and were watching it over and over again. On the sixth time Malachi stopped in front of Superdrug I caught up the remote and paused the tape. I took a chair and placed it in front of the TV.

'What is it?'

I sat so close to the screen that the static popped against my nose. I clicked the video, frame by frame, until Dove came backwards into the walkway and turned to the chemist's window again. 'I want to know what he's staring at. We're not seeing something. We're not seeing this through his eyes. There's something here . . .'

I searched the screen a little longer, trying to decode the blurry pixels, the areas of grey and black and white, and when I still couldn't figure out what I was looking at I pushed the chair back, got the Ordnance Survey map from my jacket pocket and opened it on the kitchen table. I ran my finger down the list of place names: Inverary, Inveraish, Inveranan. I drew a pencil ring round Inverary and stared at it, looking at what surrounded it. A scattering of estates, a sewage-treatment plant, a power station.

'What's there, Malachi?' I murmured, tracing the line of a Forestry Commission sector with my thumbnail. 'What's there?'

Danso got up and came to the table, looking over my shoulder, so close I could smell the dry-cleaners' chemicals on his suit. 'If we could look at this through his eyes, tell me, what would we see?'

I shook my head. 'Twenty years ago I could have told you. Believe me or don't believe me, it's true. Twenty years ago I could have told you what he had for breakfast.'

'And now?'

'Now . . .' I sighed and turned to look at him, rubbing my temple, wishing my head would stop thumping. Now, the answer was no. I didn't know.

'That's because he's changed,' Danso said, reading my thoughts. 'He's killed thirty people and it's made him a different creature. There aren't any rules any more.'

13

Danso had twenty officers on door-to-door in Inverary. He'd issued stills from the videotape to the press and was talking to profilers every hour on the hour. But the unease wouldn't let up. He wasn't sleeping. Long nights trying to catch some kip curled up on a desk or an armchair in the station had caught up with him and the chronic disc herniation in his third and fourth lumbar vertebrae had flared up. The sleeping pills his GP had given him weren't working.

'This is killing me,' he said. 'Had a Casualty Bureau meeting seven o'clock this morning. Signed two *laissez-passers*, one for the US, one for Nigeria and all before eight o'clock. I do *not* call this a civilized timetable.'

It was Tuesday morning. Angeline was due at the Glasgow Royal Infirmary at eleven, and Danso was driving us. He knew Glasgow traffic better than we did. But I guessed the real reason he'd offered the lift. There was something he had to tell us.

'George is saying how usually when something like this happens you get hundreds reported missing – ten times more than you've got bodies to match. But—' He checked in the rear-view mirror. He indicated and changed lanes, crossing the traffic on the Dumbarton Road. In the back Angeline and

Lexie sat in silence, staring out of the windows at the decaying railway bridges, the stained and graffitied pebbledash houses lining the street. 'But this thing on Cuagach happens and only twenty people come forward.'

'That's how they worked – the PHM. Cut off ties with relatives. You wouldn't expect anyone to know where they were living after all these years.'

'Yeah, but *twenty*. That's eleven fewer than the bodies we've got.'

We'd driven on for a while and passed two roundabouts before what he'd said sank in. I turned to look at him. 'You don't mean eleven. You mean ten. You just said eleven.'

'I mean eleven.'

I laughed. 'Peter, I have to tell you, I was maybe one of Mrs Leeper's worst students for sagging, but when it came to maths I was the four-foot genius. Twenty plus ten makes thirty. Always did, always will.'

'I mean eleven. That's what I want to tell you.' He glanced at me out of the corner of his eye. 'There were thirty-one people in that chapel when it blew up.'

'No. There were only thirty members of the PHM.'

He made a face, pushing out his lips and nodding, like this was a reasonable thing to say.

Like I could even be right. 'So you said. You're sure you didn't forget anyone?'

I stared at him. Then I fumbled a pen out of my pocket. I had a glimpse of Angeline watching me, her eyes puzzled and unblinking in the rear-view mirror. I scribbled down the initials of all the people I could think of on my arm. I'd been through all this before with George and I knew I was right. Blake had said thirty members. The website had said thirty. I'd met thirty.

'See?' I said, holding up my arm in front of him.

He pushed my hand away. 'I'm trying to drive.'

'There were only thirty. I'm not missing anyone.'

'They weren't hiding someone?'

'Hiding them?'

'Yeah.' He licked his lips and glanced in the rear-view mirror, checking the cars behind us. 'Pig Island was that sort of place. You say it in your statement: "the sort of place people *migrate* to when things go wrong". It wouldn't be the first time a community has taken in someone on the run. There couldn't have been a wee hidey-hole on Cuagach?'

'If there was they kept it quiet.'

'Aye, well, someone was out there. It doesn't come down to much – not much more than a wee bit of skin and hair. The rest is just – well . . .' He shot a look at the women in the back, then leaned sideways towards me and lowered his voice. 'Might not find the rest of him.'

'Him?'

'Aye.'

'Dove? Injured in the explosion?'

'Already thought of that. DNA doesn't work.'

'One of them was pregnant?'

'The hair's adult.'

I shook my head, looking out at the rows of thirties houses we were passing, the boarded-up petrol stations, the businesses: Larry's Laminate Land; Kwik-Fit; Fred's Foamwash and Valet. 'I don't know. Another hack maybe? Perhaps when I left they got another hack out there. Someone else to spread their message. Or a lawyer.'

'I don't know.' He set the indicator and crossed the traffic again. We were getting to the city centre. 'But have a think about it for me. See if you remember anything.'

The car went on, the dull rocking motion of the engine in the soles of my feet. I put my head against the window and stared up as we went under the spindly Erskine bridge; high overhead, cars teetered along it, dark against the sky. I wasn't thinking about that extra victim. I was thinking of what Dove had achieved with a bit of fertilizer and picric acid, what he could achieve on the mainland. I was thinking about Inverary and the chemist's and the

Forestry Commission land. I was thinking of one word: 'memorable'. *Why is your death going to be memorable?* It's ironic that that was how my head was working because, looking back now, I see that what I should have been concentrating on was that sentence of Danso's: *Have a think about it for me.*

Because it was this that turned out in the end to be the best piece of advice I got in the whole sorry episode: to try to figure out who that thirty-first victim was. Didn't know it at the time, but I'd learn my lesson. Oh, fuck, yes. Given time I'd learn my lesson.

Lexie

1

Dear Mr Taranici

I'm writing again because I've got this dreadful, *dreadful* sense that time is . . . I don't know, that it's running out somehow. It's quite ridiculous, of course, because as you know I'm too level-headed to believe in premonition, but I can't tell you how horrible this feels. Just horrible. At first it was sort of exciting, knowing we were in the middle of a drama all the country was reading about. But now it's gone beyond funny and, honestly, I'm wishing it had never happened.

Oakesy's keeping something from me. He and Danso are always talking secretively, looking at maps and reading through Dove's paperwork. If I ask Danso, he says don't worry, everything's going to plan: they've filed reports on all the DNA they found in the cottages, developed 'profiles' on the relatives they've traced, and all the human remains have come off the island and been transferred to a temporary mortuary (that's basically a warehouse on an industrial estate near Oban. It's big enough for them to drive the refrigerated trucks inside and Oakesy says they like that because they can unload out of sight). But, I say, if it's all going to plan then where's Malachi Dove?

I'm sorry. I can't help it. This morning I opened the window and looked at the solid grey Ballantine's factory, and the playing-fields that come away from it and sweep down almost to the front door. I've never seen a soul on those fields. They're always completely silent, the trees at the side all dark, and you can't help imagining there might be someone in those trees, just like at the bungalow, someone watching the house. No one – not the police or anyone we ask – can explain why those fields aren't being used. At night, when I wake up, I imagine something out there gathering, closing in on us. I have a nightmare of it clinging to the house in the dark: pulsing like a giant heart.

I've thought about getting away. I've worked out what to do – I can't drive the car because it's a manual, but if I told Oakesy I was going to

Mummy's and made up some excuse about my bankcard not working I could buy the rail ticket on our joint account. I've ferreted away almost thirty pounds too, just from the loose change I empty out of his shorts at the end of the day.

But, of course, I'm not going to leave. How could I leave when there's so much at stake? When I'm this close to Christophe. I can't just drop it because I'm *scared*, for heaven's sake. I had to wait it out – a whole week until this wretched doctor at the Glasgow Royal Infirmary would see us. The reply to my email was pretty quick: 'Mr Radnor regrets he cannot see you personally. Without an examination it is very difficult to make a diagnosis and ordinarily it would be appropriate to refer you to a GP. However, given the circumstances, he is delighted to refer you to a colleague.' No prizes for guessing which self-appointed arbiter of human values was behind *that*. Somehow she'd weeded out my email and stopped it getting to Christophe. Of course I knew that the moment the doctor saw Angeline he'd be on the phone to Christophe double quick and then it'd all come out and Cerberus would look pretty stupid, not passing on my messages. But in the meantime there was nothing I could do except wait. So you can imagine, given the circumstances, that by the time the hospital appointment rolled round I was jumpy. Very jumpy indeed.

Guy Picot was waiting for us in the office, dressed in something lightweight and elegant. I was surprised by how good-looking he was. He hasn't got Christophe's force of personality, of course, but he really knows how to dress. If we'd met under different circumstances, if I hadn't been so anxious, who's saying there wouldn't have been sparks between us?

'After this consultation,' I said, when we'd all filed into his office, 'will you speak to Mr Radnor directly?'

'I'll send him a letter. Out of courtesy.'

'A letter?' A letter wouldn't reach Christophe's desk. Not with her guarding the postbag. 'Can't you phone him?'

He gave me a long look. 'I'll send him a letter. And I'll send one to Angeline, *the patient*. With all the pertinent points of our meeting today. I'll need an address.'

Oakesy wrote down the address of the PO box we'd rented at the local shop and I relaxed a little after that because I'd have access to the mail every day and at least I wouldn't be completely sidelined. Guy Picot made us green tea in gorgeous half-glazed Japanese bowls (green tea in the NHS!!!), then settled down, tapping a patella hammer distractedly on the desk and looking thoughtfully at the way Angeline was sitting.

I didn't say anything, but I noticed all the questions seemed to be lifted directly from *my* email. He might as well have been reading from a script. Was she continent? Did she have mobility in both legs? What, both? But when he put her on the examination couch he didn't invite me in. He pulled the screen tight, as if he thought I was trying to sneak a look. Next thing, I thought, I'm going to be accused of *prurience*, so instead I went very quickly to the opposite side of the office and stood looking out of the window, my back very firmly to the room so anyone could see I wasn't interested in *peeping*, for heaven's sake.

When he came out he was red-faced and flustered. 'I'll be honest,' he said. 'I wasn't warned what to expect. I was expecting something smaller.' But apart from that he made every effort not to talk to me or acknowledge how unique this case was. Of course, I wasn't fooled: he managed to arrange not only an X-ray but also an MRI *in under three hours* – and how many times have you known an NHS doctor do that? He even got two radiographers to give up their lunch-hour for the MRI.

'No pacemakers? Surgical clips, pins or plates or cochlear implants?'

By one o'clock Angeline was in the MRI room, dressed in a pale blue hospital gown, going through a questionnaire with one of the radiographers.

'No IUDs?'

'What's an IUD?'

'A coil. No, never mind. We'd have seen it on the X-ray.'

Oakesy and I were in the glass-panelled control area with Guy, where we could hear what was happening through the intercom system. Oakesy sat in the corner, all preoccupied – probably worrying about the thirty-first victim Danso had been telling him about. I was next to the window watching Angeline, and Guy was at the intercom mic, barking instructions to the radiographers: 'Get her comfortable. Doesn't matter if she's on her front.' He pulled Angeline's X-rays out of the brown folder and held them up to the light. 'That's it – that's the way.'

He switched off the mic and turned away, stopping when he caught me staring at the X-rays in his hand. He knew I'd got a glimpse of them. He knew from my expression.

'Are you going to let me have a look?' I said. It had been only a few split seconds, but it was long enough for me to know there was something very odd about those X-rays. Very odd indeed. 'I'd really like to see them.'

'I'll be getting a second opinion before I share my thoughts.'

'Mr Radnor?'

'No. Someone here, I expect.'

He shovelled the X-rays away, but that grey and white and black image stayed in my head. A ghostly imprint of a human. I looked round at Angeline being arranged on the MRI table. The radiographer asked her to move her feet forward and as she did the gown moved a little and I saw behind her calf a fat, sausage-coloured slab of flesh, the skin slightly hardened like a cuticle. She realized what had happened but she didn't try to hide it. She was staring blankly at the glass window. She didn't even seem to register me – there was this thoughtful, distant look on her face. I turned back to Guy Picot.

'I know why you won't let me see. I know.'

He shook his head, opening his nostrils and continuing to watch Angeline, as if I was a fly bothering him. But I wasn't going to be put off. 'I can read an X-ray, you know – I'm not imagining what I just saw. I saw calcium. In the growth, I saw a mass of something and I'm sure it was calcium, and that means—'

'That means?'

'Bones,' I said. My voice wasn't much more than a whisper, because something vague and distant was going through my head. *Ectoderm, endoderm, mesoderm* . . . a few half-remembered words from the journal. There was a long silence while I looked at Guy Picot without blinking. *Heterogeneous elements* . . .

'But it can't be,' I murmured. 'It can't be. *She should be dead . . .*'

2

In retrospect, I can see it was right after the hospital appointment that Oakesy's behaviour, as if it wasn't bad enough already, took a turn for the worse. The next morning, when I was still half asleep, he leaped out of bed as if he'd been bitten, disappeared into the bathroom and stayed there, in the shower, for almost an hour. When he came out he looked awful, just *awful*, his skin all grey and damp as if he had a virus. He wouldn't speak to me, just slunk around looking really shifty, pale and uncommunicative, finding every excuse to keep a distance from me and Angeline, not meeting our eyes, sitting at breakfast with an uncomfortable, drawn-up look on his face, shutting himself in his room upstairs the moment he had a chance.

'What did the doctor tell you?' he asked me, later that night. We were in bed. 'What were you talking about? When you said you saw calcium on the X-ray, what did that mean?'

I tipped my head sideways and frowned at him. It was almost the first thing he'd said to me all day. He was staring at the ceiling, really unhappy seeming, moving his tongue around as if he'd found something foreign in his mouth.

'I don't know,' I said. 'There's only one thing it could be.'

'What?'

'A tumour. But the only tumour I know that's got bone in it is . . .'

'Is?'

'A teratoma. And if it was that she wouldn't have survived. They go malignant, teratomas. I'm sure I remember reading that somewhere – they go malignant.'

'Then what? What is it?'

'I don't know.'

'You must have an idea.'

'No,' I said.

'But you must.'

'*No*,' I said, irritated. 'I haven't got a clue.' Up until now Oakesy couldn't have cared less what was wrong with Angeline. Now all of a sudden he was showing this interest? And expecting me to have all the answers? 'I just told you, *I don't know*. We've got to wait for Mr Radnor to call.'

It wasn't until much later, when he'd gone to

sleep and I was lying awake listening to that ghostly wind coming across the playing-fields and rattling the windows, that it dawned on me what was going on in Oakesy's head. I rolled my head sideways on the pillow and looked at him, hunched up, the duvet pulled over his head as if he wanted to shut out the world. He must have seen the growth, like I did, in the MRI room, with its slightly unreal, rubbery-looking skin. Suddenly everything made sense – the way he'd gone around all day yellow-faced and distracted, the way he couldn't meet Angeline's eyes. I stared at the bulge of his shoulders, the duvet rising and falling as he breathed, and I pushed out a dry, irritated laugh. How typical of a man. How *bloody typical*.

Overnight a wind came up from the Irish Sea and pounded the west of Scotland, blowing round the house, rattling the windows and shaking drifts of leaves from the trees at the edge of the estate. When I went downstairs in the morning the kitchen was dark as if winter was already here. Out of the window, rain pelted the road, dark clouds trailed long fingers down to stroke the roofs and the flame-effect gas-fire in the living room barely took the chill off the air. In the night someone had left a shopping trolley on the pavement outside the boarded-up house opposite. It just sat there, occasionally moving a few inches in a gust of wind, the chain at the coin slot dangling back and forward.

'You know,' I said, when Oakesy came down for breakfast. It was just the two of us: Angeline was still asleep, her door closed tightly. He sat opposite me, not meeting my eyes, pretending to be reading the proposal he's putting together for Finn. 'You know it would behove you to hide your feelings a little better.'

He looked up at me. His pupils opened and closed a couple of times, as if he was struggling to take me in. 'What did you say?'

'Oh, come on.' I gave a short laugh. 'I know you so well. You're really upset. And it's not just because of Malachi Dove. It's her.' I jerked my head in the direction of the stairs. 'It's her too.'

He stared at me then, as if I was a complete stranger, as if I was someone who had just wandered in off the street and sat down opposite him at the table.

'Don't look so embarrassed, Oakesy. I do *know*. I know *exactly* what's going on in your head. I'm not stupid.'

He kept looking at me – so hard that a vein in his forehead rose and began to pulse steadily. 'Lexie, I know you're not stupid, I never thought you were, and I . . .' He trailed off. There was a pause, then he said, 'What's going on in my head?'

'You're disgusted.' I laughed. 'You don't like even sitting in the same room as her.'

'Disgusted?' he repeated, like a mantra. 'Disgusted.' Slowly, not taking his eyes off me, he laid down the manuscript and stood up, rather woodenly. He went to the sink, turned on the tap and scooped some water into his mouth.

'There's one basic rule, Oakesy,' I said to his back. 'One fundamental guideline for decency not only for medical professionals but for all human beings. You should try as much as possible to conceal your disgust. *Especially* from the person you find disgusting.'

He straightened then, his back still to me. He took several deep breaths, as if he was trying to control himself. Water ran down his arms and dripped off his fingers on to the floor. Just when I was about to speak he raised a foot and slammed it into the cupboard door, sending a crack shooting down to the bottom.

'For God's sake.' I stood up, stunned. 'What *on earth* do you think you're doing?'

He didn't answer. He stood there, arms dangling, head down, staring at his toenails where lines of blood had appeared at the edges. He turned, not meeting my eyes, and came to the table, dropping into his seat. He sat there in a heap, shoulders slumped, staring dully at the coffee-pot. He looked terrible.

I sat down cautiously, a little knot of anxiety tying itself in my stomach. He knows something, I thought. He knows something about Dove. 'Joe? What is it? What's going on?'

'Alex,' he said, not looking at me. 'I love you. You know that, don't you?'

I opened my mouth, then closed it. '*What?* Well – yes. Of course I know. What's that got to do with anything?'

He breathed in and out, very, very slowly, as if the effort of just sitting upright was too much. For a long time he didn't speak. The only noise was the sound of rain pounding against the window. 'Nothing,' he said eventually, in a strained voice. 'Nothing's going on. I just want you to know that I love you.'

Well, that was it – he wouldn't say any more. He went upstairs and locked himself into the third bedroom, leaving me sitting at the kitchen table and looking in stunned silence from the broken cupboard to the stairs and back again. Now, I thought, putting my hands to my head, now I know the world has gone mad.

Oakesy

1

If I've got my hand on my unreconstructed heart, when I met Dr Guy Picot – he pronounced it the French way *Ghee Peeko* – I didn't like him one bit, with his wide, sculpted neck and these big kind of classical lips, and curls that looked like they'd been carved out of soap or stone or something. Adonis of the Gorbals. It's a mystery to me how anyone can get through the day dressed like a Versace model and not feel a total prat.

He didn't say anything to start with – just hello – then sat us in a line on the other side of his desk, watching Angeline as she settled down, taking her in from toes to head, staring particularly at her feet. Lex was anxious. She kept asking Picot who he'd got the referral from, was it directly from Mr Radnor. If I'd been thinking a bit clearer I'd've noticed this. But good old Oakesy, he of the concrete head – never do listen to the important stuff, do I?

Picot asked Angeline some questions – mostly about her feet, for some reason. Then he put his pen down, looked at her carefully and said, 'Angeline.' He got up from the desk and pushed back the screen. 'I'm going to give you a gown and I'm going to ask you to get undressed. Are you OK with that?'

She didn't answer straight off. We all turned to look at her. She was staring at her hands, moving them round and round compulsively, breathing hard in and out. The rash round her mouth had cleared up, I noticed, and she'd put on some of Lexie's makeup, but it didn't stop you seeing the blood pumping round her face.

'Angeline, would you like to—'

'Yes.' She stood abruptly, her eyes wide. 'Yes.'

It was awkward – her limping away behind the screen, the sound of her undressing – and for a while there was a silence in which none of us could meet each other's eyes. Lex and me both picked up a magazine and pretended to flick through them. Then Angeline called, 'Ready,' and Picot went behind the screen, pulling on his gloves.

It was an old-fashioned screen, with green fabric strung over the frame, like something from a *Carry On* film. There was a slit in both sides and Lexie tilted her chair back as far as it would go, craning her neck to look through the gap and see what was happening back there. After a moment or two she put down the magazine silently and crept, very carefully, towards the screen. She stood, side on, her chin drawn into her neck so she could just peep through the slit.

'Hey,' I said, kind of disgusted by her. She shook her head, put a finger to her lips and was about to step closer when, from the other side, Picot tugged the screen closed with an impatient noise. She froze for a second, not looking at me, colour gathering in her face. I thought she was going to say something, be pissed off with Picot, but instead she made a little huffing sound – like 'These doctors're all the same' – snatched up the magazine from her chair and went to the window at the far end, standing with her back to the room, staring out at the car park.

I watched her for a bit, then went back to my magazine. I wasn't reading it: I was thinking about Dove, about that bridge. Spectacular. 'My death will be spectacular.' I glanced up and saw that when Picot had moved the screen he had accidentally opened one of the slits nearest to me. I could see part of what was happening in there.

I didn't move. I sat totally still, hardly breathing. I could see obliquely along one side of the table, could see the little toe on Angeline's right foot poking out from a heavy white sheet, her hand holding the side of the table, and Picot standing next to her, his gloves pulled over his shirt cuffs.

'Now, I'm not going to hurt you,' he said, his head on one side, looking down to where her face must be. 'I'm just going to look. Is that OK?'

I shot a glance at Lexie. She was still staring out of the window, tapping her nail on her teeth, not interested in me. Behind the screen, just out of my eyeline, Angeline must've nodded because Picot was folding down the sheet. 'I'm going to feel your spine and . . .' He stopped and I sat up a bit, watching his expression. He was staring down at Angeline's lower half, just out of view, and you could tell he didn't know what to say. There was a moment's more hesitation, then he must have sussed Angeline was looking at him, because he put his shirt-sleeve briefly to his head and said, 'Yes, good. Just – uh – let me see now. Turn a little – this way. That's it. On to your side.'

There was a long, long silence, when no one spoke and no one moved, and the only sound was the distant clatter of trolleys in the hospital corridors. Then he cleared his throat. 'Right,' he said. 'Angeline, I'm looking at your spine. OK? I'm

330

just going to run my fingers down it . . .' He swallowed and took a step towards the head of the table, bending sideways and moving both hands just out of sight, drawing them downwards, his tongue between his teeth. 'OK. Now, can you shuffle towards me a bit? That's it – no, stay on your side. I want to see how strong your ankles are.'

Angeline moved, and suddenly, into the small space between the screen and Picot's shirt front came the yellow underside of a foot, and then, when she'd shuffled a bit more, the section of her back that extended from her shoulder-blades to her knees. I was looking up the length of her body. The growth had arranged itself away from her legs so it lay straight down the table towards him, and I could see the exact point where it converged with her spine. I could see the eye-shaped crevice neatly creased between her thighs, just like any other woman, and I could see further up to the point of the eye, to the junction where the growth began, widening away from her coccyx. I blinked. This was weird. I put my hand to my chest. My heart was thumping hard under my shirt.

'I'll just cover you here,' said Picot, reaching under the chair for a blanket, which he placed over her buttocks, so that it hung down into the gap behind the growth, shutting off my view. 'Then I want you to tell me what you can feel and what you can't.'

I shot Lexie another look. She had opened the magazine and was leafing through it – still with her back to me, like she was making a point. I shifted very, very silently in my chair, taking care not to make it creak, so I could watch what Picot was doing. I'd seen the growth before – just for a bit, in the house on the island, but I hadn't seen its base: it was wider than I'd expected – as wide as a wrist – and very pale, with almost the quality of marble to it. I'd had this image of what she'd look like down there – I wouldn't have admitted it to anyone but I'd spent a long time in the last few days wondering about it – and it hadn't been like this. I hadn't expected anything so – I fumbled for the word – so *beautiful*. Yes, I thought, feeling like a bit of a tart for the choice of words: beautiful. That bit of flesh had something I couldn't put a name to – like a sculpture, or a piece of architecture.

'OK,' Picot said, after a while, and there was something different about his voice – a nervousness. He lifted the sheet to cover her. 'I'm – I'm . . . let me see.' He fiddled uncomfortably with his tie and stared at the telephone on the wall, like he wanted to call someone and ask for help. After a while he scratched his neck and, like someone invisible had just asked him what he was going to do, said, 'An X-ray, then an MRI. Yes – right, right.' He pulled off his gloves. 'OK. If I can arrange it, I want to do an MRI. Do you know what an MRI is?'

Angeline shifted on to her back and began to sit up so that everything I had been looking at was replaced by her left hand. 'I think so. It's a—' She broke off. She had moved upright so quickly that I hadn't had time to look away, and she'd caught me staring at her from the other side of the office: pale, bug-eyed, my magazine clutched tightly in my hands. I was frozen, couldn't drag my eyes away, and for a moment we were stuck there, holding each other's eyes, both too surprised and embarrassed to know what to do.

'Angeline?' Picot said. 'Are you . . . ?'

'Yes,' she said hurriedly, grabbing the sheet and pulling it round her protectively. She hadn't taken her eyes off me. 'I'm ready. Where do we go?'

One of Danso's PCs drove us back to the rape suite. I didn't say a word. I sat in the passenger seat, elbows on my knees, smiling rigidly at the windscreen, my head pounding. I was fighting the sinking feeling that this had been waiting somewhere inside me for a lifetime, that it had always been destined to be dragged to the surface one day.

He was a shrewd one, Picot, keeping his cards close to his chest. Even after the MRI he wasn't giving away what he thought was wrong with her.

Instead of answers, we came away with nothing except more questions and a limp, flesh-coloured surgical support. It was just a piece of bandage, boiled soft and covered with hospital laundry marks, and we all knew, when he held it out to Angeline, that it wasn't designed for her and probably wouldn't fit or make any difference anyhow. Back at the house she sat on the sofa under a duvet, one hand hidden beneath it. I couldn't see for sure, but I think she was feeling herself, walking her fingers down her body, re-examining it. I walked round the place, not knowing where to put myself, avoiding meeting her eyes. In the end I went to bed early and lay there, wondering why the fuck I couldn't get what I'd seen out of my head. That night I had an erotic dream about her.

She was sitting on the edge of a swimming-pool, her feet dangling in the water. She was wearing some kind of pink bikini thing, shorts up to her waist, the growth peeping out of one of the leg openings. It lay next to her left leg, glistening with pool water, the tip of it in the pool like it was a creature sucking up water. I was a few feet away in the pool, staring at it, mesmerized. I said something to her, something indistinct and meaningless, and she raised her eyes, smiled, and let the tip of the growth move up her left calf, pausing at the knee. I opened my mouth to speak again, but this time the water rose in a wave behind me and carried me towards her. She opened her arms and her legs and snaked the tail out, like an arm, to pull me hard against her. I woke in the sticky sheets, my heart thudding, buzzing with excitement and sadness.

'What is it?' Lexie murmured sleepily, throwing out a hand. 'You all right? You ill?'

I swung my legs round so my back was to her, put my feet on the ground and sat up to stare at my wet thighs. It was early morning – there was a faint line of light round the curtains. 'I'm fine.'

I waited for the feelings to go – a feeling in my chest like I'd just taken a drug straight in the heart, pure nicotine or one of those amyl-nitrate poppers we used to do at uni. When the blood stopped pounding and my head came back to the ground, I went into the bathroom and stood in front of the mirror, staring at myself.

Man, I thought peering at myself. Hair and muscle and dick. That's all we amount to. I looked down at my cock, still red and half hard. What is going on here, Oakes? I asked myself. What is happening to you?

2

Later that day Angeline went missing. She was gone for four hours, and it was me who found her. I took the Fiesta and drove round the deserted streets, the sound of syringes cracking under the tyres. She was half a mile away, on the main road that bordered the estate. There was a newsagent with bars on the windows and a postbox outside, and she was standing in front of them, staring at the traffic going back and forward. We'd given her some money to spend in Dumbarton and she was dressed differently now: under her leather coat she was wearing a skirt she'd patched together out of two others and a ribbed brown sweater with a McFly badge pinned to it. I watched her for a moment or two from the car, trying not to think about what was under that coat. I'd made up my mind. It was time to tell her to move on.

I pulled into the kerb, leaned across the passenger seat and opened the door. 'Hey. We didn't know where you were. Everyone's worried.'

She hesitated. Then she climbed into the car and closed the door, arranging the coat round her, rubbing her nose. I didn't look too close, but I got a sort of thumbnail image of raw eyes and veins broken in her cheeks. She'd been crying. We sat there for a long time not speaking. The billboard outside the newsagent said, '*Terrorist Experts in Nationwide Manhunt*'.

'Angeline?' I said. 'Were you trying to go somewhere? Someone's house? Do you want me to drive you somewhere?'

She shook her head and wiped her eyes. 'No,' she said thickly. 'I just wanted a walk.'

'There's nowhere I can take you?'

'I don't know anyone. Only you.' She pulled on the seatbelt, the way she'd seen Lex and me do it, and sat, her hands on her lap, looking out of the windscreen. 'I've been thinking,' she said, 'about what happened yesterday.'

I felt the muscles in my face lock solid. I knew she was looking at me, shyly searching my face, trying to make sense of me.

'I've made up my mind. If there's an operation I'm not going to have it.' There was a long, long pause. 'You think I'm right, don't you? You think I'd be wrong to have an operation.'

I should say something. I was supposed to say something – something adult. But my head had gone rigid. I reached across her and locked the door. 'Do something for me, Angeline.' I put the car into gear and took off the handbrake. 'Don't come out here again. You don't know who might drive past.'

* * *

The next few days there was this slow, pressure-cooker feeling in the rape suite. Angeline ignored what I'd said about going out on the road: every day she'd leave the house and be gone for hours. The surveillance car didn't follow her either: me and the officers had talked about it and decided to stop arguing with her, decided we weren't her keepers. Secretly I was relieved. It was easier when she wasn't around. I didn't like the way she kept watching me, like she was waiting for me to say something.

Lexie knew something was wrong. She kept staring at me and asking me weird questions until my chest was tight and my head felt like it was full of blood and I spent as much time as I could away from her, locked in the office I'd rigged up in the third bedroom, the one with the cot and puke on the wall, trying to work on the proposal. I shut myself up and wrote like crazy: two K words a day, trying to cram all my thoughts on to the hard drive, my hands clamped to my head, moving ideas around until my brain was like catfood and I knew how the Sputnik monkey felt. But it didn't matter how hard I wrote, I couldn't get two people out of my head: Angeline Dove and her dad, Malachi.

Danso and I talked about it all the time: we spent hours going through the paperwork from the cottage, pushing it all around. Every night he'd stop by on his way home from work and every night he'd bring things for us. Bribes to keep me sweet, I decided, to stop me going back to London. One day it was a bottle of Jura malt whisky. One day a pound of farmed smoked salmon. Fuck knows where he was financing it from – his own pocket maybe – but none of us complained. Lexie got one of the guys in the surveillance car to bring down a jar of capers from Oban when he came on duty and we ate them with the salmon, using our fingers, sitting in a circle like cave people. I always asked Danso about the sightings of Dove. I asked him to show me on the map where they all were and I plotted them. When he'd gone I'd spend the night looking at the map, thinking about what these random sightings meant.

Then, suddenly, on the Thursday morning, the police got a lead.

Someone had spotted a blue Vauxhall near the southern tip of Loch Awe. Within an hour someone else called in a report: Dove wandering near a stone bothy tucked up in a crevice of the nearby hills in Inverliever Forest. The police brought out the Royal Logistics Corps – used to clearing military land and unexploded Second World War ordnance. They stuck a specialized probe into the bothy window and siphoned off air into absorbent cartridges. When the explosives test came out

339

negative the support unit got sent in to batter down
the door. There was no one inside.

'Empty,' said Danso, that evening at the rape
suite. 'But the thing is, it's only a mile from a chalet
owned by one of the ex-members of the PHM. And
she was on our TI list.'

'TI?'

'Trace and Interview. We'd cleared her on
Tuesday, but then this came up and started sounding klaxons.'

I pulled on my coat.

'What are you doing?'

'I want to see it.'

'There's nothing to see. He's not there. It's just a
wee bothy with a load of crap in it.'

'There is something to see.' I pulled my car keys
out of my pocket. 'You're just not looking at it
right.'

Danso sighed. He massaged his forehead, like I
was making him tired. 'We're not looking at it
through his eyes?'

'That's right.'

'And you're going to explain to the missus why
I'm late home *again*?'

'You don't have to take me. Tell me where it is. I
don't need you to hold my hand.'

'Yes, you do,' he said, all weary. 'Yes, you do.'

* * *

We drove in convoy: me clinging to the tail-lights of his black Bimmer. We headed north along the B840 and at eight o'clock we hit the edge of Inverliever Forest – those fuck-off, dark-as-hell mountains that swept out of the night skies and disappeared vertically below the still, dark waters of Loch Avich. We were a long way north. I wondered what it meant that Dove had changed direction. He'd gone north and not south towards London. When we stopped, in a small lane that wound up along the edge of a burn into the cleft between two mountains, it was like we'd gone into another universe.

'See the chalet?'

We'd walked half-way up the path when Danso stopped and turned to look down to the road and the loch. He pointed at a small shingle-roofed house on the shore, outlined in silver by the water behind it. It was planted with a border of leylandii and as I looked a security light came on briefly – a cat or a hedgehog maybe, lighting the trees from inside.

'The family's gone now, off to their home in London. Left us with a key, but we've checked. It's clean.' He turned to the west, pointing a long finger, pale in the half-light. I looked across the sky to where the stars and a few clouds were reflected in the loch. 'The Vauxhall was over there, at the far end, just parked in a layby at teatime on Wednesday. You can't see the layby from here.

Then we've got a taxi-driver says he stopped for a whizz down here, at the bottom of this path where we've just left the cars, and he looks up and sees Malachi Dove standing in the door of the bothy, staring down at him. Said it was like being watched by an eagle.' Danso turned and began to walk up the path. 'That's when the night shift DS gets on the phone and gets me out of the first decent sleep I've had in a week.'

I followed him, keeping my eyes on his good shoes that his missus must've picked for a quiet day in the office but which kept slithering on the hummocky grass. Sheep lumbered away from us in the darkness, heavy, cloudy shadows, hoofing into the higher slopes. The wind scattered leaves and parted the grass like hair, but under my coat I was sweating. I tried feeling inside myself, trying to put a finger on my fear, but I couldn't. Dove wasn't here. He wasn't here. In front of me Danso walked with his shoulders wide, back stiffened, his face and chest open. He was scared too, I saw. But he wasn't going to tell me that.

We crossed a cattle grid and there was the bothy, tucked between two sheer rock faces. Ten feet away we paused and looked at it in silence. The roof was moss-covered, the window-frames rotted away into two dull sockets. A thin line of police tape flapped in the wind.

'It was locked when we got here,' Danso said. The wind took his voice and blew it into the empty building, battering it against the cold walls. 'The SG sergeant kicked the door down like it was a matchstick. Here.' He handed me a torch. 'Have a look.'

I approached the building and slowly opened the door, nothing more than five planks nailed together and hung from rusty hinges. It was dark and there was a smell that sent an uncomfortable prickle along my hairline. For a moment I thought I could hear breathing, something reedy and thin bouncing off the walls. I clicked off the torch and waited, my heart thudding. Then the wind changed direction and popped my ears, and I decided I'd imagined it. I shone the torch into the darkness. I saw flashes of a bare earth floor, plants growing on the inside walls, a stack of White Lightning cider bottles in the corner.

'What're they?'

There was a pile of towels bunched in the corner.

'We think he was injured. There was blood on some of them. The science boys have got them over in the labs now, trying to make a match.'

I stepped away from the bothy. I went up a small path to where the land rose so I could survey the area. I clicked the torch on and off, a nervous tic. 'What's out here?' I murmured, looking at the faint

343

greyish line of the path winding back down to the road, the glimmer of the loch beyond. 'What's here?'

'The chalet?' Danso came and stood beside me. 'It's only over there.'

'No. The chalet is *how* he knows this place . . . but it's not *why* he came here. He came for something else.'

I switched off the torch and we stood in the darkness, our ears reaching out across the mountains and the forests, pinging our thoughts like sonar against the glassy surface of the loch. I turned to Danso. He was staring at the sky, a gnawed-at, hungry look to him – the way people get when they're close to the end of their energy.

'He scares you,' I murmured, 'doesn't he?'

There was a moment's silence. Then he said, 'I've never worked a mass death before. Missed Dunblane, Ibrox, Mull, Lockerbie. Missed them all. I've never seen more than three dead bodies in the same place at the same time and that was an RTA.'

'I don't mean that. I mean *him*. He scares you.'

He hesitated, shuffled his feet. 'I'd like to know how he knew we were coming.' He glanced over his shoulder at the bothy. 'No one saw him leave. When the SG kicked the door in they thought he was in there. You'd think he had a tunnel or something, the way he got out so quick.'

'That's what I mean. He scares you.'

Danso met my eyes. He held them seriously for a long time. Then he clicked on his torch and shone it down on my shoes. They were covered with black slime. 'Sheep shit,' he said. 'Sorry. I forgot to tell you to put boots on. There're sheep all over the place here.'

Lexie

1

Dear Mr Taranici,

Please believe me when I say things have gone very wrong. Very wrong indeed. I've done so many things in the last hour, said things that I can never, ever take back. Really I think I might be going mad because the world is upside-down. The worst thing is, I don't know who to believe any more. I've discovered I'm being systematically lied to. And no, before you even think it, *I am not being paranoid*. I know it for a fact.

I was on the sofa this morning watching the news – more about the hunt for Malachi – and Oakesy was up in his room, working. It was another awful day, with rain lashing the house, and I was vaguely aware of someone upstairs moving around, but I wasn't really paying attention. It was only when I heard a door slam that I muted the TV and looked up at the ceiling: someone was walking around on the landing. Another door opened and closed. The floorboards were creaking in the bathroom, a bath was running. At first it was just that and the rain pelting down outside. Then from the landing I heard Oakesy say, very sadly, as if he was about to cry, 'I love my wife.'

I stared at the stairs, my mouth open. *I love my wife?* A toxic little bubble of suspicion detached itself from the bottom of my stomach and floated upwards. He must be talking to Angeline. But why was he talking about me? I leaned over and switched off the TV, feeling suddenly very cold. A whole stack of images shuttled down behind my eyes, unbelievable, ridiculous things, things that had been staring me in the face when I thought about it: Oakesy standing in front of the sink, kicking the cupboard; Oakesy stricken and sick-looking in the car on the way back from the hospital, echoing my words, *Disgusted? Disgusted.* And Angeline beginning to look after herself since the visit to the hospital, even washing and putting on makeup, combing her hair so it covers the bald patches, somehow getting her skin cleared up, all in all looking quite wholesome. I looked at the cupboard. It couldn't be. Couldn't possibly be . . .

And then he appeared, coming heavily down the stairs. I went to the foot of the stairs and when he saw me he stopped. He shook his head silently, as if he didn't trust himself to speak, as if what he had to say was just too awful.

'Joe,' I said faintly. 'Joe, why did you just tell Angeline you love me?'

Well, he could have answered any way he wanted and I'd have probably listened. He could have denied it, or laughed, or been affronted. But he did none of those things. He did something worse. Much worse. He said *nothing*. He just stood there, staring at me.

'It seems such a funny thing to say,' I said woodenly, feeling as if someone had put their hand inside my ribcage and was squeezing my heart. My skin went hot and cold, then hot again. 'Joe? Please, Joe, please. Tell me you're joking. Come on. This is a joke.'

'I'm sorry.' He pulled his jacket from the banisters and threw it on, pulling his keys out of his pocket. 'Lex, you won't believe me, but I'm sorry.'

He pushed past me and headed for the door.

'Joe?' I stared at him, disbelief washing up and over me. 'Joe? Wait. *Wait*—' He pulled the front door open. A gust of wind and rain came into the hallway, nearly taking me off my feet, but he leaned forward into it and went out, into the streaming day, his jacket whipping and slapping around him like a parachute, leaving me in the doorway. I stood there for a few seconds, thinking stupidly that my shoes were lying on the floor in the kitchen and I couldn't go out without them. Then I saw him hold the key up and heard the beep as the car doors unlocked and I knew then it was real and he was going. I ran out barefoot into the rain, the wind driving water into my eyes. '*Wait, Joe. Wait!*' He was already swinging into the car. He slammed the door, and as I got to the kerb I heard the central-locking system clunk closed and that made me panic. I scrabbled at the handle, the wind driving me flat against the car. '*Open the door!*' I hammered at it with my bare hands. I could see the side of his face through the greasy, rain-drenched window. He looked grey, cold. He wouldn't look at me as he reached down and turned the key.

'For God's sake, Joe. Talk to me!'

The headlights went on. The engine came to life. He took the handbrake off, twisted the steering-wheel and pulled away. The tyres sent up a massive whoosh of water from the gutters, soaking my trousers, making me take a shocked step back-wards. He got to the top of the street and the brake-lights came on, turning all the raindrops around them to rubies, then he was gone – swallowed into the dark storm, leaving me standing barefoot in the pouring rain with the wretched shopping trolley moving up and down the pavement opposite, thinking, *What? What just happened? What just happened?*

2

For those first few minutes after he'd gone I really didn't know what to do. It was like I was in a dream. I stood there soaking, thinking he was going to come back and say, 'Ha ha – got you.' When he didn't I limped back into the house, streaming with water. I stood at the foot of the stairs and stared up at Angeline's door, thinking, No, no. This isn't happening. She's deformed. She's ugly. So ugly.

I got my phone out and dialled Oakesy's mobile, my fingers numb. It was impossible to believe. Oakesy and Angeline . . . And it was *me* who'd had the idea of her staying with us *in the first place*. 'Answer it. Come on. Answer it.'

But the phone rang and rang. My head thumped as if it was going to split right open. The call went to answerphone.

'*No!* You *bastard.* NO!'

I called again and this time it clicked straight through to his messages. He'd switched it off. Didn't want to speak to me. I called him again – and when it went on to answerphone I immediately hung up and called again, jabbing my thumb furiously at the phone, three, four times, crying now, and when I still couldn't get through I went into the kitchen, shakily got his bottle of Jack Daniel's out of the cupboard, poured two inches into a cloudy glass, then filled it up with some flat cola from an opened can in the fridge. I drank it down straight, shaking like a leaf, dripping water everywhere, tears running down my face. Then I poured another and sat at the table, the phone held at arm's length, jabbing his number in over and over again. When I'd dialled twenty times and his phone was still switched off I hurled my phone into the wastepaper bin and went to the window. I stood there for a long time, holding my face, my nails digging into the skin. That's when I remembered something you said to me once.

You're an achiever, Alex.

Do you remember those words?

You are clever, Alex, whatever you think, and you've got the ability to achieve whatever you set out to do.

I paused, standing there at the window, looking at the shopping trolley, and at that very moment something inside me went cold and hard. I actually felt it freeze into place, solid, just like that. I stopped crying. I wiped my eyes. I was very calm.

And angry. Very angry. I turned away from the
window and looked up at the door at the top of
the stairs. Then I limped over to the bin and hooked
out the phone. I dialled Guy Picot's number. I'm
an achiever. I am not weak. I do what I set out to
do.

3

Guy Picot pretended he didn't recognize my voice.
When I explained who I was he was a little cool. To
put it mildly. 'Yes, Alex. I was going to give you a
call today – to let Angeline know I've sent her
a referral letter.'

'And you're sending one to Christophe?' I kept
my sentences short because I was shaking and I
didn't want him to know I'd been crying. 'He'll
contact me directly. We're very old friends and
colleagues.'

'It's more orthodox for the doctor to liaise
directly with the patient. Angeline didn't say she
wanted an intermediary.'

'Look, really, this is the smoothest way. Mr
Radnor knows I've been involved in this from the
start. He'll deal with Angeline through me from
now on.'

There was a moment's hesitation, then he said, 'The referral letter doesn't have Mr Radnor's name on it.'

I opened my mouth to say something, then closed it. I went to the bottom of the stairs and looked up to make sure her door was closed, then I went and stood at the window. Outside the rain tipped down on the dead playing-fields, streamed down the sides of the Ballantine's factory. 'I beg your pardon,' I said, in a much quieter voice. 'If you're not referring her to Christophe, then where are you referring her? You're meant to refer her to Christophe.'

'It was a very difficult decision. I had to decide between referring her to an oncologist or a paediatric surgeon. I still may be proved wrong, but I've decided on the latter. I'm passing her on to Great Ormond Street.'

'*Great Ormond Street?* This isn't something for a *paediatrician.*'

'Angeline's condition is not in Mr Radnor's field.'

'Of course it is.'

'No. Really it isn't.'

'Why ever not?'

He sighed. 'When we were talking in my office your husband mentioned something that stuck with me.'

'My husband's got nothing to do with this.'

'Angeline's mother lived near a chemical dump, that's what he said. Herbicides. Dioxins. Richard Spitz's team will explain it to you,' he said. 'They've seen the MRI scans, and they're showing great interest. They really want to—'

'Richard Spitz?' I stopped him. *Did you say Richard Spitz? The* Richard Spitz?'

'Yes. *The* Richard Spitz.'

'My God,' I said distantly, staring out at the trees bent almost double in the wind. Everything was becoming clear. I had a friend who'd once worked for Richard Spitz and I knew exactly what Guy was saying. 'My God. Now I get it.'

'Now you get what?'

'*That*'s why there's bone. That's why she's still alive. That's why.'

Guy Picot was right: Christophe has no background in what's wrong with Angeline. Her 'tail' wasn't a tumour at all. And nothing to do with spina bifida either. Which means everything I've done for her has been a complete waste of my time. Absolutely *everything*.

Oakesy

1

The landing was dark when I came out of the third bedroom – no electric lights. There was a little weak daylight coming from the bathroom where the door stood open and the sound of a bath running. I knew who was in there. I wasn't stupid. I *knew* who was running the bath. So why didn't I just go back to my work? Oh, no. That would be too easy for Joe Oakes.

I took a silent step forward and stopped in the doorway. She was in there, hazy in the steam, a towel wrapped round her, bending over the bath to swirl the water. It took her a moment or two to sense me standing at the door, and when she did she stiffened. She didn't look up. She went very still, her hands motionless in the water. A slow, hot colour crept across her bare shoulders, up the back of her long neck into her cropped hair. It seemed like for ever before she straightened, her back very stiff and strong, and turned to me.

We stood for a long time totally silent, neither of us knowing what to say. I could see in her eyes how totally full of questions she was. Her triangular little chin was down almost on to her collarbone and she was shaking violently. But she didn't take her eyes off me. She took a deep breath and put her shoulders back. It was like she was pulling all her courage up inside her, into a tight rod. She turned slightly, not breaking eye-contact, dropped her hand and in one movement lifted the towel up high – as high as her waist so I could see everything: her naked legs, the naked place the growth jutted out from at the bottom of her spine.

'Shit.' I took a step back. I steadied myself on the banisters behind me. 'Shit—' I dropped my head and stared at the floor, the blood pounding in my face. Tried to gather the right words. 'Listen . . .' I went, but my voice came out slushy and flat – like I was drunk. 'Listen. I'm sorry – I'm sorry. You've got me wrong. I love my wife. *I really love my wife . . .*'

2

In my last year at university there was a book doing the rounds of the halls of residence: *The Encyclopedia of Unusual Sex Practices*. Written by a Californian academic who went by the unlikely name of Brenda Love ('Yeah, right,' said all the undergrads, 'like that's her real name'). It was on everyone's must-read list. 'It's, like, crammed to the ears with mind-boggling things to do with your todger,' Finn told me, when he sent me a copy from the States. The closing line of the section on *zoophilia* (or *bestiality*, if you want its common-or-garden name) was the one all the undergraduates kept whispering to each other, creasing up about: 'Sex with a partner that has little intelligence, superior strength and who panics easily, is risky . . .'

Page 298: Zoophilia
- *Zoophilia involves sex between humans and animals and generally takes more forms than does sex between humans. Some of our ancestors felt that sex with animals held a magic power . . .*

There are different kinds of zoophiliacs, and if you really think your head's on tight enough you can track down that encyclopedia and read all about them: androzons, avisodomists, bestial-sadists, formicophiliacs, necrobestialists, ophidicists. But the one I kept thinking about time and again was the 'gynozoon'. A Roman obsession this, a gynozoon was a female animal trained for sex with a human male.

At university I'd read *The Encyclopedia of Unusual Sex Practices* from cover to cover, taking it all in: guys who can't get off without electric shocks, or armpit sex, or licking their partner's eyeball. (Making it up? I wish I was.) There was still a copy of that book somewhere in my study in London, but I hadn't thought about it for years. Not until now. Now I thought about it over and over again until my head was thumping. I kept thinking about the gynozoon. A gynozoon.

Page 92 I: Dysmorphophilia

- *Dysmorphophilia: (dys: abnormal. morphe: form. philia: attraction) Those who are sexually aroused by deformities in their partners. It's linked to acrotomophilia and apotemnophilia and for some dysmorphophiliacs the strong sense of compassion or fear may condition them to . . . confuse this excitement with sexual arousal. Others feel emotionally secure or in control when their partner does not have the ability to leave them for someone else. Others*

*need to nurture or rescue a sex partner to feel
love of bonding and some are simply attracted by
novelty . . .*

I walked out of the rape suite and into the pouring rain and I didn't have a clue where I was going. I just put the car into gear and went, not thinking about the turnings I was taking, half blind to my surroundings. I wanted to be out on the road, Lex and Angeline behind me. When Lexie called I switched off the phone, threw it on to the passenger seat and went on driving. On and on and on, dodging trucks and coaches, the Massive Attack CD in the deck playing until it was making a hole in my head. I didn't even notice when the rain eased off, changed to drizzle, when the passing cars switched off their headlights, and the weak autumn sun burned out from the clouds. It didn't cross my mind I was heading west. It was only when I'd been driving for two hours and saw a sign I recognized that I slowed the car down and woke up a bit. The post office at Ardfern. I was on Craignish Peninsula. The hairs went up on the backs of my hands. Something had led me back here, like it was the most familiar place I could turn.

I drove on a little further, slower now. I hadn't been here since the night I came back and picked up our stuff. The bungalow drive was barer now autumn was here, more visible from the road. I turned up it, leaning forward to study the bungalow as it evolved out of the trees, all shut up and dull-looking, its windows filthy from the earlier rain. This was the last place I'd slept a night through – instead of lying there like a torture victim, thinking either about Malachi Dove or about his daughter. The bungalow hadn't changed much.

Half-way up the track I stopped the engine. I chocked the wheels and stared out of the windscreen. Now I didn't have the mindless business of driving to deal with, I started to shake. It was early afternoon and the storm must've gone west to east, because the sun was reflecting little dewdrops of rain in the trees like diamonds. Across the loch a flash of coloured light came from the shore. I stared at it, thinking about Lex standing in the rain in Dumbarton, crying as I drove away. I balled my fist, rested it on my temple, wanting to hit myself, wanting to knock the thoughts out of my head.

'You stupid fucking arse.'

I hadn't seen her cry in years. It was the kind of crying you do after a shock, the same kind of crying I did after the massacre. I'd never wanted to see her doing it. Never had. I looked at the phone on the passenger seat. What did I do now? Did I just turn round, pick up the phone and say, *I'm sorry, babe, been meaning to mention it to you for months – our marriage is in the toilet.* Or did I lie? It was going to have to be a lie. I'd have to lie to her. I reached for the phone, was about to pick it up, when something made me stop. Something I hadn't registered properly till now. I dropped my hand and slowly, very slowly, a thought racing over me like a shiver, I raised my eyes back to the loch.

The point of light was still there. Sunlight reflecting off a window. I stared at it, my thoughts going dead slow, dead cautious. There were some cottages over there, just a few clustered round the shore. They were due south, on the other side of the loch, where the land curved round to face the peninsula. Suddenly, without knowing how I knew, I realized I was looking at Ardnoe Point. The place they found the dory.

I opened the car door and got out, buttoning my jacket, staring at the light. I'd been there once, with Struthers, three days after the massacre, just to have a look. Wasn't much to see: a few cottages, a beach that wasn't a beach at all, just a tidal mud-flat, marshy, matted with eelweed stretching dimly out to the water, one or two pieces of police tape still snagged in the weeds' clumps. The boat had been lying on its side, not tied up – another reason Struthers thought Dove had floated up here by accident, then bailed out. We'd talked about it a bit. What we'd never realized was how, if we'd just turned a bit to our right, we could've seen the bungalow across the loch.

I leaned into the car and pulled out the roadmap from the webbing at the back of the passenger seat. I opened it on the roof of the car and studied it closely, my elbow on it, looking up from time to time at Ardnoe Point, still glinting in the distance. No pen in my pockets so I used my thumbnail to make a mark on the map – a neat cross over Ardnoe Point. Then I walked backwards a few paces, going up the track until I got to the place in the bungalow gardens where you could see inland, over to where Loch Avich must be. The bothy, the place I'd gone with Danso that night, trying to work out what Dove was planning, was in the mountains over there.

I stood for a few moments, letting my thoughts slosh dreamily around. Ardnoe Point was to my left. The bothy was behind me and to my right. And the shopping centre at Inverary was . . . I snatched up the map. It took me a moment to focus. When I did my heart started to beat, very slow and deliberate, in my chest.

I will run rings around you. I will, in the final hour, will run rings around you.

The bungalow. When I looked at the four points, Ardnoe Point, the bothy, Inverary and Pig Island, they made a circle round Craignish. Round the bungalow. I slammed my hand flat on the map, my heart thumping hard. For the last week Malachi had been circling the bungalow. He thought we were still there. I raised my eyes, scanning the horizon, the trees, the bungalow behind me with its blank windows.

Where are you now?

Just like it wanted to answer my question, a car on the road slowed to watch me. I closed the map very slowly, staring at it. It was an English car, dark blue. A cold line of fear traced its way up my spine, into my hair: the car stolen from the Crinian car park was a dark blue Vauxhall. I was at least two hundred yards away but I could tell it was a bloke driving it – a bloke with sandy or blond hair and dressed in something pale: a golfing sweater, maybe. *Shit*, I thought, my heart thudding, my limbs going a bit numb. *Is that you? Is it?*

I opened the door and threw the map inside, trying to look calm. The car didn't move. I took the keys out of the Fiesta's ignition. Staying casual, even though I was shaking, I turned and began to walk towards the road. I was going to speak to him. Just talk. That's what he wanted. A flock of birds twisted and banked in the flat blue sky above us, menacing as a stormcloud, and from somewhere distant came the thin, briny cry of a curlew. I didn't look up at the sky – just kept walking, my paces even, measured, my breathing steady.

As I got nearer I could see that what I'd thought was sandy blond hair was a baseball cap, pulled down close over his ears, and just as I was about to get a good view of the driver he floored the accelerator and sped away. I broke into a run, skidding in the gravel, stopping at the centre of the road, feet planted wide, staring at the dwindling dab of darkness on the road: vanishing to the south, in the direction of Lochgilphead, away from Craignish Point.

It's not him. Of course it's not him.

I stood there, suspended for a few beats of time in a silent bubble of disbelief, that dot of colour disappearing in my retina. *Why would he be so casual? It was just a local – slowing down to see if I was on the rob.* But my blood was up now. I raced back to the Fiesta, fired it up. Not a chase car, it struggled and whined as I forced it along the road – sixty, seventy, eighty, my heart pounding. Off the peninsula and right along the coast. The car reached a forest, then abruptly, with no warning, swung to the right and we were in the flat marsh-lands near the river Add. Over a bridge and the road became a narrow canalside single-laner. The Fiesta screamed along it, passing a turning to the right – *that way, or stay on this road?* – and another, and another. Then a bridge to the left over the canal and a glimpse of red-painted narrow-boats, bikes chained to the roofs. Rusty chimneys puffed woodsmoke into the cold air.

I fumbled the mobey off the front seat and switched it on, my eyes going up and down from the display to the car in front. It chimed out a tune, the screen flaring up. Twenty-five missed calls from Lexie, and before I had time to jam in Danso's number, it jumped to life. Lexie again. I tossed the phone on to the passenger seat, and floored the Fiesta down the narrow lane. I turned another corner and saw, less than a hundred yards ahead of me, a camper-van lumbering along, fat-bellied, taking up the whole of the road, brushing the hedgerows. I jammed on the brakes and came to a halt in the middle of the road, hands clenched on the wheel, leaning forward, my nose almost pressed to the wind-screen, breathing so hard I could've run the last few miles. I was beaten. I knew it. These roads were straight and uncompromising, but they were a warren for a chase. Dove could be anywhere by now.

The camper-van waddled and swayed until it was swallowed into the distance. On the seat the mobey rang again. I pulled the car over and waited for Lexie's call to go to answerphone, then I snatched it up and jammed in the number for the Oban incident room. Got Danso to send out a couple of patrol cars. Then I drove around, slowing to peer down any driveway or farm path or layby. Every five minutes the phone rang on the passenger seat, twisting and turning on the upholstery, arsed off I wasn't answering. She wasn't giving up. I couldn't talk to her. Not now. I took a left and continued in an arc over the head of the Crinian canal. After about twenty minutes I saw one of the police cars – unmarked, but you could have spotted it a mile away – cruising slow, predator-wise, in the opposite direction, the driver and passenger both chewing hard, craning their necks and staring, *gagging* to get into a high-speed chase. I didn't acknowledge them, just drove past, anonymous. I knew it was over. All I could do now was check the same places again and again. The phone began to ring and this time I nosed the car into the hedgerow and snatched it up impatiently.

'Look, I'll call you back.'

'No, you won't,' she said coldly.

'We'll talk later.'

'Fuck you, Joe. We'll talk now. Don't insult my intelligence. Please.'

I killed the engine, pulled the phone out from where I'd wedged it under my chin and clamped it against my mouth so she'd hear me better. 'Lex, we're going to talk, but not now. I'm in the middle of something.'

'I'm going to ask you a question,' she said, in a controlled voice. 'And when you answer it's going to be an honest answer. I want to know the truth. *The truth*, Joe,' she said emphatically, like it was something I was a complete stranger to. There was a long pause. Then she said, 'Do you love me?'

'I'll come home. We'll talk—'

'I *said*, do you love me?'

I took a deep breath. In the distance a car pulled on to the road and headed towards me. I stared at it, just a dot, my eyes aching.

'It's an easy question. Not quantum physics, Joe. Do you love me, do you fancy me, do you still want to fuck me, the woman who has stuck by you for years and fucking years while you piss away your degree up a wall, or do you want to fuck some ugly shitty little *shitty* little *bitch cow*?' She broke off, breathing hard. I could almost smell her bitter breath down the phone. 'Do you know what's wrong with her, Joe? *Do you?* Have you got any idea, or are you just content to leave it to me – the one who's actually *bothered* to get herself some kind of medical training?'

I stared blankly at the road, a tightness straddling my windpipe. I wanted to sort it in my head, find a response, something to say. But I couldn't. Just couldn't get my head to work.

'She's a *freak of nature* and *if you fancy her* you

are a pervert – and you should be put out of your misery, you fucking horrible, *horrible freak*—'

'Lex, listen—'

'I'm going upstairs *now* and I'm going to tell her that she DISGUSTS YOU. You get it? And then, when you come back, you're going to go into her room and tell her that SHE DISGUSTS YOU. You're going to tell her you don't *fuck freaks*.'

She broke down into a series of staccato sobs, her breath hitching and catching. The car drew nearer, the grey sky reflected milkily on its windscreen. My hand was stony on the steering-wheel. Grey. There was a long time while I listened to her sniffle and get herself under control.

'You're not saying anything,' she muttered, after a while. 'You've gone quiet.'

'When I get home we'll sit down and talk about this.'

'No, *fuck you*, Joe. I'm not sitting down with you and—'

'Fuck you, Lexie.'

She took a furious breath, gobsmacked that I'd answered her back. '*Don't you dare talk to me like that. Don't you d*—'

'What? You get to talk to me like that but I can't do the same?'

'I'm not the fucking *adulterer* in this relationship,'

she screamed. 'Being *cheated* on gives me some rights.'

'I *haven't* cheated on you.'

'But you want to. *Don't you? Don't you?*'

I didn't answer. I thumbed the cancel-call button, switched off the phone, dropped it in my lap and put my elbows on the steering-wheel, resting my chin on them. I sat there for a long time, moving my chin back and forward so that the skin wrinkled and stretched, wrinkled and stretched, watching the car draw near and slow to a crawl to pass me: it was a 2.4 family in an SUV, two stocky, buzz-cut kids in the back, battering each other with helium Nemo balloons. Not Dove. Not him at all.

Lexie

1

After the phone call to Oakesy I was shaking so hard my teeth were chattering: actually banging against each other. I'd given him every chance – every chance – to weasel out of it. But he didn't. He just went back to that awful guilty silence. I got up and stood at the bottom of the stairs, breathing in and out, trying to stop crying, knowing I was about to do something I'd regret the rest of my life.

Going up to her room was an effort. Every step I wanted to cry. But I wasn't going to let *her* know that, of course. I stood on the landing outside her door and pushed the tears off my face, taking a deep breath, pulling myself up as straight as I could. I didn't knock – why should I? – I just pushed the door open and stood there, tall and straight, in the doorway. The curtains were closed and the bedside light was on. She was sitting on the bed with her back to the wall, looking at me in surprise, defensive and wary. Her legs were curled up under her, hidden in a mishmash skirt with grubby-looking patches of Indian silk, Paisley and suede all sewn together. My heart beat really hard when I thought about what was under that skirt. What *I* knew that *she* didn't . . .

A small pelvic girdle with free extremity, adipose tissue, muscles and a rudimentary bowel sac . . . That's what I'll be telling Mr Spitz—

'Angeline,' I said. 'I'm going to tell you something.'

'T-tell me something?'

'Yes. Now, take off your clothes. Put them on the floor, then stand in front of the bed and I'll tell you something.'

She stared at me uncomprehendingly.

'I said, take off your clothes.'

'No,' she said faintly. 'No.'

'*Yes!*' I licked my lips. 'Yes, Angeline, you will because – because *I* know what's wrong with you. I've been talking to Dr Picot.'

She stopped shaking her head when I said 'Dr Picot'. Her chin went up and her eyes locked on mine.

'I know what's made you like you are. I know what's made you into a . . .' I put my hand on the doorframe, digging my nails into the wood. I knew if I didn't concentrate very hard I might cry. *Parasitic. Acardiac and anencephalic – no heart and no head. Parasitic . . .* 'Into a freak. I know why you're a *freak*. So—' God, I had to gulp the air down to stay in control. 'So – now. Take. Off. Your. Clothes.'

She stared at me, a little pulse beating in the side of her neck, every corner of her brain processing what I was saying. An age seemed to go by. Then, just as I was about to say it again, something happened. She seemed suddenly to collect all her courage. She pushed herself off the bed on to her feet so quickly I took an instinctive step back, but she stopped a few inches in front of me, her arms at her sides, trembling like a leaf, and for a moment I just stared at her speechlessly. Then she pulled off her sweater and threw it on the floor.

I blinked very, very slowly, letting my eyes stay closed for a few seconds until my heart calmed down. Then I opened them again. She was wearing a short-sleeved T-shirt; her arms were bare and unexpectedly muscular. She was still looking at me, but her throat was working as if she was trying hard not to be sick or to cry.

'The rest,' I said hoarsely. 'Take everything off.'

She pulled off the T-shirt, raising her arms, giving me a flash of underarm hair. She was very thin with small breasts and waist, but her hips were really wide and layered with muscle. She was wearing a greying, lace-trimmed bra that looked as if it had been washed about a hundred times. She unhooked it and let it drop to the ground, showing me her tiny breasts. I had to fight not to lower my eyes.

'And the – the skirt.'

She unzipped it and stepped out of it, kicking it aside. She wasn't wearing underwear. It was just her legs, thin and a bit scarred round the knees, and her dark pubic hair, but she didn't try to hide herself. She was looking me right in the eye. The blood raced to my face.

'Turn round,' I whispered. 'Turn round and face the bed.'

She didn't move. We stood there for a long time, holding each other's eyes, and I had this sense we were teetering on an edge, that this could go either way. Something in my head was screaming for it to stop, stop.

'I said, *turn round*.'

The room was silent. Downstairs the washing-machine went into its final spin and that was the only noise, apart from us both breathing. Then Angeline swallowed. I could hear it, could hear all the ligaments and muscles clicking together.

'Whatever,' she said tightly, tears welling in her eyes. 'Whatever you tell me – I've thought about it. And I'm not going to have an operation. I'm not ashamed.'

And before I could answer she took a step away from me to the bed and turned and suddenly there it was, all displayed in front of me. I put my hand on the doorframe to steady myself, my eyes wide and fixed. The tail – except I knew it wasn't a tail – came out of her spine like a giant tree root. It went out backwards a little, then hung down slightly to the side.

A collection of calcifications in the pelvis, a single deformed long bone erupting from the sacro-coccygeal region. Parasitic . . .

Her hands hovered in the region of her back for a second, then she raised them – straight up in the air so there was nothing I couldn't look at. I could see now, now that I knew, I could see clearly that it wasn't a tail but a deformed leg.

Parasitic. A parasitic limb . . .

There was a thick, visible vein that ran along the top of it, down to the swollen tip, which must have been a crude, spade-shaped foot. I pictured what I knew was inside her: half a twin with its mouth open, drinking Angeline's blood, yawning and hiccuping and baring its bloodied teeth the way a baby does in the womb. I pictured her heart pounding, thinking of it working hard to feed her twin. I wanted to hit her. I wanted to pull at the leg, tear it out of her. It was unthinkable Oakesy could fancy her. With her looking like this . . . how *anyone* could want to . . .

I bit down hard on my tongue, a bud of blood welling through my teeth until the urge to hit her went.

'*Duplicata incompleta*,' I said, my voice coming out louder than I'd expected. '*Duplicata incompleta*. Incomplete separation.'

There was a pause. Angeline's arms seemed to waver a bit, as if they were suddenly heavier. But she raised them up again, trembling with the effort. 'I'm not going to have an operation,' she said, in a small, strained voice. 'I'm not like this because of anything I did and there's nothing—'

'A parasitic twin. No head. No heart.' I paused to let this sink in. 'Just that leg and a few vertebrae sticking up inside you.'

She sagged. She made a noise in her throat, then her whole body seemed to convulse. She toppled forward on to the bed, rolling away and trying to gather the limb up to her at the same time. Self-pitying tears ran down her face.

'Don't cry!' *I* was the one who should be crying. Not *her*. 'Stop it. Stop it now.' I took a few steps forward so I was standing above her, looking down at her body, her scarred legs. 'Stop it!'

But she was sobbing, her forehead hard against her knees, which were pulled up, showing everything down there, everything normal at the front – labia majora with a sprinkling of hair. (Don't forget I'm a professional – that's why I can be so pragmatic about it.) Her hands were clasped round the leg, holding it tight against her bottom: it ran straight against her thigh, then hung a little, stiff and scaly, as if it wanted to droop to the bed but couldn't. I crouched down so I was eye-level with her vulva, smelling its faint peppery odour. When she realized I'd moved she opened her eyes, meeting mine, and tried to sit up, this panicky look on her face. But I didn't give her time to speak. I got on the bed and pushed at one thigh, pressing it out to the side and putting one knee on it to hold it there. The other I forced down so I could see everything.

'No,' she sobbed, her hands reaching up to me. 'Please—'

But I pushed her hands away. Her vagina gaped a little. I saw a little bit of moisture there, glinting silver at me, and then I saw her smooth reddish perineum leading back, ducking away to a V shape, and behind it the flat slab of the tail, a faint pucker running along it, like the seam that leads down the underside of a scrotum. Then, and I don't know what made me, but then I inserted two of my fingers into her vagina. She gasped, but I pushed my fingers in deeper, digging them in, the idea flashing through my head that if I only dug deep enough I'd find whatever it was that Oakesy wanted. And if I found it, I'd pull it out of her, and give it to him, wrapped in a bloodied handkerchief.

'Get off. Get off me.'

She grabbed my wrists and tried to twist away, her feet scrabbling on the bed. But I followed her, moving my fingers from her vagina to her anus. I thought of membranes tearing as I pushed my fingers up there, feeling her muscles clamp on me, feeling the smooth insides of her even though she was scrabbling at my wrist, digging her nails in. The twin was in there somewhere – I pictured its face, hands, fingernails, gut, spine, all concertinaed down to a bundle of bone and muscle the size of a foetus inside her pelvis. Maybe I was going to brush against a nose or an ear. Poke my nails into its eyes.

'*Get off me!*'

She rolled away and my nails raked along the inside of her as my fingers came out. She let out a long gasp and rolled out of my reach, clamping her hands between her legs. I stood back, sweating and trembling, breathing hard, my head pounding.

'He's disgusted by you. Do you know that? You make him *sick*.' The tears were rolling down my face. 'He said that the first time he saw you he went away and puked. Did you know that?'

'No.' She lay weakly on her side, shivering and crying. 'He didn't say that.'

'Yes.' I looked down at my fingers, splayed out, sticky and shaking. 'That's what he said. Believe me.'

I went woodenly to the bathroom and washed my hands, using hot water and lots of soap, my teeth chattering as if I was freezing. I knew I'd crossed a line. I knew I couldn't go back. I kept washing and washing and washing until my hands were raw and the urge to cry had left me. Then I went into the bedroom and changed my trousers and blouse. I've made up my mind. It's time to go to London. I haven't got anything to show Christophe – but if I don't see him, talk to him, I'm going to go crazy.

Oakesy

1

People get lines in their head like a record, grooves they move along when they think they know everything they need to know. They stop trying. With Lexie, I thought I knew her so well I'd stopped thinking about her in the right way. That was why I never expected what I found when I got back to the rape suite that day.

It took two hours, dawdling along the tourist roads, stuck behind caravans chugging out sooty fumes, testing strategies as I went, the Massive Attack CD ramming itself into my head. I'd thought about Lexie so much I should have felt better when I pulled up outside the rape suite. Instead I felt like the king of all shits, caught flat-footed, and busy eating myself alive from the inside out. I couldn't go in. I had to sit for a long time, my hands on the steering-wheel, staring at the lines of grime under my fingernails, my thoughts inching laboriously into opening sentences, mentally walking myself into the house, mentally sliding into the conversation. The storms had passed. The streets were wet, glistening in the late sunlight, but the curtains in the living room were closed and I pictured her sitting in there, bolt upright in one of the blue Formica chairs, staring at me when I came in. Angeline would be upstairs.

When I'd been there for five minutes and I still couldn't think of an opening sentence, I started the car and moved it forward a little, coming to a halt at the crossroads. I looked left, right. The police surveillance car was in its usual place, facing me about ten yards to the right, parked casually, just far enough along for the officer to see the front of the rape suite. The sunlight bounced off the wind-screen and for a second or two I didn't realize there were two people in the car. Then a cloud rolled across the sun, the light dimmed, and I saw Angeline in the passenger seat, a handkerchief jammed into her eyes. The officer had his arm across the back of her seat. Not actually touching her, but only inches away.

I parked the Fiesta and jumped out, crossed the road, knocked on the window. The central-locking system disengaged and the officer shot a thumb over his shoulder. I opened the back door and stuck my head in. 'What's going on?'

'An argument.' He turned to me. He had very messy red hair and I noticed he didn't take his arm off the back of Angeline's seat. She was inclined towards him, as if at some point she might have been crying on his shoulder. She kept pinching her nose, like she was trying to hold something in. *She's a cripple, mate . . . have you noticed? A cripple. Let me tell you about what she's got under that coat . . .*

'Two young ladies. Had a wee misunderstanding.'

I got into the back and closed the door. They had the heating on full blast and one of them had been drinking. Or both of them. It stank in there like a south London minicab.

'Well?' I said to Angeline. 'What's happened?'

She shook her head, pressing her eyes with the handkerchief. The sound of her tight breathing filled the car.

'I'll know eventually, so you may as well tell me. What happened?' The officer shot me a glance in the mirror and I caught it, raising my eyebrows calmly at him. If he said, 'Don't be harsh on the lass,' I'd ask him why he had his arm round her and why he had a face like a dog's arse. 'Angeline. I asked you a question. What's been happening while I've been gone?'

She dropped the tissue from her eyes and met my eyes unsteadily in the mirror, this congested look on her face. So, I thought, it's you who's been drinking.

She's no one, Oakes, no one to you. You've known her five minutes . . .

'I took some money from your briefcase.' She wiped her nose and began to pull things out of her pockets, placing them on the dashboard in front of her. Two packets of kids' sweets, three miniature Stolichnayas, four miniature brandies and a couple of empty Doritos bags. It all went rolling across the dashboard, into the air vents and on to the floor. The officer had to pull his arm off her seat and make grabs for it all.

'Easy there, hen. Ea-*sy*.'

'She was in your bedroom and I went into the kitchen and borrowed money from you.' She jerked her chin in the direction of the Spar shop on the other side of the estate. 'Got all of this and some vodka and I'm already drunk. You see?' She pulled a handful of notes and change from the other pocket and dropped it on the dashboard. A five-pence piece rolled off, hitting the gear lever and falling tails up, an inch from my toe into the leather sleeve at the bottom of the handbrake. 'I'm a thief and I'm drunk and I'm probably *just like my father because I hate her and I hate you too . . .*'

'Hey, hey, hen, go easy on yourself.'

He put his hand on her shoulder and she dissolved into tears. I sighed and looked out of the window at the rape suite. What a shitty fucking place to be doing this, a godforsaken abandoned scheme with its crap lying around everywhere, dead lawns and the horizon bruised yellow, like there was a poisonous cloud coming up from the west. A car nosed out of the street parallel to the rape suite, the road that went to the playing-fields. When it saw our car it did a hasty right and disappeared. Fly-tippers. Offload your shite. Come here to Shitening Grove Estate and offload it. Leave it on the tracks. Someone else'll deal with it.

'Wait here,' I told Angeline, opening the door. 'When I come back we've got to talk.' I hesitated then tapped the officer on the shoulder. 'I'm going to be ten minutes. But I'm only over there. I can see you from the front window.'

He started to say something, but I closed the door on him. I stood, zipping up my jacket, turning up the collar and staring across at the rape suite. Like *High Noon* or something, which is a joke, because when I got over to the house all I was facing off with was stale air and some ageing soft furnishings. Lexie wasn't there. She wasn't in the house.

2

I stood in the living room, blinking at the chairs, the blank TV, the cold kettle. I went up and checked in our bedroom, but she wasn't there. She'd gone. I stood in the hallway for a few moments, my head thumping, thinking, She's left me. Not the other way round – *she's* left *me*. Then I went back to the car. This time the officer didn't wait for me to knock. He opened the window and looked at me blankly.

'She's not there.'

Angeline turned, her cheeks red and mottled, and looked past me to the house. 'She was there when I left.'

I put my elbow on the roof and dropped my face into the window close to the officer's. 'Well?' I said slowly. 'What time did she go?'

A line of red appeared across the bridge of his nose. Another travelled from his neck up to his forehead. There was a few moments' silence, and then it dawned on me.

'Oh, you fucking clown. You left your post. Didn't you?'

He glared at me, grinding his jaws in small, tight circles.

'You left your fucking post.' I slammed the roof of the car, making him jump.

'He came to find me,' Angeline said. She got out and faced me blearily over the top of the car roof. Her breath was white in the cold air and I could see she was suddenly panicky, looking over my head at the rape suite. 'It was my fault. I went for a walk and he came to find me.'

I didn't answer. I looked around myself at the empty streets, the bleak houses and the burning horizon. The curtains closed in the rape suite. I turned and headed for the house, a sweat breaking out over my skin. Angeline limped behind me, unsteady, worried. 'Don't panic,' she said. I could hear in her voice she was as scared now as I was. She was sobering up quickly. 'I'm sure everything's all right. She said she was going back to London. She said she was going. I'm sure she's OK.'

A J-cloth had been hung over the kitchen tap to dry. As I waited for Lexie's mum to answer the phone I watched a drip forming under the cloth, slowly fill until it was too heavy, then drop with a metallic *ping* into the sink. We didn't get on, me and Lexie's ma. She'd never quite swallowed the fact that her daughter had married me, a Scouser who didn't even make a token effort to conceal his working-class roots. Where she came from, you boasted that the kids had got into Oxbridge; where I came from, you boasted that they'd stayed out of the nick. And another thing, she'd told Lex, I didn't make enough money. Not nearly enough. So you can see it was never going to be the world's best relationship. When the phone rang six times, then shuffled over to answerphone, part of me was relieved. I didn't leave a message. I called the house in Kilburn and left a message: 'Call me, Lex, when you get in.' I hung up and went into the kitchen to make a brew.

The house was silent. Angeline had gone upstairs. Probably knew the stray voltage that would crackle up if we tried to talk just now. I listened for her as I made the tea, threw some milk into the cup, turned to put the teabag into the bin and . . .

I stopped, the bag extended on the spoon, a little pulse beating in my temple.

Lexie's bag was hanging on the back of the chair.

It was her brown leather Gap bag. Her favourite because it had straps that could make it a rucksack or a tote bag. I'd got it for her for Christmas last year – she used it all the time, swimming or shopping or the pub. She was never separated from it.

Very slowly, like a quick or unexpected movement would make the bag leap up and scuttle away, I dropped the teabag into the bin, threw the spoon into the sink, unhooked the bag from the chair and unzipped it with trembling hands. A faint smell of leather and Airwaves berry chewing-gum came up from it, and inside I found a pocket packet of tissues, a half-finished tube of Lockets, her spiral-bound diary and a spare pair of tights, still in their packaging. I fumbled it all out on to the table, my mouth dry. At the bottom of the bag was her wallet. Her wallet, her keys and her mobile phone.

I stared at the phone in my hand, at the zigzaggy signal icon, my pulse falling to a low, monotone thud. The wallet was closed, and when I opened it I found some loose change, our joint NatWest card, a newspaper cutting of her boss, her library card and a tattered picture of me, tanned and with lots of young-man hair, standing on the Tarmac in front of a Boeing 747 at Athens airport on the way back from our honeymoon in Kos.

I stared at the picture, blank and welded where I stood, all the light and sound in the kitchen muffled. *Lex, Lexie – you wouldn't have left this if you were going to London . . . would you?* I went woodenly into the hallway and began to climb the stairs, moving arthritically, clutching the wallet in my numb fingers. I was at the top when I saw Angeline, coming out of the bathroom door. I knew instantly something was wrong.

'Joe,' she whispered, her eyes bright and glittering. 'Joe. Look in the bathroom. I think you'd better look.'

3

'This is a crime scene.' Chief Inspector Danso stood on the landing with his hands in the pockets of his navy raincoat, peering into the bathroom. Earlier when I came upstairs the door had been standing half open, just enough for me to tell that no one was in there. But I hadn't bothered to push it open wide. If I had I'd have seen the shattered glass in the window above the sink, letting in a cold square of greyish outside light, I'd have seen the towels thrown untidily in the bath, the shower curtain ripped from the rings overhead. 'I'm sorry, but I'm going to have to call it a crime scene. Let's go downstairs. The Crime Scene Manager'll be here any time now.'

We went down in silence. Police car lights flashed blue outside. From the moment I'd seen Angeline's face on the landing I'd known. I'd known that whatever I thought I'd seen over at Crinian, Dove had been here in Dumbarton all the time. The driver in the cap was a *doppelgänger* – a spectre, a blind coincidence. It was only now, with Danso here and back-up cars on the way, that shock set in. As I got to the bottom of the stairs I began to keel sideways.

'Hey up.' Danso came up behind me, catching me under the arm. 'There you go, big man. That's it, through here, let's sit you down before you fall.'

He led me into the living room and lowered me on to the tattered sofa where I sat heavy, my feet planted a pace apart, my hands on my knees, staring at nothing, solemn and stony as old Lincoln in the Washington memorial. Angeline sank on to the sofa opposite me, blinking rapidly, her eyes puffed from crying. 'Still with us, eh?' Danso, bent over with his hands on his knees so he was eye-level with me, studying my face, reassuring himself I wasn't going to fall over like a skittle. He straightened and scanned the living room and kitchen. 'Have you a drop of something about the place?'

'Jack Daniel's.' I nodded automatically. 'Yes, Jack Daniel's.' I looked up at the kitchen, and then, like the noise of my own voice might drown the static in my head, I repeated it a few times, 'Jack Daniel's. Jack Daniel's. Jack Daniel's. Over there. See it? In the kitchen.'

'Will I fetch you a drop, then? Just a little – just to get your head back on, eh?'

If there was any evidence worth preserving in the living room Angeline and I had already destroyed it, walking back and forward down there, waiting for Danso to arrive. But the bizzy habits were in Danso's blood, and he went carefully, automatically tearing off a length of kitchen roll to pick up the bottle because with these break-ins they always make a beeline for the booze. When he saw the cracked cupboard door he took a step back, like he'd been slapped, holding his hands up.

'Me,' I said dully, shaking my head. 'Me. The other day. Bull in a china shop.'

He looked at it a bit longer, then slowly lowered his hands. He got a cracked Rangers mug from the back of the shelf, splashed a couple of inches of JD into it and handed it to me. The mug smelt of coffee and sour milk, but I sipped it gratefully, hearing my breath come back at me from inside the mug.

Danso went to the chair. 'This her bag, then?'

'Yes.'

'And she hasn't taken any clothes?'

'Nothing.'

'Your bedroom just as you left it?'

'It's just the bathroom. The bathroom's the only place that anyone has—' I broke off and pressed my fingertips to my throat, moving my Adam's apple in a circle as if that would stop me choking. 'Anyone has . . . you know . . .'

'Yes,' Danso said quietly. 'Yes. I know.' He scratched his head, then pinched up his trousers by the knees and sat on the sofa next to me, his giant spider's legs black and sharp and thin. 'When you came in, did you notice anything unusual about the house? Anything strike you as odd?'

I stared out of the window in silence. Danso's

driver was standing next to the car, speaking into a radio, one hand on the car roof, one on his hip so his coat was pulled back just far enough to show the glint of handcuffs on his belt. Every now and then he turned and stared off in the direction of the red line of trees, their shadows lying flat and long across the playing-fields.

'No,' I said. 'Nothing.'

Danso tapped his fingers on his knee. There was a long silence. Overhead the immersion-heater came on, a chirruping, tapping noise like a trapped beetle in a joist. 'The back door was locked.' He leaned over and stared out down the corridor, as if to reassure himself that he had remembered correctly. 'And the front door was—'

'Locked.' My mouth was numb, drugged. The words were coming out painfully – like pulled teeth. 'I used the key.'

'And is there anywhere she could have gone? Has she got any friends or relatives in the area?'

'Her ma's in Gloucestershire. She'd have used her mobile to call. But the only calls on it are to me and to the Royal Infirmary . . .' I trailed off and turned to look out of the window, a memory coming to me.

'Joe?'

'A car,' I said faintly, my finger floating up to point out at the street. 'There was a car in that road half an hour ago. It was leaving.'

Danso sat forward, frowning at me. 'A car?'

'White.' I half stood, staring at the boarded-over houses opposite. 'White or silver, maybe . . .'

'Saloon? Hatchback? Estate?'

'Saloon – I . . .' I was on my feet, throwing the front door open, walking out stiffly to stare down the road in the direction it had gone. The officers in their cars stopped their phone and radio conversations and turned to watch me. Danso came out of the house and caught up. He stood shoulder to shoulder with me, staring at the same grey piece of road between the houses. 'It was fly-tippers,' I said faintly. 'I mean, I thought it was fly-tippers.'

'Don't suppose you got a registration number?'

'It went too quickly.' I blinked, staring out at the road, trying hard to force the thoughts. There had been something . . . something . . .

'Did you see who was driving?'

'No.' *Was she in the car, you fucking twat? Did you sit there and watch him drive her away?* Something about the back of the car . . . 'I only saw it for a couple of seconds – couldn't see who was driv-ing or if there was anyone else in the—' I broke off. It had come to me in a flash. 'Boots,' I said. 'Football boots. Little ones – the ones you hang off a mirror. And a miniature Celtic strip. Right up there, hanging over the back shelf, like there could have been kids in the car. That's why I didn't think anything of it.'

As information went it was piss-poor, but it was all I could force out of my memory. Danso took it to the officer, and he sent a PNC marker on his radio. Danso's face was tense as he turned, a little apprehensively, to scan the fields and the empty streets behind him. Then we traipsed back inside, feeling beaten. I sat down next to Angeline. Upstairs the immersion-heater began to knock rhythmically, as if it had come loose from its moorings.

'I'm sorry,' Angeline said quietly. 'I'm really sorry.'

I looked at her. She was still in her coat, bunched-up and miserable-looking, her chin almost on her chest as if she was beyond crying or moving. That flushed-drunk look had gone. Now she was wiped clean of colour. Her feet in the brown boots were turned inwards, like she was trying to disappear. 'I shouldn't have left the house.'

'It's not your fault,' I said. 'It isn't.'

'It's my dad. My dad. And I shouldn't have gone out. You told me not to. It's just that we – Lexie and I – we had a fight and . . .' She broke off. 'If I hadn't been staying with you he'd never have come here.'

I shook my head sadly. 'It's not your fault.'

She nodded and tried to smile but I could tell she didn't believe me. Danso sat down and was about to speak when the noise from the immersion-heater interrupted him. He turned his eyes to the ceiling. 'That's a noisy wee set of apparatus up there.'

'Everything's falling apart in this place.'

'I'll speak to maintenance about . . .' He trailed off as the knocking got louder. Now Angeline and I turned our eyes upwards to stare at the place on the stained Artexed ceiling where the sound was coming from. For a long time none of us spoke. Then Danso lowered his eyes and met mine. A little wash of pale pink was already creeping across his cheeks. He swallowed and gave me a pained smile. 'Joe,' he said evenly, as if he was asking me nothing more serious than what time it was. 'Before you called us, did you check all the rooms upstairs?'

4

'I need some space here.'

'And I don't? I've got to get this Hartmaan's in. You told the consultant you'd keep out of our way.'

The forensic examiner, a female GP from the south of Glasgow, was arguing with a liaison nurse from the Burns Unit. The doctor's cardboard kit sat on a chair in the Glasgow Royal Infirmary's Intensive Care Unit, open, spewing out sealed tubes and latex gloves. The nurse kept having to squeeze past it as she moved round the bed where Lexie lay motionless, legs swaddled in webbed petroleum bandaging, monitors on mechanical arms hovering above her, three different tubes connecting to taps on the Venflon central line going into her neck.

'Why's that green?' said the doctor. She was pointing to the catheter bag. 'Is that something you're giving her?'

'Propofol.' The nurse pushed past her. 'Neurologist doesn't want her moving around. Wants deep sedation until they know what swelling she's going to get from that head injury. Now, would you like to check her fluid output or do you trust me to manage?'

'Just trying to do my job,' the doctor muttered. She bent and took a sealed tube from her bag. 'Just trying to do my job.'

Danso watched from the corner of the private room, face grey, arms folded. He'd asked me to leave for this bit, but I'd said, no, I wasn't leaving her, whatever happened. I sat inside the privacy screen on a wobbly plastic chair, silent, watching numbly as the doctor examined Lexie's limp hands, carefully scraping under the fingernails, sealing the wands into test tubes, each labelled and dated, checking the wall clock for a time and handing the tube to Danso to sign. It was seven o'clock and the day had gone in a blur. Lexie was alive. Alive. But no one could figure out why. She should be dead. That was what they kept telling me.

I turned stiffly, like my head might explode. Angeline was there, sitting a few feet away, white and shocked, staring unblinking at me. All day long I hadn't spoken to her. I hadn't even acknowledged her.

'You'll talk to her,' I said. 'When she wakes up you'll tell her what to do.'

She opened her mouth. It looked to me like she was moving in slow motion. The inside of her mouth was pink. 'What?' she whispered. 'What did you say?'

'What to do now she's . . .' I paused and turned to look at Lexie again. They'd put her on a dark blue air mattress that was supposed to take the pressure off the burns that ran all the way down the backs of her legs. Her airways were clear, none of the burns circled her legs, and the consultant said all of this was promising. But no one was pretending there'd be any getting away from the disfigurement. That was hers. For life. The first paramedic to arrive at Lightning Tree Estate had gone pale when he saw the burns. I remember him trying to wrap her legs in clingfilm, the crime-scene manager yelling at him to *hurry up, hurry up*, and I knew from everyone's faces there wasn't much could be done about those burns. 'It's the pensioner syndrome,' someone muttered in the confusion. 'Saw it once on an old stiff I got called to. Died in bed. When I got there he'd been simmering on an electric heating pad for six days.'

The noises from the immersion-heater hadn't been the sound of it switching itself on: that had already happened a long time before I got back to the house. What Danso, Angeline and I had heard from the living room was Lexie's heels drumming out a reflex tattoo on the hot-water tank. It was a neurological spasm, a tic, because she was unconscious when I opened that cupboard door. She'd been placed on top of the tank, legs astride the copper pipe that led up to the tank in the attic, her arms flopped backwards. Her mouth was open and her head was back against the wall, not lolling but alert and upright even though her eyes were closed. That weird angle to her head wasn't an accident: she'd been pinioned there, her head jammed over and over again into a nail that stuck out of the wall. He'd done it so hard, and so many times, that there was a hole in the back of her head the size of a shot glass and he must have thought for sure she was dead. He'd have loved to see my face when I found her.

I'm fucking with your peace of mind, Joe.

The doctor unsnapped the kit from its

Cellophane and began to lay out its contents. A dull ache started in my back and my knee joints: the tiredness that sets in after an adrenaline jag. I knew what that kit was. I knew what she was going to do. Lexie's legs were burned so badly because Dove had removed her tights and knickers before he hauled her up on the tank. The lagging had come loose so the top of the hot copper tank had been in direct contact with her thighs and buttocks for two and a half hours. I managed everything else, all the stuff about the nail rammed through her skull, about the bruises on her face, the red welts on her neck where he'd strangled her, but that detail of there being no underwear . . . It was that detail took my legs out from under me, sent me dry-heaving over the kitchen sink.

Danso helped me like he was my father: he kept close to my face, talking to me constantly, kept me from losing it. He stayed with me while we went to the station and I went through the miserable process of giving DNA, because, yes, we were still sharing a bed even though the sex was pretty much dead and buried. I let the arse of a doctor take what he needed: hairs and a tube of blood. I spent the rest of the day trying not to picture a lab technician somewhere in Glasgow sorting my DNA from Dove's.

I'm fucking with your peace of mind, Joe.

The nurse stopped what she was doing and watched as the doctor pulled a speculum from the kit. 'Is that what I think it is?' she asked. 'Did the consultant tell you that was OK?'

The doctor peered at her over the top of her glasses. 'As a matter of fact, yes. I believe he did give his permission.'

'Because that burn to the perineum. That's really complex. You know that, don't you?' She moved closer to the bed, to where the doctor was pulling the sheets down, gently moving Lexie's legs apart. 'It's the worse for swelling.'

I looked up and found Danso's eyes on mine. I knew what he was saying: *You don't want to be here for this, you don't want to be here.* I held his eyes, the blood pumping in my head. The doctor peeled the wad of bandage from between Lexie's legs, careful not to move the catheter tube – and that was enough for me. I stood shakily and left the room, standing in the corridor and breathing carefully. A moment later there was a click and when I turned Angeline stood behind me, expressionless. She had unbuttoned her coat in the warm hospital air and was clutching a tissue in her right hand, maybe to dab her forehead or her eyes.

'What?' I said. 'I had to come out here. I can't watch that.'

'I know.'

She stood there for a while, looking at me, saying nothing.

'What? What do you want?'

'Joe?' she said quietly. 'When she wakes up?'

'Yes?'

'When she shows you. You won't . . .'

'Won't what?'

'You won't let her see you're disgusted?'

I stared at her. For a few minutes I wasn't getting it. 'What?' My head was so drum tight, nothing was sinking in. 'What did you say?'

There was a pause. Then she said, 'Don't let her think she disgusts you.'

'Angeline.' My voice was stiff. 'I didn't say it. Whatever you think . . . I never said it.'

5

Nine the second morning Lexie's ma arrives, trailing luggage. Bony calves in expensive hosiery poking out from under her tweed skirt. A Harrods astrakhan hat crammed on to springs of auburn hair.

'This was always going to happen, Joe,' she says crisply, as she comes in. 'And forgive me if I blame you. You and your job.'

I don't answer. I watch her kiss Lexie. I watch her summon the nurse to clean the thin line of saliva that runs down Lexie's chin. I watch her survey the room and get comfortable, hang up her coat and hat, arrange her belongings, and sit down primly, one hand on her skirt because I'm definitely enough of a pig to try getting a look at her knickers, the cacky old mare. And I don't say a word.

We sit like this for thirty-six hours, locked in a monumental battle of wills: the first to wilt, to give up the vigil, is the loser. I spend my time slumped in my chair, staring sullenly across the room, a leaflet they've given me crumpled in my hand: *Managing the Future After Burns: Psycho-Social Needs*. She sits upright, her mouth pursed as she peers at the *Telegraph* crossword over the top of her specs. I keep studying her, making sure she never tries to switch on her mobile phone. We've all been told not to have any contact with the outside world, not even with relatives and friends, and I'm not going to give her a chance. Because the police have got a problem.

At first when the word came through about Lex everyone up at Oban was secretly relieved: Malachi Dove had done his bit to fuck with my head and it had taken out just one person, not hundreds like they'd been afraid. But now they saw the catch: in Dove's head his job was over because he thought

Lex was dead. Reality was different. A local reporter had got wind of a 'domestic' at the rape suite. He hadn't connected it yet to the Pig Island massacre, but when his usual police contact stonewalled him over it he knew there was more and he was starting to dig. Danso was going crazy trying to contain it: he knew Dove was finished now, but Danso wanted to be sure before they let anything out to the papers. We wanted Dove's body. There were blinds on the private room and every nurse and doctor who came through was warned not to speak to anyone. Not even a friend. Still, you got the feeling that any time now the bag was going to split and it was all going to come out. If Lexie's ma so much as moved her hand near to her phone I was going to be on her.

Angeline had been trying to get us to leave the room, to get some proper rest – there were couches in the relatives' room we could stretch out on, and she'd call us if anything happened. She kept limping in and out of the room, ferrying coffee and Snickers bars, asking when they were going to wake Lex up. At eleven a.m. on day two she brought in four doughnuts in a pink-and-white-striped box. There was a blue picture of a chef's hat on it. She placed a napkin on the chair next to Lex's ma and carefully put two doughnuts on it.

Lex's mother looked down at them and gave a

small laugh. 'And they say the nation's youth don't know how to eat properly.'

Angeline paused, and for a moment I thought she was going to take the doughnuts back. But she didn't. Instead she straightened and moved calmly to my chair, putting the box down and setting the coffee next to it. 'My mother's dead,' she said, addressing no one, but making us both raise our eyes to her. 'My mother's dead, but she was beautiful. She was beautiful and she was kind. And she loved me.'

I looked at her. Somehow in the last two weeks her hair had grown enough to cover the bare patches of scalp. It was brushed and there was even a bit of light reflected in it. She looked like she'd put some mascara on and there was something defiant about her as she stared at Lex's ma.

'Yes,' she said, almost trembling with the effort of keeping her voice in control. 'And you know what? I think she was right. I think she was right to love me.'

She rested a napkin on top of the doughnut box, and, like nothing had been said, like we weren't both staring at her, she sat on the chair in the corner, pulled the lid off her coffee and drank.

6

Autumn was coming, and out of the window, level with the third floor, the monuments and mausoleums of the Necropolis towered dark against the cloudbanks. On the roadway below the ward patients stood in dressing-gowns and slippers, smoking quick and intent, trying not to look up at those grave markers, at the austere statue of John Knox. Angeline sat in silence, watching me from the opposite side of the hospital room.

It was the third day and it had been a morning of skin. The Burns Unit nurse brought in a fringed tape to measure for pressure garments, leggings that would stop the scarring and make sure Lexie could move her joints when she healed. She'd have to wear them for a year and a half, said the nurse. A technician from the Myskin labs came to take biopsies. Where he worked, they could take small pieces of skin and grow them into sheets ready to graft back. At lunchtime the plastic surgeon started pushing the neurologist a bit: he wanted to debride Lexie's legs, snip away the dead flesh. The neurologist hummed and hah-ed but in the end they settled on that afternoon. By the evening Lexie would be out of theatre and in a high-dependency ward on the Burns Unit. Awake. She'd know all about her future, about the clinical-psychology services, and about how her skin was being grown in a lab a hundred miles away.

In the chair next to Angeline, the Ice Queen was dozing, her chin on her chest, a society mag crumpled on her lap. When Danso arrived he didn't come into the room, probably didn't want to face her. Instead he stood at the door with Struthers, looking like Columbo or something in his crumpled raincoat, and tapped on the windowpane, beckoning to me and Angeline.

'We're taking you for coffee,' he said, when we came out. He was holding the day's local newspapers and you could see it in their faces: something was up. Especially Struthers. He looked like he'd been given an extra pint or two of blood overnight. 'Something's changed and we're taking you for coffee.'

Danso set off in the direction of the hospital cafeteria and, without hesitating, I followed, keeping pace with him, going through the plastic crash doors, out through the car park, the drizzle plastering our hair to our heads. Struthers hung back with Angeline, offering his arm to her as she limped along.

'I'm going to tell you this now,' Danso said, as we went ahead of them through another set of plastic doors, back into the main building, our feet squeaking on the polished floor. He didn't turn to look at me: he kept his eyes on the door of the cafeteria at the end of the corridor. 'I'm going to tell you while he can't hear.'

'Struthers?'

He nodded. 'It's not why we're here but it's important to you and I wanted you to hear with a bit of privacy.'

'You wanted me to hear what?'

'We got the results back. This morning. From the forensic examiner.'

I was in mid-stride. I let the step hesitate a bit, my foot slowing in mid-air, then continue down in slow motion. It hit the floor and I carried on at the same speed. Like he hadn't said anything at all.

'They came back,' I said, my voice level. 'And?'

'And he left nothing. Nothing under her finger-nails. No hair, no skin.'

'She'd have fought.'

'Yes. Three of her nails were torn off. The others . . .'

'The others?'

'He'd cleaned. Scrubbed. They watch so much crime TV they all know how to cover their forensics these days. She'd have been unconscious.'

I kept walking, letting this settle on me.

'What does that mean, Peter, *he left nothing*?'

Danso stopped. We'd reached the café and he stood, his hand resting on the door, looking at me seriously. A ghost scene of him as my father played briefly in my head. I'd had that before, with Danso.

'He didn't get to her, son,' he said, resting a hand on my shoulder. 'Why did he leave her naked? Who knows? But he didn't touch her, so you can let that go.'

I stood there, getting an embarrassing urge to put my arms round him because a huge, paralysed section of my mind had clicked a bit and started to function again, like an iceberg coming free of the icecap. Then Struthers and Angeline appeared at the end of the corridor, coming towards us, and the moment was gone. Next I knew we were in the café, pulling off wet coats and finding a table near the radiators.

7

Danso drank tea from a stainless-steel pot and the rest of us had coffee in plastic filters that dripped all over the table. We ate damp ginger biscuits from heavy white plates still hot and cabbagy smelling, like they'd come straight from a dishwasher. The cafeteria was a Turkish bath, the tea urns and the hotplates steaming the place up, making the windows drip with condensation.

Danso and Struthers kept us waiting. They fed us snippets of information that hadn't got anything to do with the big news. They said they thought Dove had found us through the rental car. Somehow, Christ knew how, he must've picked me up on one of my drives, maybe from Oban police station, and had been watching the rape suite for days. They told us there had been seventy-eight public sightings of the saloon car, because it turns out a Celtic kit hanging over the back shelf isn't such a rarity in that part of Scotland. They showed us a tiny column in the *Glasgow Herald* saying the police were refusing to confirm or deny an attack in Dumbarton, which had left one woman critically ill in hospital.

'Which reminds me . . .' Danso wiped his mouth and looked at me. 'Something else I wanted to ask you.' He swallowed his mouthful of biscuit. 'The car. You sure you didn't see that car parked?' He pulled a biro from the inside of his jacket, and uncapped it with his teeth. He unfolded a napkin and made some rudimentary lines on it. 'See, we think it could have been parked here.' He made an X on the road that led to the east of the estate along the playing-fields. 'What do you think?'

'Could have been. When I saw it,' I pointed to the parallel road, 'it was here – on this road.'

'So, let's get this straight. You'd driven in from

here,' he marked the west road, 'from where your babysitter was, so you stopped here, facing this way, and you saw him here, parallel to Humbert Place.'

'Yes.'

'So he'd parked either here or here. Anyone on this road, or walking in the fields, would have seen him.'

'Anyone except our babysitter.'

Danso cleared his throat. 'We're just trying to plot his movements on the estate.'

'Because you want to get your lad off the hook?'

He sighed. 'Joe, I'm sorry. I see you think we came here to antagonize you. But we didn't. The officer wants to apologize to you when his disciplinary's over.'

I breathed out and sat back, my arms folded, giving him a disbelieving smile. 'Please. Don't jerk me around.'

'I'm serious. He wants to say sorry. It'd do him good to speak to you. What do you think?'

I grinned brightly at him, then at Struthers. A fake, face-splitter of a grin. 'What do you *think* I think? Did you really think I'd say yes?'

Danso ran a finger inside his collar, uncomfortable. 'Aye. That's how we thought you'd feel.' He glanced sideways at Struthers. 'We didn't think he'd be happy. Did we?'

'We didn't.'

'OK,' Danso said. 'I'm not going to force the—'

'I mean it. I'm not going to speak to him. I don't want to hear him whingeing about how difficult it was to see Dove on that estate.'

'That's not why we're thinking about Dove's movements.'

'Then why?' I put my hands down, looking at them both. I could feel a beat of anger flaring in my temple. 'What other reason do you need to know *which way* he drove on to the fucking *estate* to put *my wife* in a fucking *coma*?'

'Because,' Struthers interrupted, his face a bit red, 'we want to know when he posted this.' He pulled a brown envelope from his briefcase and put it on the table. 'That's why.'

There was a moment's silence. Me and Angeline stared at the envelope.

'He cleaned up the house,' Danso said irritably. 'I told you – there was nothing of him in there, nothing. Couldn't even place him on the estate until this. It's the only evidence we've got.' He opened the envelope and tipped out the contents. There were two black-and-white photographs and a manila envelope sealed in plastic evidence sheaths. 'Posted in the box on the estate some time before the collection at three on the day he did Lexie. If it's what we think it is, then everything's going our way.'

'Everything's going our way?'

'Everything.' He looked at me, then at Angeline, then back at me. 'It's a suicide note. He's telling us when he's going to do it.'

8

The envelope wasn't stamped. It was addressed to Danso at Oban and it contained the two photos of Malachi Dove gone from the study on Pig Island. The first showed him posed with Asunción, Angeline's mother. It might have been the wedding because she wore flowers in her hair and he had one in his lapel. The second was the photo of him praying. Lying on his back, dead-looking. When we saw it me and Angeline both reached out.

'Uh-uh,' Struthers warned. 'No touching. I had to sell my soul to the productions officer to get these for the afternoon. He's got "continuity of evidence" written on his heart – I bring them back covered in your prints he'll have my knob on a stick.' He gave Angeline a sickly smile. 'Sorry, pet. Pardon the French, eh?'

'They're his,' Angeline said, staring stonily at him. 'They're from his study.'

'Aye. We know. They're covered in his latents.'

Danso turned the photos over to show lines written in a small, curled hand. He pushed the picture of Dove and Asunción towards us. We leaned forward and looked at the writing. Straight away I felt the tug in it.

'It's about you,' said Struthers. 'It's about you and Alex.'

I pulled the photo nearer.

I have ploughed with your heifer, my friend [he'd written]. *And now that you have paid the uttermost farthing you are bound in fetters of iron, your torment is as the torment of a scorpion when he striketh a man. To live in grief is worse than death. In your days you shall seek death and you shall not find it: you shall desire to DIE, but death shall flee from you . . .*

A nasty smile twitched on my face. The words were dragging me back to the old days in Albuquerque when he was my adversary and my head was full of the *cojones* he spouted, and I was young and angry enough to have stabbed the bastard. Except this time I was the winner, because Lexie was alive. It was like one end of my life was being brought round to touch the other end.

'And this is the one you'll really like,' Struthers said, after a while. It was the back of the prayer photo. 'See if he's telling us what we *think* he's telling us.'

He'd divided the top of the page into two columns, one headed *Taken by God* and one headed *Taken by the Antichrist*. Under the Antichrist heading he'd written *Judas* and *Ahithophel*. Under the God heading he'd written: *Abimelech, Samson, Malachi Dove*. And at the foot of the page were a few lines:

> *I was wounded in the house of my friends and now my harvest is past, the summer is ended, my days are as grass, the wind passeth over them and they are gone. As the hart panteth after the water brooks, so panteth my soul after thee, O GOD I will fly away. No man taketh it from me, but I lay it down of myself, here, at the end of my fifty years.*

There was a long silence. In the kitchen someone dropped a stack of plates. A door banged. Someone laughed. But at the table none of us spoke.

'At the end of my fifty years?' I said, after a while. Struthers and Danso nodded. They were looking from me to Angeline, watching us filter the information. Waiting to see if we came to the same conclusion. 'His birthday?'

'That's what we think.'

'Which is the twenty-fifth of September,' said Angeline, faintly.

'Exactly.'

'And that is . . .'

'Tomorrow.' Struthers nodded. 'Tomorrow. All we have to do is keep Alex out of the papers for another twenty-four hours.'

Which was how we came to spend the whole of the next day on the edge of our seats, waiting for the day to crawl across the sky and be over. Thinking that if we could get past his birthday we'd be OK. Which is all very fucking funny, all a fuck-off laugh at my expense, when you consider that by the time his birthday was over it wasn't Malachi Dove I was thinking about. I'd forgotten to give a shit about him, and where or how they were going to find his body. Because by the night of his birthday the only thing I was thinking of was Lexie and how come it had worked out that she was dead. Of septicaemia. Nine-thirty on 25 September. Age: thirty two.

Part Three

LONDON
FEBRUARY

Oaksey

1

Ten empty Newkie Brown bottles hanging on the wall . . .

There were ten empty Newkie Brown bottles lined up on the bog seat. Ten. I lay in the bath staring blankly at them, trying to work out how long it had taken to drink them. I couldn't talk myself into getting out of the bath and all the way over to the toilet, but I needed a piss – had needed one for the last twenty minutes, so I could have been here for, what? An hour? Two?

It was four months since Lexie died ('Sepsis,' the consultant had said. 'She would have been vulnerable to sepsis from the moment she was admitted and I find it difficult to believe you weren't warned of the possibility') and I suppose it'd be fair to say I'd let myself go. I didn't know if I was more depressed that she was dead than I was depressed Dove had won, after everything. Every time some-one found a corpse in Scotland, bones mashed into the side of a rock or something bloated bobbing like a dirty tarpaulin in the sea, they thought it was Dove's body. But it wasn't. I'd thought he was going to be easy to find. So I'd been wrong about that too. Some days I thought I knew the answers, others I knew I didn't.

On the floor my mobile rang. I dropped my hand over the side of the bath and grabbed my jeans, shaking them until the phone fell out of the pocket.

'Are you supposed to use mobiles in the bath?' I asked the phone, staring at it. The display said: *Finn. Answer?* 'I don't know. I mean, will it kill me if I do?' I opened the phone. 'I'm in the bath,' I said. 'This could kill me.'

'Fucking great,' he said. 'It's two in the after-noon, you're in the bath and I'm sitting staring at an empty in-box. Was expecting fifteen thousand words and a synopsis by nine this a.m. At the latest. Instead I've got six slush-pile manuscripts and a Ghanaian asking me to ship money into his bank account.'

I didn't answer. I'd been dragging my feet, wait-ing for Dove's body to pop up before I committed to a book deal. But I knew I was losing it: a lot of what had happened out on Cuagach had already been released – the public knew about the pig corpses, the gargoyles, what life in the Psychogenic Healing Ministries was like. Two ex-members had already signed publishing deals for their stories. The story, the whole purpose behind the last six months, was slipping through my fingers.

'He's dead, Oakes. Dead. Can you hear me?'

I lifted my foot out of the water and studied it. It was pink and wrinkled into magnified folds, like the skin on a baby rat. I tried to turn the hot tap on with my toe, but it wouldn't budge.

'*Oakes*,' Finn snapped. 'Can you hear me?'

I pushed the tap harder. When that didn't work I changed my strategy and stuck my toe up it instead. I looked at it for a moment or two, then laughed. I was thinking about an old film where a plumber comes into the bathroom and finds some blonde or other with her toe stuck in a tap. I laughed again, liking the way my voice echoed off the walls.

'Oakes, you are weirding me out here. You're laughing. Can you hear yourself? *Laughing*.'

'Yeah,' I said. 'I know. I've got my toe in the tap. It's funny.'

There was a long, cold silence. 'Joe, you can sit there laughing because you've got your toe in the fucking tap, but out here in the real world there are articles every day about what happened on Cuagach – something only this morning about his Mexican wife, Asunción. She died on the mainland two years ago, did you know that?'

'Yes. I knew.'

There was a moment's silence. I stared at my toe. Even more like a rat now. A rat with its nose up a tap.

'Oakes, you're hurting for money, am I right?'

I pulled my toe out, letting my foot splash into the water. 'Yeah,' I said dully. 'You're right.' I'd gone a long time without a paycheck. My syndication-agency accounts stood at zero. Worse, when I got back to London I'd discovered the hole Lexie had got herself into without telling me. She'd run up an overdraft of over three K on our joint account, paying her therapist seventy quid a pop. There was a P45 in the mail, too, from the clinic. Another part of her life she'd forgotten to mention.

'And then,' said Finn, 'yesterday I hear how some hack from Glasgow is auctioning *his* story. Reckons he's interviewed some of the major players in the police *and* the clean-up crew out on the island. Says they let him inside the temporary mortuary and what he's saying is there're photos.'

'*I've* got pictures from the mortuary,' I said coldly. 'I told you already—'

'I know, but that was *more than four months ago.*'

'Yes. And in those four months I lost my wife.'

Finn sighed. 'I'm sorry, I really am. But you're acting like you're on some fucking candyfloss cloud floating across the sky. Now, listen. I'm going to tell you what to do.' I could hear him switch off his computer and swivel round in his chair. 'First, get me those words. Don't worry about Dove, just do it. Then I want you to talk to that kid.'

'Kid?'

'The one who pulled the video hoax. The one arsing around with the devil suit. He's important to the story. Did you speak to him yet?'

I hesitated. I looked at the winter sunlight making stars of the condensation on the window. Angeline was out there in the garden. She'd come down to London with me, waiting until they found Malachi's body and the probate began. I knew it was a mistake. I'd given her the front room with the fold-out guest futon, the one printed with the bright orange flowers that Lexie had been nuts about, and she stayed in there day after day, the door closed tight, coming out only to cook or to go into the garden. She spent hours outside, digging and planting vegetables, sometimes even in the dark. But most of all she spent time watching me. She would sit at the kitchen table, her chin in her hands, and stare at me, like she was expecting me to say something. It'd got so I didn't look at her. I

knew if I did I'd have to go into a part of my head
I didn't want to open.

'Well?' Finn said. 'Have you got an interview
with the kid? Without an interview it comes across
like you've taken your eye off the ball. It comes
across sloppy.'

'Then you know what?'

'What?'

'That's probably because I am sloppy. In fact,
you know what? I'm so sloppy that right now I'm
pissing in my bath-water. It's gone cold, so I'm pissing in it while I'm talking to you.'

There was a pause. Then he said, 'No, you're
not. Don't talk sick.'

'I am.' I closed my eyes, relaxed my muscles and
the urine leaked out of me across my thighs. 'Told
you.'

'Jesus, Oakes. What's happening to you? What's
happening? You've got to pull yourself
together . . .'

I dropped the phone on the floor and lay back in
the bath. The condensation hung like teardrops
from the ceiling – the whole bathroom was soaked
with steam. No wonder it's cold: the bathroom is
stealing my heat, I thought, and suddenly I was
crying. I was trembling and crying and holding my
hands up to my face, shaking my head and crying
like a baby. I got up, sobbing angrily. *You just*

LONDON

pissed yourself, for fuck's sake. Where's this going to end? I unplugged the bath, turned on the shower and stood under it, exhausted, self-pitying sobs jerking out of me while the cold water rained down on me and the pissy water disappeared down the plug-hole between my toes.

2

Me and Lex had lived in that house just off the Harrow Road for almost four years. The Victorian semis round there all had driveways and side entrances and were highly desirable, according to the local estate agents, who kept poking their leaflets through the letterbox. But I knew my house let the neighbourhood down, with its peeling windows and the cellar stuffed full of crap the previous owner had left: paint pots, kitchen tiles, a rusting old fridge-freezer I'd never had the guts to open. When me and Angeline got back from Scotland in December – after four months of the house being locked up – you could smell the cellar coming up through the floorboards. The first thing I did, while she put on the heating and swept dead flies from the windowsills, was go down there and open the door to the garden just to let some air in.

That was five weeks ago and I hadn't thought about it again. I'd opened it and never got round to closing it.

It was Tuesday. The day after Finn called. I sat under the diseased old apple tree, hunched against the cold in my thin sweater, and stared at the cellar door, trying to find the energy to get up and do something about it. In the corner of the garden Angeline was forking over the hard clay, her breath hanging in the air. When I came out to the garden to be with her like this we almost never spoke, and in spite of the small sounds of her breathing and the fork clicking against a pebble, a silence had come down over the garden that felt like it belonged to the darkest part of winter. If this had been the weekend the neighbours would be out in the alley that ran along the bottom of the fences, wheelbarrowing bags of mushroom compost and topsoil down to their gardens, but today the neighbourhood was deserted. We were the only people outside and all the windows looking down at us were blank sockets, bare branches reflecting back from the panes.

Angeline worked intently, jamming the fork into the ground, making small grunts, occasionally stooping to pull out a root or a piece of stone and throw it into a pile. She wore a scarf, mud-congealed boots and a thick hemp skirt. Her hair had grown in, very dark and curly. Whenever she bent, the extra limb strained against the fabric of the skirt in shadowy outlines.

'What?' she said, straightening up. The work and the cold had brought the blood to her face and against the stony colours of the garden her skin was vivid. She pushed some stray strands of hair back into the scarf. 'What're you staring at?'

'Nothing,' I said.

'You're staring at me. What's wrong? You know what's under my coat – you saw it – so why are you staring now?'

I let all my breath out at once. My pulse began to move a bit. So today was the day we were going to talk about it.

'Well?'

'Well what?'

'You saw it, but you've never once said what you really think.' She was flushed now. Her knuckles, where she was pressing the fork into the ground, had gone white. 'Joe? What did you think? Of my twin? My twin?'

I stared at her, not blinking. I couldn't answer. Just couldn't get a single word out. I didn't know what I thought. I'd read Lexie's letters. I'd spoken to Guy Picot and somewhere I had a vague idea I'd dealt with it, fitted it somehow into my head. But I was finding good ways of not thinking about it. It was locked away somewhere. Just locked in a place I didn't want to go.

'Well?'

I stood, avoiding her eyes. I crossed the frozen ground to where the wind had opened the gate to the alley just a fraction, so a section of shingled ground was visible through the crack. I waited for a second or two, wondering if I could say anything. Nothing came to me. I pulled the gate closed, kicking a stone against it to jam it there. I looked at the gate, at the stone wedged at the bottom, then turned back to Angeline.

'You know something? You know when I'll feel better?'

'No. When will you feel better?'

'When they've found your dad's body.' I went and closed the cellar door and stood, brushing my hands off, looking up at the featureless blanket of cloud above us. 'But I suppose you know that already.'

In the kitchen I opened a bottle of Newkie Brown and sat at the table. Outside it was getting dark and the clouds had that heavy look, like they might start spitting out hailstones any minute. I sat on the chair, upright, my hands on my knees, my heart thudding. I tried to read the paper. But I couldn't. On the wall the clock was ticking dead loud.

After about ten minutes the door opened. At first I thought it was the wind, but then she came in, bringing rain and dead leaves. She didn't see me sitting there in the dark. She stopped on the mat and stamped the mud off her feet, so hard you'd think she was pissed off with the floor. She levered one boot off with her heel and was about to start on the other when she realized I was there. She froze, one boot on, one off. Her eyes rolled round to me.

'What?' I said, guilty of being in my own kitchen. 'What?'

She shook her head. She began to say something, but instead closed her eyes and suddenly she was breathing very fast and hard, like she was ill. Then all these tears came out of her eyes and dribbled down her face and on to her chin.

'Oh, Christ.' I was on my feet next to her, not knowing what to do. I kind of patted her shoulder cautiously, not leaving my hand there for too long. The way you'd pat an animal you thought might bite. 'Oh, Christ. I'm sorry. I'm sorry. I really am.'

She turned away from me so her face was against the wall, put her hands over her ears and just cried and cried, like she was crying for everything that had ever happened to her. We stood there, me kind of shocked, useless, without the guts to put my arms round her; her with her forehead pressed into the wall, her shoulders jerking up and down.

'*When's it going to be over, Joe? When?*'

'When's what going to be over?'

'This. This – this . . .' She could hardly get the words out, she was trembling so much. '*You're paralysed, Joe, just paralysed, and I don't know why. I mean, you read the letter. You know what she did.*'

'What who did? Lexie, you mean?'

'*Yes, Lexie. You know what she did. Why c-can't you forget her?*'

'Why can't I . . . ? No. It's not just her – not just her any more.'

'*Then it's my dad. It's about him.*'

'Yeah, him,' I said. 'Him too. It's about lots of—'

'*And that's just as bad. Can't you see – can't you see? If you let him stop you writing then he's won. He's won again and you're just sitting there and letting the world go past us both.*'

'Yes, but – hey, hang on –'

She lurched past me, out of the kitchen, up the stairs and into her room. I stood for a second, listening, not knowing if I was supposed to go after her. I could hear her moving things around, and after a couple of minutes I went into the hallway, following the trail of mud from her single boot up the stairs. On the landing I stopped. The bedroom door was open. She was in there, hobbling around, pulling things off the shelves in big handfuls. I hadn't been in her room for weeks. She'd filled it with library books and notebooks. Sheets of paper printed off the Internet.

'James Poro.' The moment she saw me on the landing she flung a book on the floor. It was open at a black-and-white photo. I didn't have time to register it before another book came down. And another. 'Lazarus-Joannes Baptist Colloredo, Betty Lou Williams . . .' She turned to the shelves, sorting through the other books, leaving me to blink at the one on the floor. It showed a photo of a traffic-stoppingly pretty girl in a frilled prayer-meeting dress. Arranged in her lap were four small limbs, plump and black against the white dress. If there was a head you couldn't see it: it was buried in the girl's stomach. I went from the limbs to her face and back again.

'Betty Lou.' Angeline limped over to me, holding more books. She squatted down, the books wedged between her knees and her chest, and put her hand on the girl's face. She wasn't crying any more. The tears had dried on her cheeks and there was a fixed look in her eye. 'Betty Lou's twin was epigastrus. Do you know what that means? No. Why would you? It means the twin is attached here. To your chest.' She opened another of the books and slammed it down. 'Most of them are epigastrus, but some are like me. Look at this – Frank Lentini. He was just like me, an extra leg. Look, Joe, look where it's attached.'

I held up a hand, stalling her. I couldn't process it all, this science fiction, this Victorian bestiary she was showing me. 'This isn't real. This isn't real.'

' "The deeper aspect of the parasite is composed of large, cystic and tubular structures." ' She picked up a piece of paper and read, her voice fierce: ' "And solid organs resembling liver and—" '

'Angeline—'

' "*Resembling liver* and spleen. There are rudimentary gastrointestinal structures, some bowel sac, for example, a rudimentary genito-urinary system, severe skeletal anomalies compromising the autosite's vertebrae . . ." ' She held up another book, pushing it in front of my eyes so I had to look. 'It's real, Joe. It's real.'

This book showed a young man with a small *pagri* on his head. He was smiling graciously into the camera and holding up two tiny limp arms protruding from the front of his embroidered tunic. A matching pair of legs dangled below, reaching just below his belt. '© Barnum and Bailey collection', said the photo tag line. 'Until the era of prenatal scans and microscience, circuses were littered with parasitic twins.'

'That's Laloo. He was famous. Made a fortune. But you know the worst thing for him? For Laloo?'

I pushed the book away. I sat down with my back to the doorpost, my hands on my ankles. I couldn't look any more.

'The worst thing was he couldn't stop his twin urinating.'

'Please—'

'He never knew when it was going to happen. He couldn't stop it happening. And you think *I*'ve got problems.'

She stood in the doorway above me, breathing hard, the colour darkening in parts of her face: the tips of her ears, her nose, her mouth. The shadow of a branch outside the window moved back and forward across her face. It struck me that I'd never really studied her face before, never taken it in, never noticed she was pretty. All I'd ever thought about was her body. I dropped my eyes, heart thumping. Couldn't look at her.

'Joe,' she said, in a low voice. 'Joe, you can't let me keep this secret any more. I can't not talk about it. I can't be on my own with it any more.'

I sat there, my face hot and rigid, staring at the fabric of her skirt, fighting the feeling that this moment had been crashing towards me all my life. Face it, old man. Do it. Do or die. I cleared my throat and knelt up, tipping forward so the change in my jacket pockets jangled softly on the floor. I reached across and put my hand under the hem of her skirt. She stiffened, but I didn't take my hand away. I found her small warm calf and circled it with my thumb and forefinger. The cuff of her boot pressed against my wrists. We stayed in that weird position for a long time, not looking at each other, the only noise the wind blowing in the attic over our heads.

'You're not on your own,' I said, after what seemed like for ever. 'Can't you tell?'

3

'Well, isn't *this* the arsehole of London?' Finn came in, flicking the rain off his coat, like Kilburn rain came out of the sewers instead of the bottled Evian stuff they got in Chiswick. It was Thursday. He'd come over because I'd told him I was ready to talk. 'I'd forgotten how crap it was. I mean, the sheer turdiness of it is awesome.'

He pulled off his coat, dropped it over the chair. He wore a suit, but hints of the subversive Finn lingered – ironic 1970s sideys almost to his jawline, a shiny kipper tie fixed with a Playboy pin. A Zenner symbol stud in his ear and his vague out-ofseason suntan. He bent to check his reflection in the hall mirror, swiping at the raindrops scattered in his hair. Then he paused and looked sideways at me.

'You don't look as bad as I expected.' He patted my arm. He wasn't going to say it, but he was worried about me. He's my cousin. Some things don't need to be said. 'I mean, you look crap 'n' all, but not as crap as I expected.'

'You don't have to stay long,' I said, checking my watch with great deliberation. 'I'll kick you out at eleven.'

'Yup.' He held up his hand. 'Good to see you too.'

We went into the living room. Angeline was standing near the kitchen door pulling on her gardening coat and fastening the scarf round her head. When she saw Finn she came forward, smiling, one hand extended in greeting, the other pushing the stray curls off her forehead. She moved smoothly, coming across so regal, so weirdly at ease, her brown eyes focused and serious, that I was a shabby coach tourist next to her, in my fading shirt and chinos.

'Finn, this is Angeline.'

'Angeline. Hey!' Finn said, holding up his hand to salute her. He took her in, her hair, curly and dark, her small nose, kind of moulded-looking, like it was made of china. There was even a bit of lipstick on her mouth. 'How's it going?'

'Fine, thanks.'

'Wicked, Angeline,' he said. 'Wicked to meet you.'

'Angeline was just going into the garden,' I said. 'Weren't you?'

She held up her gardening gloves. 'I'm afraid I'm an addict.' She went into the kitchen calmly and out of the back door. When she'd gone, there was a pause. Then he turned and stared at me, a look of amazement on his face.

'What?'

'*What?*' he mouthed. 'You never said a word about her. She's totally *fit*.' He went into the kitchen and drew back the curtain. He stood on tiptoe, his nose against the glass so he could see her moving round the garden. 'What's wrong with her? She got a limp or something?' He turned to look at me. 'Is she hurt?'

I stood silently, looking at him without expression.

'What?' he said. 'What you looking at me like that for? The girl's got a limp, I'm asking you about it. Don't get PC on me here.'

'Come upstairs. I've got something to show you.'

'What?' He dropped the curtain and followed me bad-temperedly to the staircase. 'You going to seduce me?'

In the study I switched on the light and fired up

the laptop. 'I've got the proposal. A proposal and the first ten chapters.'

'So you've seen the light. You're really ready to go?'

I hesitated. I drummed my fingers on the desk. Didn't meet his eyes.

There was a pause, then Finn seemed to read my mind. He shook his head and sighed. 'Dude, the man is dead. Dead and gone. If he wasn't we'd have heard.'

'Yeah. Yeah, I know.' I paused. I kept trying to imagine Dove's body – somewhere up in the Highlands. 'If we do it, how long've we got before publication?'

'Depends on which house takes it. If they're really pushing . . . three, four months?'

'Three months?'

He sighed. 'Oakes, pardon my rudeness, but you get me over here because you say you're ready.'

'I am. I am ready. I've thought about it. You're both right. You and—' I nodded towards the window. 'You and Angeline. You're right.'

'She pulling your strings for you? What's she got to do with anything?'

I was silent for a moment, holding his eyes steadily. Then I swivelled the chair round to face the computer, clicked on the media-player icon and found the tourist video. 'Ever seen this? Did I ever show you this?'

'Sure.' He leaned forward and watched Angeline's hazy figure crossing the beach. 'It's weird as all fuck. Knobhead kids. Have you spoken to him yet? Like I said?'

'It's not a kid.'

He turned his eyes to me. 'What?'

'Not a kid.'

'Oakesy,' he said, smiling cautiously, 'you told me it was a kid.'

'I lied.'

'Then who was it?'

I looked back at him, then turned my eyes slowly to the video.

'What?' he said. The video played again, Angeline walked across the beach. The colours from the screen moved over Finn's puzzled face. He frowned, opened his mouth, then closed it. He looked at me and I could see the beginnings of something dawning. Slowly, almost woodenly, he put his hands on the desk and peered closer at the video, watched it for a moment or two, then turned and let his eyes drift out of the window to the garden.

'No,' he whispered. 'No fucking way . . .' He was suddenly pale under his tan. 'You're kidding me.' Slowly, moving like in a dream, he went to the window and stared into the garden for a long time. Angeline was out there, tapping a plank into place beneath the gate, edging it under the cross-bar to keep the gate firmly closed. Then he turned and looked at the computer screen, licking his lips, a look of half revulsion, half excitement in his eyes. 'What the fuck is it?' There was a line of sweat on his forehead. 'What the fuck has she got down there?'

'A parasitic limb.'

'A para-*what*?'

'A limb. Part of a twin that never formed right. You'd call it a Siamese twin. It's not weird, Finn. Whatever your face is saying, it really isn't that unusual.'

'Not *unusual*?'

'No.' I clicked the video off. 'It's not. There are kids born like this every year.'

His eyes got even wider, filtering all the information. Then the clouds parted for him – and he got it. 'Shit, shit, I mean *shit* I've just come in!' He sat down abruptly on the sofa, staring at me in awe, his hands on his temples, like he was trying to keep his brains from falling out of his skull. 'Holy fucking Christ. You're *dicking* her, aren't you? That's what this is. You're dicking her.'

'Yes,' I said quietly. 'Yes, I am.'

4

When he'd gone I went to bed. It was still daylight. I took my clothes off and I lay on my back, watching the grey sky out of the window. After a while Angeline came in from the garden. She'd taken off her coat and scarf and was wearing a belted olive-green cardigan. When she came into the room I rolled on to my side, my head resting on one hand, looking at her.

'Hi.'

'Hi.' She'd come up because she knew I was there. But she was timid. It was new to us, this. It hadn't really sunk in. 'Well,' she said, when I didn't say anything. 'I'll – I'll come to bed.'

She undid her belt and cardigan and dropped them. Underneath she wore a skirt and a thin-strapped vest, showing her narrow shoulders. She took it off, unzipped the skirt and stepped out of it, and then she was naked, wearing only a pair of grey knee-high socks. You could see the long muscles in her legs even though she wasn't moving.

She gave a small laugh. Shy. She stayed for a moment or two, resting her left foot on the right. She knew I was looking at her body. Peeping from behind the calf was the end of the extra limb, tapering unevenly to the battered, deformed foot resting against her ankles. I pictured its roots high up

438

inside the smooth basket of her stomach: a bundle of limb, bone and sinew packed away inside it. Something else living inside her. I looked at her belly, at the little crease above her pubic hair.

'Well?'

'Well what?'

'I've been thinking about it all day.'

'Finn?'

'What did he say?'

'He said.' I scratched my head. Tried not to smile. 'He said he loved it.'

There was a pause. A smile twitched at the corners of her mouth. She got into bed, pulled the cover up and mirrored me, her elbow on the pillow, her head resting on her hand, holding my eyes, fighting to keep a smile off her face. We looked at each other without speaking. In the slanting light from the window I could see microscopic details of her face: fine downy hairs, cushiony diamond creases of the skin. Last night we'd sat here on the bed for two hours. She'd been half turned from me and the limb was lying on the sheet between us. She let me examine it. I'd held in my hand the pea-sized nodules inside the skin where toes were meant to be. I'd moved them around, letting them click and grind against each other. I'd rested my hand over a swollen place half-way up the limb, where the flesh strained against the skin:

a weird tension of muscle tethered to bone. A knee.

'And did he think it was weird? Me, I mean. What did he think?'

'He thought you were beautiful.'

'Beautiful?'

'Yes.'

There was a pause while she bit her lip, fighting the smile. 'What? Really? Beautiful?'

'Really.'

'My God,' she said, and now the smile came, breaking out, showing her small teeth. 'I can't believe it.' She shivered, half laughing, lifting her shoulders and squirming in delight under the covers so that her cold knees touched my legs.

'Excited?' I said.

'And scared. Really excited, but really scared too. Both.'

We'd talked about it: about how much she needed people to know all about her. I had to remember she was nineteen years old. Just nineteen. And I was thirty-eight. I'd forgotten what it was like to want normality the way you want a drug. For her being public, very public, was the fastest route to normality she knew. Didn't matter what I thought. In a closed-off section of my calloused old head I sort of knew I had to put my unease to one side. I nodded, tried to smile. Tried for more enthusiasm.

'It's going to be three months,' I said. 'So, not long.'

'Not long?' She grinned and shivered again. 'Three months seems like for ever.' She shuffled towards me, pushing her face close to mine, her swimmy eyes magnified so I could see my own face in them: grey, drawn, not at all certain. 'For ever,' she murmured, tilting her face sideways and putting her mouth over mine, the breath from her nose warm on mine. Her hand came up, fumbling round my neck, pulling me closer.

I closed my eyes and kissed her. I reached under the covers and dragged her body hard towards me, thinking if I pressed her stomach tight enough to mine the anxiety would go away and I'd stop thinking, *Three months, three months is nothing. And they still haven't found Malachi . . .*

5

We were in Finn's office when we got the news. That was the irony. We were actually signing the book deal. Angeline was sitting neatly at Finn's desk, wearing a coat I'd never seen before with embroidery on the sleeves and fake fur round the collar, and she was dead excited and flushed. I was next to her, wearing this huge sweater because I was cold all the time, these days, and trying not to think about this sick feeling in my stomach. Finn had been brokering the contract for days, and although it wasn't the total off-the-scale deal he'd hoped for, it wasn't bad. 'Enough to keep you in Newkie Brown for a couple of years.' And I was going to be paid separately for the photos too, so that was a little icing. Still, my guts were in knots over it. Just three months.

'Now,' Finn said, 'initial these pages and sign here – on the last.' He handed Angeline this big show-off fountain-pen. She was going to be joint signatory on a clause that tied her into publicizing the book. 'Because,' said Finn, pushing up his sleeve to bare his suntanned arms and the dingy old Glastonbury braid, 'you are the best-kept secret, Angeline, after where Saddam hid all that uranium – which, as we all know, was up Tony Blair's arse.' He winked at her. 'The press are going to be all over you. We're going to make sure we play it right.'

There were a few moments' silence. The winter sun came through the giant arched window and on to her curly head as she leaned over the contract. No one spoke. The only noise was the scratching of the pen. She lifted her head and handed it to me and, with a moment's hesitation, I pulled the contract over and signed quickly, turning the pages and initialling fast before I changed my mind. There were ten pages and it was the exact moment I lifted the pen off the paper that the mobey rang in my pocket. It was Danso.

'Joe,' he said, 'where are you?'

'London.'

Sitting at the desk opposite, Finn was looking at me, silent.

'Got your car?'

'Yes.'

'OK. Would you do me the honour of getting into that car, and bringing that lass with you?'

A beat of unease went through me. 'Yeah,' I said cautiously. 'Probably could, if you tell me where you are.'

'Dumfries, just over the border.'

'Dumfries? And what's in Dumfries?'

There was a pause. When he spoke his voice was low, excited. 'Joe, we think we've got him. We really do, Joe. We think we've got him.'

Dumfries in southern Scotland is a good hundred miles south of Pig Island. It lies near the English border on the Solway Firth to the west of Lockerbie. They'd picked him up at eleven o'clock the night before in a forest two miles outside the town and now he was lying on a mortuary block in the Dumfries and Galloway Royal Infirmary.

It took me and Angeline five hours to drive there, and it was dark when we arrived, but Danso was waiting for us outside the undertaker's loading bay, looking calm, a little pleased. He came forward to open the car doors. Angeline had been shivering with nerves most of the way but when she got out of the car she managed a small smile.

'Hello there, lassie.' Danso held out his hand to her, slightly surprised to see her so confident. 'You're looking very bonny, I must say. Suits you, does it? London?'

She shook his hand. 'I suppose it must do.'

Struthers came out of the hospital mortuary, pulling on his coat, and when he saw her he paused for a second, a little flush coming to his face. 'Hi,' he said hurriedly, when he realized we were all watching him. He wiped his hand furtively on his trousers and gave it to her to shake, his eyes on her face. 'It's been a long time.'

She had changed. It had happened so gradually I hadn't noticed it. But now, seeing the men following her with their eyes as she made her way to the lighted building, I could tell she was a different woman entirely from the one they'd first met shivering with fear at the Oban station. She'd left the embroidered coat on the back seat and was wearing a tight, ribbed sweater and a greyish skirt. She'd put her hair back in a beaded slide she must've got from Lexie's drawer. She looked like she was going to a dinner party. Struthers kept shooting glances at the skirt out of the corner of his eyes as we went into the building.

Two men waited in a wallpapered side-room: the family liaison officer and the pathologist, dressed in a suit and tie, his reading glasses tucked into the breast pocket. They stood to introduce themselves to Angeline, explaining who they were, why they were there, what was going to happen next. *The procurator fiscal has asked me to perform a post-mortem . . .*

Danso waited a moment or two, then put a hand on my arm and beckoned me back into the corridor where we couldn't be heard.

'Joe,' he said, closing the door behind us, 'just needed to say something. This character we've got on a slab, he's carrying no ID. The doctor's think-ing he won't be getting any prints because of slippage.' We stood against a painted pink panel on the wall, our faces sick-looking in the fluorescent lights. 'Do you know what that is? That's when the skin starts to slide off.'

'Decomposition?'

'Aye. And you can't get a print off it.' He went and peered through the glass panel into the waiting room. Inside, Struthers had brought Angeline a cup of something and was standing facing her, not speaking, just watching her with this arsey smile on his face. 'Discussed it with the chief. We're going to back ourselves up before we go public, get DNA. But that'll take till next Monday and, the idea goes, this is the quickest way for us to get the PM done.' He cleared his throat. 'But, look, when I say there's slippage on his fingers . . .'

'Yes?'

'There's some on his face too – that's what I'm trying to tell you. I almost called and said, "Forget it, we'll wait for the DNA." Not sure I want her to go through this.'

We both watched Angeline through the glass panel. She was standing in the middle of the room, holding herself straight, listening to what the pathologist was saying. She was holding the drink in both hands. Usually her hands would be hovering self-consciously behind her. The back of the skirt stood out from her small waist like a bustle.

'But you know what?' Danso said, smiling slightly. 'You know what? Not sure now what I was worried about. The way she looks right now she could handle anything.'

The smell in the mortuary was nothing like I expected. It was fresher and sweeter, even tame in its way. Even the viewing room didn't smell of death. It had the whiff of a newly cleaned industrial kitchen, vases of fresh yellow flowers in each corner. Seven or eight seats were arranged round the walls, a Bible and a blue box of paper tissues on each one, and along the far end of the room, side on, a linen-covered shape lay on a trolley. A mortician in a white coat stood next to it, watching as we all filed in. His hand was resting on the white-and-blue-striped towel that covered the corpse's face.

'You're aware of the circumstances of the discovery of this body,' the pathologist said. 'You know there could be some discolouration on his face. If this is your father he might not look exactly the way he did when he was alive.'

'I know.'

He nodded, studying her carefully.

'Well now,' he said. 'You take your time. Look for as long as you want and if you need a break we'll take you out and you can have a breather. Come back inside later. We've got all the time in the world.'

'I'm ready.'

I held my breath, my heart knocking at my ribs. The mortician folded down the towel. Dove lay on his back, just his face showing, the sheet pulled up to conceal the rope he'd hanged himself with. The first thing I thought was, Christ, he's thin. He must've lost about five stone. He looked totally different: his jaw was so far relaxed it melted into his chest, his jowls drooped in folds, touching the sheet. His thick fair hair was reduced to sparse patches on the skull and his skin had lost that burned-looking red colour – even under the skim of makeup the mortician had used you could see it was yellowish-brown, the weight of it pulling at the rest of his face so you could see the sharp bone in his nose. I stared at him, not blinking, listening to my breath going in and out. In my head I'd been here, in this mortuary, a hundred times, looking at his dead body.

'Angeline,' said the pathologist, clearing his throat, 'are these the remains of your father, Malachi Dove?'

She turned to me, her hand over her mouth. I put my arms round her and she buried her face in my chest. 'My God, my God.'

'Angeline?' said Danso gently. 'What's happening with you, pet?'

'*Yes*,' she muttered, nodding into my sweater. '*Yes*. It's him.'

'Are you sure, lass? You sure you don't want another wee keek just to be sure? You can take your time. He's lost some weight – living rough all this time.'

'Doesn't matter,' she whispered. 'Doesn't matter.'

'Doesn't matter?'

'No. It's him. I'd know him anywhere.'

'You all right?' After the viewing Angeline went to get a cup of water with Struthers and I went outside for a ciggy. Danso came to stand with me, his hands in his pockets, looking out at the car park, the ferroconcrete fire escape that led up to the Pathology Unit. 'Don't look happy to me.'

I shook my head. I took a drag on the ciggy and looked up at the stars. It was a clear night, just a few clouds, horror-movie clouds, floating across the sky. 'I've been waiting half my life for this.'

'Aye. I'll bet you have.'

'And you know what's weird?' I turned my eyes sideways to him. 'What's weird is I never pictured it like this. Always thought it'd be different.'

'Different how?'

I gave a short, dry laugh. 'Don't know. S'pose I couldn't ever get rid of what he said: "My death will be memorable." Do you remember? "Memorable."' I turned to look at the mortuary. The windows threw square panes of light on to the gravel. 'Not like this.'

'You mean you thought it'd be staged?'

'Yeah.'

'It was.'

I blew out some smoke. 'It was?'

'Yeah.' He pulled a clear plastic wallet of photos

from inside his coat and handed them to me. 'Not supposed to show you these, OK?'

I put the ciggy between my teeth and held up the photos so the light from the lit walkway overhead fell on them. At first I thought I was looking at a bundle of clothes caught in a tree. Or a parachute tangled up. Then I recognized hands, and I could make out the outline of a body among all the material, stiff like a scarecrow, the head flopped down on to the chest.

'Rope round here,' Danso said. 'Round the trunk. Jumped out of the tree, rope broke his neck. The branches caught his arms. This stuff here is some groundsheet he had wrapped round him – been living up there rough for weeks.' He paused. 'Look at him Joe. He looks just like an angel, doesn't he?'

I didn't answer. I was staring at the groundsheet, the way it extended from the outspread arms like wings.

'An angel. That groundsheet was flapping like mad in the wind. Put the creeps up the lads – you could hear him before you saw him. Blak-blak-blak coming out of the trees. And smell him too.' He sniffed the air, like the smell was still in his nostrils. 'And smell him.'

I handed him the photographs, flicked away the ciggy and sat down, back against the big door the undertakers used, elbows on my knees, head down.

'Joe? You OK, son?'

I nodded, but I didn't look up. I was staring at the ground between my feet, pictures going across my head like a train: Finn's ma; me and Lexie; the evil way Dove dissolved out of the trees and lay on top of me. Danso wanted me to jump up and punch the air or something. I knew that was what he wanted – it was what I'd always pictured too – but I couldn't do it. All I felt was this great fucking ocean of tiredness open up inside me, and spread and spread, until I knew I was tireder, much tireder than I'd ever been in my life.

6

In London spring was on its way. There were winds and floods. Half of East Anglia and Gloucestershire was under water and Londoners sat glued to the television, watching cars floating down high streets like driftwood, thanking God they lived in a city civilized enough to have a flood barrier. The back gate had been forced open again. I put it down to the high winds, but the neighbours said it had happened in their gardens too, and probably a tramp was living in the neighbourhood. Nobody had seen him, but they were sure he was there. Everywhere he left trampled lawns, scraps of tissue and Twix wrappers that had to be picked up on gardening forks. He was using the back alley to sneak into gardens at night, trying to find a warm place to sleep. Some of the other gardens had the locks broken off their sheds.

The world didn't seem real to me. With Dove gone, it was like the plug had been pulled on my life. The tiredness thing wouldn't let up. I slept long stretches, nine, ten hours, but I'd wake up tireder than before and end up asleep at my desk, hands flopped on the keyboard, sending long strings of letters on to the screen. It crossed my mind to see a doctor, but I kind of guessed what the answer would be – *Have you been under any stress recently, Mr Oakes?* And then it would come out – Lexie dead, the way I didn't feel better that it was all over, worry about the book. Before I knew it I'd be in counselling, clutching a Seroxat script. So instead I kept going, pushing forward like I was under water, ignoring this perpetual drag on me.

After ten long days I got the manuscript off to the editor. The publishers' art department had been sending us visuals of the dust-jacket and now they'd arranged a photo session for Angeline in some studio in Brixton. This was something Finn and me and Angeline had spent a long time talking about – how to show her to the world. She wasn't going to let the deformity itself be photographed, so we'd decided on a still from the video, and for a modeller who worked for a medical-supply company to make and photograph a fibreglass cross-section of it. The publishers were going to send her up to Pig Island later in the month to get some shots of her at the chapel, but they wanted some studio portraits too. Just head and shoulders. It happened on the first Monday in March. The beginning of spring and, looking back at it now, it turned out to be the beginning of another kind of change in the air.

'Well?' I said. 'How do you feel?'

We sat in the makeup room looking at each other. She hadn't taken off her outdoor clothes: she still had on her coat and a knitted stripy beanie pulled over her hair. I'd brought the JD with me and now I opened it, poured her some in a plastic cup and handed it to her.

'You going to be OK?'

'I don't know.' She took it and shivered, shooting an anxious look at the door. We'd been let in by the janitor to an empty studio, but now the others were arriving. We could hear voices out there. 'They've seen the video. I wonder what they're going to think. Of me.' Her eyes went across the room at a rack of dresses pushed into the corner. They were covered with Cellophane but you could see the long skirts trailing the floor. She'd been fitted and measured for these, specifically so nothing would show. 'But whatever I wear, it doesn't matter. They'll still know.'

'You can change your mind,' I said. 'I'll have Finn tear up the contract. You only have to say the—'

'No. No, really.' She gave a small, nervous laugh. She pulled off her hat and ran a hand through the short curls, raising her eyes cautiously to the mirror, getting a shy look at her face, bare and colourless. 'I'm going to do it. Of course I am.'

When the makeup girl came in I left them to it and wandered into the studio, thinking about what she'd said: *What will they think of me?* The studio was in a warehouse with polished concrete floors, ceiling cross-braces painted black, and big, unlit studio lamps standing like sentinels in the dark corners. A roll of white paper hanging from an overhead brace had been pulled down to the floor and a small swivel stool placed in the centre. An assistant wandered around setting up lights, snapping open diffusers, all the time chatting in a low voice to the photographer, who was bent over the top of his camera, peering into the viewfinder. The photographer was in his early twenties and looked like he wrote for an alt music mag like *Mojo* or *NME*, with his faded print Bob Marley T-shirt and his jeans hanging round his arse. They didn't see me come in so I got quite close and I'd listened to them for a few minutes before I sussed they were talking about disabled people modelling.

'There's this whole, like, obsession with it at the moment. Marc Quinn and that pregnant bird, Alison Lapper.'

'Yeah, and Aimee Mullins . . .' said the assistant. 'Both totally cool.'

'And personally, I'm, like, this is *so*, you know, so *about time too*.'

'I know.'

'It's so overdue, it's just not funny. It's time they—' The photographer broke off suddenly and straightened, looking far off into the corner of the studio. Me and the assistant both turned to see what he was looking at. The dressing-room door had opened and Angeline was there, blinking shakily in the studio lights. She was wearing some silver number that had a neckline half-way down her stomach and looked like it cost half my yearly salary, and she was a totally different person: the makeup girl had slicked her short curls back against her head like a black helmet, fixed false eyelashes on her, and outlined her mouth in lipstick like red plastic. Her hands were shaking but her face was as composed as a shop-floor dummy, almost glassy it was so perfect. She swallowed, then began to walk, slowly, sort of tentatively, putting one foot in front of the other, like she thought she might fall. No one breathed while we took her in and the studio went totally silent, just the sound of her heels clicking on the floor echoing round the high roof. She got to the edge of the lights, hesitated, then stepped on to the paper, walked quickly to the stool and sank on to it like it was a life raft.

'Fuck.' The photographer let out an amazed whistle. Just soft, under his breath. 'Fucking hell.' He shook his head, then tugged up his jeans and went to stand on the paper about two foot in front of her, looking at her curiously, like he was asking a question. There was a long pause. Then he goes, all surprised, 'You're beautiful, Angeline. You're totally fucking gorgeous.'

At first she stared at him, like she couldn't work out what he'd said or who he was. Like he might be telling her off, maybe. Then something inside her sort of cracked open and all this colour spilled out under her skin and her cheeks went pink. 'Thank you,' she whispered shyly. 'Thank you.'

He gave a disbelieving laugh, still staring at her. 'You,' he said, 'are totally, totally welcome.'

Not taking his eyes off her, like she might run

away if he did, he walked backwards to the camera. He lifted up his hands – the way you'd pacify a skittish animal.

'Don't move,' he said, glancing down at the viewfinder. 'Don't move.' And before she knew what was happening he'd taken a photo. The flash fired and he was winding on the camera.

Angeline blinked at him. 'Did you do it?'

'Yes,' he said, switching the camera to display and squinting at the screen. He looked up at her. 'See how easy it's going to be?'

It was so weird that afternoon to stand there, outside the lights and watch her kind of . . . I don't know the word, but *expand*, maybe. Like she was growing under the attention. It was like each time the flash fired the muscles in her face relaxed a bit more until the doll look softened and she looked, even I have to say it, awesome. And no one was treating her weird or patronizing. No one was stupid about the way she had to sit, half tilted over because she was never comfortable on a stool and had to grip the sides of it. Instead they were treating her like she was something cool.

When they'd done about twenty shots they got her changed, put her in a different dress, different hair and stuff. During the day she went through about six different dresses, most of which looked totally fucking ridiculous to me, like some of those makeover boudoir get-ups but must've been some kind of style statements because everyone else seemed to get them. Even Angeline. By three o'clock I had to sit down. I was getting tired. And there was something else. I was starting to get arsed off with the photographer.

At first it was great, seeing how happy he was making her, but now he was getting sort of tiresome. The way he kept up with this *beautiful, beautiful* shit, it was getting on my tits. I started watching him a bit more closely. I went further into the shadows so they couldn't see me, and stood there, fiddling impatiently with my keys, spinning them on my finger, pulling them on and off the ring, trying to stop myself saying, 'What? Do you fancy her or something? Stop staring at her.' So when, at the end of the day, we were all knackered and I thought, At least it's over, he went up close to her, dropped his face, and said something really quiet, I stopped spinning the keys and went very still, watching them closely. Angeline's smile went. She sat there, her eyes on the floor, and listened to him talk, tucking the hair behind her ear and thinking about what he was saying. He finished and straightened, took a step back. 'Well?'

'Hey,' I said, coming closer to the set so I could feel the lights on my face. 'Angeline?'

But she didn't turn to me. She didn't even seem to

hear me. Her eyes were locked on his. There were a couple of beats, then she gave a small nod.

'Hey,' I murmured. 'Angeline?'

No one reacted. The photographer went and unscrewed the camera, took it off the tripod and lay down on his stomach, resting on his elbows with the camera raised to his eyes. He was focusing on her skirt hem and, suddenly, catching us all by surprise, she reached down, grabbed the fabric and lifted it to her knees.

I've got the photo from that moment and I still look at it, even today. Her thin ankles, the little sweaty footprints of her feet on the background paper, but most of all the third, broken and squashed foot, heavier-looking, but you can tell it's made out of the same flesh as the other two, and it's hanging there, with its own shadow. Turns out it's the best shot in the book, the one everyone talks about. But at the time I was ready to kill the photographer.

When they'd finished, when she'd gone to get her makeup off and someone had brought round coffee and a bottle of sparkling rosé, I took my glass and made sure I sat near him. Wanted to keep an eye on him. I wasn't having him talking to her on his own again.

He was lounging on a sofa, half on his back, idly running his charity bands up and down his arms. If he knew I had the arse with him he didn't show it. 'So,' he said, all casual, 'what happens when it all comes out?' He paused to drain his glass, and swivelled his eyes to me. 'When I was watching her all I could think was, What if her dad reads the book? What's he going to think? See, if it was me I'd be hiding in a hole.'

I looked at him steadily. 'Malachi Dove is dead. How can he read the book?

'Is he?'

'Don't you read the papers? They've been talking about it all week.'

'Oh, that body. In Dumfries. But they never confirmed it. Never said it was definitely him. Did they?'

'No,' I said, in a slow voice, like he was a child not listening properly. 'They're waiting for DNA before they do. But it was him. He. Is. Dead.'

Angeline came across the floor then, holding an opened can of diet Coke. We both looked up. She was wearing a white dressing-gown and I could see where her makeup had been taken off: a line round her neck. Above it, she was pink and shining, glowing more than she had a right to after five hours under the lights.

'Hey,' said the photographer, getting up and smiling, a really fake smile like he was dazzled by her. 'Have a seat.'

She sat down, tucking her curls into two pins above her ears. 'I'm *sooo* tired,' she said, with a smile. She looked at me. 'I'm so tired.'

'You were great,' I said, but I had to force it out.

'Hey, Angeline.' The photographer leaned sideways and shoved a hand into his back pocket. He pulled out a card. Held it out to her between two fingers, so delicate you'd think it was some exotic butterfly, not a bit of cardboard. 'I work with her all the time. Her work is lush – just lush. Edgy. Real. Know what I mean?'

She took the card and looked at it. Her mouth twitched a little.

'What is it?' I said, leaning over. 'Let's see.'

There was a moment's hesitation before she handed me the card. I had to pull it a bit to get it out of her fingers. Just a bit. I flipped it over and stared at it, my face set. The features editor of the *Daily Mail*. What was going on? I turned to the photographer, moving my head stiffly. 'Well? What's this?'

'She's really wanting to do something on Angeline.'

The fucking features editor of a national newspaper knew about Angeline? How had that happened? I leaned forward and tapped his knee, getting him to look at me, wanting to tell him to sit upright, stop slouching. 'That's OK.. That's fine.

Except we're negotiating the serial rights on this story and it's not with the *Mail*.' I paused to make sure he'd heard that. 'OK?'

'Sorry, mate.' He held up the glass to me, like he was toasting our status as a couple. 'Didn't want to interfere. Not my job to make waves.'

I stood up. 'Come on,' I said, holding my hand out to Angeline. 'Let's get you dressed.' But she didn't get up. She sat there, staring at my hand. 'Come on,' I repeated. 'It's time to get dressed and go. Let's give your friend some time to read his contract.'

Angeline sighed and rolled her eyes. 'OK,' she said, in a sarcastic voice. The same voice Sovereign always used with her mother. 'I'm com*ing*.'

She finished the Coke and dropped the can into the bin. She held up her hand, thumb at her ear, pinkie at the corner of her mouth, and smiled at the photographer. 'Call me,' she mouthed, and walked straight past me, sauntering off to the makeup room, her feet in the towelling slippers slapping lazily on the floor, the way I'd seen hookers in Tijuana walk. I stood and watched her and all I could think about was when I was a teenager in Bootle. Back then the local fathers used to line up outside nightclubs waiting for their daughters at kicking-out time. They'd get out of their cars and put their elbows on the roofs. They'd look casual, but you could tell what they were thinking. They were thinking if one of those arseholes in the club had laid even a *finger* on their little girl he was going to get a hiding he'd never forget.

7

We travelled home in silence, Angeline in the passenger seat chewing gum she'd picked up somewhere. She kept fiddling with the radio, trying to find Choice FM, until I reached over and switched it off. I'd made up my mind we weren't going to speak to the photographer again. I didn't like his interfering and I didn't like the knowing way he talked about Dove. The body in Dumfries was him, no one had said it wasn't. In the morning I'd call Danso – just so I could hear the DNA match from his mouth. Even so, when I got home I went into the back garden and nailed the gate closed. Then I double-checked the cellar door and trundled the lawnmower up against it.

Inside, the phone was ringing. As I came into the kitchen I heard Angeline's hurried footsteps on the stairs, and her breathless 'Yes? Hi?' I came into the hallway and stood there, my coat half off, staring at her. 'Yes,' she was saying into the phone. 'It's me.' A giggle. 'I know – he told me all that.'

She noticed me then in the doorway and turned

away to face the wall, twiddling her hair round her fingers, resting one foot on the other and jiggling up and down as she spoke. 'No, that's *OK*. Honest. I *wanted* you to call.'

I stood there in silence, toying with the idea of putting my fingers on the phone connectors. Instead I pulled off my coat and went and sat at the kitchen table in the semi-dark, moodily necking a bottle of Newkie Brown. The fathers outside the Crosby nightclub kept coming back to me.

'Joe?' When she finished the call she appeared in the kitchen doorway, eyes bright, chin lowered, a little-girl smile on her face. 'I've been naughty, haven't I?'

'You're going to do it?'

'Friday.'

'Friday? You really think that's safe? Before we know if it was your dad or not?'

'But it was him.'

'He looked so different.'

Her shoulders slumped. 'Not this again.'

I sighed and rubbed my temples wearily. 'I don't know. I really don't know. I don't like it.' I dropped my hands and looked at the window, thinking about the security locks on them. They hadn't been used in years – like we had anything worth robbing – and I couldn't remember the last time I'd seen the key. It was probably in the old coffee jar on the basement shelf. Danso, I told myself again, would've called if there was a problem.

'Joe,' she said, coming and putting her hands on my shoulders. She swung her leg over my legs and sat on my lap facing me, her skirt bunched up between her thighs so her legs were exposed. I could smell the coffee she'd drunk and the cold cream they'd used to take off the makeup. 'Why don't you believe me? It was him.'

'And *why* can't *you* wait until we're sure? They'll have the DNA any time now. I'm going to call Danso in the morning.'

'But it was him, Joe. And, anyway, it's not like I'm going to say anything.' She shifted a little, pulling the skirt out of the way so her bare thighs pressed against my jeans. 'I won't say where I live.'

'You're going to have to wait till I've spoken to Finn. You could mess up the contract if you're not careful. He's not going to like it.'

'He is. He'll love it.' She took my hands and eased them up under the skirt, forcing my fingers between her legs. She hadn't got knickers on. She was damp and warm and I could feel the hard pressure of the deformed leg pressing down on my knuckles. 'I promise, I promise,' she whispered, closing her eyes and moving her hips in a circular motion. 'I won't say a word about you.'

8

She wasn't trying to antagonize me. She totally wasn't. I wasn't in her thoughts at all, I knew that. All she was doing was wanting to be heard. She was nineteen, for Christ's sake, and if everything she did when the *Mail* came to interview her seemed like she was giving me the finger, it was my own fault.

I'd talked to Finn and he didn't love it. Not one bit. He'd gone through the contract with a fine-tooth comb and unless she talked about the massacre itself there wasn't a thing he could do to stop her, but he was furious. I'd called Danso over and over again and I kept getting his answer-service, so I left all these messages telling him to call me if the DNA didn't match. But he didn't get back to me. It was starting to seem like I couldn't stand in front of this landslide and hold it back. All of which made *me* the bad tempered-arsehole boyfriend during the *Mail* interview, hovering behind the journalist and signalling to Angeline over her head if I thought she was giving stuff away.

She kept losing her grip – being careless about what she was saying. At one point she said, 'I can't talk about that because Joe and I . . .'

'Angeline,' I said significantly, 'you're, uh—'

'Oh, yeah,' she said. 'What *was* I thinking? What I meant to say was . . .'

I spent the rest of the time staring at her furiously, waiting for the wrong word, the wrong expression. After a while she got fed up with me hovering and took the journalist into the kitchen, where the pair of them sat in a girlie huddle, drinking tea and smoking. I kept making excuses to come in: to boil the kettle, or wander through into the garden. Every time I did it they'd stop giggling and turn to me with sweet, empty smiles, waiting politely for me to go so they could get on with the interview.

I didn't know if she'd stuck to her promise until the article came out three days later. It was a Monday, and although I'd set the alarm for seven, when I woke up the bed was already empty. I knew where she'd gone – down to the newsagent's to get the paper. I was still in bed, rubbing my head and trying to wake up, when the phone rang. It was Danso, his usually austere voice weary and tense.

'Well, you sound crap.'

'I feel it. Been up all night and come straight here to the airport. We're on the Tarmac now.'

'We?'

'Me and Sancho Struthers. My travelling companion.'

'Not off to Miami, then. Or do you take him on your holidays too?'

He didn't laugh. 'Joe,' he said, 'are you going anywhere today?'

'Me? Only the corner shop. I'm staying in. Got a book to write.'

'We're on our way to Heathrow. Be with you in a couple of hours. Need a little *consultation* if that's OK.'

'A consultation? What's up?'

He hesitated. 'It's a lot to go into on an open line, Joe, if you're with me. Shall we hold it till we're face to face?'

I threw off the covers and swung my feet out of bed. Something in his voice had set a bell ringing in the back of my head. 'It's not him, is it? That sad sack on the slab in Dumfries, that's not Malachi. I've left messages, Peter, about this. Been waiting for you to call.'

There was a silence. Just the sound of static on the line and the steady thrum of a small-engined jet.

'Peter? Can you hear me? I said, it's not him, is it?'

'It's not him,' he said eventually. 'The DNA's wrong.'

'Fucking *knew* it.' I stood up. 'He found someone who looked like him. The suicide note, everything, he just wanted you off his back for a few weeks.'

'No. We don't think he did this one – think it's coincidence.' He lowered his voice – probably getting the evils from the other passengers. 'The Dumfries guy's an ex-squaddie, not been right since Desert Storm. Threatening suicide for years.'

'Peter,' I said, pacing up and down the room, tapping out the words in the air, 'how long does DNA take?'

'Not long. It's—'

'Exactly. Not long. You said Friday – that's three days ago. You've known three days, and I've left messages asking you to let me know if—'

'Joe, listen—'

'To let me know if there wasn't a match and in the meantime Angeline's gone to the fucking newspapers and given them her story.' I went to the window and flicked open the curtains, expecting to see her coming down the street. 'He'll read it this morning and know where she is and—'

I broke off. Something in the street outside had caught my eye.

'Peter?' My blood had gone a bit slow, a bit cold. '*Peter, you bastard?* What's happening? What aren't you telling me?' I opened the window and leaned out, my breath steaming in the air, condensation wetting my naked shoulder. 'There's a fucking squad car in the street outside with his lights on. What the fuck's going on?'

'He's from Salusbury Road. Joe? *Joe!* Listen. He's just there as a precaution.'

'A *precaution*? Jesus fucking Christ – you'd better tell me what's going on.'

'Maybe you'll stay in the house today. You've got no reason to go out, eh? Cancel the shopping trip. I'm going to text you the number of the local nick – they know all about the situation.'

'The situation?'

'The plane's taxiing, Joe – I'm getting the evil eye from the stewardess.'

'Listen,' I hissed, 'Angeline's out. What am I going to do about—'

'Just relax. There's nothing to worry about,' he said, and the phone went dead in my hand.

I punched in 1471 then 3 but his answer-service picked up. I hung up and stared at the phone, the blood thumping in my ears. 'You bastards,' I said. 'You *knew* about this.' I looked out of the window. The streetlights were still on, the orange mixing with the flashing blue light. When I went to the bed and put my hand on the side where Angeline slept it was cold. The newsagent's was only a five-minute walk. Fear came up into my mouth like stomach acid.

I put on jeans and went down the stairs, pulling on a T-shirt. Every step was a bit closer to panic. By the time I got to the hall my teeth were chattering. I ran outside in my bare feet, hesitated, went back and unhooked the keys from above the phone, then slammed the front door tight behind me. In the car opposite the police officer turned his head in my direction as I came down the path. I couldn't see his face – it was behind the sun visor – just his chapped hands resting calmly on the dashboard. I ran into the middle of the road, the cold biting my feet. I turned to check both ways up the street and was about to continue over to him, to hammer on the car window, when I saw her in the distance, coming down the road towards me.

It nearly snapped me in half, the relief. I limped back and leaned on the gate, getting my breath, lifting my head to watch her approach. She was carrying three newspapers and her eyes were bright.

'Joe!' she said, speeding up when she saw me. 'It's in here!' She waved one of the papers at me. 'She said I'm beautiful.'

'Come inside.'

She hesitated, her smile fading, her arm falling slack at her side. 'You haven't got any shoes on.'

'Just get inside.' I took her arm and led her down the path, not speaking. Inside I locked the door and bolted it, put the chain on. She stood in silence as I locked the back door, up-ended the coffee jar on the floor and sorted through the keys until I found the security key. I went round each room locking the windows. I drew all the curtains, then went back to the hallway and took the newspaper from her limp hand.

'Is this it? The article?' I put it on the kitchen table and began to leaf through it. 'Does she say we're living together?'

'No,' she said, unwinding her scarf. Cautious. 'She doesn't mention you at all.'

I found the page and placed my hands flat on it, leaning down to study it. Above me the electric ceiling light moved in a slow circle, its shadow rotating across the newspaper like a divining stone. The article was a two-page feature, a large head-and-shoulders shot of Angeline in the centre, and two insets: one of Dove and one taken offshore at Pig Island, the police tents and boats clustering round the village.

I skimmed the text rapidly. It was standard who-what-why-when journalism: the horror of the massacre, the number killed, Malachi Dove on the run, Lexie's death, all covered in the first para-graph. Then it went on to describe Angeline. There was her favourite line: *a beauty, hints of a piercing intelligence*. It said she had been disabled from birth and walked with a limp. Nothing more specific than that. Then there was a synopsis of her life on the island, her impression of the murdered cult members, finishing with a reference to the book, due in August. I didn't get a mention.

I bent nearer and examined the photo, looking at the reflection in her eyes, half expecting to see my own face there, standing in the shadows of the studio, anxious and jealous-looking. But there was nothing. Just the photographer's flash.

'Joe. You'd better tell me. What's happening?'

I shook my head and sat down at the table, pressing my fingers into my temples. I needed a painkiller. I pulled the paper towards me and stared at it glumly.

'*But, Angeline says, the members of PHM treated her well. "They were all so sweet to me. I think they knew what was happening to me."'*

'They were so sweet?' I looked up at her. 'Is that what you said? "I think they knew what was happening to me?" Those are not the words I remember.'

'No.' She coloured. 'I didn't want to . . .' She rubbed her nose, embarrassed. 'I didn't want to sound bitter.'

'Didn't want to sound *bitter*?' I sighed. 'Listen, you think you know what you're doing but this is dangerous crap we're dealing with. It wasn't smart talking to them.'

'It's just self-preservation.'

I looked at her stonily, my words coming back at me like an echo. 'You think this is self-preservation?'

'Yes. Yes. I do.'

'You know what it sounds like? You know what it sounds like to me?'

'What?'

'Not only does it sound like you've given a different story from the one I'm giving, which is going to be a bit fucking embarrassing since that part of the book is already with the publishers—'

'Please don't swear.'

'Listen,' I said, holding up my hand. 'Let me finish. Not only does it sound like that, but it also sounds to me like antagonism. It sounds like you're baiting your dad.'

'*Baiting* him?' She blew a little air out of her nose. 'Well, that's stupid. How could I be baiting him? He's dead.'

I dropped my hand from my head and looked at her seriously. 'Sit down.'

'Why?'

'Just do it.'

'Joe?' she said, sitting at the table opposite me, her face paling a little. 'You're scaring me.'

'They're coming down from Oban to speak to us. Something's happened.'

'All the way from Oban?'

I sighed. 'Angeline, you think you saw your dad in that mortuary but . . .' I put my hand over hers '. . . it wasn't him. They ran a DNA match.'

She snatched her hand away from me, all the colour leaving her face. 'What're you talking about?'

'It wasn't him. I know you ... I know you *wanted* it to be him, and I know why – but it wasn't.'

'My God,' she whispered, putting both hands to her face. 'My God, you mean it, don't you? You really mean it. It wasn't him.'

'It's not just your fault – they wanted it to be him as much as you did. But looking at it now, I think you and Danso both, you were clutching at straws.'

She breathed in and out a few times through her nose, moving this information around her head. Then slowly, very slowly, she raised her eyes to the kitchen window, to the curtains drawn tight against the morning. She turned and looked down the corridor to the lock on the door. 'Oh, no,' she whispered. She put a hand to her throat. 'This is a barricade, isn't it?' She looked at me. 'Isn't it? A barricade? They think he's on his way.'

I didn't say anything for a long time. Then I took her hands. 'They'll be here in two hours. There's a police car outside. We're going to be fine.'

9

For the last few days the skies over London had been draped swollen over the rooftops, inert, not breathing. But late that morning, just before lunch, the clouds gave up their stalemate. They dropped a barrage of hailstones on the little terraced houses of north London, which bounced off the roofs like buckshot, danced pogo in the street.

We didn't speak much that morning, but I was sure Angeline and me were both thinking the same thing: that Malachi was clever, that he could slip through air vents and up chimneys and through knotholes in the floorboards. She had turned on all the lights, looked under the beds and checked inside every cupboard. Then she went to sit in the living room and tried to read her newspaper. But she couldn't concentrate. From time to time she'd get up and go to the french windows, flick open the curtain and stare at the rain-drenched garden. 'There's someone in a tree,' she said at midday, putting her nose against the glass. I came to look. It was a police officer, dressed in boots and a blue sweater with epaulettes. When he saw us he waved. We raised our hands in reply. After that Angeline stopped peering out at the garden. She left the curtains closed.

I wasn't content with the locks on the windows:

I'd hammered nails into the runners of the sash windows to seal them and closed up the letterbox with packing tape. I took a torch into the attic, ripped my jeans as I crawled around checking all the tiles, every brick, every rafter, every rotting roll of insulation, the hail clattering on the roof inches above my head. It was like hearing hell fall out of the sky.

'The cellar,' I said, when I'd finished. Angeline looked at me from the sofa, where she sat biting her nails and anxiously watching the clock. 'I'm going to check the cellar.'

'Do you have to?' She sprang to her feet and limped after me to the cellar door. 'Can't you stay up here? They'll be here in a minute.'

'I won't be long.'

I went down the rickety steps, fumbling with the torch. Angeline stood at the top of the stairs, watching until I disappeared from view into the gloom. I'd bolted the garden door from the outside and pushed the lawnmower against it, but now I hammered an extra four nails into the wood until I was sure it would never move. When I'd finished I sat down on an old deck-chair and clicked off the torch, letting the darkness come to rest round my head and shoulders. It smelt of moss and petrol in here, and something older, more familiar. Overhead Angeline had left the doorway and was in the kitchen, making the floorboards creak.

I switched on the torch and shone it up into the braces under the kitchen floor, listening to her moving about, watching the little puffs of dust coming out of the ceiling. She'd stiffed me with those comments about the PHM. She couldn't see it, but she'd totally stiffed me. I was going to have to talk Finn into getting that bit of the manuscript retracted. I let the beam travel down the wall into the box-vaulted recesses that stretched out under the front garden. Everything was as I remembered it, all the crap piled up, the fridge-freezer glinting dully at me. Strange how nothing down here had changed when upstairs everything was so different.

The doorbell rang. I went up the steps, clicking off the torch and running the bolt on the cellar door, giving it a kick to wedge it into place. 'They're here.' I went to the front door. I switched on the porch light and pressed my face close to the window. 'Yeah?' I called. 'What d'you want?'

'It's us,' came Struther's dry answer, raised above the clatter of the hail. 'All the way from sunny Oban.'

I pulled off the chains and bolts and opened the door. They stood huddled in the porch, cold and sombre in the overhead light, their shoulders wet with hailstones. In the dark street beyond, another marked police car waited, lights flashing lazily, its driver turned in his seat to watch us, resting his elbow on the steering-wheel.

'Our ride from Heathrow,' Danso said, when he saw me looking. 'I admit I wasn't expecting that kind of co-operation from the Met, the stories you hear.' He leaned back and cast his eyes around the front garden, first over one shoulder, then the other. 'Joe?' he said, peering past me into the warm hallway. 'Hate to bother you, son, but it's cold out here.'

I stepped back to allow them in, placing the torch nose down on the windowsill. 'He's not dead.' They came in and I shot the bolts. I put the chain on and turned to them, my back to the door. 'Is he? Not dead. And you know where he is.'

Struthers nodded. 'We know where he is.'

'Listen,' said Danso. 'Can we—' He looked around the hallway. 'I think we should go and sit down for this.'

I stared at him, suddenly angry. 'He's here, isn't he? In London. And you've known it for days.'

'I think,' Danso said, more slowly and deliberately this time, taking in me and Struthers with his tone, 'we should sit down for this.' He put his hand on the living-room door. 'This way, is it?'

We went into the living room, me angry, Danso weary, his feet dragging. Struthers came behind, ostentatiously checking out the room, lifting the curtain and peering out at the police cars in the road. 'Nice place,' he said, dropping the curtain and looking around at the posters and the drab houseplants. 'But, then, it's a nice job you've got.'

'There you are,' Danso said, raising his hand to Angeline. She'd appeared at the kitchen door, wiping her hands on a tea-towel. 'Hello, wee lassie. Saw you in the paper this morning. You're famous.'

'Hello,' she said, with a weak smile. She looked at Struthers. 'Hello.'

'Hello,' he muttered, standing stock still staring at her, at the low-cut sweater, the glitter of something at her neck, her hair caught up in a slide so little curls just covered her ears. 'How are you?'

'Yes. Yes, I'm—' She swallowed and put the tea-towel on the counter. She limped into the living room and stood in front of Danso. 'It wasn't him, then? That's what Joe said. The man you showed me, it wasn't Dad.'

'We're so sorry, hen.' He gave her a sad smile. 'So sorry you had to go through all that.'

'I'm sorry I made a mistake.'

'No.' He shook his head. 'Don't be.'

We all stood for a moment, looking at each other, embarrassed. 'Well,' she said, with a tired shrug, 'you'd like a drink?' She pointed at my drinks cabinet, at the VSOP Armagnac Finn got me last birthday. 'I've got brandy. Or some gin. There's lime-flavoured tonic water in the fridge. Oakesy only drinks Newcastle Brown Ale and you won't want that.'

'No, thanks, pet, we're on duty.' He indicated the sofa. 'Can we?'

'Sorry,' she said. 'Of course.'

Struthers took off his coat and draped it over the sofa arm. He dropped down, settling himself comfortably with his legs stretched, patting the sofa and nodding approvingly, like he was in a show-room, testing the furniture. 'Joe,' Danso lifted up the tails of his coat and sat down on the sofa, with a soft 'ooof' like any movement pained him, 'we need to ask you a few questions.'

'Ask me some questions? What about I ask you some questions and what about you give me some answers? Is Malachi in London?'

'If I give you my assurance you're safe, would you believe me?'

I hesitated.

'I mean it, you're quite safe. You and Angeline. But we've got to follow up a new line of investigation and that's where you come in. Bear with us, son. It's going to sound like we're going round the houses a bit.'

'But we're not,' Struthers said, still checking out

the sofa, bouncing his arse up and down to test the springs. 'We're going somewhere.'

I sat on the other sofa opposite them, moody. There was an empty glass on the table between us – the G and T Angeline had been drinking. 'Well?' I folded my arms, trying to calm down. 'What?'

'Look, I know we've done this to death,' Danso put his elbows on his knees and leaned forward to look at me, 'but, see, it's that car again. I want to go back and think about that car you saw outside the house the day Lexie was attacked.'

'The saloon?'

'Because the surveillance PC's version is different from the version you gave us. The lad's saying you first came to the house from the east. From the road that ran along the bottom of the playing-fields.'

'That's right.'

'Right?'

'Yeah. But I never saw the car parked up. I've thought about it and I'm sure.'

Danso sighed. 'Joe, Joe, why didn't you tell us this earlier? You never said you came from the east.'

'Didn't I?'

'No. You said you'd come along the main road, that you'd parked opposite the police car.'

'Yes, but I . . .' I closed my mouth. Opened it, and closed it again. 'So? So I forgot. What difference does it make?'

'It means that when you drove up to the main road you'd already been to the house.'

'Yes. I mean, no, not *inside* the house. No. I'd stopped *outside* the house. In the car.'

'Joe?' Struthers leaned forward, elbows on knees like Danso. 'Remember when we went out to Cuagach?'

I looked from him to Danso and back again. 'Yeah,' I said cautiously. 'For the forensics. Why?'

'Remember how I asked you if you'd been in the chapel? And you said only for a few minutes to take photos? You can't think back now, I suppose, and recall something else happening in there?'

'Something else?'

'Something that would have left your DNA?'

'No. Fingerprints. I told you, probably just some prints. Can you get DNA from prints now? Maybe you can.'

'I'm thinking about blood. Remember our thirty-first victim? Our hair and skin on the floor? Blood.'

'*Blood?*' I blinked at him. I wasn't getting it, just wasn't getting it at all. 'No. Not blood.'

'Nothing happened that could have left traces of your blood, hair and skin? A fight, maybe? Because the DNA on that thirty-first victim? Remember him – in the chapel? It turns out to be yours, Joe.'

'What?'

'Your DNA. You're our thirty-first victim. And

remember that crack in the cupboard at the rape suite?'

I shook my head, holding up my hands and appealing to Danso: 'Hang on, hang on. Where's this going?'

'Sorry. I don't think you heard me – let's try again. That crack in the cupboard at the rape suite? Do you remember when it got there?'

'I said, where's this going?'

'You told my boss here you cracked the cupboard when you were having a fight with your wife. When was that fight?'

'That's it,' I said, pointing a finger at Struthers, fixing him in the eye. 'I *said*, where the *fuck* is this going? My DNA's in the chapel, so fucking what? I got a twatting off Dove and they took me somewhere. I was half-conscious so it could have been the chapel, for all I fucking know, but *what* has it got to do with a fucking *cupboard*?'

'Don't point at me. Put your hand down.'

'*I said, what has that got to do with a fucking cupboard?*'

'That's enough.' Danso cleared his throat and looked up at me with watery eyes. 'I didn't want to do it like this, but please,' he pointed at my finger, 'please drop your hand.'

'What's going on?'

'Your *hand*, please, Joe.'

I lowered it slowly, narrowing my eyes at him. 'Come on, old man. What's happening here?'

'I'm sorry.' He shuffled inside his jacket and pulled out his warrant card, putting it on the table in front of me. He couldn't meet my eyes. 'You know who I am anyway – but let's make it official. That's me, DCI Danso, and I am cautioning you, Joe Oakes, under section fourteen of the Criminal Procedure of Scotland Act, 1995.'

'*Cautioning* me?'

'You're going to be questioned about a series of murders in Argyllshire at the end of August and in the first week of September 2005, which we believe you may have been involved in.' He put the card back into his pocket and said, 'You're not bound to answer, but if you do your answers will be noted and may be used in evidence.'

I stared at him, thinking, *This is a joke. This is someone's idea of fun . . . What, Danso old boy, are you wearing suspenders under that suit? Is that the gag?* I sat back in the chair, swallowing hard, shaking my head very slowly. 'No,' I muttered, looking from one to the other and back again. 'No. This is a joke.'

'We're doing this under Scottish law, Joe, under our cross-border powers, and that means we're detaining you. If I'm going to be strict about it I'd say I don't even need to give you a solicitor, but I wouldn't do that to you.'

'We *could* just question you for four hours. Imagine that – you and me on our own for four hours.' Struthers raised his eyebrows. 'I don't know about you but I could look forward to that.'

I gave a weak laugh. 'No fucking way. Stop it now.' I looked from one to the other, still hoping to see the crack of a smile, the wink: *Aah – had you going!* 'Stop, because you're talking bollocks. It started off funny but now it's just arse. Let's end it here.'

But Danso was watching me seriously, a film clouding his eyes. Struthers was smirking, his arms folded across his chest like he was concealing a weapon. I thought of the blue police lights flashing silently on and off in the street outside, and something dull clenched under my ribs. They'd been here all day. It wasn't to protect us. It was to stop me leaving the house. Angeline lifted my arm and pulled it round her shoulders, burying her face in my chest. I put my hand on her head and pressed it into me, not taking my eyes off Struthers. I hated him at that moment more than I've ever hated anyone. 'Well?' I hissed. 'You'd better start giving me some answers.'

His eyes were cold. 'The only time I've ever seen DNA receptors like you left in the chapel is after a fight.' He took a notebook from his coat pocket and opened it, uncapping a pen. 'You didn't like the

PHM much, did you? We spoke to your publishers this morning. They were saying how you—'

'*I wasn't even on the fucking island when he killed those people.*'

'Aye. That's the problem. Malachi didn't kill "those people".'

'Oh, please, what toss is this now? *Of course he did.*'

Struthers and Danso looked at each other. Danso rearranged his coat, pulling the two sides neatly together and smoothing it down. 'Joe,' he said quietly, 'he couldn't have.'

'Couldn't have?'

'No. He was already dead.'

I stared at him. I knew the blood had left my face.

'That's right. He'd already been dead more than a week.'

'What?' In my arms Angeline raised her head, wiping her eyes. 'What did you say?'

'He was dead when it happened,' said Struthers. 'You'll hear all the science bit in court – got some bearded creep from Edinburgh University lives and breathes insects. Turns out that early winter we got in Argyll was a jackpot for a forensic entomologist.'

'OK,' Danso said warningly. 'Let's not hand him our case on a plate.'

But Struthers was sitting forward, smiling at me

487

like a pitbull on a leash, his eyes watering. 'Aye, turns out there are things that insects just can't do to a body when it gets that cold. See, me, I never knew that. Never knew it, but sounds like some insects just won't lay eggs if the temperature's wrong. See, if he'd gone in the ground after the killings in the chapel he wouldn't have had—'

'OK,' Danso said. 'Let's stop this now.'

'Where was he?' Angeline sat up and stared at Struthers, pushing her hair from her eyes.

'On Cuagach, hen. Near your home. Contractors found him. Cleaning up the chemicals. This time we know it was him. The DNA works. Aye,' he muttered, staring red-faced at me. 'Shoved head first in a mine shaft – and your boyfriend's stamp all over the place. He took photos of the pig too. Something else his publishers told us. Bit of a souvenir collector when it comes to photos.'

'Look,' I said reasonably, 'this doesn't work – he was seen after the massacre. Loch Avich for a start.'

He shook his head. 'The DNA from the bothy didn't match.'

'Didn't match?'

'No. It was just some dosser. Dove was already dead. And now it's all unravelling. What's funny is that all the time we were trailing him round Argyllshire there's nothing to place him on Argyll the whole of September.'

I stared at him. 'Nothing to place him there?'

'It's true.' He shrugged. 'Strange but true. We caught up with the wee sods who had the Vauxhall from Crinian Hotel car park. Glasgow neds, like I always said.'

Angeline made a small sound and tried to stand, pulling herself up slowly and shakily. Her face was drawn and smeared, her head a little wobbly. She put out a hand to steady herself, like she felt faint, and instantly Struthers was on his feet, supporting her under the elbows, lowering her back to the sofa. 'There you go, hen. There ye go.'

She sat for a moment, breathing in and out, her hands pressed to her temples, staring at me like everything was falling into place. 'You didn't like him,' she muttered. 'You never liked him. You didn't like them either. The Garricks – you said you didn't trust them.'

'When did I say that?'

She didn't answer. She turned to Danso pleadingly, tears in her eyes. 'Can I go, please? I can't stay here in this – in this – place with – with him.' She made a low, furious sound in her throat, and raised her foot to kick me viciously in the calf with the tip of her stiletto. '*Why did you do it?*'

'Fuck off,' I said, holding my hand out to stop her doing it again. '*Fuck off.*'

'Hey! Hey! Come along now . . .' She tried to

kick me again, but Struthers pulled her away, turning her to look at him, holding her face. She was weeping uncontrollably now, wiping her nose and shaking her head. 'Let's not see any more of that, wee lassie. You hear me?'

'I want to go. *I want to go.* I'm not staying here with *him*.'

'Callum, for God's sake.' Danso waved his hand at Struthers. 'You're FLO-trained, aren't you? Take her somewhere. Have you got somewhere to go, lovey?'

'*No!*'

'No one to visit?'

She shook her head again. Then something occurred to her. She wiped her eyes with the palms of her hands, taking breaths to stop her chest heaving. 'Yes. Paul. I can go to him.'

'Paul?' I echoed. 'Who the fuck's Paul?'

She looked at me, full of contempt. 'You didn't even bother to find out his name.'

'That fucking arty photographer? How long have you and him been friends, then?'

'That's enough.' Danso flicked a hand in the direction of the street. 'Get her out of here. Meet me at Salusbury Road.'

As Struthers pulled her to her feet, the warm, creamy expanse of her right breast slid briefly into view from her sweater, then back as she straightened. She shook her hair, tucking a curl behind her ear, taking care not to look at me. I sat totally still, numb, silent. My head was pounding. *Mineshaft*, I was thinking. *Wedged in a mineshaft*.

'Was there a carcass on top of him?' I asked Danso distantly, not taking my eyes off Angeline. She was letting herself be led to the door. In the hallway they paused so Struthers could sort through the coats, looking for hers, asking her, did she need a handbag, keys, phone? A wash of unreality came over me. I felt like something old and poisonous had fastened its mouth over mine and was breathing silently and steadily into me. 'An animal? One of the pigs?'

'I suppose if someone wanted to disguise the smell of a corpse it's a good idea . . .'

'Yeah. A dead pig. It would have disguised the smell. And my fingerprints . . . they were . . .' I paused. Struthers was taking Angeline out of the front door and on to the garden path. Now he'd transferred his hand from under her arm to round her shoulders. She was leaning against him, steadying herself against his chest as she limped away to the street. For a moment I was back on Cuagach, a cold wind blowing, her voice, thin and fleeting: '*Stop it watching me . . .*' 'They were on a chemical drum, weren't they? My fingerprints. That's where you found them?'

'I've got a case to build, Joe. You understand that. What we're going to do now is take you down to Salusbury Road and question you.'

'But they were. Weren't they? My prints. On a chemical drum.' I stood, heading in a trance for the front door. 'A drum wedged in front of him.'

'You'll need to stay here, Joe. Until I've got some men in.' When I didn't stop he raised his voice behind me. 'You're *detained*, Joe. *Detained*.'

I threw open the door. In the dark street the blue emergency light flashed on and off, shadows racing up the neighbouring houses. The hail had stopped and Struthers stood at the police car, closing the door on Angeline. As I came down the path he went round to the other side and got in. Danso was coming up behind me. I wrenched the garden gate open. '*Hey!*' I said, hurling myself at the car, shaking the handle. '*You! Angeline.*' I banged a fist on the window. 'Open this. Open the fucking door.'

Out of the corner of my eye I could see uniformed police jumping out of the other cars. I could hear Danso breathing behind me. 'Joe,' he said. 'Come on, son.'

'Open the fucking door,' I bellowed. The driver flashed me a nervous glance, just a small glint of eye under the cap, and put the car into gear, taking off the handbrake. Struthers was leaning forward, urging the driver on. '*No! You fuckers!*' I grabbed the door trim, digging my nails in, shouting at Danso who was behind me, hands on my shoulders. 'I put the fucking drum in the shaft *for her*.' I banged on the window. Blood vessels popped in my temples. '*Angeline. Open this fucking door.*' Flecks of spit shot out of my mouth. '*Angeline. You bitch. You BITCH. You evil bitch.*'

Suddenly, with a whoosh of cool air, the electric window slid smoothly down and Angeline's face appeared close to mine. Everyone on the street became very still. The driver re-engaged the hand-brake and Struthers sat back with a jerk. 'What did you say?' She leaned close to me. Her breath was sour, like something was erupting from her. 'Just then, what did you say?'

'*I said, you evil fucking bitch.*'

'Joe.' She reached a hand up to my face. 'Joe. You don't believe in evil. You don't believe in possession and you don't believe in evil. You said it yourself.'

'Shut *up*!' I bellowed. 'Shut up!' Out of nowhere hard arms wrapped round me, pinning my hands down. Someone was frisking me, searching my pockets. I twisted in their grip, banging my leg on the car and sending someone's cap flying off into the gutter. '*You arseholes.*'

'Joe, whatever it is you've done . . .' More tears came to her eyes. She looked pityingly at my struggles. '. . . I don't blame you. You must remember that, I don't blame you.'

She sat back in the seat, letting the electric window slide calmly up to close off her face. I stopped struggling and stared at her. She crossed her stockinged legs and next to her Struthers lowered his chin to get a look. There was a bit of a pause, then the driver took off the handbrake again and the car pulled neatly out into the road. For a split second I thought I saw something coiled and dark, like smoke or a spirit, lifting itself out of the car and hovering near the roof, then the driver reached the end of the road, hesitated, put the indicator on, turned and disappeared from sight, leaving me standing in front of my own house, held back by two police officers, nothing better to do than watch the car drive away.

THE END

Acknowledgements

Thank you to everyone at Transworld, particularly my utterly dedicated, 24/7 editor Selina Walker, and also Patrick Janson-Smith (keep trying, PJS, and one day I might forgive you for leaving Transworld). To Jane Gregory for being my rock – and a brilliant, flaming, red-headed rock at that. A loud cheer too for the Hammersmith office: Anna the traitor, Claire, Emma, Jemma and Terry.

To everyone in the Strathclyde police force: DC Dee Bradbury and DC Gary Brown for fitting me in between pregnancies and attempted murder charges, and DS Allan Derrick (glockenspiel king). To Dr Awny Lutfy (FRCPath) of The Dumfries and Galloway Royal Infirmary; to Sisters Rosalyn Bonner and Jackie Iverson, and especially Nurse Practitioner Breeda McCahill of the Glasgow Royal Infirmary Burns Unit. To Mr Richard Spicer

(FRCS) of the Bristol Royal Hospital for Children for the insights into the sacrococcygeal growth and its complications, and to explosives expert David Hargreaves for detailed explanations of how to make things go bang. Thank you to Minette Walters for teaching me more about the publishing industry in four days than I've learned in the last eight years, and most of all a huge hug to Mairi Hitomi for being my best chum and for teaching me how to get ma geggy round Glasgae slang.

Thank you also to: my mother, my father and my little brother; Jim Brooks; Broo Doherty; Simon Gerard; Pat Mallows (website king); Murf and Margaret (OWO Murphy); Karin Slaughter; Gilly Vaulkhard; the Downings, the Laydons; the Heads; the Roberts. A special hurrah for everyone at Bath Spa MACW (especially Tracy and Richard), everyone at Appletree and the Larkhall yummy mummies: Helen, the two Kates, Konny, Mel, Ness, Olivia, Rebecca. But most of all: love and a thank-you that goes on for ever to you, Keith, and our little girl, Lotte Genevieve.